Pamela Evans was ~~born in~~ the Borough of Ea~~ling~~ ~~children. She is married and has two sons and now lives~~ children. She is married and has two sons and now lives in Wales. She has had nine novels published, all of which are available from Headline, including *A Barrow in the Broadway* ('a long, warm-hearted London saga' *Bookseller*), *Lamplight on the Thames* ('a good story and excellent observation of social change over the past forty years' *Knightsbridge and South Hams Gazette*), *Maggie of Moss Street* ('a good traditional romance and its author has a feeling for the atmosphere of postwar London' *Sunday Express*), *Star Quality* ('well peopled with warm personalities' *Liverpool Post*), *Diamonds in Danby Walk* ('a heart-warming family saga' *Newtownards Chronicle*), *A Fashionable Address* ('very readable' *Bella*), *Tea-Blender's Daughter* and *The Willow Girls*.

Also by Pamela Evans

Part Of The Family

Pamela Evans

KNIGHT

First published in 1995 by
HEADLINE BOOK PUBLISHING

First published in paperback in 1996 by
HEADLINE BOOK PUBLISHING

This edition published 2001 by
Knight an imprint of Caxton Publishing Group

10 9 8 7 6 5 4 3 2 1

ISBN 1 84067 370 2

Typeset by Avon Dataset Ltd, Bidford-on-Avon, B50 4JH

Printed and bound in Great Britain by
The Guernsey Press Co. Ltd, Guernsey, C.I.

Caxton Publishing Group
20 Bloomsbury Street
London
WC1B 3JH

To Colin and Glynis, affectionately...

Chapter One

Behind the bow windows of the smart Kensington town house, with its white-painted stucco and shiny black railings, dinner was just beginning in the dining room. The menu was rather mundane this evening as the family was not entertaining – just Brown Windsor soup, best fillet of beef with a variety of vegetables, and baked plum pudding and custard.

'Just think . . . in a few days' time I shall no longer have to plough my lonely furrow as the sole female of the family,' Meg Verne remarked lightly to her two sons as Dora, the maid, moved silently and nimbly among them with a silver ladle, pouring soup into china bowls.

'You're quite happy then, to be gaining a daughter, as they say?' said Philip, her eldest, whose wedding was this coming Saturday.

'You bet I am,' replied Meg, whose full name was Marguerite. An attractive, vivacious woman in her late-thirties, she wore her tar-black hair waved softly back into a coiled knot, complementing her embroidered white blouse which was tucked into a floor-length skirt, her rigidly corseted shape curving dramatically beneath them. 'At least it'll help to create more of a balance in this male-dominated family.'

'I'm glad you're pleased . . . you hear such tales about mothers and daughters-in-law, don't you?' remarked Philip, who was tall with an athletic build and the same striking dark looks as his mother. 'Sometimes there's all out war between them, apparently.'

'Yes, I gather some women have a problem letting go of their sons and I'll probably shed a few tears at the church when I actually . . . er . . . hand you over to Emily,' confessed Meg whose busy life wasn't conducive to maternal possessiveness. 'It is the end of an era, after all, but it's the natural order of things . . . and I'm very fond of her.'

'I should think you'll be jolly glad to get rid of him, won't you, Mother?' teased younger brother Neville, who favoured the paternal genes and was as fair as his brother was dark.

'Don't listen to him, Philip,' she protested mildly, her sloe eyes hinting at a smile. 'I'll miss you around the house, of course, but it isn't as if you're going far. You'll only be around the corner in Cedar Square.' She frowned, unfolding her starched white napkin and spreading it over her lap. 'Not that I'll make a habit of descending on you uninvited, naturally.'

'Don't be silly. You'll be welcome at any time,' Philip assured her.

'Thank you, dear,' she said graciously, though made a mental note to treat any such open invitation with caution.

'You must be mad to want to get married so young,' interrupted Neville, nibbling his bread roll as Dora served him.

'I'm not that young.'

'Good grief, you're only two years older than I am.'

'Men are later to mature than women, so they say,' said Meg, 'and some men may well be too young at twenty-two to

2

settle down. But Philip knows his own mind.'

'A girl like Emily could talk a chap into anything,' said Neville, taking up his spoon as Dora moved away. 'She's got everything. She's beautiful, clever, and one of the snappiest dressers in London.'

'Sounds like you've got designs on her yourself,' laughed Philip. Speckled sunlight shafted through the lace curtains between the red velvet drapes and caught his black wavy hair.

They sat in a resplendent room with a vast expanse of polished floor. The wood panelling along one wall was hung with tapestries, the floral wallpaper offset a variety of paintings and wall plates, and the glossy dark wood furniture reflected light and movement in its gleaming surfaces. The air was fragrant with good food, polish, clean linen and the plump velvet-like blooms set amid lustrous green leaves in a blaze of colour inside the crystal rosebowl on the sideboard.

'You're quite safe, don't worry,' laughed Neville. 'She's gorgeous but definitely the marrying kind and that isn't on my agenda . . . and not likely to be for ages yet.' He grinned wickedly. 'Still, I expect you'll have a mistress tucked away before very long, eh, Phil?'

'That's a bit crass, isn't it, when a chap's about to celebrate his nuptials?' said his brother evenly.

'It's what married men do.'

'Oh, really Neville! It isn't clever to make such rash, uninformed generalisations,' his mother interrupted with asperity. If it had been her younger son about to embark upon matrimony, she really would be worried. As likeable as he was, even her biased maternal eye could detect a definite lack of maturity. Neville didn't have a fraction of his brother's

3

common sense. But then Philip was mature beyond his years; he'd always been the serious one. While he tended to be a little too conscientious and responsible, Neville just coasted through life without a care in the world. 'So let's have no more of that sort of talk in this house, if you please.'

'As you wish, Mother,' conceded Neville breezily.

She turned to Philip. 'Well, I suppose this will be the last time I shall have the job of seeing you off to anything before Emily takes over. So are you all ready for Saturday? You have the ring, you've collected your suit from the tailor . . .'

'Don't worry, everything's under control,' he assured her with an affectionate grin. His mother was a really good sort. He'd always been close to her, unlike his father with whom he'd never had any kind of rapport.

'At least I can let you go with an easy mind,' she said. 'Emily will probably make a better job of looking after you than I ever have.'

The daughter of a partner in a stockbroking firm with whom Meg's husband, Humphrey, had been at school, the bride-to-be was entirely suitable to join the Verne family. She and Philip had first met at the wedding of a family friend and the parents on both sides had been delighted when they'd hit it off. As Neville had just said, Emily was beautiful, clever and well turned out. The ideal wife for Philip, in fact. Meg's only slight reservation concerned the young woman's strange moods – times when she became extremely odd and very melancholic. Still, everyone had their little idiosyncrasies, she thought, and Philip didn't seem to mind. As he quite rightly pointed out, there were far worse faults than moodiness.

They were interrupted by the maid. 'Excuse me, madam,

but will the master be eating at home this evening?'

Meg thought about this for a moment. 'Yes, Dora, but I'm not quite sure what time he'll be in. I shouldn't think he'll be too long.'

'Right you are, madam,' said the girl and walked neatly from the room, long black skirts rustling around her feet.

'Did your father say why he was staying late at the factory?' Meg asked, looking from one to the other of her sons.

'No, he just said to tell you we were to start dinner without him,' Philip informed her. 'He had someone with him in his office when we left. An important customer, I think.'

'Well, if he's too late getting home, I shan't see him before I go out,' she murmured almost to herself.

'Going anywhere nice?' enquired Neville, out of duty rather than interest. He was far too engrossed in his own social life to be curious about his mother's.

'Just to visit a friend, dear,' she said casually.

'Oh, right,' said Neville, whose thoughts had already moved on to his own arrangements for the evening. He and a group of friends were going to a newly opened nightclub in the West End where they played the new ragtime music and you could dance the 'Bunny Hug' and the 'Turkey Trot' until the small hours.

Unnoticed by Neville, a look had passed between Philip and his mother as she replied to Neville's question, a slight nuance of her expression answering the query in Philip's eyes.

Meg was a woman with a large appetite for altruism, a genuine philanthropist who thrived on working for the common good. Always happiest in the thick of things, she didn't limit her contribution to committees for worthy causes but was personally involved in raising money for such lifelines as soup kitchens, shelters for the homeless and outings for poor families.

She unashamedly used her middle-class position to this end, organising social events to raise funds and often losing popularity with prosperous companions who preferred to shut their eyes to the poor and needy or blame them for their own poverty. She hoped she wasn't a glory-seeking do-gooder. She certainly tried not to be. Her motivation came from a genuine need to redress the balance in appreciation for the blessings that had been bestowed so liberally on herself and her family.

To those less fortunate, the Verne family must seem to be unfairly steeped in privilege, she was well aware. For as well as enjoying the considerable rewards of a successful family business, some accident of nature had tipped the biological scales in their favour and made them all exceptionally good-looking – a combination guaranteed, understandably, to inspire jealousy.

Although basically honest, there was one area of Meg's life in which she considered subterfuge to be a necessary expedient. If Humphrey knew what she really got up to when he thought she was out visiting friends, he'd demand that she withdraw her support, something that her belief in the cause ruled out.

Only Philip knew her secret. The dear boy was that rare breed of man who was in sympathy with the fight for women's suffrage. But then he'd always had a feeling for the oppressed – which womankind certainly was in this so-called modern age of 1910. It was incredible to someone of Meg's enlightened opinions that such a large proportion of the population was still blind to the injustice of depriving women of the right to vote.

She was recalled to the present by the appearance of a tall, distinguished man with steely grey eyes and fair hair, turning white around the hairline. At forty-five, Humphrey Verne was still in excellent shape and cut an impressive figure in his dark business suit.

'Sorry I'm late, my dear,' he said, slipping into his place at the head of the table and addressing his wife at the other end. 'I was held up by an important customer.'

'That's all right, Humphrey.' She considered him for a moment. 'You're looking very pleased with yourself this evening. Has something nice happened?'

'It certainly has! Royal patronage for the company to be precise,' he said, beaming as Dora appeared with perfect timing to serve him. 'We've been asked by a firm of royal couturiers to make the silk that will be used for some of the Coronation robes next year.'

'Oh . . . how exciting,' exclaimed his wife with enthusiasm.

'Yes, indeed,' he said, spreading his napkin over his lap.

'Will it be the material that will be used for the actual Coronation robes that King George and Queen Mary will be wearing at the ceremony?' she asked.

'No, that's being manufactured by a firm of silk weavers in Essex,' he explained, his face unusually flushed. 'We're to make the silk to be used for the clothes that will be worn by some of the other royal guests.'

'Well done, Humphrey.' She turned to her sons who had both gone to work in the family silk-weaving business with their father after leaving boarding school. 'Congratulations to you all . . . it's a tremendous honour.'

'It'll certainly be a boost for the firm,' said Philip, who was the production manager.

'Indeed it will,' agreed Neville, managing to inject a note of dutiful zeal into his tone. Work was far too dull for such a committed hedonist and he made an art form of avoiding it though officially supposed to be learning the business.

'A few more silk-weaving firms could do with that sort of patronage,' said Philip who was very concerned about the general state of the British silk-weaving trade which had been declining steadily since about the second half of the last century. The main reason for this worrying state of affairs was the fact that French woven silks were allowed into Britain free of duty, while British silks exported to France were subject to a duty of thirty per cent. With cheaper French silks flooding into the country, many British manufacturers found it hard to compete.

'Never mind about other firms,' snapped Humphrey, frowning darkly at his son. 'This is our moment of glory.'

'I'm not denying it,' said Philip. 'But we're a large, old established company, we'll survive even without this . . . unlike some of the smaller struggling silk mills.'

'Huh! I suppose you'd rather we turn the job down and recommend it goes to a more needy firm,' said Humphrey sarcastically, over-reacting as usual to anything Philip said.

'Of course not,' he retorted. 'I was merely making an observation. We all know that if the government doesn't do something about duty free imports, silk-weaving will die out altogether in Britain eventually.'

'That's a gross exaggeration,' said Humphrey sternly, shooting his eldest son a withering glare. 'Trust you to spoil the good news by looking on the black side.'

'You know how strongly Philip feels about cheap foreign

silks pouring on to the market, dear,' put in Meg in an effort to dampen the animosity that flared up at the slightest provocation between these two. If only Humphrey would try not to make his feelings for Philip so obvious.

'None of us is happy about it but this is hardly the moment . . .'

'All right, Father,' interjected Philip in a conciliatory manner to stop this escalating into a major row which would upset everyone. He was angry with himself for letting his father's hostility affect him. After a lifetime of being on the receiving end of it, he really ought to have total immunity. 'My timing wasn't very good. I didn't mean to pour cold water on your exciting news. I'm sorry.'

'Oh, right. Apology accepted,' grunted Humphrey with thinly veiled reluctance. He thanked the maid for his soup, and, as though forcing an interest, said to Philip, 'So . . . are you all set for the big day on Saturday?'

'Yes, all ready.'

'That's the stuff.' He turned his attention to Neville. 'How about you, young man, are you going to make a good job of being his best man?'

'Rather,' said Neville.

Only the totally insensitive could fail to notice Humphrey's different attitude towards his younger son. Philip had accepted long ago that Neville was the apple of their father's eye. Philip didn't mind that. What did upset him was the fact that he himself felt no sort of bond with his father at all. Despite his very best endeavours to penetrate the barrier between them, Humphrey remained cold and aloof.

Fortunately, it hadn't caused trouble between himself and

Neville. His brother was a bit of a chump at times but he didn't have a malicious bone in his body. And, credit to him, he never tried to capitalise on their father's favouritism. In fact, Philip got the impression that he was rather embarrassed by it.

Inevitably, the conversation drifted back to the line of business in which the Verne family had been involved since the seventeenth century. At that time Humphrey's Huguenot ancestors had fled to England from France, after persecution in their own country, and set up in business in London's Spitalfields.

Eventually most of the silk community in East London had begun to move out of the capital in search of cheaper premises, many of them settling in Essex. Philip's grandfather, however, had considered it beneficial to stay in London and had set up a factory in a poor area of North Kensington. That shabby district was vastly different to fashionable South Kensington where Humphrey and his family now lived in leafy Eden Crescent, even though the two areas were geographically adjacent. Humphrey Verne had taken over the firm from his father when Philip was just a small boy.

'The workers will be tickled pink about the royal order too,' Meg was saying. 'Even apart from the glory, it will make them feel more secure in their jobs.'

'They're going to have to work damned hard though,' pronounced Humphrey firmly, 'because we'll still have our regular customers to please.'

'Our workers won't object to that. In the majority they're a fairly diligent lot,' began Philip.

'They get good treatment from us, that's why,' interrupted Humphrey. 'You look after your workers and they'll pay you back in loyalty. The reason we don't suffer from the discontent that is so common lately among the working classes is because we give our people a fair deal.'

'Exactly,' agreed Philip. 'As I was about to say, they're a good crowd . . . apart from a few trouble makers.'

'Some people will always find an excuse to make trouble,' growled Humphrey.

'A few certainly will,' agreed Philip, thinking of one of their workers in particular who was a very disruptive influence indeed.

'I reckon I must be the only woman in London who'll be mother to both the bride and the groom at the same wedding,' declared Polly Carter that same evening to her family who were gathered around the scrubbed wooden table in the kitchen of their small rented house in North Kensington for a meal of faggots and pease pudding, bread and margarine and plenty of strong tea.

'How's that then, Ma?' asked her eldest son, Stan, who was the bridegroom in question.

'Wake up, Stan, you're slow on the uptake tonight,' said Lizzie Smith who was to marry him this coming Saturday. 'Because your mum's been a mother to me as well as you since my parents died, of course.'

'Oh, yeah,' he said absently, brushing an insistent bluebottle away from his face with an enormous hand. 'I wasn't really payin' attention. I've other things on my mind.'

'Such as?' Lizzie wanted to know, greenish-brown eyes shining with interest.

'Well . . . I was talking to the maintenance man on the way out of the factory tonight. Apparently he was workin' in the corridor outside the guvnor's office this afternoon, fixing the gaslight.' He took a large swallow of tea, vivid blue eyes peering at them all over the rim of the mug. 'Anyway, he reckons he heard someone in there talking to the boss about an order for material for the royals for the Coronation next year.'

'Ooh, how terrific!' enthused the exuberant Lizzie, concealing her disappointment that her fiance was not sharing her happy anticipation of their forthcoming wedding which currently filled her thoughts.

'I dunno so much about that,' said Stan, a sudden burst of fury suffusing his face so that it matched his wild red hair. 'There'll be plenty of slave-driving goin' on, you can bet your life on it. Well, I won't have it! I'll get everyone out on strike if they try to pull a fast one. They'll get a good price on this job, so we'll have to make sure they give us a decent rate and pay overtime for those people who aren't on piece work: labourers, overlookers and so on.'

'It's quite an honour for the firm though, isn't it?' remarked Lizzie.

'They'll soon turn honour into dough to line their pockets,' declared Stan hotly. 'Ruddy capitalists with their posh house in the south of the borough. Honestly, they might as well be on another planet, it's so different there from the conditions their workers have to put up with round here.'

'Oh, no, don't start all that again, Stan,' protested Lizzie for there was no stopping him once he got on to politics and his precious socialism. 'The Vernes'll see to it that we do all right out of this royal job.'

'They better had too or I'll be on to the union sharpish!'

'Calm down,' said brother Bobby, an easy-going type who

could never understand why Stan expended so much energy in anger about things that might never happen. 'The Vernes are all right as guvnors go.'

'Stan's right,' grunted Luke, the most moody and taciturn of the four Carter brothers. 'They'll want blood out of us to meet this order.'

'I don't think the Vernes are bad to work for,' said the youngest Carter, seventeen-year-old Roy, a gentle, thoughtful boy who usually managed to see the best in everyone.

'You're lucky to have someone like Stan to worry about his workmates, and he's right to be concerned that you get your fair dues out of this royal job,' said Polly, turning to her husband and adding, 'Aint that right, Will?'

Deeply immersed in thoughts of a few extra quid to be made in addition to what he earned as a labourer on the railway, by selling some dodgy gear for a bloke he'd met in a pub, the man who went under the misnomer of 'head-of-the-house' had to be nudged and have the question repeated.

'Oh, yeah, luv, whatever you say,' he replied, because the only route to a comfortable life for him was to agree with his wife regardless of his true opinions. Polly was a good woman but a very domineering one who took a dim view of opposition from anyone, and simply wouldn't tolerate it from her nearest and dearest. Will didn't really object – he needed someone like her beside him to take control. Raising four sons needed constant strength of character and the ability to exert discipline. Since Polly outshone him in both departments he was happy to stand aside and let her rule the roost.

'Well, speaking personally,' said Lizzie, changing the subject rather than disagree with the woman to whom she owed so much, 'I'm going to have better things to do with my time while I'm away on honeymoon than to worry about what's going on at the factory!'

Their raucous laughter brought colour to her cheeks. 'Honestly, you lot have one track minds,' she said, rolling her eyes and tutting, her face bright with lighthearted indignation.

'Yeah, stop embarrassing the girl,' said Bobby who was her favourite among her future brothers-in-law. He and Lizzie were both eighteen and as children had rarely been apart. It had been the awe-inspiring Stan, however, with his broad shoulders and charismatic personality, who had stolen Lizzie's heart as she entered her teens.

'All taken in good fun though, eh, Liz?' said Will.

'There's not much choice in this house, is there?' she grinned. A slim, pretty girl with straight, corn-coloured hair, she was wearing a cotton blouse and long floral skirt that made her perspire and wonder why shorter clothes couldn't be worn by women in summer. And as for her damned corsets, they were about as comfortable to wear as concrete and ought to be abolished in her opinion.

'Aren't you going to stand up for your future wife then, Stan?' suggested Roy lightheartedly. Being the youngest of this exuberant crowd, he was usually on the receiving end of teasing and family jokes.

'If she can't defend herself against you lot by now, she's making a mistake in marrying me,' laughed Stan, who loved Lizzie but in rather a vague sort of way. Romance, and everything else for that matter, took second place to the role of champion of the working classes which was becoming almost an obsession with him.

'Don't worry, Lizzie, you and me'll stick together against all these men,' said Polly with affectionate levity. 'We're completely outnumbered. Gawd knows what I'd have done if you hadn't come into the family to give me a bit of feminine support.'

Until ten years ago Lizzie had lived next door to the Carters in scruffy Thorn Street. Aunt Polly, as she'd always called her then, had been her mother's closest friend. When Lizzie had been orphaned by the influenza epidemic of 1900 that had claimed so many lives, Polly and Will had taken her in to save her from an institution. As she'd grown up, Lizzie had come to realise how hard it must have been for them to have coped with another mouth to feed. The boys had been financially dependent on their parents then so money had been short.

Things were better now in that respect. Lizzie and all four Carter brothers worked at Verne's Silk Mill, and handed over money for their keep to Polly every Friday. But Lizzie tried never to forget her debt to them, especially Polly whose kindness had been her salvation in those dark days. The Carter family had made a bewildered little girl feel as though she belonged with them from that very first moment, the four boys cramming into one bedroom without complaint so she could have the tiny attic room to sleep in.

Surrounded by this warm and caring atmosphere, the tragedy had gradually receded and she'd become the daughter Polly had always wanted. On Saturday she would legally become a Carter. This meant a lot to her for she loved them all dearly, with the exception of Luke.

Mentally distancing herself from the strident voices as they all fought to be heard, she glanced around the familiar room. Cooking smells permeated everything and were tinged with a hint of carbolic. A steamy emanation from the local laundry drifted in on the sooty air through the open sash windows, across which yellowing net curtains guarded the family's privacy.

It was a long room with a hideous black-leaded range at one end and a chipped dresser at the other. The dresser was a homely muddle of cheap ornaments, old newspapers, socks for darning, ash trays, cigarettes, matches and various other incidentals of everyday living. There was a sink with a single water tap and a tin bath hanging on a nail on the wall. The latter was taken down on family bathnight, filled with water heated in pans on the range and used in front of it by them all in turn. The rest of the house comprised a parlour, two bedrooms and an attic room. The lavatory was in the back yard.

In meditative mood, Lizzie observed her surrogate family. First there was Polly, a warmhearted but redoubtable lady of large proportions with bright red hair which sprang from its bun at the back of her neck and flew about in wispy curls. She had a shiny round face and bright blue eyes that were startling against her white freckled skin. She was wearing a well-worn white blouse with the sleeves rolled up and a black skirt with a pinafore tied around the waist. Her age was no secret – they all knew she would be forty next year – the boys enjoyed teasing her about it.

Then there was Stan who was the light of Lizzie's life. At twenty-one he was a great bear of a man, tall and muscular with the same colouring as his mother. He was not handsome in the classical way – his face was too chunky, being square and solid-jawed with a snub nose and broad mouth – but he had a raw magnetism that Lizzie found irresistible and she loved every bit of him from the top of his thick springy hair to his size eleven feet.

Sitting next to Stan was Roy, still a spotty pubescent with endless limbs and a bristly thatch of flame-coloured hair.

Bobby was, without doubt, the good-looking one of the family. He had the same colouring as his father as well as his clear-cut features, light brown laughing eyes and mop of chestnut hair. Bobby's dazzling smile, sportsman's build and gift of the gab made him well fancied by the girls at the factory even though he was going out on a regular basis with Lizzie's best friend, June.

A year younger than Stan was Luke, a saturnine individual and the only member of the family with whom Lizzie wasn't at ease. He had mousy brown hair and piercing grey eyes that unnerved her. Even now that she was an adult, she tried never to be alone with him, the memory of his cruel childish tricks still too vivid. She shivered at the recollection of the assortment of creatures he'd used to persecute her. Huge black spiders had been slipped down her back to crawl wildly among her underclothes. Slugs and earthworms had greeted her when she'd got into bed. Every so often a dead mouse would be in her shoe when she'd put her foot into it. He'd even placed a poor deceased sparrow between her bedsheets once.

Then there had been that awful time he'd tied her to the iron bedstead by her hair and stolen her knickers. She could still feel the agony of her locks pulling against her scalp as she struggled to get free, but even more painful was the humiliation of having her privacy so cruelly violated.

Although he'd made his dislike of her obvious through these heinous acts, he'd never actually told her why he resented her being in their family, and she'd never told anyone what he did to her when no one else was around. She'd longed to snitch on him but to do so would have seemed like a betrayal of the others, somehow, his being a part of their family and their being so good to her. Thankfully he'd eventually grown out of such puerile pranks, but she'd never quite been able to lose her fear of him.

Now her attention was drawn by the wedding talk.

'What are the arrangements for Saturday, then?' Will was asking. 'I mean, Stan and Lizzie can't both go to the church from here, can they? It wouldn't be right.'

'I've told you a dozen times, Will Carter,' said Polly with mild impatience, 'Stan's staying with his mate, Arthur Brown, on Friday night and going straight to the church from his place. It's unlucky for the bride and groom to see each other the night before the wedding anyway. Don't you ever listen?'

''Course I do,' he retorted. 'But I can't be expected to remember everythin' that's said in this house since you lot never stop jabbering!'

The meal was over and they were lingering over a final cup of tea amid clouds of cigarette smoke when there was a knock at the front door.

'I'll go,' offered Lizzie. 'It'll probably be June.'

'Will she have come to see you or Bobby?' Polly idly wondered.

'Me, I should think,' said Lizzie, scraping her chair back on the quarry-tiled floor, and rising. 'She said she'd probably pop over for a chat about Saturday. You know, with her being my bridesmaid.'

'It isn't my night to see June anyway,' declared Bobby, on the defensive. 'I'm going out with me mates in a minute.'

'I don't know what you and June find to talk about, Lizzie,' remarked Stan in a jovial manner. 'You walk to and from work together, you eat your sandwiches at dinner-time together, and you still find plenty to rabbit about of an evenin'.'

'That's what friends do, isn't it? Anyway, I've never seen you and Arthur lost for words.'

'You can chatter till your teeth fall out for all I care,' he said casually. 'I'm off out to a party meeting when I've finished this cuppa tea anyway.'

'Again?' queried Lizzie lightly.

'Yes, again.'

'Some girls have other women as rivals,' she said jokingly. 'With me it's politics.'

'Not complainin', are you?' grinned Stan, leaping up and blocking her way as she went to open the kitchen door to the hall. He swept her into his arms and kissed her thoroughly while the family observed them matter-of-factly.

'No, Stan, I'm not complaining,' said Lizzie breathlessly when he released her, then she hurried from the room to answer the door.

'Ah, it does you good to see 'em together like that, dunnit?' said Polly.

'I don't know so much about that. I think it'll be a bloomin' good job when you two are married and in your own place,'

19

the long-suffering Will remarked mildly to Stan. 'All this canoodling about the house gets on my nerves. If it isn't you and Lizzie, it's Bobby and that girl of his.'

'Go on! You'll miss us when we move out, Dad,' said Stan with a booming laugh. 'We keep you young and remind you of what you and Mum used to get up to.'

Strange how children always think in the past tense as regards parents and that sort of thing, thought Polly, as she and Will exchanged a private look.

June lived with her family in a house opposite the Carters' in Thorn Street, and had been Lizzie's soulmate ever since either of them could remember. A short, dark-eyed girl with a plump round face and a mass of black hair, she was only slightly less outgoing than Lizzie.

'Have you heard the news?' she burst out excitedly as she and Lizzie trekked down the hall to the nucleus of the house where the Carter family still sat.

'What news is that?'

'Well, there's a rumour going around that we're gonna be working on cloth for the royals ... for the Coronation next year,' June informed her brightly.

'Oh, yeah, Stan's heard something about that too.'

'Must be true then. I mean, with him being in the know with the union and that.'

'He got it from the maintenance man, apparently.'

'Oh. Well, I expect they'll tell us officially tomorrow.'

''Course they will ... if it's true,' agreed Lizzie as they approached the kitchen door. 'But please, June, can we talk about my wedding on Saturday? It *is* supposed to be the most important day of my life, after all. Anyway, we'll have quite enough of work tomorrow.'

'Ugh, don't remind me! Wedding talk is much more fun.'

Chapter Two

The noise was deafening on the ground floor at Verne's Silk Mill the following afternoon with all the power looms in operation. Lizzie was so used to the reverberating clatter of the machines and the strong smell of hot oil from their constant use, she barely noticed them. She was miserably aware of the excessive heat in here, though. It made her head throb and her clothes feel sticky against her skin.

Unfortunately, a high temperature had to be maintained because warm hands were essential to the efficient handling of silk thread. At the moment her fingers were slightly swollen and damp as she struggled with the lengthy and laborious job of entering a new warp of silk thread on to the old warp already on the loom.

Painstakingly, she twisted the threads which were to run the length of the scarlet and gold upholstery brocatelle. Leaving the task for a moment, she went to check another of the power looms under her supervision which was frantically rattling out a plain tabby weave. The floor shook beneath her feet from the vibrating machines – sturdily constructed with cast-iron frames and beechwood parts – as flying shuttles tore to and fro, carrying the weft thread from one side of the loom to the other across the warp to make silk fabric in a glorious variety of designs and colours.

She could just see the top of Stan's fiery hair as he attended to his looms at the far end of the room. Bobby, who was training to be an overlooker so was responsible for setting up the machines for weaving as well as maintaining and repairing them, was doing something to one about halfway down the vast weaving shed which was liberally endowed with windows to maximise on the use of natural light.

Although Verne's produced a variety of silk weaves, they were best known for their upholstery and curtain fabrics, many of which adorned the homes of the aristocracy. Their reputation was second to none in the silk industry which was why, Lizzie guessed, they were being trusted with the royal order which was outside their usual specialist field.

Her job was oily, noisy and frustrating; even when things were running smoothly it was boring. But when she took a piece of woven silk off the loom she was rewarded with a deep sense of satisfaction. She was glad now that a lack of alternatives had forced her into the trade at the tender age of thirteen, because silk was such a lovely material to work with.

Over the years, she'd been involved in a variety of jobs at Verne's so was familiar with the whole process of silk-weaving. She had run errands, swept floors, had even worked upstairs on the warping floor with June for a while where raw silk from China, after being sent to the dyers, was wound from the hanks on to wooden bobbins ready for weaving.

Nowadays she worked permanently on the weaving floor and brightened the long hours of repetitive labour by creating elaborate fabric designs in her mind, knowing they would never see the light of day for it wasn't done for someone in her position to make suggestions to Verne's creative team of designers. Her favourite outlet for her artistic energies was a fantasy in which she was running her own silk-weaving company and working out her own patterns for the cloth. Her days were happy enough, though. Work at the looms was certainly more satisfying than labouring around the factory which was the lot of Luke and Roy.

She was about to resume work on the warp when she became aware of a disturbance at the far end of the factory floor. Oh no, she thought, craning her neck to see what was going on. I might have guessed Stan would be involved.

Weavers were abandoning their machines and assembling around him. Lizzie's heart sank as she watched him climb the iron stairs that led to the production manager's office, stopping halfway and using the steps as a platform from which to address his audience. She couldn't make out what he was saying from this distance but guessed it concerned the announcement Philip Verne had made this morning about the royal order and all the extra work it would entail. For some reason Stan saw this as a threat rather than an opportunity. Quivering with apprehension, she left her position and hurried towards the gathering.

'Us workers must stick together, rise up against the management who'll take all the glory and pay us as little as they can get away with,' he was saying, shouting to make himself heard, his face gleaming with perspiration, huge wet patches soaking the shirt under his arms as he waved them about emphatically. 'We'll have to watch them every step of the way, make sure we get a decent rate for the job and proper overtime for those on time work. If you're not already in the union, I urge you to join.'

Lizzie felt sick. Had he lost his mind altogether, to be carrying on like this in the firm's time and on their premises? Despairingly, she knew she was powerless to do anything about it. Stan would give up when he was good and ready and not a minute before.

If the boss hears him remonstrating and recruiting union members when he should be working, he'll be out of a job, she thought gloomily. What a rotten start to married life that will be!

Philip Verne was busy at his desk upstairs in the factory office. He'd just finished checking the latest production figures and was about to take them to show to his father, who was based in the general offices at the side of the building, when the sound of trouble drifted up to him from the weaving floor. Shouting could be heard over the noise of the machines.

Deciding to investigate on his way through the factory, he hurried from the office on to a small balcony area overlooking the weaving floor and leading to the stairs.

Mm, I might have known it would be Stan Carter, he thought, perceiving the scene below and immediately getting the gist of Carter's oratory. As usual he was doing the company down.

'All right, Carter, that's enough, you can do that sort of rabble-rousing in your own time,' he said in a firm but reasonable tone. 'Everybody back to work now, please.'

A sea of faces stared up at him on the balcony: some with hostility, others with compunction. As a general drift back to the machines began, Carter bellowed to his workmates, 'Don't go just because of him!'

Most of them ignored him but a few ardent supporters lingered as Stan turned and shouted up to Philip. 'We're not living in the dark ages now, you know, Verne. We don't have to take everything you chuck at us. We've got trade unions . . . we won't be exploited!'

'The management at Verne's has no intention of exploiting you,' Philip announced to the crowd below. 'As I told you this morning, all of you will be well rewarded for this royal job. It will be a good chance for you to make some extra money. Now back to work, please.' As there was no other way to the general offices than through the weaving floor, he started down the stairs only to find his way blocked by Carter. 'Let me pass, please.'

'Arrogant bastard,' hissed Stan, remaining steadfastly where he was.

Being at close proximity to Carter on the stairs, Philip was shocked to see the degree of animosity in the other man's eyes. He hates me . . . he *really* hates me, he thought, stunned by this realisation because he had a good relationship with the workers in general. 'Don't try to make problems where there are none, Carter,' he advised evenly. 'Now out of my way, man.'

'I'm not going anywhere, mate,' announced Stan, who had lost all sense of reason in his ardour for the cause. This was theatre, he was the star in his own production. All eyes were upon him and it was wonderfully exhilarating. 'Why should I do what you tell me?'

'Because I pay your wages is the best reason I know,' replied

27

Philip with determined calm. Of course he ought to dismiss the man on the spot for such disruptive behaviour. His father wouldn't think twice about it. But judging by his unhealthy rage, the man had quite enough problems already. 'Now out of the way, I have a factory to run.'

As Philip lifted his foot to continue down the stairs past Stan, the latter raised his hand in a halting gesture then spread himself across Philip's path. But Stan's foot slipped on the iron step and he lost his balance, bumping down the stairs to end in a dazed heap at the bottom.

Numb with horror, Lizzie watched her husband-to-be jeopardise their future. 'What the devil does he think he's doing?' she said to Bobby who was standing next to her as Stan blocked Philip Verne's way. 'He won't be helping anyone if he loses his job.'

'He's certainly pushin' his luck this time,' agreed Bobby worriedly. 'I dunno what gets into the daft bugger, I really don't.'

Seeing Stan raise his hand in what looked to be a threatening manner, Lizzie thought he was going to burn his boats altogether by putting his fist into Philip Verne's face. But in the next instant he was sitting on the floor at the bottom of the stairs, looking bewildered.

Instantly she was at his side, anger outweighed by concern for him. 'Stan, love . . . are you all right? Have you broken anything?'

He considered the matter and decided that nothing felt painful enough to be seriously damaged though he guessed there'd be bruises tomorrow. His pride was severely dented though. As he was helped to his feet by his pal Arthur and by Bobby, it occurred to him that there was political capital to be made out of this accident.

'Are you all right, old man?' Philip Verne asked with genuine anxiety. 'What happened, did you slip?'

'You know very well what happened,' declared Stan, raising his voice for the benefit of the onlookers. 'You bloody well pushed me!'

Philip was lost for words for a moment. 'I didn't touch you,' he exclaimed at last.

Stan turned to the crowd which had reformed. 'You don't believe that, do you? You saw what happened,' he told them, knowing that wasn't likely because he'd had his back to them in front of Verne.

Philip finally lost patience with this infuriating man who did nothing to assist the cause he professed to represent. 'I didn't push you and you know it,' he said in a tone that sent a respectful hush through the crowd. Stan Carter was out to destroy the relationship Philip had built with the workforce since his father had put him in charge of the factory a year ago, an association that was based on mutual respect. Too soft and he'd be seen as weak; too harsh and he'd come out of this as the villain. What he daren't do was to let Carter be seen to intimidate him. 'But I ought to have done. And now I ought to shove you right out of the door and tell you never to come back. You're lucky it's me and not my father who's caught you stirring up trouble. He'd have you out of this factory so fast your feet wouldn't touch the ground.' Philip stared at Stan grimly. 'If you're not satisfied with the conditions here at Verne's, perhaps you might be better suited elsewhere.'

29

'Oh, no, please don't sack him, sir,' said Lizzie impulsively. 'Stan doesn't mean anything . . . it's just his way.'

Philip's dark eyes met hers, querying her interest in the matter while Stan looked ready to explode with fury.

'Me and Stan are getting married on Saturday, same as you.' The Verne wedding was common knowledge in the factory. 'He really needs this job.'

Perhaps it was her spirit that touched him, or the sincerity in those clear green eyes. Maybe he was particularly responsive to weddings at the moment because of his own. But for whatever reason Philip found himself sympathising with her, convinced she was worth more than marriage to a bigot who probably didn't even begin to appreciate her unquestioning loyalty.

'I'm not sacking him,' he told her mildly. 'Though God knows I ought to. I'm merely suggesting an alternative if he isn't happy working for us.'

The gathering dispersed, leaving Lizzie, Stan and Philip.

'He is happy . . . 'course he is. Aren't you, Stan?' she said, fully aware of the rage her intervention was causing.

'Well,' said Philip, throwing him an enquiring look, 'which is it to be, Carter? Back to work or a parting of the ways?'

Lizzie's nerves were jangling as she waited for Stan to reply. She wouldn't put it past the stubborn fool to lose the job out of sheer damned cockiness. But she couldn't interfere any further without undermining his self-respect. This must be his decision.

The two men stood locked in conflict. Philip had never been the recipient of such hatred before. Even his father's dislike didn't have this sort of ferocity. Those piercing blue eyes were transmitting poison into his very soul, making him feel both threatened and sad that anyone could be capable of such feelings towards him.

'Well?' he said again.

Lizzie watched Stan's facial muscles working and guessed he was in combat with his pride. She sensed that something profound had happened to him this afternoon – that this incident wouldn't be easily forgotten. When he spoke his tone was so subdued, it was barely audible.

'All right, I'll go back to work.'

'Righto. Look sharp then before any more production time is lost,' said Philip, and left through the swing doors.

Outside in the corridor he leaned against the stone wall, feeling shaky and emotionally exhausted. He was annoyed with himself for being upset by a cretin like Carter. That poor bride of his was going to need some mettle, embarking upon a lifetime with him. Oh, well, that's their business, he thought, and hurried along the corridor towards his father's office, still smarting from Carter's venom.

Stan turned on Lizzie as soon as they were out of the factory that evening.

'Don't you ever interfere in my affairs again,' he ordered, walking alongside her while his brothers fell into step with June behind them. 'Answering for me as though I was some snotty-nosed kid! We're not married yet, you know, Lizzie . . . and even when we are I won't have you fighting my battles for me. Just what do you think I am, eh? Some sort of a half wit who can't speak up for himself?'

'I had to say something, Stan, or you'd have ended up without a job.'

'So what? I'd have got another one,' he retorted.

'Just like that? Oh, do grow up, Stan,' she said sharply. 'London isn't exactly crowded with silk mills.'

'All right, so I'd have looked for some other sort of job.'

'And they're ten a penny, I suppose?' she said cuttingly. 'Anyway, you're experienced in the work at Verne's.'

'I don't care.'

'All right. So if you felt so strongly about it, why didn't you resign then?' she challenged him.

He thought for a few moments. 'Because it suited me not to. One day I'm gonna show Philip Verne what it's like to be on the receiving end,' he declared vehemently.

'I don't see how you can since he's the boss.'

'I don't know either, but one day it's gonna happen, I can promise you that,' he said dramatically.

'Oh, give over for Gawd's sake and let's change the subject,' said Lizzie because listening to Stan in this mood was about as entertaining as an empty bandstand in the rain.

But she was forced to relive the whole thing again over tea as he related his version of the incident to the family.

'That's the management classes for you,' said Polly, slicing a saveloy which she was having with peas and mashed potato. 'I've a good mind to go and sort that Philip Verne out myself. Pushing you down the stairs indeed! You could have been seriously injured.'

'He said he didn't push Stan,' Lizzie pointed out.

'Whose side are you on?' Polly demanded to know. 'If Stan said he was pushed, then that's what happened.'

'You saw him do it, Lizzie,' said Stan who had by now convinced himself it was true. 'You know very well you did.'

'No, I didn't,' corrected Lizzie.

'Nor me,' put in Bobby.

'Are you calling your brother a liar?' asked Polly, who demanded unquestioning loyalty from each family member.

'No, I'm just saying that I didn't see what happened,' replied Bobby. 'None of us did. Stan had his back to us when he was talking to Verne on the stairs.'

'You know the Carter rule,' declared Polly, 'we stick together, no matter what.'

'Yeah, I know all about that, Ma,' said Bobby with a hint of irritation. 'All I said was . . .'

'What about you, Lizzie?' interrupted Polly. 'I hope you believe Stan? Marriage is no good without complete trust, you know.'

Lizzie didn't reply. Until recently, Polly's opinions had automatically been hers too. But this was changing nowadays though she knew better than to air her conflicting views. Now, as Polly waited for her answer, Lizzie was plunged into frightening confusion. The loving atmosphere she so cherished seemed suddenly oppressive; she felt trapped in this close-knit circle – imprisoned by the intensity of her feelings for them. She longed to escape from Polly's overpowering presence and the family that, for so many years, had been the foundation of her existence. Increasingly, she was feeling the need to assert her own personality.

She could have wept with sheer frustration at this unwanted intrusion into the contented pattern of her life. For this was hardly the moment to embark upon a voyage of self-discovery, when she was about to make the ultimate commitment to Stan and become even more closely involved with his family.

33

But she couldn't make herself believe him about the incident on the stairs. She was certain he'd seized the opportunity to blame Philip Verne as a way of gaining support for his crusade against management. This didn't mean she loved him any the less – or that she wouldn't stand by him under any circumstances. It simply meant that she accepted his failings and loved him despite them. But to admit all this to Polly was a recipe for disaster so Lizzie just sighed and said, 'Of course I believe him.'

'I'm very pleased to hear it,' said Polly, pouring tea from a huge brown pot. 'People like the Vernes are brought up to be bullies. They've too damned much of everything, that's the trouble. Good food, lovely clothes . . . and I could never trust people as good-looking as they are.'

'Oh, come on, Aunt Polly, you can hardly blame them for what's nature's doing,' said Lizzie, unable to restrain herself.

Polly gave her a sharp look. 'Maybe not, but having so many privileges must make you more selfish and less sympathetic than the rest of us . . . it stands to reason.'

'Does it?'

'Yeah, o' course it does. It's the way human nature works.'

Frankly Lizzie found such sweeping generalisations rather unfair. The Vernes had always seemed reasonable to her. The old man was a bit of a cold fish but Philip seemed a nice enough bloke from the little she knew of him. It wasn't his fault he looked like one of those romantic heroes who drew women in their thousands to the Bioscopes.

'Anyway,' said Bobby, perceiving Lizzie's distress and wishing his brother would be a little more sensitive to her feelings, 'you and Stan will be going down to Southend for a few days at the weekend to enjoy yourselves so you can forget all about the factory and the Vernes then.'

'We bloomin' well intend to, don't worry,' said Lizzie, throwing him a grateful look and feeling much better suddenly. Her peculiar mood must just have been the pre-wedding jitters she had heard so much about.

'I'm so happy, Stan,' said Lizzie as she strolled along the Front at Southend-on-Sea on her new husband's arm in the evening air. They both looked extremely snazzy, she in her going away outfit, a pale blue dress with a white collar and straw hat decorated with white ruched trimmings, he in his navy blue wedding suit with white starched collar and tie, much of his red hair confined beneath his best cap.

'I feel dead chuffed an' all,' he said, patting her hand affectionately.

'You're enjoying married life so far then?' she said, smiling up at him.

'Not half.' He squeezed her arm and grinned into her face which was flushed with excitement, a few wisps of golden hair falling on to her brow. 'You look a real treat in that titfer, Lizzie. I'm proud to have you on my arm.'

'Why, thank you, Stan.' At that precise moment, with him in tender mood beside her, Lizzie had everything she wanted in the world. They only had a few days away – they couldn't afford to take too much time off work – so she was savouring every blissful moment. Just an hour on the train from Fenchurch Street and they had left the smoke and grime of London behind and were in the playground of the working classes.

'I'm glad the rain has stopped at last,' she continued.

They had spent the first day of their honeymoon damply sitting about in cafes or wandering around the amusements in the Kursal trying to keep out of the rain because Mrs Betts closed the door of her boarding house to guests between breakfast and high tea. Now it was a pleasant summer evening, mild but with a moist smell about it. Rain wasn't far away.

'Cor, I'll say! I thought I was gonna get webbed feet,' Stan said lightheartedly.

'I'm very glad you didn't,' Lizzie laughed girlishly. 'I like your toes just the way they are.' She paused, meeting his eyes. 'In fact, I like your feet . . . your hands . . .'

'And?'

She teased him with silence for a moment. 'I'm just mad about your big blue eyes!'

'And the rest,' he whispered in her ear, though he needn't have worried about being overheard because everyone was far too busy enjoying themselves on the crowded promenade to notice. They were all here – mum, dad, grandma, grandad and the kids, gangs of friends, courting couples, honeymooners.

Sunday best dresses and fancy hats were out in force among the rowdy crowd. People ambled towards the pier while others headed for the thrills and spills of the Kursal amusement park or the evening performance at the Hippodrome. The pubs were packed to overflowing.

'Fancy some cockles, luv?' asked Stan.

'No, thanks. I'm still full from Mrs Betts' boiled ham and mashed potato. Anyway, cockles can give you typhoid,' she warned because a recent outbreak of the disease had been blamed on badly cooked cockles and the public had been warned not to eat them.

'Don't be daft,' he said, pointing to a seafood stall next to one piled high with coloured sticks of Southend rock. 'There's a notice on that stall saying that their shellfish have been sterilised by the latest improved apparatus. I'm having some. Can't come to Southend and not have a plate of cockles.'

They leaned on the promenade rail while he ate his seafood, inhaling the bracing air and the sour smell of Southend mud mingled with the pungent mixture of brine, fried fish and candy floss. The beach was less crowded than it had been earlier as holidaymakers and day trippers took to the town for their evening entertainment, but there were still quite a few people on the sands. Intrepid paddlers rinsed their toes in the waters of the estuary but the bathing machines had finished for the day and stood abandoned in rows. Doubtless inspired by copious amounts of Southend beer, a picnicking crowd nearby was singing tunelessly, accompanied by the unmelodic strains of a mouth organ.

'Let's go dancing at the Kursal Ballroom,' suggested Lizzie impulsively.

'What, with my big feet?'

'Yeah, why not?'

'I thought we were gonna wander along to the pier then have a couple of drinks,' said the unimaginative Stan.

'Oh, go on. I really fancy going dancing,' she persisted. 'It'll be ever so romantic.'

'All right then. As long as you don't mind me treading all over your feet.'

'Nothing could upset me this evening,' she told him.

Indeed, her happiness seemed indestructible as they shuffled around the floor in the magnificent Kursal Ballroom with its ornate balconies overlooking the dance floor. On the flower-fringed stage a dance band interspersed slow dreamy numbers with the upbeat 'Alexander's Ragtime Band' that got the younger element trying the daring new animal dances.

Lizzie was positively glowing when she and Stan strolled back to the boarding house in the gaslight through a town that looked set to enjoy itself until the small hours. Lights were still glowing in windows everywhere and singing could be heard from all directions.

'I'm having such a good time, Stan, I wish it could last forever.'

'Mmm.'

'I don't fancy going home at all.'

'Nor me,' he said, his arm encircling her waist.

'It's being here on our own that's so lovely,' she sighed.

'Yeah. Back to work on Wednesday and that bloody Philip Verne!'

'He won't be there,' she said, feeling a sudden chill. 'He'll be away on honeymoon, same as us . . . though I expect he'll be away for about a month so you can forget all about him for a while.'

'How can I do that?' said Stan, and she knew from his altered tone that she had lost him. 'The bugger's right in my system. I hate him, Liz. I really hate that man.'

'Shush, Stan,' she said gently, trying to restore the loving atmosphere. 'Don't spoil everything by thinking about him. Just think about us, you and me, and what we're going to do when we get into bed.'

'That's all very well but that man gets right up my . . .'

'Oh, for Gawd's sake, forget about him,' she snapped as they turned in at the gate of their boarding house. She was deeply hurt that he could spoil their few days away together by bothering about someone else. Surely every woman had the right to feel like the most important thing in her husband's life on honeymoon, even if she never felt that way again afterwards. It certainly illustrated the depth of his loathing for Philip Verne, she thought miserably, that it outweighed his feelings for his new wife.

Philip and Emily were having coffee alfresco at a cafe on the Left Bank of the Seine, having dined earlier on the fashionable Right Bank near the Champs Elysées where they were staying. They were almost at the end of their second week here in Paris. In a few days' time they were to travel by train to the sunny Riviera for the final fortnight of their honeymoon.

Eager to sample as many different areas of the city as possible, they explored a different district each evening. This boulevard had a particular feeling of joie de vivre because it was filled with people attracted by the street entertainers. Jugglers, musicians and puppeteers worked their magic beneath the chestnut trees in this broad avenue, fringed by cafes and shops aglow with gaslight on this summer's evening. A tangle of traffic filled the road, horsedrawn cabs and carriages battling for supremacy with motor cars and bicycles.

'Are you happy, darling?' asked Philip.

'Very,' said Emily, looking across at him and smiling.

'You look lovely.'

The word was hardly adequate to describe Emily whose

looks turned heads wherever she went. Even amid the glamour and elegance of the Champs Elysées her beauty did not go unnoticed. This evening she looked stunning in a white silk blouse and pale green skirt with matching bolero, the outfit finished with a green and white hat with a large brim and satin trimmings. The colours looked well with her luxuriant brown hair and sherry-coloured eyes that seemed-almond shaped against her perfect features.

'Thank you, Philip.'

They sat in comfortable silence watching the events around them. On the pavement nearby a group of dancers with garishly painted faces were performing to the velvet tones of a clarinet; further along a sword swallower displayed his peculiar expertise to the crowds. At a table a group of young people were having a noisy and animated discussion in French.

'Politics, I should think,' remarked Philip, recognising a few words from his schoolboy French.

'Yes, I think so too,' she said. 'That's what I love about the Left Bank, it's so wonderfully bohemian . . . humming with life and teeming with intellectuals exchanging ideas.'

'Even if we can't understand what they're saying!' he laughed.

'It doesn't stop us feeling their energy, though, does it?' she pointed out, her eyes very bright as though she had been infected with sudden new vitality. 'You can feel it bubbling around you . . . everywhere.'

'I quite agree.'

'Wonderful.'

'The Right Bank has certain charms too,' he said.

'Oh, yes, the shops there are out of this world.'

'We must do some shopping before we leave,' he said. 'Perhaps you'd like something special in the way of jewellery?'

'You're spoiling me.'

'Pure self-indulgence, I assure you,' said Philip. 'My pleasure comes from pleasing you.'

He was deeply in love with her and imbued with a kind of desperation to make her happy. At times he sensed that she didn't reciprocate with quite the same intensity, that she functioned at some deeper level to which he was not privy. She sometimes seemed to withdraw right into herself as though he wasn't there at all, talking about how heartbroken she was not to have had a career as a school teacher. Apparently her parents had been more interested in her potential as a wife and had refused to allow her to stay on at school to get the necessary qualifications. He found it strange that she had never mentioned this before they were married.

But being with her for twenty-four hours a day on this honeymoon trip had made him realise just how superficial their relationship had been during their genteel courtship, when they had only been together for limited periods and often in the company of others. Now he suspected that a very complex personality existed behind that immaculate façade.

'And I wouldn't be human if I didn't enjoy being spoiled,' she said.

'Oh, Emily, I'm so very honoured to have you as my wife.'

'The feeling is mutual, Philip.'

In the gaslight her skin looked pale and translucent, her features so perfect they might have been made of porcelain. A light breeze stirred the trees. Seeing her shiver, he said, 'Would you like to go inside?'

'No, thank you, darling. I like sitting out here watching the world go by.'

He ordered more coffee. Sipping the bitter liquid, he could feel the throb of Parisian life around him. The air was thick with the spicy aroma of coffee and cigarettes mingled with the sweet scent of perfume and cakes. Aimless hordes of people thronged the pavements, stopping to look at the sights and filling the cafe tables. A group of young men in open-necked shirts sat down at the next table and began discussing poetry in English.

'Such a life force,' said Emily. 'So hard to imagine death hovering among such strong vibrations of life.'

Surprised by such an incongruous remark, he said, 'Why should you even try to imagine it, dearest?'

' "In life we are in death",' she quoted gravely with a drastic change of mood. 'It's all around us . . . everywhere. Some say it is the finer existence.'

'Possibly,' he said, troubled by her train of thought. He had noticed during this last two weeks that she had a tendency to probe very deeply into things. 'But hardly the sort of topic for two young people on honeymoon?'

'I don't see why not,' she said, and he noticed how oddly bright her eyes were suddenly, staring at him in a most peculiar way.

'It's a bit morbid for my taste, that's all,' he told her.

One of the dancers began moving among the crowd, collecting coins in his hat. He paused by their table and Philip dropped some change into the collection for which he was thanked in French. The man's glance lingered on Emily for a moment in sheer admiration. His eyes were heavily outlined in black against a white-painted face, looking eerie in the lurid glow of the cafe lights.

Smiling, he went on his way. Philip absently watched him weave through the tables, stopping now and then to exchange a few words with the customers. Philip was startled by a sudden hand on his arm.

'Take me back to the hotel,' said Emily urgently, gripping him tightly, her lovely eyes wild with fear.

'What is it?' he asked anxiously. 'Whatever's the matter?'

'That man . . . he's been sent by the devil to get me!'

'He's just a performer, dear,' he said soothingly, taking her hand in both of his.

'He's going to kill me,' she said, trembling, her face ashen.

'Of course he isn't, Emily.' He looked worriedly into her eyes and squeezed her hand reassuringly. 'No one is going to harm you . . . no one at all.'

'He is . . . he is!'

'Don't be silly, darling.'

'Take me back to the hotel,' she urged again, her voice high with terror. 'Make love to me, Philip.'

That was much more in keeping with his mood and he brightened considerably. 'With pleasure, my love,' he said. 'Just as soon as you've finished your coffee, we'll make our way back.'

'No, now,' she said, leaping from the chair, her voice breaking with tears.

'Hey, steady on,' he said. 'I'm as eager as you are but I haven't paid the bill yet.'

'*Garçon . . . garçon!*' she called, making a frenzied gesture to a nearby waiter. '*L'addition, s'il vous plaît.*'

The bill was hurriedly settled and they tore through the crowded boulevards, Emily dragging at his hand like a terrified child until they reached their hotel suite where she headed straight for the bedroom.

The next morning Philip had angry scratch marks across his shoulders and back. The modest lady who had slept by his side since they'd arrived in Paris hadn't been recognisable in the frantic creature who had drawn blood from his body last night.

Observing his reflection in the mirror as he shaved, he tried to define her uncharacteristic behaviour. She loved him, of that he was sure, but it hadn't been love, or even lust, that had been behind her passion last night. As exciting as it had been, it had left him uneasy.

In retrospect, it seemed to him as though she had been driven by sheer terror – almost as though she'd needed his love-making to blot out sinister thoughts, to feel life at its zenith as an antidote to the shadow of death that had haunted her.

Even stranger was the fact that she seemed to have forgotten all about it this morning and was her normal composed self. When she'd seen the scratch marks inflicted by her own nails, she'd had no recollection of having made them. In fact she was quite concerned as to how they'd got there. She didn't seem to have any memory of their hasty retreat from the cafe last night, either – or her fear of the dancer with the painted face. The only possible explanation could be that she'd had some sort of emotional fugue caused by all the wedding excitement.

As she was her usual demure self this morning, he thought

it was probably best not to upset her by mentioning it, and to carry on as though nothing had happened. It wasn't something he would forget though.

Chapter Three

'Now, now, there's no call for that dreadful noise, Mrs Carter,' reproached Mrs Toms, the midwife, as Lizzie's tortured shrieks reverberated through the tenement house in Bessle Street where she and Stan had rooms. 'You'll disturb all the other tenants.'

'Bugger them!' gasped Lizzie, unable to think beyond the excruciating pain that had had her at its mercy for what felt like a lifetime.

'That's not very nice now, is it?' coaxed Mrs Toms in the manner of an indulgent schoolmistress as she applied a cool flannel to her patient's forehead.

'Neither is this, mate.'

'It's the most natural thing in the world, dear.'

'So's death.'

'That's a bit morbid.'

'Not really . . . at this moment it would be a blessed relief,' puffed Lizzie. 'You won't catch me coming back for a second helping of this.'

'The times I've heard that!'

'I mean it.'

'Childbirth is a woman's ultimate fulfilment,' stated Mrs

47

Toms, waxing lyrical. 'You are experiencing pain at its most glorious.'

'Glorious be buggered!' she exclaimed. 'It's ruddy torture.'

'Language, if you please,' admonished the midwife primly. 'Anyway, you'll forget all about the pain the instant you clap eyes on the baby. Everyone does. You're nearly there. A couple more big ones and it'll all be over.'

'Never again,' the young woman gasped, soaked in sweat, her knuckles white as she gripped the iron bedstead, dreading the next contraction but desperate to get to the end of this ghastly business. 'I'll not let my husband near me . . .'

'If I had a shilling for every time I've heard that, I'd be a rich woman.'

'Oh Gawd, there's another one coming . . . oh, no . . . oooh . . . waaah . . .'

'Give it everything you've got, there's a dear. That's it . . . it's coming now. The head's out. Just one more almighty shove . . .'

The baby was born as the May afternoon advanced into evening, a nine-pound boy with a mop of bright red hair like his father's.

'Oh, he's beautiful,' said Lizzie, immediately captivated, the agony of labour already fading. 'He's all Carter, no doubt about that.'

'Yes, he's certainly got his daddy's colouring,' agreed Mrs Toms.

'Is Stan home from work yet?' enquired Lizzie, eager to share her joy with him.

'Yes, I believe he's in the other room with his mother.'

'Could you ask him to come in here, please?' requested Lizzie.

'Certainly not. This is no place for a man,' Mrs Toms stated categorically. 'I can't allow a male person in here . . . at least, not until I've cleaned up and got the baby looking decent.'

'Oh,' said Lizzie in disappointment.

'Your mother-in-law is making some tea. She'll bring you in a cup as soon as it's brewed,' said the midwife by way of consolation. 'There's nothing quite like that first post-natal cuppa.'

There was only one thing Lizzie wanted at this precise moment and that was her husband's company but she knew better than to undermine the authority of Mrs Toms whose word was law during a confinement in this neighbourhood. Never mind that this was Lizzie's own home.

'I suppose Mrs Carter Senior will be looking after you during your laying in?' the nurse remarked chattily as she bustled about the room.

'Yes, that's right.'

'Handy having her just around the corner to help out.'

'Mmm.'

Polly appeared a few minutes later, brimming with emotion and carrying a tea tray. 'My clever Lizzie,' she said, smacking an exuberant kiss on her cheek then peering at the baby who was being made decent by Mrs Toms on the washstand with water that had been boiled earlier by Polly in the communal kitchen on the ground floor. 'You've given me my first grandchild . . . and he's the spitting image of Stan too!'

Still sore and exhausted from the birth, Lizzie found Polly's capable presence reassuring as she joined forces with Mrs Toms, the two of them seeing to the baby and holding forth about the technicalities of childbirth. It seemed an age before the two superintendents of the maternity room allowed Stan into this female preserve. They wouldn't let him over the threshold until the baby was washed and tightly cocooned in a shawl, and Lizzie was looking presentable in a clean cotton nightdress with her hair freshly combed. Even then he was told not to stay long for his wife needed to rest.

'How are you feelin', love?' he asked, perching on the edge of the bed and glancing briefly at the baby she held cradled in her arms.

'Happy but worn out.'

'You'll be all right once you've had a sleep.'

'Mmm.'

'He's certainly a whopper.'

'Yeah, no wonder he gave me such a hard time on the way out!'

'Aah, ne' mind, it's all over now,' he said fondly.

'Thank goodness, though it wasn't really too bad,' she heard herself saying from the favourable viewpoint of retrospect.

'What shall we call him?'

'I rather fancy Jed . . . Jed Stanley Carter,' she said, listening to the sound of it. 'What do you think?'

'Sounds all right to me,' he said absently as though she only had part of his attention.

'Good, that's settled then.'

'Ma will be coming in with a supper tray for you soon.'

'Why not have yours with me in here, to keep me company?' she suggested happily.

'I've already had mine.'

'Oh!' She was unable to hide her regret.

'I couldn't wait for you, love, because I'm going out.'

'Out? Oh, of course, to wet the baby's head,' she surmised.

'But surely you can do that later on tonight?'

'I'll have a drink with my dad and brothers later on, o' course, that's traditional, but first I have to go to a union meeting,' he explained. 'Arthur's coming to call for me soon so I'll have to go and get washed and changed in a minute.'

'Well, I think you might have stayed at home with me for a while tonight, Stan,' she said with more than a touch of asperity. 'I mean, today *is* rather special.'

'So's the meeting, love,' he informed her breezily. 'It's crucial that I keep up to date with what's going on, for all our sakes. I've gotta keep up the good fight for us workers against the plutocrats, you know that.'

'It's really important to me that you stay with me, for a little while at least.' It was inconceivable to her that anything else could possibly equate with the wonder of what she had just experienced. 'I need you, Stan.'

'I'll be back before you even notice I've gone,' he said, patting her hand in a casually patronising manner. 'Ma will be here looking after you. She said she'll stay till I get back. Anyway, you don't want me around keeping you awake when you need to get some sleep.'

'Please stay, Stan.'

'I won't be late.'

Huge, eloquent tears rolled down her cheeks.

'Hey, this isn't like you at all,' he said, for Lizzie wasn't the clinging type. 'Whatever's got into you? There's nothing to cry about.'

'I know, I'm just being silly,' she said, mopping her face with the handkerchief he handed to her and becoming more composed.

'That's my girl,' he said, leaning over and kissing the top of her head before making a hasty exit.

As the door closed behind him, she felt fresh tears falling. She knew she was being completely irrational for it was a recognised fact that childbirth was outside the male interest. But she couldn't help feeling let down by Stan – much as she had on her honeymoon when he'd allowed Philip Verne to take first place in his thoughts. Was she being unreasonable or was it natural to want to share this momentous occasion with the other part of the equation?

She forced herself to face the truth. Stan hadn't been with her in spirit even when he'd been here beside her. He'd already been at the union meeting. Long ago she'd accepted the fact that she came a poor second to his outside interests so there was no point in being hurt by his behaviour tonight. Usually she took it all in her stride but now she just couldn't get to grips with her emotions which seemed magnified to make everything register with bruising intensity. And to make matters worse there was the growing suspicion that the search for personal kudos played a large part in Stan's apparent quest for democracy.

'Oh, dear. In tears, are we?' said Polly, sailing in with a supper tray which she put down temporarily on top of the chest of drawers.

Lizzie buried her face guiltily in her handkerchief.

'Don't worry, love. Having a baby does that to some women. It'll pass.' With the efficiency of the well practised, she removed the baby from his mother's arms and put him into his crib by the side of the bed before placing Lizzie's supper tray in front of her. 'You'll feel better once you've had something to eat.'

'Silly, isn't it?' sniffed Lizzie. 'I'm so happy really.'

'Have a good cry,' said Polly, offering her a clean handkerchief and patting her hand reassuringly. 'Then eat your supper. I've made you some nice beef tea to build you up and make your milk good and nourishing for young fella-me-lad.'

As had happened so many times in the past, Lizzie was soothed by this kind but overbearing woman. She couldn't tell her what had really triggered off this upset, though, because Polly was blind to Stan's faults and took any criticism of him as a personal insult.

'All the family send their love,' said her mother-in-law cheerily. 'They'll be coming to see you and the little 'un as soon as you're feeling up to it.'

'I'll look forward to that,' said Lizzie, feeling a little better.

'Oh, and by the way, Bobby and June have set the date for their wedding. It's going to be January of next year,' she said, hoping that a spot of family gossip might lift Lizzie's spirits.

'That's good. It'll be nice to have a wedding to look forward to.'

'Yeah, I'm very fond of June. She's one of our own.'

Sounds of movement were coming from the crib. A few gentle snuffles quickly escalated to an ear-splitting din.

'How can anything so small make such a racket?' said Lizzie, who was somewhat unnerved by this new responsibility.

'He's making sure we know he's there,' said Polly lightly. 'They all do plenty of that. I knew you should have eaten your food while he was quiet. You won't get your meals in peace like you used to . . . not with a new baby about the place.'

'I suppose not,' said Lizzie, as Polly lifted young Jed Carter from his crib.

* * *

'Well done, darling,' said Philip that same evening to his wife who was sitting up in bed at their home in Cedar Square proudly holding their firstborn in her arms. He peered at the tightly wrapped bundle and gently pulled the shawl away from his face. 'He's a fine boy.'

'I'm glad you approve.'

'What a clever girl you are.'

'I didn't produce him all by myself.'

'No, but I got the easy part.'

'I won't argue with that.'

Together they studied their new offspring.

'Who do you think he looks like?' she asked contentedly.

Actually, he was far too new for Philip to see anything more than a wrinkled scrap of humanity but he was too sensitive to say so. 'I'm not really sure,' he said. 'Let's hope he inherits your good looks.'

'Diplomatic as ever,' said Emily.

'Not really. I mean it.'

There was an added radiance to her, he thought, as she sat propped against the pillows, a white, lacy bed-jacket draped attractively around her shoulders.

'Babies get better looking as they get bigger,' she said.

He nodded in agreement. 'But what about you, darling? How are you feeling?' he asked with genuine concern for he was uxorious in the extreme and considered it his duty to make his wife's life as easy and pleasant as possible. To this end, he'd taken on a nurse to live in when Emily drew near her time and had employed the services of a Harley Street gynaecologist throughout the pregnancy. A nanny had been put on the staff well in advance and was already in residence.

'Rather weak and *very* tired,' she said, 'but that's only to be expected, isn't it?'

'You'll get your strength back during your laying in.'

'Oh, yes. Two weeks will make a world of difference.'

The baby started to whimper then to emit lusty screams.

'Shall I ask Nanny to take him?' suggested Philip worriedly.

'Yes, I think perhaps you'd better, dear, so that we can talk in peace.'

At the touch of a bell a uniformed nanny appeared and whisked the crying baby away to the nursery.

'About a name for him,' remarked Emily. 'I don't want to inflict either of his grandfather's names on him. Humphrey or Albert would be too cruel. Will your father be offended, do you think?'

The only time Philip's father had pretended an interest in the forthcoming baby was when his wife had forced him into it. 'No, of course not,' Philip assured her.

'That's good. So how about calling him Toby?'

'I like that.'

'That's settled then, Toby Verne it is. Mmm ... I think that sounds quite nice, don't you?'

'Perfect.' Seeing Emily so serene and happy, it was as though her unbalanced behaviour in Paris had never happened. Apart from her characteristic mood swings there had been nothing to mar a blissful ten months together.

'Are you going to celebrate the birth this evening in the traditional boozy way?' she enquired.

'I thought it would be rather nice if we were to drink a toast to Toby up here with you when the grandparents arrive to see him,' he said. 'They're on their way over now.'

'Lovely.'

Everything was indeed lovely. Was it too perfect to last? he found himself wondering.

No sooner had Lizzie got used to coping with one baby than she was pregnant again. Almost a year to the day after Jed's birth, Bruce arrived, followed just under a year later by a sister, Eva. Three children in as many years kept her fully occupied but she loved them all to distraction.

Her days were long and arduous, though, because she wove silk at home for a master weaver who ran a business using only outworkers. The pay was abysmal but he supplied her with a handloom, delivered the materials and collected the work. She was only too glad of the chance to earn a few shillings because, although they could just about manage to live on Stan's wages, there was almost nothing left over after the rent and food for clothes and other eventualities.

Wanting more for her children than ragged second and third hand clothes and a diet of bread and dripping, Lizzie was at her loom every morning before anyone else was up. A few hours' work without the children under her feet was worth double that done in their demanding presence.

Space was something of a problem because they only had two rooms – the bedroom in which they all slept and the living room in which they did everything else. Fortunately the latter was quite spacious so Lizzie was able to fit her loom in by the window to catch the light. She covered it with a sheet when it wasn't in use as protection against busy little fingers.

No matter how much work she had on, she always took the

children out in the afternoon for some fresh air. They usually shopped in the Portobello Road or High Street, Notting Hill, then went to the park or to visit Polly or June. If it meant working all night at her loom to make up the time, she never missed this ritual which she considered essential to the children's well-being. Their whole day revolved around the outing.

One chilly autumn afternoon when Eva was about six months old, Lizzie trekked to the shops at Notting Hill pushing the high black perambulator. Eva was sleeping inside and the two boys were sitting on the end, warmly clad in woolly hats and mittens. She went to the butcher's for a hambone to boil for stew for tomorrow's dinner and purchased some vegetables from a street barrow.

She had just emerged from the grocer's with a twist of tea, a ha'porth of sugar and a few other items when she noticed a well-dressed woman wearing a sash in the official purple, white and green colours of the Women's Social and Political Union. She was standing in the gutter selling the newspaper *Votes for Women*.

Lizzie was tempted to buy a copy for she supported women's suffrage in principle even though she had neither the time nor the freedom to go to their meetings or work as a volunteer. But if she were to spend a penny on the newspaper, she'd leave herself without enough money to buy the children the few sweets she'd promised them.

As she stood mentally debating the question, she saw two rough-looking young men come out of a side street and approach the suffragette in an unmistakably threatening manner. Such was the volume of their abuse towards the woman and her cause, the vile invective could be heard above the harsh hubbub of street noise – the rattle and roar of traffic, much of it horse-drawn, and the shouts of street traders announcing their wares.

Horrified, Lizzie watched as the two men began physically assaulting the suffragette. One was pushing her, the other dealt her a blow to her head. She seemed to be putting up a fight, she even managed to hit one of them with her large handbag, but the unequal odds soon took their toll and she fell to the ground.

Leaving the pram in a row of others lined up outside the grocer's shop, Lizzie rushed to her assistance, burning with fury and ready to do battle with the attackers. But by the time she got there, they had gone, frightened off by people hurrying to the woman's aid.

'You poor thing,' said Lizzie, first on the scene. 'Here, let me give you a hand up.'

'Thank you.'

Gently, she pulled the woman to her feet and placed a reassuring hand on her arm. 'You all right, love?'

'Yes, I think so,' said Meg Verne, her olive skin suddenly pale. 'I'm rather shaken up, though.'

'I should think you are! If I'd got here a minute sooner those louts would be the ones feeling shaken, I can tell you,' said Lizzie, gathering the copies of the newspaper that were scattered in the gutter and handing them to Meg as other onlookers lost interest and moved on. 'With two of us they wouldn't have stood a chance.'

'I managed to catch one of them with my bag,' said Meg.

'Yeah, I saw you having a go. Two against one isn't fair

though,' said Lizzie, 'especially as men are more powerful than us. Well, physically anyway.'

'In every way,' said Meg. 'Which is why I'm out on the streets selling these . . . to try to even things up a bit for us girls.'

Seeing her at close proximity, Lizzie realised why she looked vaguely familiar.

'Well, I'll be blowed, it's Mrs Verne,' she said, introducing herself and explaining her connection with her family firm. 'You visited the factory a few times while I was there. I didn't expect to see you on this side of town.'

'We're trying to get our message across to women in all areas.' Meg looked worried. 'I'd appreciate your not saying anything at home about what I was doing here, though. If your husband mentions it at the factory, it might reach my husband's ears and he'll make it awkward for me to carry on. I wear the banner with pride but only when Humphrey isn't around. Discretion is definitely the better part of valour in this particular instance. He's a dear but stubbornly opposed to our campaign.'

'Don't worry, your secret's safe with me.' Lizzie looked across the road. 'I have to go now, I've left my nippers in the pram outside the grocer's.'

'Yes, of course, you get along, dear. Thank you for your help.'

Lizzie was about to go on her way when she realised by the woman's colour just how shaken she must be.

'Look, I only live a few minutes' walk from here,' she told her. 'Why not come home with me and have a cuppa tea and a sit down? You look really done in.'

'It's very kind of you but I'm sure you've enough to do . . .'

'Nothing that can't wait. I was only gonna take the kids round their gran's for an hour. It won't hurt them to miss that for once. I'll pop into the sweet shop on the way home, though, to get 'em something to keep 'em quiet.'

'In that case, thank you,' said Meg, whose legs were feeling decidedly unreliable. 'I do feel a rather pressing need to rest for a while before I carry on.'

Ten minutes later she was comfortably ensconced on an elderly sofa drinking a cup of strong, sweet tea in a room that should have been squalid but was surprisingly snug. It was a mystery to Meg how anything so tatty and overcrowded could be made to look homely. A shabby brown three-piece suite circled the fireplace at one end of the room and oddment dining furniture was neatly arranged at the other. Numerous other artifacts added to the conglomeration – something covered in a dust sheet by the window; a kitchen dresser; a forlorn wooden stand bearing a chipped enamel washing-up bowl; and a water jug standing next to a grim gas cooker.

Her hostess moved the fireguard, which was strung with damp, steaming washing, and stirred the coals into a red glow. The two little boys were sitting on the floor happily immersed in two ounces of Dolly Mixtures shared between them in separate paper bags, and the baby was asleep in the bedroom in her cot.

Meg was still trying to work out how this hovel of a place had been made into a cosy home. She came to the conclusion that it was all down to the copious use of soap and polish, the careful choice of pretty curtain material added to the creative arrangement of cheap ornaments, and a vase of fresh chrysanthemums in the centre of the table which was covered with a maroon, tassel-edged cloth.

'Vastly different to what you're used to, I expect,' remarked Lizzie, noticing her guest's scrutiny.

'I can't deny it,' admitted the visitor. 'I was just thinking how nice you've made it look, though, my dear.'

'We manage,' said Lizzie sipping her tea and feeling surprisingly easy in the other woman's company.

Meg's curiosity finally got the better of her. 'Would it be terribly rude of me to ask what is underneath the dust sheet?'

'Of course not,' smiled Lizzie. 'It's a handloom. I'm an outworker.'

'I say, you certainly have your hands full, don't you?'

'Well, I don't have time to sit about doing nothing, put it that way,' smiled Lizzie. 'But it helps us to make ends meet, Mrs Verne.'

'Meg, please,' she requested casually before continuing, 'I admire you for your industriousness.'

'I don't have any choice, Mrs . . . er, Meg,' she explained. 'We each have to make the most of our capabilities, don't you think?'

'Yes, that's a maxim I've always lived by, too.'

'I have good weaving skills, three lovely kids and a husband with a wage that can only just feed us and pay the rent. If I want shoes on the children's feet and jam on their bread, I've gotta work to get 'em.'

'It must be hard.'

'We're used to hardship round here,' said Lizzie. 'We just have to make the best of things.'

'You don't strike me as the sort of person who finds it easy to resign herself, though,' said the other woman conversationally. 'Any more than I do. I wouldn't be out on the streets campaigning for women's rights if I did.'

'With respect, Mrs Verne . . . I mean, Meg,' said Lizzie, 'women of your class are in a position to try to change things. You have the time and the money to support causes. I can't even afford the suffragette newspaper without taking food out of my kids' mouths. I certainly can't take an active part in the campaign because I'm working every hour God sends. People like you have servants to see to your domestic chores – nannies to look after the children . . .'

'We do have quite a few members from the working classes, you know,' Meg informed her. 'But, yes, I agree it is more difficult.'

'Impossible for some of us.'

'Inequality of the sexes runs right through the social classes,' Meg pointed out. 'Women in your position are forced to work in menial jobs while we are not allowed to work at all – which is why we have time to give to worthy causes.'

'I know which I'd choose!'

'We have our frustrations the same as you,' explained Meg. 'Many middle-class women want more from life than what the home has to offer. Some are struggling to enter the professions on equal terms with men but only a few have succeeded. We want a time to come when a woman qualifying as a doctor isn't so rare that it warrants attention in the newspapers.'

'You're right about me,' said Lizzie, feeling able to put her thoughts into words about this for the first time. 'I do find it hard to accept that my circumstances will never change.' She waved a hand at the room. 'I may not be an intellectual but I know I want better than this. I want more than working all day to make someone else rich while my children live hand to mouth in cramped conditions. But I don't have the means to change anything ... without money I'm powerless ... so resignation is my only choice.'

'Yes, I can see what you mean,' said Meg, deciding that she liked this bright young woman.

'I'm not jealous of your possessions,' explained Lizzie, 'but I do envy you the power to make things happen.'

'There isn't much I can say to that,' said Meg. 'It's all a bit of a lottery, isn't it? I mean, which class we are born into.'

'Mmm ... I suppose so.'

'Of course, one occasionally hears of someone from the lower classes bettering themselves significantly.'

'Not often enough, though,' said Lizzie. 'It beats me how anyone manages it without funds to get started.'

'I don't know the answer to that either.' Meg rose with reluctance for she found Lizzie's company most enjoyable. 'Anyway, I must be on my way. Time to sell a few more papers, spread the word and bring in a bit more cash for union funds.'

'You're still going out in the streets with them then, after what happened?'

'Of course. Our movement is not for the faint-hearted.' She picked up her large black leather bag. 'Some of our members have been very badly beaten while out selling newspapers. We're unpopular with a lot of people ... and not just the general public either. We have to walk in the gutter to sell our newspapers or be charged with obstruction of the pavement by the police.'

'Get away!'

'It's true.'

Lizzie felt a strong rapport with Meg even though she knew she would probably never see her again. They had a lot in common despite their different backgrounds.

'Look, my dear,' said Meg, taking her purse out of her bag, 'you've been so kind to me. I'd like to show my appreciation.'

Lizzie's face hardened. 'Thank you, but I don't need payment for behaving in a normal civilised manner.'

'Oh, dear, I didn't mean to offend you,' said the older woman, biting her lip. 'It's just that . . . well, you said yourself that things are not easy for you and I'd like to help in a small way.'

'You misunderstood me, I wasn't hinting at a handout.'

'I know you weren't but I really would like to . . .'

'No, thank you,' interrupted Lizzie coolly. 'And I'd rather you didn't embarrass me by mentioning it again.'

Seeing the quiet determination in her eyes, Meg knew she was beaten. Despite all the odds against it, Meg was convinced that at some point in her life Lizzie Carter would find a way out of her present circumstances.

'All right, my dear,' she agreed gently, 'just as you wish.'

Glancing idly through the window down into the street, Lizzie's heart took a sudden dive.

'Oh, Lor. You'd better take that banner off and put it in your bag along with your newspapers,' she suggested anxiously. 'My mother-in-law is coming this way.'

'She's not a supporter, then?'

'I'll say she's not,' confirmed Lizzie. 'She thinks women should stay at home and keep out of politics. If she gets wind of what you're up to and tells my husband, it'll be all round the factory tomorrow.'

'Thanks for the warning.'

Together they stuffed the incriminating articles into Meg's bag, giggling like naughty schoolgirls.

'What on earth was that Verne woman doing at your place, Lizzie?' asked Polly on the way upstairs, having been briefly introduced to Meg in the hall as Lizzie showed her out.

'She came over poorly in the street,' explained Lizzie, 'so I brought her back here for a sit down and a cup of tea.'

'Oh, you did, did you?' said Polly critically.

'Well . . . yes.'

'What was she doing in these parts anyway?' Polly demanded aggressively.

'I saw her in Notting Hill High Street,' said Lizzie, evading the question.

'Surely she wouldn't be shopping round there?' declared Polly. 'Knightsbridge is for the likes of her.'

'Maybe she was on her way somewhere?' suggested Lizzie innocently.

'Walking in the streets? They have a bloomin' great motor car complete with chauffeur. It just doesn't make sense,' exclaimed Polly who sensed she wasn't being given the whole story.

'I really couldn't say. I didn't pry into her personal affairs,' said Lizzie.

'I can't think what came over you, taking her into your home.'

'She wasn't feeling well, what else could I have done?'

'You should have taken her into a shop,' said Polly quickly. 'They'd have looked after her until she was well enough to get a cab home.'

'Well, it's done now and I can't see that it matters,' insisted Lizzie. 'She's a very nice woman actually.'

'You shouldn't try to make friends with a Verne,' said Polly aggressively.

'I gave her a cup of tea and shelter for half an hour or so,' Lizzie informed her. 'I didn't invite her for Sunday dinner.'

'There's no call to be sarcastic,' snapped her mother-in-law who couldn't bear the thought of any member of her family engaging in activities of which she wasn't fully aware. 'Are you going to tell Stan that she was here?'

'If I think of it, yes. Is there any reason why I shouldn't?'

'He won't like it,' said Polly with a grave shake of the head. 'You know how he feels about the Vernes.'

'I couldn't just ignore someone who was sick just because their name happens to be Verne.'

'Plenty of people would have been only too willing to help her.'

'Look, I'm sorry if it upsets you, but I'm not prepared to turn a blind eye when someone's ill just because my husband has a paranoid grudge against their family.'

'Who are you callin' para . . . er . . . loopy?' Polly wanted to know.

'When it comes to the Vernes, Philip in particular, that's exactly what Stan is,' said Lizzie clarifying her thoughts on the subject for the first time.

'How can you say something like that when the man pushed Stan down the stairs?' Polly reproached her. 'He could have been seriously injured if he'd fallen awkwardly.'

Lizzie remained silent while she wrestled with seething irritation towards her mother-in-law whose narrow viewpoint increasingly infuriated her. It wasn't lack of courage that prevented Lizzie from battling things out to the bitter end with her, but obedience to a lifelong bond of respect, love and gratitude. To articulate her doubts about Stan's version of that wretched incident on the stairs would genuinely wound Polly, even after all this time, and hurting her was something Lizzie tried never to do. She reckoned she owed her that much.

'It's all in the past,' she said patiently, 'don't you think it's best forgotten?'

'Stan won't forget it.'

'You and I can, though, can't we, Mum?' she said addressing her in the affectionate manner that had become normal practice soon after she'd legally become part of the family.

'I'll not forget it,' came the stubborn reply. 'Families should stick together. The Vernes would certainly close ranks against us if the occasion were ever to arise, make no mistake about that.'

'If you say so,' sighed Lizzie wearily.

Fortunately they'd reached her rooms and Jed eased the tension between them.

'Hello, Gran,' he said, running up to her and hugging her legs in delight for all the children adored their indulgent grandmother. 'Have you got anything for us in your bag?'

'Now then, Jed, what have I told you about asking your granny for things?' admonished his mother.

But she was wasting her breath.

'Well . . . I might just be able to find something in here,'

Polly was saying, delving into her shopping basket and producing a bag of broken biscuits which she handed to him with a huge grin. 'Give 'em to your mum to share between you and Bruce at tea time.'

The tension between the two women seemed to have passed and Lizzie was glad. Since her slavish devotion to Polly had first shown signs of weakening just before her wedding, Lizzie had been through troubled periods over her feelings for her. Sometimes, when Polly was being particularly dogmatic, Lizzie almost hated her and was then guilt-ridden for ages afterwards. But it was becoming increasingly difficult for her to go along with her mother-in-law's wish for all members of the Carter clan to be of one mind.

Watching the older woman sitting on the sofa with her beloved grandchildren by her side, Lizzie was reminded of her loving heart. Polly would willingly go without food herself rather than see any of her family go hungry.

But it was her determined need to possess all those who she loved that turned her into a monster, and Lizzie didn't know for how much longer she could take it. She did know, however, that it couldn't go on forever. One of these days it was going to come to a head, and that was going to be very painful for them both!

Chapter Four

There was quite a gathering at Polly's for high tea on August
Bank Holiday Monday 1914. Lizzie and Stan and the children
were there as well as Bobby and June with their twins, Keith
and Jamie, who were a year old. The family, en masse, had
spent an enjoyable afternoon at the Bank Holiday fair on
Shepherd's Bush Green.

With her entire brood in attendance, Polly was in her
element. 'We'll have to get a bigger table soon if the family
expands any more,' she chirped hopefully as they all sat down
to tinned meat and salad, doorsteps of bread and margarine, a
bowl piled high with winkles, and an enormous caraway seed
cake.

'Well, I hope I'm not the one to oblige,' grinned June, whose
little son was busily encrusting her clothes with half-chewed
bread and jam while his brother made messy inroads into a
soggy crust on Bobby's knee next to her. 'I've quite enough to
do with these two.'

'I'm happy to leave it to Luke and Roy to add to the Carter
numbers, too,' laughed Lizzie.

'They'll have to find wives first,' said Polly, only half
joking. 'I want no stroppy fathers knocking on my door.'

'It's about time those two left home and set up on their own,' said Will who liked the idea of a shorter queue for the lavatory.

'They might be leaving sooner than you think,' remarked Stan on a more serious note. 'With war about to break out.'

'We'll all have to go, come to that,' Bobby pointed out. 'They reckon they're gonna be recruiting for volunteers.'

'Surely they won't expect married men to join up?' said June.

'It's *every* young man's duty to fight for his country,' stated Stan categorically.

'I still can't see why things that are happening miles away in Europe have anything to do with us here in Britain,' said Polly, whose stomach had begun to churn at the idea of her sons going to war.

'From what I can make out from reading the papers, Germany has been planning to take more territory by force for some time,' said Roy, studiously picking a winkle out of its shell with a pin.

'And if they do go ahead and attack Belgium, we'll have to step in and help because of some ancient treaty in which Britain promised to defend Belgium,' added Luke.

'Quite right too,' said Roy who was an ardent supporter of justice. 'The Germans can't be allowed to get away with that sort of thing.'

There was a murmur of agreement.

'And all of this because some Archduke was murdered in the Balkans?' put in Lizzie.

'That was just the excuse the Kaiser had been waiting for to put the German military to the test,' explained Bobby.

'It doesn't seem right that we should be drawn into a war

over something that's nothing to do with us, though,' said Polly.

'Don't worry, Ma, the Germans'll soon step into line once the Carter brothers get on the job,' said Stan lightly.

'They will an' all,' she said, brightening with a sudden surge of patriotic spirit. 'No one tangles with my boys and gets away with it.'

'Hey, hang on,' said Lizzie. 'War hasn't even been declared yet.'

'Just a matter of time, love,' said Stan cheerfully.

'Any minute now, I reckon,' agreed Bobby.

Lizzie found it most peculiar that the men awaited dire news with such enthusiasm.

'They're just like little boys hungry for adventure, aren't they?' June remarked to Lizzie later as they walked home together in the summer evening. 'They can't wait to join up.'

'I was just thinking the same thing myself, actually.' Their husbands were walking on ahead. Stan was carrying Jed on his shoulders, Bobby was doing the same with Keith. The other children were sleepily ensconced in pushchairs being pushed by their mothers. This happy procession was a familiar sight for the two young families lived in close proximity and saw a lot of each other. 'Still, men are conditioned from birth to be keen on duty to King and country and all that.'

'I don't relish the idea of Bobby going into the army,' said June.

'I'm not mad about the idea of Stan going either but I suppose we'll just have to put up with it if it does come to that.'

'They say it's just as much our duty to give them a hero's send off as it is theirs to go.'

'Everyone's talking a lot about duty lately,' observed Lizzie. 'Mother-in-law is doing her nut at the thought of them going.'

'Cor, not half! She gets withdrawal symptoms if she has to go a day without seeing her precious boys. Having them away overseas will pole-axe her.'

'Bobby calls to see her every day. Never misses.'

'So does Stan.'

'I hope my children are as dutiful when they grow up.'

'It isn't just duty, though, is it?' remarked Lizzie thoughtfully. 'They go because they really want to see her.'

'We all do. Let's face it, she's a very compelling sort of a person.'

'Mmm . . . even though we all have to dance to her tune.'

'I think she's bossier with you than she is with me, you know,' said June. 'Maybe because she considers you to be a daughter rather than just a daughter-in-law.'

'You're probably right.'

'She really *does* think the world of you, you know, Lizzie.'

'Yes, I know, but all due credit to her, she treats her daughters-in-law equally.'

'Just about. You've always been the favourite, though,' declared June. 'It's only natural . . . she brought you up.'

'You do feel as though you're part of the Carter family though, don't you?' enquired Lizzie.

'Sort of but not like you are. I mean, they all adore you.' She paused and looked at Lizzie with a wry grin. 'I used to be absolutely green about you and Bobby when we were kids. I hated you at times.'

'Oh, why?'

'Because you and he were such a pair,' she explained. 'I always thought it would be Bobby and not Stan you'd marry.'

'You should have told me how you felt. I could have put your mind at rest.'

'Some things are too painful to talk about at that sensitive age,' June confessed.

'Looking back on it, I suppose Bobby and I could have given the wrong impression. We were always very fond of each other, still are, but never in that way,' Lizzie explained. 'Stan was the one I fancied. You were the one Bobby was after.'

'I had to chase him hard to make him realise it though, didn't I? I made all the running at first.'

'It worked out all right, though, didn't it?' said Lizzie. 'The two of you seem very happy together.'

'We are. That's why I dread the thought of him going away.'

'He and Stan will be among the first to join up, I reckon,' said Lizzie. 'Judging by the way they're talking.'

'Mmm.'

Lizzie thought that June would probably suffer more as a grass widow than she herself would because Bobby was much more of a family man than Stan whose marital interest had declined in direct proportion to his growing obsession with socialism. Most evenings he was out with Arthur and their cronies, attending some meeting or putting the world to rights in a pub somewhere.

'Still, at least we'll have each other for company,' said Lizzie.

'Yeah.'

'It's really good the way things turned out, isn't it? You

know, us ending up related,' said Lizzie.

'I'm glad.'

'Me too. It would have been hellish if Stan's brother had married someone I didn't get on with,' she remarked. 'With the Carters being such a clannish lot.'

They strolled on in the pale glow of the gaslight. People stood about chatting on street corners in the summer evening, many returning from Bank Holiday outings. Singing could be heard in the distance. 'Land of Hope and Glory' rose evocatively from somewhere not too far away. Lizzie could feel a current of excitement on the streets as the population drew together to face the uncertainty of the future.

She felt a sudden surge of sisterly feeling for June as they awaited the unknown together. Lizzie had always been the stronger partner in their friendship but at this vulnerable moment she felt comforted and strengthened by June's presence in her life.

Following the German invasion of Belgium the next day, war was declared to a nation fired with patriotic fervour. People poured on to the streets waving flags and singing the 'National Anthem'.

As the days and weeks passed, war fever grew. London was awash with flags flying, appeals to enlist, men in khaki and special constables. Influenced by dreadful anti-German stories in the newspapers, Londoners became infected with hatred for anything even remotely connected with Germany.

There were street parades, and concerts to raise money for the war effort, and the recruiting offices were flooded with men eager to join up. All the Carter boys were among their number and Polly threw a party to celebrate her 'brave boys' having taken the King's shilling.

Stan went away one foggy morning in late-autumn. Having seen him say goodbye to the children upstairs, Lizzie went down to the front door with him to see him off.

'You look after yourself now,' she said emotionally, for she still loved him for all his faults.

'Don't you worry about me,' said Stan, hugging her tight. 'You take care. I won't be gone long. It'll all be over by Christmas, everyone knows that.'

Neither of them seemed to know quite what to say next so after an awkward embrace he was gone, striding off into the smog, giving a final wave before he turned the corner.

Patriotism was all very well, thought Lizzie, sniffing into her handkerchief, but it didn't take away the aching void she felt in the pit of her stomach. Composing herself, she went upstairs to her children.

Philip Verne walked out of the factory gates one wet February lunchtime and headed for South Kensington on foot for it had become unpatriotic to use a motor car for private business. His hands were thrust deep into the pockets of his raincoat and his head was down. He was so deeply engrossed in thought, he barely noticed the heavy rain.

A guilty conscience was his wearisome burden. It shadowed his every waking moment and filled his dreams at night. He didn't need his father's implied disapproval, his pointed talk about patriotism and every fit young man's duty or his over-emphasised pride in his younger son, Neville, who hadn't hesitated for a moment before joining up.

'Must do our bit for King and country, what?' he'd said lightly. 'Give the Germans a trouncing and all that.'

And never a word of criticism about the fact that his brother hadn't followed his example. Philip respected that. Beneath his pleasure-seeking superficiality, Neville had the sensitivity to respect the fact that it was every man's personal decision.

It was over six months since the outbreak of war. More than half a year of street parades, recruiting campaigns and Lord Kitchener pointing his accusing finger from ubiquitous posters and urging men to JOIN YOUR COUNTRY'S ARMY. It had been hell for Philip.

The factory had changed dramatically too. All the eligible men had disappeared almost overnight to join up and Verne's was no longer engaged in the weaving of luxury silks. They now worked with viscose fibre known as artificial silk as well as cotton and wool blends to make fabric to be used for uniforms.

Splashing through the puddles on the broken pavements of North Kensington, through narrow streets of terraced houses with dusty windows and broken doors, Philip was aware of sour smells seeping from the houses. Many of them had their doors open despite the weather and small, ragged children stared out wistfully, waiting for the rain to stop so they could resume their street games. Shabbily dressed women, weighed down with shopping bags, passed him on the street, seeming to scowl at him accusingly. He expected to be given a white feather at any moment.

Entering the more salubrious ambience of his home territory, where elegant houses were arranged in smart squares, leafy avenues or stylish crescents, he continued on past his own home in Cedar Square and into Eden Crescent.

'I hoped I might catch you at home at this time of day, Mother,' he said, as he was shown into the dining room of the family home by the elderly housekeeper, Mrs Todd, the only member of the Vernes' domestic staff who hadn't left to go on to war work.

'I'm only here long enough to have a bite to eat, dear,' she said, smiling at him from her seat at the table. 'Won't you join me?'

'I'd love to, but no . . . Emily will be expecting me.'

'Yes, of course. I know you always try to get home to have lunch with her.'

'Still busy with your voluntary work?' he asked.

'I'll say. As one door closes another one opens, as they say,' she said, referring to the fact that at the outbreak of war most members of the WSPU had put their political campaign to one side and concentrated their energies on fighting the war on the home front. Within a week of going to war, the government had released all suffragette prisoners on the understanding that their violent activities would cease.

'So what's on your agenda today?' he enquired politely.

'I'm helping to set up a workroom for destitute women. Somewhere they can earn money sewing while helping the war effort,' she explained.

'What a good idea.'

Meg waved her hand towards a chair nearby. 'But you've obviously something on your mind so sit down and tell me about it.'

He did as she asked and she continued with her meal. 'Well, I do have something of a dilemma actually and you're the only person I feel I can talk to about it.'

'It's about your not having joined up, isn't it?' she said, putting her knife and fork down and giving him her full attention.

He nodded.

'And you haven't done so because of Emily?' she suggested.

'You guessed.'

'Well, I knew it wasn't because of cowardice.'

'I appreciate your faith in me.'

'If a mother doesn't have it, who does?'

'Certainly not Father.'

'Don't take it personally. It's all black and white to him. He thinks every eligible man should go and fight for his country regardless of any other commitments. Anyway, he's never actually seen Emily when she's ill . . . he doesn't know the extent of the problem.'

'I feel I can't leave her. No one else can cope with her when she's sick.'

'I can understand your concern.'

'As you know, she can go for months being as normal as you or I, and I think she's better then it starts up again and I know she isn't. She never will be.'

'It's a dreadful worry for you.'

'She's completely demented when she's having a bad patch, convinced all the demons in the world are after her. I feel I must be close at hand to look after her. I'm afraid she might physically damage herself. She can be quite self-destructive at times, as you know.'

'Is there nothing more the doctor can do?'

'No. He just keeps me supplied with laudanum to give her.

And he comes if I call him and gives her a shot of something if she's really bad.'

'It's a terrible thing to say but I think that miscarriage she had that left her unable to have any more children is a blessing,' said Meg sadly. 'I mean, even with the best domestic help money can buy, a child still needs a stable mother.'

'Toby seems surprisingly well-adjusted,' said Philip. 'I try to protect him as much as I can and Nanny is very good. Of course, the problem is only intermittent. When Emily is well no one would know there's anything wrong with her.'

'The trouble with this kind of illness is that it has to be hidden away like a guilty secret,' she said.

'Oh, yes . . . apart from the doctor and trusted staff it must never go outside the family, for Emily's sake,' said Philip firmly. 'I won't have her made into a figure of fun.'

'It must be heartbreaking for you, dear,' said Meg, leaning towards him with her elbows on the table.

'Seeing someone you love in such a bad way isn't pleasant but I won't have her put into an asylum,' he said vehemently. 'It's my duty to look after her at home.'

'But now you're being tormented by this other duty?' she suggested.

'That's right.'

'It would be easier for you if they introduced conscription, you wouldn't have a choice then,' she said.

'Perhaps.' He shook his head despairingly. 'I just don't know what to do, Mother. They urgently need more men at the front and I feel my duty is on the battlefields of France . . . but I'm needed here with Emily too.'

'Well, if you really feel you should enlist, I'll do everything

79

I can to help here with Emily while you're away,' she said. 'Your housekeeper could let me know whenever she notices the signs and I'll go straight to her. I can be there within minutes.'

'You'd be prepared to take the responsibility, then?' he said. 'Emily isn't easy to deal with when she's ill.'

'I'll manage. We each have to do what we can to help out in these difficult times, don't we?' Meg gave him a hard look. 'I'm proud of you for your devotion to your wife and God knows I don't want you to go and fight – there are men dying out there in their thousands in France – but I know you'll never be able to live with yourself if you feel you've failed in your duty to your country.'

'Yes, I know that too.'

'The decision must be yours, though.'

'We both know that I don't really have a choice,' he told her gravely, but the tension had lifted from his face now that his decision was made. 'I've hung back long enough. I'll call in at the recruiting office before I go back to work.'

Although Lizzie could manage on the separation allowance the government paid to wives of soldiers away at the front, there was very little left over for incidentals, so when she lost her job life was grim. The fact that the allowance was often paid late didn't help matters either.

The war had had a serious effect on the economy. Many industries were cutting back on their operations. The fact that the wealthy were cancelling orders for clothes and luxury goods in a patriotic urge to economise had put her employer out of business and Lizzie out of work. Women's employment of any kind was hard to find. While the men were away fighting, the scope of female support was limited to knitting for the troops.

But early in 1915 things began to change rapidly. As more and more men enlisted and businesses were short staffed, the solution became obvious to employers who began to replace the men with women in banks, shops and offices. It didn't end there either, as June pointed out to Lizzie one wet February afternoon over a cup of tea at Lizzie's place.

'I saw a woman road-sweeper in Hammersmith the other day.'

'Get away! Who'd have thought that a female would ever be employed to do standard men's work like that?' said Lizzie. 'Mind you, there was a woman driving a delivery van in Notting Hill last week.'

'They reckon they'll even be taking them on in munitions factories if the war goes on much longer too.'

'Yeah . . . I heard something about that too,' said Lizzie thoughtfully. 'There's talk of the government providing nurseries for working mothers in some areas, though I don't know if there'll be any round here.'

'I'm not sure if I'd fancy leaving mine in a nursery,' said June.

'Me neither.'

'I was talking to a woman in the market who knows someone who's just started on the trams as a conductor,' said June, 'she said the pay's ever so good. A darned sight better than we get working at home.'

'Really? I wouldn't mind working on the trams,' said Lizzie. 'I'd like to do my bit for the war effort.'

'I wouldn't have the nerve,' confessed June. 'I'd never be able to control a tram full of people.'

''Course you would,' said Lizzie, 'and it's better than staying at home feeling useless while the men are away fighting.'

'You're more confident than me . . . always have been.'

'You'd soon improve, working among the general public. And at least we'd be doing something for our country,' said Lizzie, enthusiasm growing by the second. 'It would mean we'd have that bit extra to spend on the kids too.'

'But we can't go out to work because of them.'

'I wonder if Mother-in-law would be willing to look after them for a few hours each day?' suggested Lizzie. 'I wouldn't mind leaving mine with her and if their cousins were there too, they'd all have a whale of a time. You know how she dotes on her grandchildren. It would help to take her mind off her boys too. She worries about them dreadfully.'

'She'll probably refuse on principle,' June pointed out. 'She's dead set against mothers going out to work and leaving their children unless it's absolutely unavoidable.'

'Things are different in wartime,' said Lizzie. 'It's up to all of us to do our bit.'

'We could ask her, I suppose,' said June doubtfully. 'Though you'd better do it, you're more likely to get her to agree than I am.'

'I'm not so sure about that but I'm willing to give it a try. And there's no time like the present,' said Lizzie exuberantly. 'Come on, kids, we're going round to see Granny.'

'It isn't that I mind having the kiddies, you know that,' said

Polly when Lizzie had put the question. 'But I believe a mother's place is at home with her children.'

'In normal times, maybe,' agreed Lizzie. 'But there's a crisis on . . . we're needed to keep the country running.'

'Yes, I know that,' said Polly, but she didn't sound convinced.

'You could look on it as your contribution to the war effort,' suggested Lizzie. 'After all, you're the only person we'd allow to look after our children while we're out working.'

'That's blackmail,' protested Polly, though the idea of having her grandchildren to herself without parental interference was very tempting. 'I do my bit. My fingers are practically dropping off from all the knitting I've been doin' for the troops.'

'Now's your chance to do something else as well,' said Lizzie. 'They say you earn good money on the trams, so we'd pay you properly for minding them.'

'As if I'd take payment for looking after my own grandchildren!' Although Polly was genuinely aghast at such a suggestion, she couldn't help thinking how useful a few extra shillings would be now that she only had one wage packet coming in. She hated not being able to treat the kiddies as she used to when all the boys were at home.

'You'd be a fool not to,' said Lizzie.

'We'd insist,' agreed June.

'The kids would be thrilled at the idea of spending more time with you. They love coming round here,' said Lizzie.

The thought of having the five adored children under her sole authority for part of each day was finally too much for Polly. 'You'd better get down to the tram depot to get yourself signed up then, hadn't you?' she said, grinning.

Lizzie and June were too excited to bother about the rain as they hurried to the bus-stop to catch the bus to Shepherd's Bush.

'Polly'll be in her element if we do go through with it,' said Lizzie. 'The kids adore her. They'd do anything to please her.'

'And she can take any amount of that,' laughed June.

'Can't we all?' said Lizzie. 'Dear old Polly, she's a good sort.'

'Hey, Liz. Look who's over there,' said June, glancing across the road at a tall, well-dressed man in a raincoat striding in the opposite direction.

'It's Philip Verne, isn't it?'

'Yeah, it's him all right.'

'He's on his way back to the factory after a late lunch, I expect,' surmised Lizzie. 'He wouldn't dare use his car, not these days.'

'Huh. Very nice too,' snorted June.

'Why the sour attitude?'

'Well, there's him all done up to the nines and leaving his factory just when he feels like it while our husbands are out in the trenches doin' God knows what.' Her voice rose with rage. 'Just look at him! Fit and strong and walkin' the streets in peace and comfort while men are dying at the front. I've a bloomin' good mind to go over there and tell him just what I think of cowards like him.'

'Calm down, June.'

'Why should I?'

'Because there's probably a very good reason why he hasn't

84

joined up yet,' Lizzie heard herself saying.

'Why are you sticking up for him?' demanded June, her fury exacerbated by Philip's expensive clothes which were completely out of place in this poor area.

'I'm not. Not especially.'

'Yes, you are, you're defending him,' June insisted. 'Though Gawd knows why.'

'He's never struck me as a coward, that's all,' said Lizzie.

'So why isn't he in the army then?' June wanted to know.

'Perhaps he hasn't got round to enlisting yet. Perhaps he's been held back for business reasons or something.'

'Held back, my eye! It's time he got down the recruiting office like any fit man should,' June retorted as the object of her fury passed out of sight. 'He deserves to be given a white feather, that one. I'd do it myself if I had one.'

'Not while you're with me you wouldn't because I wouldn't let you,' said Lizzie who was fiercely opposed to the cruel practice some women had of pinning a white feather to the lapels of any man seen in the streets in civilian clothes.

'Why not? He'd deserve it.'

'How do you know that?'

'It's obvious.'

'No, it isn't,' insisted Lizzie. 'You never know why a man hasn't joined up . . . there could be any number of reasons. You could pick on someone who's been prevented from enlisting by bad health, for instance.'

'Surely you're not suggesting Philip Verne isn't fit? A tall strapping man like him.'

'I'm not suggesting anything,' said Lizzie, as fierce in defence as June was on the attack. 'All I'm saying is, you can't tell what problems people have just by looking at them.'

'Stan wouldn't be pleased to hear you defending a Verne,' snorted June.

'You should know by now that I don't have the Carter mentality, that dictates we all share certain opinions just because we share a name.'

'But Philip Verne is Stan's sworn enemy!'

'If Stan wants to waste energy in hatred, that's up to him,' Lizzie exclaimed. 'But I'm not going to do the same, and he knows it. Life's too short for petty grievances.'

'So you think it's right that Philip Verne is still here living in comfort while your husband is at the front?'

Lizzie halted abruptly in her step and turned to June. 'Don't be ridiculous . . . *of course* I don't think that,' she said with sharp emphasis. 'All I am saying is that he could have a very good reason for not being there. It isn't up to us to judge when we don't know the facts.'

'All right, keep your hair on. Anyone would think you were sweet on Philip Verne the way you're carrying on.'

Lizzie was too angry even to express herself in words. She wasn't sure why she'd been so rattled by June's accusations except, perhaps, because she had a natural abhorrence of unconsidered judgements and victimisation – of anyone, not just Philip Verne!

By the time they got to the tram depot the argument was forgotten in their apprehension of the task at hand. The place was noisy and grimy and crowded with people. Drivers and conductors chattered loudly as they came off duty; fresh crews were heading towards their outgoing vehicles. Harassed supervisors clutching clipboards were rushing about purposefully.

Having made the reason for their visit known, Lizzie and June were told to wait outside the Depot Manager's office until Mr Beasley had time to see them.

Eventually they found themselves in an untidy, paper-strewn office sitting across a desk from a fraught little man with tufted black hair and a greying moustache.

'So you're looking for work as conductors on the trams then?' said Mr Beasley gruffly, owlish eyes resting on them only briefly before darting towards the window into the busy depot.

'Yes, that's right.'

'You realise it's shift work?' he informed them aggressively, dragging his attention away from the window.

'What will that entail, exactly?' enquired Lizzie.

'It means you'll have to take your turn working evenings every so often.'

'Oh . . . well, I suppose that's fair enough,' said Lizzie.

'You'd better be sure about it now because it'll be no use coming to me later on, when you're already in the job, with some tale about not being able to do the evening shift because of some domestic problem . . . or because your kids aren't well, or you're feeling a bit off colour, or some other damned feminine problem,' he told them with blatant hostility.

'That's funny. I thought the transport companies were trying to persuade women to come on to the trams, having lost so many men to the services,' said the outspoken Lizzie acidly. 'But you wouldn't think so to hear you talk!'

'If it was left to me I'd have no women around the depot at

all,' he told her bluntly. 'I think they should stay out of the way while the men get on and fight the war and run the country. A woman's place is at home where she belongs. Unfortunately it isn't up to me. I've been told to employ women, so that's what I have to do.'

'You might be pleasantly surprised,' suggested Lizzie with a withering stare. 'Some of us are quite capable. Why, some of us can even do joined up writing!'

'It's a question of horses for courses, my dear,' he countered with asperity, running a worried hand over his brow. 'After all, I wouldn't try to tell you how to run a home . . .'

'And we've no intention of telling *you* how to run a tram depot,' Lizzie riposted. 'But we do want to do our bit to keep the country going. So are you going to consider us for a job, or shall we try elsewhere?'

'I won't put up with troublemakers in my depot,' he announced, somewhat unnerved by her spirit.

'And we won't put up with being treated like imbeciles,' said Lizzie, finally losing her patience and standing up with an air of finality. 'So we'll go and find work somewhere else. I understand they're letting the weaker sex into all sorts of jobs these days.'

'That's right,' echoed the slightly less bold June.

With one accord they marched for the door.

'Wait a minute,' he said.

They turned.

'Yes, what is it?' enquired Lizzie.

'Perhaps I might have seemed a bit . . . er . . .'

'Insulting?' she finished for him.

'I'm under a lot of strain,' he explained, holding his head

dramatically. 'The war has thrown transport into chaos.'

'Is that any reason to be so damned rude?' said Lizzie.

'No, I suppose not.'

The two women stared at him without moving.

'All right, I'm sorry.'

'So are we,' said Lizzie.

'Er . . . look, ladies, I really do need more people to man the trams,' he said, looking very harassed indeed.

Lizzie and June walked slowly back towards his desk.

'Well, if you ask us ever so nicely we might just be able to help,' said Lizzie with a wicked grin.

He ran an eye over them. 'Mmm, you're both young and healthy. Is either of you interested in becoming a tram driver?' he asked, astonishing them.

'Not me,' said June in a tone that didn't invite persuasion.

'Would I have enough muscle?' enquired Lizzie thoughtfully.

He shrugged his shoulders. 'Before the war I'd have said no, but I'm desperate for drivers, and you'd soon toughen up.'

'No, I think I'd rather be a conductor,' she began.

'I could arrange for you to work together after training if one of you were to sign up as a driver,' he interrupted.

Lizzie didn't hesitate for long. 'All right, I'll give it a try.'

'Good.' He pushed some papers across the desk. 'You'll find full details of our terms and conditions in the leaflet. If you can fill in the application forms, I'll have them dealt with right away.'

Wondering what on earth she had let herself in for, Lizzie sat down next to June at his desk and dipped a pen into the ink.

Chapter Five

Lizzie stood on the open platform of her tram with her hands on the controls, left one on the lever that made the vehicle move, right one firmly upon the big brass handle that would bring it to a stop.

It was a cold November afternoon with angry grey skies and a savage wind that penetrated the thick dark overcoat of her uniform and turned her ears numb beneath her cap. The tram clunked to a halt and there was a reshuffle of passengers, all thickly swathed in hats and mufflers, faces screwed against the elements. Those boarding the vehicle fought to find a seat inside rather than climb the curved staircase to the windswept, open-topped upper deck.

'Not long till the end of the shift now, thank Gawd,' said June, standing next to her friend with her ticket machine strapped over her shoulder. 'I think my feet are gonna drop off with frostbite if I don't get into the warm soon.'

'I can't feel my toes either,' said Lizzie, who often felt quite nauseous from exposure to the weather on bitter days like this. 'Still, in less than an hour we'll be home by the fire.'

'Ooh, what a lovely thought!'

'Are we all set to move then, June?' asked Lizzie as her

friend ushered the last passenger on to the vehicle.

'Yep.' June gave a hearty ding-ding on the bell as confirmation then disappeared inside the cab to collect the fares.

Working the lever, Lizzie soon had the tram clanking and rattling onwards towards the next stop on its route back to Shepherd's Bush from Uxbridge where they'd simply swung the trolley, which was attached to overhead electric wires, around ready for the return journey. Lizzie had moved to the controls at the other end of the vehicle.

She'd been in the job for the best part of two years and was extremely happy in her work. She enjoyed the freedom and the fresh air and the sense of involvement in the world outside her Bessle Street rooms. It was only in weather like this that she looked back on her home-working days with affection.

As promised, Mr Beasley had arranged for her and June to work as a team and they'd been on the Shepherd's Bush to Uxbridge route for most of the time since training. Not being a woman of muscular proportions, Lizzie had found the driving physically challenging at first for a great deal of strength was required to work the levers. The ache in her arms and shoulders had been chronic until she'd got used to it.

Inevitably life had fallen into a routine. As hectic as it was fitting the job around family commitments, and callous as it seemed with Stan away fighting in France, it was a way of life Lizzie had come to value. The war had been good to her. It had given her financial relief and a degree of personal fulfilment, albeit driving a tram for long periods could be tedious and exhausting in the extreme.

The children had quickly adapted to her working regime

and were perfectly content to spend part of the day with their granny. Jed was at school now and Bruce would be starting quite soon, leaving only Eva at home during the day. They were all healthy, well-balanced kids, though the intrepid Bruce frequently robbed his mother of breath with his total disregard for danger or gravity. A dedicated daredevil, he shinned up trees – walls – fences – anything. Only the other day she'd caught him balancing on the window ledge of their rooms, several floors up.

Despite all the hard work involved in childminding, Polly seemed to thrive on it. Lizzie guessed that the children's exuberant presence helped to keep at bay worrying thoughts about events on the other side of the Channel. Lizzie and June insisted on rewarding her for her services so she had money in her pocket to spend, in common with many other women as female labour had expanded into a vast number of trades previously considered to be 'men's work'. This had escalated even more with the introduction of conscription earlier this year which forced men into the services whether they liked it or not.

Letters from Stan were rare and uninformative as all the mail was censored. He sounded cheerful, though according to rumours about what life was *really* like in the trenches which came from the wounded who were being shipped home in their thousands, he didn't have much reason to be. His health and safety were continually on Lizzie's mind but her job on the trams kept her sane.

'Acton High Street . . . anyone else for Acton High Street?' called June, whose confidence had increased with doing the job. 'Hurry along there, please, folks. Too cold to hang about now.' She grabbed the sleeve of a filthy urchin of about twelve. 'Hey, where did you spring from, you little horror? I haven't had any fare from you.'

'I lost me ticket.'

'And I'm Mary Pickford!'

'I did, missus, honest.'

'Go on with you,' she said in a firm but sympathetic tone, 'it's too bloomin' cold to argue. Just don't let me catch you stealin' a ride on my tram again.

'Cheeky young tearaway,' she said to Lizzie after he'd gone. 'But I reckon the tram company can afford to give him a ride. Poor little devil, he looked as though he could do with a good meal too.'

At last they drew into the depot and the two women went off duty.

'I've been thinking,' said Lizzie as they walked towards Thorn Street to collect the children, 'how about you and me giving Polly a night out on Saturday? Gertie Gitana is on at the Shepherd's Bush Empire this week. It should be a good show.'

'Ooh, Polly would love to see that. So would I for that matter,' enthused June.

'That's what I thought.'

'Any particular reason for this sudden burst of generosity?'

'Well, I know Polly can be a bossy old bat at times but her heart's in the right place and she's good to us and the kids,' said Lizzie.

'Yes, I know.'

'And she never goes out anywhere socially.'

'That's true,' agreed June. 'She hardly ever even goes to

the pub with Will. Household shopping is about the limit of her outings, and she spends most of the money we give her on her grandchildren.'

'You're right.'

'A night out will do her good.'

'It'll do us all good to go out, come to that,' said Lizzie. 'I can't remember the last time I went out anywhere just for fun.'

'What about the kids, though?'

'I've thought of that. I'll ask Will to baby sit for us,' said Lizzie. 'He has plenty of nights out at the local with his mates. It won't hurt him to stay in and let Polly have some light relief for a change.'

'If anyone can persuade him, you can,' said June.

'I'll certainly do my best.'

'You girls are spoiling me rotten. Tea out, fourpenny seats in the stalls at the Empire, and beer in the interval,' said Polly as Lizzie handed her a glass of stout in the bar of the Shepherd's Bush Empire on Saturday evening. 'I don't know what I've done to deserve it.'

'It's for bein' such a smashing mother-in-law,' said Lizzie.

'Hear, hear,' agreed June.

'Don't be so soft,' Polly protested, but she was very touched by their gesture. Her eyes were shining beneath the brim of her best black feather-trimmed hat which she wore with a dowdy, floor-length grey coat.

The younger women, who were both still only twenty-four, were much more fashionably attired with large squashy berets worn jauntily at an angle on their bobbed heads, and calf-length coats.

Polly raised her glass. 'Well, cheers, girls. Thanks for everything. I'm havin' a lovely time.'

They had made a real outing of it. They'd done a spot of window shopping and had Welsh Rarebit and muffins in a tea-shop before getting to the theatre in time for the first house. This had included the usual assortment of turns: a singer, a comedian, a troupe of rather clumsy clog dancers, a magician, and a performing poodle who had brought the house down by cocking its leg against the leg of the table it was supposed to jump over.

'And the best is still to come,' Lizzie reminded her.

'Not half! So let's drink up and get back to our seats,' said Polly.

The auditorium was packed and buzzing with excitement. Humanity at its most ebullient cheered, booed and whistled through a parade of entertainment of the brightest, brashest kind. There were jugglers, a team of acrobats, a baritone, another comic and, at last, the top of the bill came on to rapturous applause. Gertie Gitana, resplendent in cornflower blue, entranced the audience with her warm personality and melodious singing voice. She closed the show with everybody's favourite, 'Nellie Dean', to cries for more and hundreds of feet stamping their appreciation in the aisles.

'Oh, girls, I don't know when I've enjoyed myself so much,' said Polly as they walked towards the bus-stop. 'It's taken me right out of myself. I feel like a new woman.'

They chattered about the show all the way home and Polly was full of it when they got in.

'The girls have really done me proud, Will,' she effused, taking off her hat and coat, her cheeks pink with excitement.

'Gertie Gitana was lovely. She sang all my favourites.'

'That's good. I'm glad you've enjoyed yourself, love,' he said in an unusually subdued tone.

'Have the children been all right?' asked Lizzie, noticing a certain tension about him. 'I hope they haven't been playing you up.'

'Good as gold, the lot of 'em. I put 'em in the boys' beds like you said.' They had agreed beforehand that the children would sleep at Polly's tonight to save dragging them out in the cold night air. 'Not sure if they're asleep though. They were larking about up there for ages.'

'Sounds familiar,' said Lizzie.

'There was one almighty thump, I had to go up to investigate.'

'Bruce?' guessed Lizzie.

'He'd jumped off the top of the ruddy tallboy!'

'That's typical,' she said, unable to stifle a grin but puzzled by her father-in-law's strained manner. 'I'll go up and see them.'

'I'll come with you,' said June.

Upstairs all was quiet and the children were sleeping soundly.

'Will seems a bit odd tonight, don't you think?' whispered June on the landing.

'Perhaps he found the children a bit too much of a handful.'

'Possibly.'

'Something's happened while we've been out, that's for sure,' said Lizzie. 'He's obviously upset about something.'

Back downstairs in the living room Lizzie said, 'Is something the matter, Will?'

He bit his lip and avoided her eyes.

'Will?' said Polly, catching his mood with anxiety. 'What's the matter? Were the children naughty or something?'

Slowly shaking his head with a weary sigh, he took something out of his cardigan pocket. The sight of the official envelope produced instant silence. Lizzie felt the colour drain from her face and saw the same thing happen to June as they waited to know which one of the brothers it concerned. Beads of icy perspiration suffused Lizzie's skin. Polly stared at her husband as though struck dumb – no one seemed able to say a word.

'Which one of them is it?' Lizzie managed to utter at last, her voice high pitched and unnatural.

His face swam before her eyes as she watched his mouth form the words. 'Young Roy,' he said, clearing his throat.

'Is he . . . has he been . . . or just missing?' asked Polly in a staccato tone.

He coughed. His face seemed as grey and stiff as stone. 'Sorry, love. He was killed in action,' he said, slipping a supportive arm around his wife's shoulders. 'Here, you'd better read it for yourself.'

Lizzie was deeply ashamed of the relief that surged through her with the knowledge that it wasn't Stan. She was greatly saddened by this news, of course, but it wasn't quite the same thing as hearing that you'd become a widow.

Polly took the letter and looked at it, the paper quivering in her trembling fingers. 'My youngest . . . my baby,' she muttered almost to herself. 'Twenty-three years old and wiped out. Where's the sense in that . . . can anyone tell me?'

None of them seemed able to give her an answer.

'If it's any comfort, love, he was a hero. He died for his country,' Will managed at last in a strangled voice.

War is obscene, thought Lizzie, anger inflamed by grief. It was senseless slaughter in the pursuit of power. Glory . . . what use was it to Roy now? But that sort of talk wouldn't help Polly at this moment, so she just said, 'June and I will make some tea. Come on, June.'

She left the room with her sister-in-law behind her and headed for the kitchen. Roy's death was a tragedy for the whole family but an earth-shattering disaster for his mother. Polly would need the support of her daughters-in-law in the weeks to come. But at this precise moment, Lizzie suspected that the only arms she would want to feel around her were those of her husband.

'Well, well. What have you been doing to yourself, eh, Captain?' asked the VAD with determined cheerfulness as the stretcher was carried into the field hospital behind the lines on the boggy battlefields near Ypres.

'Nothing too serious,' mumbled Philip. 'Slipped in the mire and caught a German bullet. Got it in the shoulder, I think.'

Philip was smothered in mud, and blood was staining his shirt in the area of his left shoulder. He was in a high fever, shivering violently, his face suffused with sweat.

'The doctor will be with you in a minute,' she said gently. 'We'll soon have you fixed up and feeling a bit more comfortable.'

'Thank you, nurse,' he whispered weakly through parched lips. 'You're very kind.'

Her confidence was totally false. She'd seen too many cases

like this – men with bullet wounds and a high fever. Talking to you one minute and buried the next. But hope must spring eternal in this job. You must never let doubt manifest itself in the patient's presence.

The stretcher bearers left and she began gently to remove Philip's khaki shirt ready for the doctor to inspect the wound. Steeling herself, she forced her eyes to focus on the gaping hole in his shoulder, sticky and moist with blood.

Her body felt heavy with exhaustion and she wanted to be sick. She had never been able to get used to the stench of burnt flesh and rotting bodies. Witnessing such suffering out here in France had dulled her fear of horror but not her outrage at the atrocities the men were forced to endure. They called it war but to her it was mass murder – on both sides.

An overworked doctor appeared at her side and kneeled over the patient who had slipped into unconsciousness.

'His name's Verne, doctor,' the nurse informed him. 'Captain Philip Verne.'

'Ah, this is the great man, is it? I've been hearing splendid things about him from the chaps in the ward,' said the doctor, examining the wound. 'Apparently he went to help a couple of his men who were wounded but still alive after a skirmish, and managed to catch a stray bullet himself.'

'The fool.'

'A brave one though by all accounts. This isn't the first time he's shown exceptional courage on the battlefield,' said the doctor. 'His sergeant major says the captain has a reputation for caring about his men and reckons he'll be recommended for a medal.'

'I hope it isn't awarded posthumously.'

'I hope so too,' said the doctor gravely.

'What are his chances?'

'We'll operate to remove the bullet but it doesn't look good, I'm afraid,' he told her. 'There's obviously an infection. He's in a dangerously high fever.'

Lizzie's face was stinging from the rain which had been blowing into it for the whole of the shift. She was chilled to the bone and wet right through. Although she was shivering, she was also damp with perspiration caused by the heavy oilskins she was wearing over her uniform. The wind was sweeping the rain across the streets horizontally and people out on this wet Sunday afternoon lost their hats and had their umbrellas blown inside out. Poor June had her work cut out keeping passengers from killing each other to get a seat inside the tram. Thank goodness this was their last run today. When they got back to the depot they could go home.

The number of people in mourning seemed to grow by the day, she thought, noticing so many black clothes on the streets. Sundays were always a grim reminder of what was happening across the Channel because most people wore dark clothes on the Sabbath for a year after a bereavement.

This line of thought reminded her that the Carters would soon be coming out of mourning for Roy. The worst part of his death for Lizzie had been her inability to ease Polly's suffering. Oh, she'd offered support and sympathy in bucketloads, but she'd known in her heart that nothing could ease a bereaved mother's pain.

Glancing idly ahead of her as she waited for the signal to proceed from June, who was busy seeing passengers on to the tram, Lizzie noticed a woman dressed in a black hat and coat hurrying towards the tram, waving her arms frantically for them to wait. As she drew closer and boarded the vehicle, Lizzie perceived a certain familiarity but couldn't remember where she'd seen her before. They were almost back at the depot before she realised that the woman was Meg Verne, a thinner, shabbier version than she remembered.

Anxious to pay her respects to the lady who was obviously in mourning, she hopped off the tram when they stopped outside the depot and watched the passengers off, hoping Meg hadn't already alighted somewhere along on the route.

'Hello, Meg,' said Lizzie as the passenger stepped off the platform, clutching her hat against the wind. 'Remember me?'

The other woman stared at her blankly. 'I'm sorry, I'm afraid you have the advantage . . .'

'Lizzie Carter.'

Still no spark of recognition.

'We met once before the war. You were a suffragette . . . you were attacked . . .'

'Lizzie, my dear,' said Meg at last, her pale face brightening slightly. 'Forgive me for not recognising you but there isn't much of you showing underneath all those clothes, is there?'

'There certainly isn't.'

'I see you're doing your bit for the war effort then.'

'That's right.'

'I'd have been amazed if you weren't, someone like you.'

'I get paid, so the family and I benefit as well as the war.'

'So I should hope.'

'You're keeping busy too, I expect?'

'Yes.'

102

'What are you up to these days?'

'Still involved in charity work,' explained Meg, trembling against the wind. 'It wouldn't be right for someone like me, who doesn't need the money, to do paid work, would it? That really would put people's backs up.'

'I suppose it might.'

'No might about it,' said Meg emphatically. 'Anyway, I'm involved in several projects. I'm helping to raise money for war orphans – I'm also busy with a refuge we're running for homeless women in Acton. I've just come from there, actually. There was a problem that needed sorting, Sunday or not. It's a good job there are people like you to drive the trams now that the war has put paid to private motoring.'

'I guessed you'd be involved in something,' smiled Lizzie.

'Well, you know me – I like to keep occupied.'

'Me too.'

'I've never forgotten you, you know,' said Meg, looking at Lizzie, her eyes narrowed as though remembering. 'Three children you have, if my memory serves me?'

'That's right.'

'All fit and thriving?'

'Yes, thanks.'

'And your husband?'

'He's in France . . . alive as far as I know. His youngest brother was killed at the Somme though.' She cleared her throat, knowing she must acknowledge the other woman's circumstances. 'But I can see that you're in mourning.'

Meg's dark eyes filled with tears and she struggled against them. 'Yes. My son died in France, I'm afraid.'

'Poor Philip. I'm so sorry,' said Lizzie with feeling.

'Not Philip, my dear,' she corrected, her voice ragged with emotion. 'It was his younger brother, Neville.'

'Oh.' How odd that it hadn't occurred to her that Neville might be the casualty. She'd not even given him a thought. 'I really am sorry.'

'Thank you . . . it's a cruel thing, isn't it, this war?' Meg's face had creased with pain.

'It certainly is.'

'I nearly lost both my sons to it, as a matter of fact.'

'Really?'

'Yes. Philip has been in France most of the time since he enlisted and he was wounded recently at Ypres,' she explained. 'He's recovering in hospital here in England at the moment.'

'Will he be going back to the front?' enquired Lizzie.

'Oh, yes. There'll be no stopping him once he's well again. Duty and all that.'

'Ingrained in the male psyche?'

'Indeed.'

Seeing June hovering nearby, Lizzie said, 'Well, I must be going now. We have to take the tram into the depot.'

'I must be on my way too,' said Meg. 'It was lovely to see you again. Take care now.'

'You too.'

She hurried off into the rain, a bold figure but a forlorn one too in her dark mourning clothes. Yet Lizzie got back on the tram feeling somehow cheered by the meeting.

Humphrey was having tea by the fire in the drawing room when Meg arrived home, cold, hungry and exhausted.

'Mrs Todd has made you some tea, I see,' she said, kneeling

down by the fire and holding her hands out to the flames.

'Yes. Though how anyone can enjoy the bread we are having forced on us these days is quite beyond me. Lord knows what they put in it to make it that revolting colour,' he complained, referring to the fact that 'standard bread' was an unappetising shade of grey.

'Powdered potatoes or beans,' she informed him sharply. 'They mix it with flour because of the shortage of grain.'

'Damned muck!'

'It can't be helped in wartime,' she snapped, impatient with his grumbling. 'Food is in short supply thanks to German submarines attacking the food convoys. There's talk of rationing being introduced before long.'

His answer to that was some furious tutting.

'I sorted everything out at the refuge,' she said conversationally. 'We've a woman with a real need for shelter. We thought we were going to have to turn her away because the place is already bursting at the seams, but we managed to find her a . . .' Her voice tailed off as she realised that he hadn't heard a word she'd said.

Her husband had taken Neville's death very badly. He seemed to have slipped into a world of his own since they'd received the terrible news several months ago. He'd lost interest in everything to the point where she felt she'd become invisible. Once a reasonable man, nowadays he rarely spoke except to complain. At one time he would have been concerned for her if she'd come home cold and tired. Now he barely noticed. When he wasn't out at work, he sat miserably in his armchair with hardly a word to say.

'Is there any tea left in the pot?' she enquired.

'I should think so,' he said absently.

She went to the tea-tray on an occasional table and opened the lid of the teapot. 'There's plenty here. Would you like another?'

'No, thanks.'

Meg poured one for herself, then put a slice of bread on to a small plate and began spreading it with butter.

'Moping about isn't going to bring Neville back, you know, Humphrey,' she said. 'He's dead and we both have to accept it.'

'Why him, Meg . . . why him?' he asked, his face twisted with anguish.

'Take a look out on the streets,' she advised him, spreading some jam on her bread. 'Most of the population is in mourning. We're not the only ones to have lost someone.'

'Why him though?' he repeated mournfully.

She looked up slowly as she realised what he was getting at.

'Why Neville and not Philip you mean?' she said bitterly.

'I didn't say that . . .'

'It's what you meant though.'

'Philip's always been your favourite,' he said accusingly.

'And you've always resented him . . . and made sure he knows it!'

'No, I haven't.'

'You have, Humphrey. I've watched you hurt him again and again over the years.'

'I've done my best. I've provided well for him,' he said defensively. 'He should be damned grateful that I . . .'

'He doesn't know he has anything to be grateful for,' she

cut in quickly. 'He has no idea that he has any reason to be any less in your eyes than Neville was.'

'That's the way you wanted it.'

'It was a joint decision,' she reminded him. 'We both thought it would be better that way.'

'Yes, all right,' he muttered. 'I have tried, you know.'

'Have you?' she asked, her voice full of accusation.

'Of course I have.'

'I'm not so sure about that,' she told him. 'From the minute Neville was born you differentiated between the two.'

'All right, so I favoured Neville a little,' he admitted. 'What's so terrible about that? You've done the same thing with Philip. That's why you're not so cut up as I am about losing Neville.'

'How do *you* know how I feel about losing Neville?' she demanded, rage scorching through her at his thoughtlessness. 'You're far too busy licking your own wounds to bother about me. When I heard the news, I wanted to die. I wished it had been me instead of him. And what made it harder to bear was not having your support . . . knowing that all you cared about was your own damned pain. Neville was my son too, Humphrey. I'm grieving just as much as you are but life has to go on. It isn't fair to other people to sit about feeling sorry for yourself. We nearly lost Philip too. I just pray to God that he survives this terrible war.'

'And you think I don't?'

'I think that if losing Philip would bring Neville back, that's what you would choose,' she told him with brutal candour.

'That's a terrible thing to say, Meg.'

'Maybe, but it's how I see it.'

'I go to visit him in hospital quite regularly,' said Humphrey defensively.

'Only out of duty.'

'These are serious accusations you're making.'

'They have to be said. Your recent behaviour has forced me to speak out, but I should have said something years ago about the way you've treated Philip.'

His face creased and twitched, on the verge of tears. 'Have I really been so awful lately, Meg?' he asked.

'Absolute hell to live with.'

'I'm sorry, I didn't mean to be . . . I've been feeling so low.'

'Me too.'

'So what now?'

'Let's try to help each other through this bad time, shall we?'

He nodded. 'About Philip . . .'

'Go on.'

'I've tried to feel all the right things for him, I really have,' he confessed, 'but somehow it's just never happened.'

'Well, perhaps if we are fortunate enough to have him spared in this war, you can try harder. Make it up to him when he comes home?'

'I'll do my best.'

But she wasn't confident of Humphrey's ever having a proper relationship with Philip. The feeling just wasn't there. 'If you can't be paternal towards him, just try not to make him feel as though you wish him dead.'

'As if I would!'

'Not deliberately, of course, but your feelings are painfully obvious at times, Humphrey.'

'Are they?'

'I think you know they are.'

'Sorry.'

'Don't apologise to me, just try to get along with Philip.'

'Let me pour you another cup of tea, dear,' he said in a conciliatory tone.

'Thank you.'

Knowing they had weathered some sort of a crisis, Meg felt better than she had in ages.

Private Stan Carter climbed out of his flooded dug-out in a trench near Passchendaele. He was soaked to the skin in the driving rain, cold, itchy and depressed. Lice thrived in his hair and on his body, while nearby rats fed on the rotting bodies and dead horses that littered the battlefield which heavy rains had turned into a bog.

'Here you are, Carter . . . one between four of you,' said the sergeant, handing Stan a Maconochie 'dinner in a tin'.

'Ta, Sarge, I'd better be careful I don't get fat,' said Stan sarcastically, spooning his share into his mess tin and passing the Maconochie on to the man next to him.

For months the men had been stumbling through slime and mud, battling with the enemy in appalling conditions, seeing guns and horses sink out of sight in the morass.

'Oi, oi, the toffs are about,' said Stan to his mate Charlie as an officer came down the trench and engaged in conversation with their sergeant. 'I bet he doesn't have to share a Maconochie with three other blokes up there in his luxury dug-out.'

'That's a safe bet,' agreed Charlie, hoping that Stan wasn't going to start holding forth about the officers again. Stan was a good bloke – a loyal mate – but he didn't half go on.

'Why should they have better conditions than us, tell me that?' insisted Stan, almost breaking his teeth on a rock-hard biscuit because they had no bread, the rain beating on his tin hat and trickling down his neck. 'We're all fighting the same war, after all.'

'It's just the way things are, mate . . . nothing we can do about it.'

'Some of 'em even have beds, you know,' Stan went on.

'Only old wrecks that are found in the ruins of villages,' his mate pointed out.

'It's still the officers that have anything that's found in the ruins, though, isn't it?' said Stan gloomily.

'O' course it is. They're not gonna let us have them, are they?'

'They should put numbers in a hat and give us all a chance.'

'Don't talk daft.'

'It *isn't* daft.'

''Course it is. Anyway, how could we have a bed in the main trench?' asked Charlie.

'You couldn't, which is exactly my point. I mean, why should officers have different living conditions to us?'

'Call these living conditions?' said his pal, shivering, rain blowing into his bloodshot eyes. 'Dying conditions, more like.'

'Even so . . .'

'Put a sock in it, Stan. None of us is comfortable out here in the trenches,' said the other man with rising impatience. 'No one. Not even the officers.'

'They're still better off than us, any day of the week.'

'They have to carry the responsibility,' Charlie pointed out wearily.

'That's just a piece o' cake,' was Stan's answer to that.

The officer finished his business with the sergeant and lingered to have a few words with the men.

'All managing to keep cheerful, eh, chaps?' he asked heartily.

'Yessir,' was the response.

'Jolly good . . . keep it up.'

'Ruddy ponse,' complained Stan when the officer was out of earshot. 'They're all the same, the upper classes.'

'No point in getting all steamed up about it,' said Charlie.

'They think they're God's gift.'

'Someone's got to be in charge, it stands to reason.'

'He puts me in mind of the boss's son at the factory I used to work in back home, you know,' said Stan as though the other man hadn't spoken.

'Get away.'

'Now he really is an evil sod . . .'

'Is he?' said Charlie who was far too wet and miserable to take much interest in Stan's crusade against his superiors. Charlie's feet were swollen with trench foot and his bones felt as though they were crumbling into little pieces with the cold.

'Pushed me down the stairs once, you know,' continued Stan.

'Did he really?' said Charlie in perfunctory manner.

'Yeah, he did,' confirmed Stan, who had come to believe this to be true. 'It was a good few years ago but I've never forgotten it.'

'Mmm.'

'He tried to make out I slipped, the bugger, but there were plenty of witnesses who saw what happened and know otherwise.'

'I bet you wouldn't mind being back at the factory taking orders from him now, though, would you?' said his mate. 'Anything's better than being in this bleedin' hell hole.'

'I'll make him pay for humiliating me like that,' said Stan, ignoring the other man's comment.

'Mmm.'

'Oh, yes, one of these fine days he'll pay dear for what he did to me.'

The conversation was interrupted by the sergeant with some fresh orders.

'I'll sort that swine out, good and proper, one day,' muttered Stan as soon as the sergeant had finished.

'Who, the sergeant?' queried Charlie who was only half listening.

'No, the guvnor's son at the factory, of course!'

'Blimey, Stan. You wanna get your priorities sorted out and concentrate on fighting the Germans,' advised Charlie. 'Never mind about some bloke in a factory back in Blighty.'

Stan didn't reply. Just the thought of Philip Verne filled his guts with fire. He didn't have any trouble killing Germans as long as he imagined them all to be Philip Verne!

Chapter Six

The war dragged on and food shortages worsened. Rationing was introduced for sugar in December 1917, rapidly followed by other items. Goods that weren't officially rationed were often hard to find so Lizzie seemed to be either out driving her tram or standing in a food queue.

Everyone had been heartened when America had joined the war with its fresh troops and huge industrial strength. But still there didn't seem to be any sign of an end to the hostilities and the return of the fighting men, apart from the wounded, of course, who continued to pour into the capital in their thousands.

Air raids became more frequent and were mostly at night, the bombers following the moonlit Thames to London. According to the newspapers, the change from daytime to nocturnal attacks had come about because of improved British defences from anti-aircraft fire and fighter planes.

At the first warning sound of the maroons, Lizzie would wrap the children up and hurry round to Thorn Street with them. They would all take shelter in Polly and Will's coal cellar, playing games and singing loud songs to drown out the noise and ease the tension. The children thought it was a great lark, especially as June and the twins were usually there too.

Fortunately there hadn't been a raid while Lizzie was out driving her tram. She dreaded that the bombers would come over when she wasn't at home with the children.

Her luck ran out in this respect one moonlit February night when she and June were on late shift. The ominous thump of the maroons sounded on their last return trip, as they were approaching West Ealing. Most people stayed calm at the onset but the shrieks of terror from a few nervous passengers quickly engendered panic, causing a general exodus from the tram as people fled to find shelter rather than stay out on the vulnerable streets.

Lizzie would have given anything to be at home with her children, but since this wasn't possible she knew she must stay in control and do the job she was paid for.

'Are there any passengers left on the tram?' she asked when June appeared at her side on the platform.

'A few but most of 'em scarpered at the sound of the guns.'

'I don't blame them,' said Lizzie. 'I feel like doing the same thing myself.'

'Hope the nippers'll be all right,' muttered June anxiously at the thunder of distant explosions.

'Mmm. So do I. But don't worry, it's probably the docks the Germans are after,' said Lizzie in an effort to reassure.

'It has been known for the Zepps to drop their load off target,' June reminded her with growing tension.

'Stop worrying. The children will be perfectly safe with Polly and Will. They'll take them down the cellar,' said Lizzie.

But June was grey with worry.

'Look, there's nothing we can do so there's no point you working yourself up into a state,' Lizzie wisely pointed out.

'I don't know how you can be so calm!'

'I'm not . . . inside,' confessed Lizzie. 'But we have to get the tram back to the depot and look after the passengers and that's all there is to it.'

An elderly man appeared on the platform in a state of considerable distress.

'Help me, for Gawd's sake,' he begged shakily. 'It's the wife . . . she's taken sick . . . started gasping something terrible, then passed out cold.'

Lizzie brought the vehicle to a standstill and hurried into the car where June was bending over a woman who was slumped across the seats with her eyes closed.

'I reckon she must have had an 'eart attack,' gasped the old man, quivering with fear. 'It's all these guns and explosions . . . they've scared her to death.'

'She's still breathing,' June informed them tremulously.

'Don't worry, sir, we'll soon get medical help for her,' announced Lizzie, managing to sound confident though she hadn't the foggiest idea how she was going to find a doctor at this time of night in a strange neighbourhood.

'There's a hospital not far from here,' said a woman passenger helpfully.

'Thank God for that. We'd better not move her in case we make things worse,' declared Lizzie efficiently. 'Put a coat over her to keep her warm and I'll run round to the hospital and ask them to send an ambulance. Can you cope with things here, June?'

'Well, I suppose so, but try not to be too long,' she said, her voice tight with fear as the thud and rattle of gunfire echoed around the streets and the sky was illuminated with a network of moving search lights.

Having been told how to get to the hospital, Lizzie raced there, returning to the tram in the ambulance, whereupon the unconscious woman and her husband were whisked off to the hospital.

'Poor old dears,' said Lizzie. 'I hope she'll be all right.'

'Mmm,' muttered June, still looking very pale and anxious.

'Right, crisis over,' declared Lizzie with determined cheerfulness. 'So let's get this tram home to bed.'

But no sooner had she uttered the words than she found herself with another problem as a loud bang sent June into a screaming fit.

'Hey, come on now, calm down,' urged Lizzie, stifling her own panic and slipping a comforting arm around her friend's shoulders, shielding her from any prying eyes inside the vehicle. 'The explosions aren't as near as they sound. Probably miles away on the other side of London, I shouldn't wonder.'

Poor June was helpless and continued to emit a high-pitched shriek.

'Shut up, June, for goodness' sake,' demanded Lizzie with a sharp change of tone. 'We *are* in charge of this tram. It's our responsibility to stay calm and make sure our passengers stay that way.'

Her friend was hysterical, laughing, crying and wheezing horribly.

'You'll upset the passengers if they get wind of this performance.'

But June was not to be pacified. 'I can't stand it . . . the bombs'll kill us all. We ought to be at home with the kids. Oh dear . . . oh dear . . . oh dear . . .'

'Oh, well. Sorry, June, but there's only one thing for it,' Lizzie said, giving her friend a sharp slap across the face.

The result was immediate.

'I'm sorry, Lizzie,' she said, rather dazedly.

'Don't worry, it could happen to anyone,' Lizzie assured her. 'Sorry I had to resort to violence but if anyone had seen you in that state on duty, and been feeling spiteful enough to report you, you could find yourself in serious trouble back at the depot.'

'Yeah, I know. Thanks.'

The tram was without passengers for the last few stops. From her position at the controls, Lizzie could see the urban skyline etched darkly against an orange glow from distant fires in the dark sky, patchworked with search lights. The guns were still booming out from Wormwood Scrubs. The two women were leaving the depot, both feeling mentally and physically drained, before the raid finally came to an end.

'What a night, eh?' said June as they walked home.

'Not half,' agreed Lizzie. 'Wouldn't want too many like that.'

When Lizzie and June were on late shift all the children stayed the night at Polly and Will's so that they got to bed at a decent hour. After calling at the house to check that they were all all right, and the children had gone to sleep after the raid, Lizzie and June made their weary way home.

Climbing into her cold, empty bed, Lizzie was imbued with loneliness and longing for Stan. She needed him with such desperation tonight, it was like a physical pain. 'Oh, well, there's no point in being miserable about it,' she muttered into the freezing room, and curled up into a ball, hugging a stone hot water bottle.

In the spring the newspapers seemed to carry bad news every day. The Germans had broken through the lines of British and Allied troops on the Western Front. Field Marshal Haig urged the troops to fight on to the end, 'With our backs to the wall', because 'Victory will belong to the side which holds out the longest'.

'That man isn't human,' protested Lizzie to June and Polly after reading about this in the newspaper. 'Hasn't enough blood been shed on both sides?'

By August, however, reports were more promising as the Allies moved forward again, forcing the enemy to retreat. German soldiers were deserting and turning against their military commanders and the Kaiser who abdicated and fled to Holland.

The guns finally fell silent across the battlefields of Europe in November. Lizzie and June and the children were at Polly's when the maroons, that had hitherto warned of impending danger now boomed out a glorious message of peace. Hugging each other and sobbing with sheer relief, they tore into the street to join the celebrations, waving flags and cheering as church bells rang out across London and people thronged the pavements, dancing and singing. The children were almost beside themselves with excitement.

When Will appeared with the news that the factory he'd worked in for the duration of the war, had closed for the day to mark the occasion, they all went inside to drink a toast with the bottle of sherry Polly had stashed away in anticipation of the occasion.

'To all our fighting boys,' said Will, raising his glass. 'To those who won't be coming back as well as those who will.'

Glasses were raised to Roy and the three women wept openly. Even Will was on the verge of tears. The excited children were eager to go back outside where the revelry was reaching fever pitch. None of them had ever seen anything like this before.

'Let's go up West this afternoon,' suggested Polly excitedly. 'There'll be plenty goin' up there, I bet. There'll be fireworks and all sorts.'

'June and I have to go to work,' Lizzie reminded them.

'Yeah, we're on afternoons this week,' June added.

There were wails of disappointment and requests for them to ignore their duty.

'I think a lot of the factories have closed,' Will pointed out hopefully. 'And I bet the shops'll send their staff home.'

'Maybe, but we have to keep the transport running or people won't be able to get about to enjoy the celebrations,' replied Lizzie whose conscience wouldn't allow her to behave as she would have liked. 'You lot go up West and we'll see you up there later on when we've finished work. We'll make a definite time and place to meet.'

'If you can get to us through the crowds!' said Will.

'We'll do our best, won't we, June?' Lizzie assured them.

'You bet.'

'Just think, girls,' said Polly happily, 'you won't have to go out to work for much longer. The men will soon be back to take up their positions again, manning the trams.'

'Yes, that's true,' said Lizzie, experiencing a pang of regret. She wondered how she was going to adjust to normal life again after being part of the 'outside world' for the best part of four years. Still, the war had altered society and changed women's roles in it, giving them the chance to show what they could do and opening up all sorts of opportunities. Surely things wouldn't revert to the old status quo with women expected to be only servants and cheap labour for dressmaking and laundry establishments?

With a few exceptions that *was* what happened. Property-owning women over the age of thirty gained the right to vote, but females in general were forced back into pre-war roles as servicemen were released from the army much more quickly than the government had anticipated after threats of mutiny around the country if the war-weary men were not sent home with all possible speed. It soon became unacceptable for a woman to be employed in any sort of 'men's work' as there were so few jobs for anyone.

The euphoria of the Victory celebrations soon paled into insignificance for Lizzie who found herself without paid work of any kind. Her tram-driving days ended with the war when men who'd been employed in war supplies as well as servicemen returned to their old jobs. Outwork in her old trade was non-existent for the silk trade had not got properly underway again.

But it wasn't all gloom. The Carter brothers came home to great rejoicing, Bobby and Luke managing to get back just after Christmas. Without prior warning, Stan walked in the door one bitter afternoon at the end of January while Lizzie was at the table cutting bread for the children's tea. It was the moment she had lived for for almost four years – and it was a bitter disappointment.

'Stan?' she said uncertainly, for his physical appearance had altered drastically. The big, burly man she had seen off to the war was now emaciated, his great square face thin and gaunt, his neck scraggy.

'Hello, Liz, how are you, love?' he said, as though just returning from a game of darts at the local.

'Stan,' she said again, feeling ridiculously shy as she went over to where he was standing just inside the door. 'You're home at last then?'

'That's right.'

'Oh, it *is* good to see you.'

'You too.'

'So . . . how are you?'

'All right.'

Abandoning the embarrassingly stilted conversation, she flung her arms around his neck and kissed him hard. The instant their lips met she knew things had changed between them. He made no response whatsoever – it was like kissing a door.

Before she had time to dwell on this, however, a small voice chimed in. 'Who's that man, Mummy?' asked Eva curiously. 'And why are you kissin' and cuddlin'?'

Turning to her daughter, she said, 'This is your daddy, darling. Don't you remember him?'

'No.'

The younger generation weren't alone in their lack of recognition.

'I would never have known them,' admitted Stan. 'They've all grown so big.'

'You've been away a long time. We've a lot of catching up to do.' Lizzie cleared a place on the sofa for him to sit down, almost as though he was a visitor. 'Come on, love, make yourself comfortable.'

'When will tea be ready, Mum?' asked Bruce, casting a wary eye over their 'guest'.

'How can you think of your belly when Dad has just come home from fighting in the war?' admonished his brother Jed gravely, freckled face crimson with indignation. He took a step forward and thrust out his hand. 'Hello, Dad. Welcome home.'

'Hello, son.' Stan shook his hand, throwing Lizzie a quizzical look.

'Yes, it's Jed,' she confirmed.

'So grown up, and Carter from top to toe,' he said, and glancing at Bruce added, 'Both boys are come to that. They have the Carter colouring.'

Bruce pushed himself forward. 'I can climb to the top of a lamppost, you know,' he announced boastfully.

'Go on. Can you really, son?' replied Stan awkwardly. 'You'll have to give me a demonstration later.'

'Don't encourage him,' said Lizzie with forced levity, 'I have enough trouble with him and his antics as it is.'

Eva, who never took a back seat for long, squeezed to the fore between her two brothers. 'I'm a big girl now, I go to school,' she told her father proudly, green eyes round and solemn. 'I'm in the same class as the twins 'cos we're all nearly six.'

'Are you now? That's nice,' said Stan stiffly, obviously ill-at-ease with all this childish attention and finding it difficult to hold his own. He put his hand out a foot or so from the floor. 'You were just this high when I went away, do you know that?'

'I'm much bigger than that now,' she said firmly.

'So I can see.' He looked closely at his golden-haired daughter and turned to Lizzie. 'She's the dead spit of you.'

'So I'm always being told.' She set her face into a smile. 'Anyway, I'll leave you all to get to know each other again for a few minutes while I go downstairs to get some water to make tea.'

Filling the kettle under the tap in the communal kitchen, her hands were trembling. She felt dreadfully uneasy in Stan's presence – almost as though she was frightened of him. Putting the filled kettle down on the wooden draining board for a moment, she stared unseeingly out of the window, her eyes resting on the peeling brown paint on the lavatory door in the backyard. She tried to soothe her jangling nerves by telling herself it was only natural she should feel strange after so long apart from her husband. It was simply a matter of being out of the habit of having him around. Other returning soldiers' wives were probably experiencing the same thing.

There would have to be a period of adjustment during which she must be patient. Stan had been through a terrible ordeal – he would need care and attention and time to recover, time to get used to family life again. Judging by his reaction to her embrace, he was feeling equally as strange about her as she was about him.

Once they had adapted, it would be just like old times. Yes, she was worrying unnecessarily, she told herself as she hurried upstairs with the kettle to boil on the gas ring. Everything would be all right eventually.

She was still trying to convince herself of this as violent March winds whistled through the ill-fitting windows and the air in their rooms was heavy with soothing pine and eucalyptus vapours released from the bronchitis kettle she was using to help her poor influenza-ridden family to breathe more easily.

One after the other they had fallen ill, the children and then Stan. Rumour had it that this was the worst 'flu epidemic since 1900. People were dying in their thousands. Having lost her parents to the disease all those years ago, Lizzie was especially diligent in caring for her patients, following the advice that was being given generally to carers of 'flu victims – to keep them warm in bed and give them aspirin.

Fortunately they were all up and about again before she herself fell victim to the bug. Stan's lack of sympathy and support was total. Not only did she find this hurtful but infuriating too. He didn't so much as make a pot of tea or wash a cup and saucer while she crawled around feeling like death and struggling to keep the household going. He was far too self-absorbed to bother about her or the children and spent all his time out with Arthur Brown in some pub or other, complaining about the state of the country and spending the little money she'd managed to put by out of her wages from the trams as well as his army back pay.

'A mother has to be about to turn her toes up before she

can give in and go to bed when she's feeling poorly,' said Polly whose assistance had been sought by Stan that morning after Lizzie had almost passed out. 'Whereas if a man has so much as a runny nose he expects to be treated like an invalid.'

'It doesn't have to be that way, though, does it?' said Lizzie.

'No, but it always will be. It's just the way things are.'

'It wouldn't hurt Stan to make an effort when there's a crisis,' said Lizzie weakly, grateful just to be able to lie down and rest her aching head on the pillow. 'Instead of getting you to come round here and help out when you've quite enough to do at your own place.'

'Nonsense, it's what I'm here for. To help the family when they need me,' she assured her daughter-in-law heartily. 'You can't expect Stan to take over the domestic chores when he's been away fighting for the best part of four years.'

'I wasn't expecting him to *take over*,' Lizzie corrected, burning and shivering simultaneously with fever and the sub-zero temperature in the bedroom. 'But it would be very much appreciated if he would give me some support while I'm feeling so rotten.'

'That isn't Stan's way, is it?' defended Polly predictably. 'He's a man of the people, out there fighting for the common good.'

Charity begins at home, Lizzie thought as Polly handed her some aspirin and a glass of water, but she just said, 'He's changed a lot, don't you think?'

'In what way?'

'He's moodier and more bad-tempered than he used to be.'

'Stan's never been an easygoing man, we all know that,'

Polly reminded her, slipping a hot water bottle between the sheets.

'No, but he's on a really short fuse now,' said Lizzie. 'He flies into a rage at the slightest little thing. Has no patience at all with the children.'

'He's bound to be edgy after what he's been through,' said Polly. 'There isn't one of those boys who were out there in France who'll ever be the same again.'

'I know all about that.'

'You'll just have to be patient.'

'June was saying that Bobby seems to have settled back into civilian life without too much trouble.'

'Oh, well, you know Bobby. He's always been one to have a laugh and a joke, no matter how he's really feeling,' said Polly, and Lizzie certainly couldn't argue with that.

'Yes, I suppose that's true.'

'Once Stan gets back to work, he'll be just like his old self again, you just wait and see,' said Polly, bustling about the bedroom with a duster, tidying up as far as she could given the lack of space.

'I hope so,' sighed Lizzie wearily. 'I really do.'

All the Carter brothers had been promised their old jobs back once things got back to normal at Verne's whose government contract had apparently ended with the war. Stan had visited the firm almost as soon as he got back from France to find out what the situation was. Apparently, Verne's were only using a fraction of the normal workforce but were hoping to expand the numbers once orders gained their pre-war momentum.

Rumour had it that Philip Verne was going to be heading

the company in the future, with his father in a less prominent role. It was a recognised fact among the workers that Humphrey Verne had never been quite the same since the death of his youngest son.

As for Lizzie, she planned to return to weaving at home as soon as things picked up in the economy generally.

Now Polly was saying, 'I brought round a nice pot o' mutton stew for your tea tonight. Enough for all of you. It only has to be warmed up . . .'

'Oh, good.'

'I've peeled the spuds an' all.'

'Thanks ever so much.'

'I've given the other room a bit of a going over, too.'

'It's really good of you.'

'Now, is there anything else you'd like me to do before I go?'

'You've done quite enough and I'm very grateful,' said Lizzie.

'No trouble at all, love. If you need me again, just send one of the kids round when they get in from school,' said Polly kindly. 'And I'll come straight over.'

'What would we do without you?' muttered Lizzie faintly.

Polly was feeling positively blissful, Lizzie knew that. In fact, she wondered if people like her, compulsive organisers whose lifeblood was feeling indispensable, had some sort of immunity to illnesses like influenza that debilitated the rest of the population. Polly had just finished nursing Will and Luke through 'flu but showed no signs of falling victim herself. The germ just wouldn't dare impose itself on her, thought Lizzie, and deprive her of the pleasure of having the family rely on her.

'You'd manage,' her mother-in-law said with unconvincing modesty.

'I suppose I'd have to.'

'Anyway, I'll be off now, love. I've gotta do a bit o' shopping on the way home. Are you sure you'll be all right?'

'Certain.'

'Tata then.'

'Tata. And thanks again.'

Lying back after she'd gone, her head hot against the pillow, Lizzie's glance wandered critically around the room which was hideously overcrowded. Crammed together were two double beds, one for her and Stan, the other for the children. Packed into the room also was an ugly old wardrobe, a chest of drawers and a washstand with a jug and bowl.

Not a spare inch in which to move about and no such thing as privacy. Lizzie had been painfully aware of the latter since Stan had been back. The children were growing up, becoming more aware. What if they were not actually asleep at 'certain' times? Stan was not an affectionate husband by any means but he was a demanding one. The war hadn't changed that.

An unexpected surge of anger raised her temperature even more as she lay there in the lumpy, smelly bed, surrounded by all the hallmarks of poverty. There must be something better than this for us, she thought, the depressing effect of her illness exaggerating the shabbiness and making everything seem more squalid. Our children deserve more than this from life. The least they should have is a proper home with space in which to breathe.

Whereas Stan constantly promoted this theory and believed it should be brought about by a democratic government, Lizzie found herself with a sudden urgent need to better things – in reality not just theory. On the heels of this came the thought that it should be possible to make it happen through her own efforts.

After all, she was intelligent and very quick to learn. She was certainly bright enough to manage a small business. She also had excellent silk-weaving skills. Unfortunately, she lacked the money to get started. That was what was so damned frustrating!

Philip was in an armchair in the sitting room, reading the newspaper. Emily was seated opposite, busy with some needlepoint embroidery. A brass clock ticked on the marble mantelpiece and a log fire crackled cosily in the hearth. Outside, as darkness fell, March winds howled through the budding branches of the trees in the square.

The papers seemed to be full of industrial trouble recently, he thought gloomily. There had been a general strike in Scotland and the London Underground had been brought to a standstill by workers demanding shorter working hours.

Still, it was good to be home again even if his homecoming had been fraught with problems. He had arrived back to the disturbing news that his father no longer felt able to cope at the head of the firm, which was barely managing to stay in business, and Philip himself was to take over as Managing Director. This meant he was immediately faced with the awesome task of putting the company back on its feet again and leading it into the new peacetime era.

There had been no time to recuperate from the war. He'd had to get back to work right away: chasing orders, looking up old contacts, considering the possibility of manufacturing cheaper, blended silk fabrics and artificial silk to keep the prices down in these difficult times. It was going to be a slow process but he was confident of an eventual return to their former glory for Verne's, despite the ever present threat of foreign competition.

He'd suffered a setback in his efforts when he'd been laid up with a severe bout of 'flu from which he was still recovering. If that wasn't bad enough, his shoulder, in which shrapnel was still embedded, acted up painfully, and Emily had had one of her 'bad spells'.

All of these things he could take in his stride. What really stuck in his throat was his father's continued hostility towards him. Philip had been devastated to hear of his brother's death when he'd been home from the war on sick leave. He'd hoped he might be able to console his father somehow – perhaps replace the male companionship he had lost in Neville. He'd thought they might have been united in their grief, that they might have had something to offer each other.

But his father was even less communicative than before. In fact, Philip received the distinct impression that Humphrey resented the fact that he had come back from the war and Neville hadn't. He tried not to make his feelings obvious when Mother was around, of course, but at the factory there was no pretence.

Philip was recalled to the present when Emily began to speak.

'I thought we might go down to Berkshire on Sunday, to visit Toby at school?'

'Yes, if you wish, dear.'

'Perhaps your mother would like to come with us?' she suggested.

'Yes, I'll ask her.'

'No point in inviting your father, I suppose,' she said.

'We can mention it to him,' said Philip, 'but I doubt if he'll come. I think the factory is about as far as he goes these days.'

'It's a pity the way Neville's death has changed him.'

'He'll snap out of it eventually, I expect,' said Philip.

'I certainly hope so.'

They chatted companionably for some time about trivial matters, eventually being interrupted by the maid with a tray of cocoa and biscuits. Emily looked happy and healthy, her beautiful eyes clear and serene, her brown hair swept off her face smoothly into a knot at the back.

Times like this with Emily were Philip's halcyon days. When they were happy together, as they were at this moment, it was hard to imagine that it was ever any different. But it was! Oh, yes, it could change in an instant. This sane, composed woman could quite suddenly be plunged into some inner hell which made her completely irrational and out of reach, a poor obsessed creature with voices in her head that dictated her actions. A few weeks ago, she'd been found wandering near Kensington Gardens with no idea how she'd got there.

It was an intermittent condition and periods of sickness could be far apart. According to his mother, Emily had been well for a stretch of almost a year once while he was away at the war. At other times she would be ill for months. The medical profession had nothing new to offer by way of treatment.

His wife was a constant source of worry to Philip. He lived in fear that he would be forced to have her committed to an asylum, so confided only in their trusted family doctor who did what little he could to help.

Philip also employed a nurse-cum-companion to be with her while he was out at work during the day, a woman with impeccable references sworn never to discuss Emily's condition outside the house. Fortunately, Toby was away at prep school so at least he was protected from it as far as was possible.

Although Emily's illness was an enormous strain for Philip, he still loved her deeply and went to great pains to make her happy. Inevitably, however, her erratic health meant that his role had become more that of guardian than partner. Naturally, he would have liked a more normal marital relationship. He was often lonely and longed for someone with whom he could really share his life, the bad things as well as the good.

He would find it comforting, for instance, to be able to discuss with her the problems he was having at the factory. But he felt duty bound to spare her from anything that might cause her worry. His marriage to Emily was rather like living with a beautiful but delicate flower which was hyper-sensitive to the slightest change in atmosphere.

His thoughts turned back to his work and the challenges that lay ahead, exciting despite the difficulties. Theoretically he had his father's support; it was after all his company. But in his heart Philip knew that Humphrey would be only too eager to criticise, and although it would not be practical or beneficial to himself, he secretly wanted his son to fail miserably. The only reason Humphrey had handed over the reins to Philip was because he no longer felt able to hold them himself.

Philip felt a sudden surge of determination. His father might well have cause to criticise his business methods but he'd not be able to fault the end result for the company. Because Philip was going to make a success of the firm if he had to die in the attempt!

Chapter Seven

'Hello, love,' said Lizzie, welcoming her husband home from work one evening in the autumn. 'Had a good day?'

'I've been to work,' said Stan gruffly, sinking heavily into an armchair and unlacing his shoes. 'Not on a bloody outing.'

'That doesn't mean you can't have a good day, surely?' she suggested hopefully.

'It does if you work at Verne's,' he pronounced, laboriously removing his shoes and unfastening the collar from his shirt.

'Oh, dear. What's happened now?' she asked, rather wearily for Stan had not settled back to work with any degree of contentment.

'Philip Verne, that's what's happened,' he said, taking the mug of tea she handed to him and guzzling loudly. 'That bloke should have been strangled at birth.'

'What's he done this time?'

'He doesn't have to do anything in particular to make life unbearable,' he snapped. 'Just his presence at the factory does that.'

'I suppose the man can't really avoid being there, as he runs the place,' said Lizzie with noticeable asperity.

'That's right, take his side!'

'I'm not.'

'Yes, you are. It's easy for you to do that,' retorted Stan. 'You don't have to put up with him day after day. You've a nice cushy number, staying at home all day weavin' with no one breathing down your neck.'

'I wouldn't call it cushy,' objected Lizzie who laboured long hours at her loom to subsidise Stan's income and help satisfy the seemingly insatiable appetites of their three growing children.

'You wouldn't, eh? Well, I wouldn't mind it, I can tell you.'

He would loathe being in the house all day without his cronies around him, she was certain of that. But it would serve no useful purpose to point this out to Stan because he considered himself to have drawn the short straw in life and wouldn't be convinced otherwise. Her hopes that a return to employment might improve his temper had proved to be false. He seemed to become more belligerent by the day. His passion for socialism and a fair deal for his fellow man seemed to have given way to blatant self-pity.

'I've no complaints,' said Lizzie truthfully for she was pleased to be gainfully employed again. 'But I don't get paid for doing nothing. I work damned hard for every penny.'

'All right . . . all right . . . don't go on about it,' growled Stan.

She turned her attention to a pot of savoury mince which was simmering on the gas stove. That last remark was typical of him. He could wear holes in her ear drums with his carping but if she said more than two words she was accused of 'going on' or nagging.

'He told me to stop reading the paper,' Stan informed her querulously.

'Philip Verne did?'

'Who else?'

'But he wouldn't stop you doing something like that in your break, surely?' When Stan didn't reply, she turned slowly to him. 'It wasn't during your break, was it?'

'So what if it wasn't? I was only having a quick glance to see what they had to say about the rail strike. It's not a crime, is it?'

'Was it really just a quick glance?'

Actually he'd almost finished reading the paper from cover to cover by the time Philip Verne had spotted him, sitting on the window ledge near his looms which were standing idle. But he wasn't going to admit that to Lizzie. She'd only say he was wrong and take Verne's side. 'I'm not a liar. If I said it was a quick glance, that's what it was,' he told her.

Lizzie was so tired she felt as though she'd been physically beaten. She'd been on the go all day, fitting in the shopping, cooking and cleaning with work at the loom. She still had to serve a meal, wash the dishes, work her way through a pile of ironing and get the children to bed before she could snatch a few minutes' relaxation. By that time it would be bedtime.

'All right, I'll take your word for it. But, remember, you really need that job, Stan.'

'That's it, start nagging again.'

'I'm not.'

'You are! You're always at it. You've become a real nag, a proper old fishwife.'

'London is crowded with people looking for work,' she said
mildly, ignoring his insults which had lost their power to hurt
through their sheer frequency. 'There's plenty who'll be only
too eager to replace you at Verne's. It doesn't do to upset the
management too often.'

'Do you think I don't know that, woman?' he shouted.
'That's the part that gets me.' He banged his mug down on the
floor and clutched his stomach with both hands. 'Gets me right
here in the guts . . . the fact that they have all the power, they
control my life!'

'It's the same for all the workers, so why not just accept it
like everyone else?' she advised, desperately trying to forge
some sort of communication with him.

'You'd love that, wouldn't you, me being a yes man?'

'No, not really.'

'Oh no, not much you wouldn't!'

'Surely it can't be *that* bad working at Verne's?' she said.
'I was quite happy when I was there. And Bobby and Luke
don't seem to mind it.'

'Well, I do,' he bellowed furiously. 'I hate every single
minute I spend in that factory . . . and having you remind me
that there's no alternative only makes things worse.'

'But, Stan, I . . .'

'Oh, shut up, you stupid bitch! You know *nothing,* nothing
at all, so stop trying to tell me what to do.'

'Oh, Stan, please listen,' she begged, her eyes hot with tears.

'No, I won't listen to you telling me to kowtow to the likes
of Philip Verne.'

'That isn't what I'm telling you to do,' she protested, her
voice raised in frustration because he wouldn't even try to see

her point of view. 'I'm just suggesting that you calm down and try not to let him upset you quite so much. All right so you don't like the man, but is that any reason to let him ruin your life?'

He leapt up and lunged towards her, face white with temper, hand raised to strike. As she instinctively drew back, he lowered his hand, his face twitching with tension.

'Oh, I've had enough o' this, I'm going to get changed,' he said in a deep guttural tone. 'I'm going out with Arthur as soon as I've had somethin' to eat.'

Trembling with reaction, Lizzie turned back to the cooking, her eyes blurred with tears. This sort of altercation was becoming all too frequent between herself and Stan. Her husband was obviously desperately unhappy and she seemed to have lost the ability to communicate with him.

The Carter children had been playing in the street and were on their way upstairs in pursuit of nourishment when the sound of their parents quarrelling echoed along the unwholesome landings of the tenement house. Huddled together, they stood outside the door of their rooms, listening in a frightened silence.

Eva dissolved into tears.

'Stop snivelling,' said Jed who was an impatient child.

Softhearted Bruce was much more sympathetic, however. 'It's all right, sis,' he said, slipping a comforting arm around his adored sister's shoulders. 'Mum and Dad's rows don't usually last very long, you know that. I expect they'll stop shouting at each other in a minute.'

'Daddy shouldn't shout at Mummy like that,' she sobbed.

'It's her own fault that he does,' retorted Jed whose devotion to his father bordered on hero worship. 'She shouldn't tell him he mustn't upset that horrible man he works for.'

'Daddy's always in a bad mood. He's always shouting at someone,' wept Eva.

'No, he isn't.'

'Yes, he is.'

'Stoppit, you two, and listen!' intervened Bruce. 'It's all gone quiet in there now. We'll wait a few minutes, and if it stays like this we'll go on in.'

Lizzie had been correct in judging her husband to be deeply unhappy. All the pleasure seemed to have gone out of life for him lately. Nothing was any fun any more. His job was boring, his wife got on his nerves because she opposed his views, and the children were so boisterous he felt like murdering them most of the time. Even politics had lost its appeal.

About the only thing that gave him any sort of a buzz these days was his private war with Philip Verne. There was nothing he enjoyed more than stirring him up and seeing his 'pretty' face creased with worry.

The morning after the row with Lizzie, Stan was really in the mood for a quarrel with Verne and waiting for the opportunity to start one. The fact that he was putting his livelihood at risk was as nothing against his lust for battle.

Waiting until he saw Philip Verne heading in his direction on his way through the factory to the general offices, Stan lit a cigarette and stood by his looms with it in his mouth. To make certain that his transgression did not go unnoticed, he looked directly at Philip, inhaled deeply and blew a cloud of smoke into his face.

'Have you gone mad, Carter?' asked Philip incredulously. 'You know smoking is strictly forbidden on the factory floor.'

'Go on, is that a fact?' drawled Stan, observing the other man with open insolence.

'You know perfectly well it is,' barked Philip. 'So put that cigarette out at once before there's an accident and this whole place goes up in smoke!'

Stan made no move to obey him. Creating ripples in the other man's calm little pond was almost a physical pleasure. What a life he had, eh? Coming back from the war to find himself running the firm. Oh, yes, it was all right for some. It was common knowledge among the workers that old man Verne couldn't stand the sight of his eldest son, so the more problems Stan caused for him, the more reason his father would have to find fault with the way he ran the factory.

'Put it out, man, do you hear me?' yelled Philip to make himself heard above the noise of the machines.

The only response was a second exhalation of smoke.

Philip knew this was a declaration of war. For some reason best known to himself, Carter wanted to give him a hard time. Philip ought to dismiss him on the spot. He certainly had good cause. There were rolls and rolls of fabric ready for delivery and tons of raw silk on the premises. It would only take a misplaced spark and there would be a conflagration to light up the whole of London.

But he remembered the young girl who had once pleaded for Carter's job a long time ago. She would be the one to suffer if he was put out of work, not Carter himself. He was the sort of man who would spend all his time at the pub with his dole money, bemoaning his lot to his mates and complaining he had been unfairly dismissed, while his wife struggled to feed the family. Well, Philip wasn't going to give him the opportunity.

'All right, if you won't put it out then I'll do it for you,' declared Philip, removing the cigarette from the other man's mouth and stamping it out under his shoe.

Without another word Philip walked away and left through the swing doors. Stan Carter was a nuisance and a threat but he was damned if he'd be beaten by him.

Stan was full of malice towards Philip Verne at lunchtime when he and Arthur stood smoking in the yard after finishing their sandwiches.

'I'm really gonna fix him this time,' he announced vehemently. 'That man's made a fool of me once too often.'

'Come on, Stan, you were well out of order this time. You know very well that smoking on the factory floor is against the rules,' said Arthur who hadn't seen the incident and only had Stan's version of it. 'If the place goes up in smoke, we'll all be out of a job.'

'Snatching the fag out of my mouth as if I was a piece o' dirt,' ranted Stan, ignoring Arthur's common sense. 'Well, that's the last bloody straw, mate. That man is gonna get a real pastin' to teach him a lesson.'

Arthur was beginning to feel worried about his pal's state of mind. Stan had always had a bit of a thing about Philip Verne but since they'd been back at work after the war, he'd been like a man possessed.

'Don't be a fool, Stan,' he wisely advised. 'Let it go.'

'No fear.'

'You'll get yourself into real trouble if you carry on like this.'

'I'm not letting anything go,' insisted Stan, puffing on his cigarette furiously. 'That ponce is gonna be made to pay.'

'You've a wife and kids to feed, remember?' warned Arthur.

'So?'

'So . . . beating up the boss is the surest way I know of getting the sack.'

'He won't sack me, don't worry,' said Stan with a logic based entirely on the lust for physical violence. 'When I've finished with him he won't rile me again in a hurry.'

'You be careful.'

'Don't worry about me,' he said with a kind of elation, as though excited by what he had in mind. 'Philip Verne's the one you should be worrying about.'

Arthur changed the subject, hoping Stan would forget all about this crazy plan. He would end up in court for assault if he wasn't very careful. But it wasn't Arthur's place to interfere. You should never try to come between a man and his personal principles.

Philip was catching up on some paperwork, after hours, in the factory office which he had continued to use since becoming Managing Director because of its convenience. He could get more done in an hour after everyone had gone home than in a whole afternoon while the factory was operating. Most evenings he stayed on for a while after the machines had closed down. He mustn't make it too late, though, because of Emily. Even as the thought came, he felt himself tensing. As much as he loved his wife, the demands of her condition were a strain while he was under such pressure at work.

He paused at the sound of someone coming up the stairs. He guessed it was his father who was familiar with Philip's habit of working late. It was unusual for Humphrey to still be around at this time, though. Philip frowned. He hoped this didn't mean he was in for one of Father's fault-finding lectures.

The door opened slowly.

'Evening, Mr Verne.'

'Carter,' said Philip in surprise. 'How did you get in here?'

'Been here all day, ain't I?' said Stan.

'Yes, but . . .'

'I stayed on after the others left,' he explained, 'waited in the toilets while the caretaker locked up.'

'But if you wanted to see me, why didn't you come up to the office during normal working hours?' asked Philip, guessing the man had come here to make trouble.

''Cos I want to be sure there's no one else around while I see to my business,' Stan informed him gruffly.

'Business . . . what business?' said Philip, his mouth drying with apprehension. 'Is it a pay rise you're after, or something?'

'I wouldn't say no to one of those,' said Stan, marching purposefully across to Philip's desk. 'Later on we can talk about that.' He moved round to where Philip was sitting with his back to the window. 'But my actual reason for bein' here is to teach you to show a little respect.'

Before Philip could utter another word, he was grabbed by the lapels of his suit and dragged from his chair.

'What the devil . . .'

'Right, you bigheaded sod,' said Stan, pushing him against the wall and holding him rigidly by the arms. 'It's time you learned a lesson.'

Philip didn't have quite so much brawn as Carter but he was no weakling. The surprise element, however, added to his shoulder wound and the fact that he was not a naturally violent man, gave his attacker the advantage.

'Lesson . . . what lesson? What's all this about?' he asked breathlessly.

'I'll tell you what it's about, mate. For years you've been getting right up my nose,' said Stan, staring into Philip's face, his blue eyes glinting insanely. 'I hate your guts, do you know that? I loathe and detest you.'

'Yes, I've rather gathered that,' gasped Philip.

'Oh, you rather gathered that, did you?' he said in an exaggerated impersonation of Philip's cultured accent.

'But I've never understood why,' continued Philip, struggling to hide the fact that he was in pain from his shoulder so as not to add to Carter's power.

'I'll tell you then, shall I? It's because of your arrogance . . . the way you lord it over the people who work for you.'

'Well, I certainly don't intend to lord it over anyone. I've always tried to be fair to our workers.'

'Don't make me laugh,' snorted Stan. 'The way you ponce about in your fancy clothes with your la-de-da talk, giving out your orders . . . it makes me wanna throw up!'

'Someone has to be in charge,' Philip pointed out. 'How would you know what to do if someone like me didn't tell you?'

Stan didn't answer that.

'Do you think you'd enjoy the responsibility of management?' asked Philip rhetorically, hoping to talk the man into a calmer frame of mind.

''Course I would.'

'It isn't all a bundle of laughs, you know,' said Philip. 'There's a lot of worry to the job. It's my responsibility to keep orders coming in so that people like you have a job to come to every day, and to make sure our standards are kept up so as not to lose customers.'

'Sounds like a doddle to me.'

'If the customer isn't satisfied with the finished fabric, I take responsibility . . . not you lot down on the factory floor.'

'Responsibility and worry? Don't make me laugh,' sneered Stan who had never considered the other side of the question. 'You've never had to worry about a thing since the day you were born. Everything's laid on a plate for the likes of you.'

'Not necessarily.'

He gave a dry laugh. 'Oh, do leave off. I mean, what happens after the war? The squaddies all come back to find themselves out of work while you come back and walk into the job of Managing Director of this place.'

'And you think the job's a piece of cake, I suppose?' said Philip.

'Not half!'

'You *really* believe that taking over as the head of a silk-weaving business when the economy is at an all-time low, competition from abroad cutting our throats, is easy?'

'Compared to trying to feed a family on the pittance the

government pays a man in unemployment benefit, yeah, I'd say it's easy,' announced Stan. 'You don't even know the meaning of the word worry.'

'Worry isn't the sole prerogative of the working classes, you know,' said Philip, trying not to wince from the pressure of Carter's bruising grip on his arms. 'Everyone has their share at one time or another.'

'Rubbish! You've charmed lives, the lot of you.'

'Not all problems stem from being poor.'

'Name one that doesn't?'

Philip could have done so very easily but he wasn't prepared to bring his private life into this. 'I didn't invent the system, Carter,' he said, greatly weakened by the pain in his shoulder. 'I just try to do my best according to the responsibilities I've been given.'

'You control my life! You have the power to say whether I eat or whether I starve!' ground out Stan.

'None of us is free, we're all reliant on others,' Philip managed to utter. 'You answer to me. I answer to the people who buy our cloth. Without them neither of us has a living.'

'This is my only authority,' said Stan, and dealt Philip a blow to the jaw. As the other man reeled from the blow, he hit him again and again until he fell to the floor.

Philip had seen enough physical violence in the war to last him a lifetime; he had no intention of giving this man the brawl he was obviously hoping for.

'All right, Carter,' he said, struggling dazedly to his feet. 'You've made your point . . . now get out of here.'

But Stan was enjoying himself far too much for that. In some dark corner of his mind he knew he had gone too far but

147

nothing mattered to him now except the desire to beat this man and keep on beating him – to squeeze the very life out of him so that he would never have to look upon his hateful face again.

Grasping Philip by the arms once more, he threw him backwards against the desk, put his hands around his throat and began pressing . . . harder . . . harder . . .

Struggling to remove the pressure from his throat, Philip felt the air leave his body. The pain in his left shoulder had become excruciating now, even though the other shoulder and arm had gained in strength over the years to compensate for the defect.

He felt helpless, doomed to die at the hands of a man whose personal inadequacy had produced deadly paranoia. With the instinct of someone whose life was under threat, Philip made a supreme effort to gain his freedom by raising his foot and pushing it against Carter's stomach. It made no difference – the hands still clutched his throat. Choking and beginning to accept the inevitable, he gave one last thrust with his foot. Miraculously his assailant moved back. The pressure left Philip's throat.

His vision was blurred as he fought to catch his breath. Distantly, through the confusion in his mind, he heard a crash and the tinkling sound of glass breaking. As his sight cleared, he saw the broken window and realised with horror that Carter must have fallen through it. Still numb from his ordeal, he moved woodenly to the window. In the fading light he could just make out a figure lying on the cobblestones below.

Trembling all over, Philip rushed down the iron staircase and out into the yard, his chest pounding with the wild overbeating of his heart. Going down on his knees, he bent over the other man whose eyes stared unblinkingly towards the darkening skies. Breathless with fear, Philip felt for a pulse . . .

Chapter Eight

The jury had come back into the courtroom. The judge had asked if they had reached a unanimous decision and was answered in the affirmative. An electric hush descended on the court as they waited to hear the verdict.

Philip stood very straight in the dock. He'd passed beyond fear into a peculiar state of numb acceptance. It was four months since Stan Carter's death – four months of deep trauma. Nothing before had affected him so profoundly. He'd been forced to kill in the war, of course, but had conditioned himself to think of it as an unavoidable job of work; that had been the only way to stay sane in combat. Being responsible for Carter's death, however, albeit accidentally, felt very different and Philip's remorse was all-consuming. Memories of that fateful incident blackened his life.

The charge against him was murder but the evidence corroborating his plea of self-defence was substantial. The heavy bruising from the beating he'd taken and the marks on his neck from the attempted strangulation had all been taken into consideration and used in his defence. The significance of these facts had also helped his lawyer to secure bail for him, so at least he'd been spared the ordeal of four months in prison.

Apart from keeping to the conditions of his bail by reporting daily to the police station, he'd tried to hang on to his sanity by maintaining his normal daily routine while waiting for the case to come to court. He'd forced himself into the factory every day, guessing that the workforce was reviling him behind his back. Carter had, after all, been one of their own.

Bobby and Luke Carter and Arthur Brown had left the company in a gesture of support for Stan Carter's mother whose opinion about her son's death had been splashed all over the local papers. As far as she was concerned, it had been a clear case of premeditated murder and Philip should receive the appropriate punishment.

He had been advised by his solicitor against any contact with the Carter family until after the trial. This hadn't pleased him because he'd wanted to visit Stan Carter's widow, to offer compensation as well as condolences. But this could be misconstrued as an admission of guilt, apparently, and would be most unwise.

Now, he glanced across at his parents in the public gallery. The whole thing had been too much for Emily who had been under sedation for most of the time since it happened. His mother gave him a confident smile which he recognised as a token of her faith that justice would be done and he would leave the court a free man.

She had accepted his story without question or reproach. His father had been rather more censorious, however. 'I can't understand why you allowed things to get so out of hand,' he had exclaimed. 'You should have called the police the minute the damned fellow appeared in your office. It must have been obvious he was up to no good since he was on the premises after business hours without permission and therefore trespassing. If you'd managed to get help this whole thing could have been avoided.'

Philip had been over the incident a million times, analysing every second of it until his head ached, searching for a point during the proceedings at which he might have changed the course of events. It was obvious that Carter had come to his office that evening after his blood. So would it have changed anything if Philip had tried to do what his father suggested? He thought not – the night watchman had yet to come on duty and Carter would have ripped the phone out of the wall if Philip had made a move to use it.

But to give his father due credit, he'd been fully behind his son and fierce in his defence of him to outsiders, even if he did grumble to Philip himself about the whole 'damned business' being a blasted nuisance. Philip suspected that his stand had more to do with the family reputation than fatherly affection, but at least the old boy hadn't been against him for once and he appreciated that.

The judge was speaking.

'How do you find the defendant – guilty or not guilty as charged?'

There was not a movement or a sound as all eyes turned to the jury foreman.

'Not guilty, milord.'

A roar of approval spread through the room for the evidence in Philip's favour had been solid. His numbness was pierced by relief so strong it brought tears to his eyes. But his moment of relief was cut short by a disturbance in the public gallery.

'Murderer!' shouted Polly Carter, jabbing her finger at him, her face contorted with venom. 'You ought to swing for what you did to my son. I hope you rot in hell!' She turned her attention to the judge. 'There's one law for the rich and another for the poor. If one of us had done what he did, we'd have copped the death penalty. Those who can afford clever lawyers to con the jury can get away with murder. It's a bloody disgrace . . .'

She broke down sobbing and was led from the court by her two sons.

Philip was surrounded by supporters. His solicitor shook his hand, his father patted him on the back, his mother hugged him. Even people he had never seen before wished him well, for public opinion had been very much in his favour.

'I knew it would be all right,' said Meg as they made their way from the courtroom. 'It was obvious to anyone with half a brain that you'd acted in self-defence.'

'To everyone except the Carters,' Philip pointed out.

'Well, yes, but his mother is bound to be feeling bitter,' said Meg. 'I'd feel the same in her position. I feel terribly sorry for her.'

'Me too,' said Philip.

'At least she has her family around her, and they seem very supportive,' remarked Meg.

'I didn't see Carter's wife in court today,' said Philip.

'She wasn't there,' said his mother. 'I noticed that.'

'She must be going through hell,' said Philip grimly. 'Losing her husband and being left to bring the children up on her own.'

'Mmm,' agreed Meg.

'You'll have me in tears in a minute,' said Humphrey

sarcastically. 'Don't forget that if Stan Carter had had his way, you and I would have been the bereaved ones, Meg, and it wouldn't have been accidental!'

'True enough,' she agreed with a solemn shake of the head. 'But you can't help feeling sorry for the family, can you?'

'Not unless you're completely callous,' said Humphrey. 'But I really think it's time we put the whole thing behind us. I'm sure you agree, don't you, Philip?'

'Yes, I suppose you're right,' he replied, but he knew he'd never be able to turn his back on it. The Carters weren't the only ones whose lives had been shattered by the death of the eldest son. His own had been too.

'Why not go and have a lie down, Mum?' suggested Bobby when the Carter family got home from court and gathered in Polly's parlour.

'Good idea,' agreed June. 'I'll bring a cup of tea up to you in the bedroom.'

'No, I wouldn't be able to rest,' said Polly, her eyes swollen from weeping. 'In fact I don't think I'll ever sleep again knowing that our courts let murderers go free to walk the streets and do it again.'

'Come on now, love, be reasonable,' said Will gently. 'Philip Verne isn't really a criminal. He isn't likely to kill anyone else.'

'He's done it once, he could do it again,' was her acerbic reply.

'We are all capable of murder under certain provocation,' he pointed out. 'That's a well-known fact.'

'Decent people don't do it though, do they?' she said. 'But

he did. He's a murderer, Will, and it's no use you trying to say different.'

'He says it was an accident and the jury believed him. Don't you think we should try to do the same?' he wisely suggested.

'Never!'

'Look, Polly, the court says Philip Verne was defending himself and us believing otherwise isn't gonna bring Stan back,' he said with unusual firmness. 'And it certainly won't make us feel any better about losing him.'

'Defending himself, my arse!' she exploded. 'That Verne bloke has always had it in for Stan. He told us about it many a time. I reckon he asked Stan to stay behind that night with the idea of doing him over. Yeah, he wanted rid of him 'cos Stan was a thorn in his side. He was a problem 'cos he wasn't afraid to speak up for his workmates. That's right, isn't it, Arthur?'

He didn't reply for a few moments. 'Yeah, 'course it is, Mrs C,' he agreed at last, but felt very uneasy about doing so.

'And as for Lizzie not being at the court today . . . well, I'm gonna have a few hard words with that young lady!'

'I think she's probably been finding the case too upsetting,' said June, protective of her friend. 'It's only natural.'

'We *all* found it very upsetting, June,' cut in Polly hotly. 'But we didn't run away from our obligations.'

'I'll go and make some tea,' said June and disappeared into the kitchen rather than add to her mother-in-law's suffering by disagreeing with her. Poor Lizzie was having a really hard time at the moment, and having to listen to Polly raving yet again about Philip Verne was about the last thing she needed and probably the reason she had stayed away from court today.

That and the fact that she was working all hours.

'It was Lizzie's duty to come today to show her solidarity with the family,' continued Polly. 'She should have been there, showing a united front with us.'

''Course she should,' put in Luke. 'She should have been there.'

'She was probably too busy at her loom,' suggested Bobby. 'The poor woman has enough to do trying to make enough money to keep them all now that she's on her own. It isn't as though Stan left her provided for.'

'We've all had to make sacrifices for his sake,' insisted Polly. 'You and Luke and Arthur only have your dole money and the bit you make odd jobbing since you left Verne's as a mark of respect to Stan. Lizzie knows we'll not see her and the kids go hungry. Families like ours stick together at times like this.'

'She's not actually family though, is she?' Luke pointed out.

'Of course she is,' said Bobby, appalled at his brother's suggestion.

'Blood's thicker than water,' remarked Luke coolly.

'Not so far as Lizzie's concerned, it isn't,' snapped Bobby, glowering at Luke.

'It is as far as anyone's concerned,' he argued. 'It's a well-known fact.'

'Lizzie's been part of the Carter family for practically the whole of her life,' retorted Bobby, eyes hot with rage. 'She doesn't need a blood tie to qualify as one of us.'

'Technically she isn't a Carter, though,' insisted Luke irascibly.

'She's probably more loyal than you are . . . if truth be known,' blasted Bobby.

'Now, now, that's enough, you two,' reproached Polly. 'About the last thing I need today is a quarrel.'

June returned from the kitchen with a tray of tea which she handed around. Polly continued to hold forth about the dreadful miscarriage of justice until June said she had to go to collect the twins from school.

'I ought to be going now an' all,' said Arthur, rising.

'Oh, are you not staying for a bite to eat with us, then?' said Polly.

'No . . . thanks for asking, Mrs C, but I've things to do.'

'See you down the Labour Exchange in the morning, then, mate,' said Bobby casually.

'Well . . . er . . . no . . . you won't as a matter of fact.'

'Oh, why not?'

'I'm leaving the area.'

All eyes rested on him, waiting for him to explain.

'I'm gonna try me luck up North,' he informed them.

'You're leaving London?'

'That's right.'

'Well, stone me!' exclaimed Bobby.

'There's nothing much about round here in the way of work in our trade, is there?' said Arthur. 'So I'm gonna head for Macclesfield. There's plenty of silk-weaving firms in that town so I've heard. I'm hoping to get myself fixed up with a job.'

'Cor, you're a dark horse,' said Polly with a hint of criticism. 'You've never said you were thinking of moving away.'

'I've only just made up my mind for definite,' he explained.

'Being a single man, I can just up and leave without making too many plans.'

'We're sorry to see you go, but good luck to you,' said Will, and this was echoed by the rest of the family.

Having said his goodbyes, Arthur marched down Thorn Street feeling brighter for having shed his burden. At least in Macclesfield he wouldn't have to listen to Stan's mum canonising him. Nor would he have constantly to bite his tongue against telling her the truth – that her beloved Stan had had every intention of beating up Philip Verne that night and, in Arthur's opinion, had brought about his own untimely death.

He had thought the world of Stan. He'd even committed moral perjury by omitting to mention what Stan had said to him on the afternoon he died; that he was going to give Philip Verne a real pasting to teach him a lesson. Arthur had kept quiet about it out of respect for Stan's mum's feelings. It must be heartbreaking to be robbed of another son after losing Roy to the war. She needed someone to blame; it was perfectly understandable that she couldn't accept that Stan might have brought it on himself. In due course she would probably be more able to face the true facts. In the meantime, he would leave her with her illusions.

Thank God the verdict had gone in Verne's favour. Arthur couldn't have remained silent and let him take the death penalty. That was why he'd waited around until after the trial.

He stopped at the corner and looked back along Thorn Street. It was bleak and grey on this winter afternoon, rain falling in a sticky drizzle. Small children played outside despite the weather, huddled in forlorn little groups on the greasy wet pavements chalked with hopscotch games while underfed dogs barked and prowled in the gutter for scraps of food. It'll be a long time before I'm around this way again, thought Arthur sadly. If I ever am again. But I can't stay, not knowing what I do.

Then he went to his home a few streets away, packed a bag and headed for the railway station and his new life.

Chapter Nine

Philip was assailed by nausea as he entered the tenement house in Bessle Street one day a week later and climbed the stairs to the third floor, having been given the necessary information by two women gossiping in the street.

The wooden stairs and landings were bare and broken and a gagging stench permeated everything – a mixture of mustiness, damp, dirty clothes and mouse droppings. God, what a way to live!

He rapped his knuckles on a door with brown flaking paint.

'Come on in, June,' came a voice from inside. 'The door's on the latch.'

Feeling ridiculously nervous, he called out, 'Er . . . actually it isn't June.'

'Who is it then?'

'Philip Verne.'

After a long silence, the door opened – just a fraction.

'Well, you've got a nerve,' said Lizzie, peering at him quizzically, two angry red stains on her cheeks standing out against her pallor.

'Perhaps, but . . .'

'No perhaps about it, mate,' she snarled. 'You've got a

161

bloody cheek showing your face here after what happened.'

Aware of doors opening all along the landing, he said, 'Actually, it's a bit public here. I think it would be better for both of us if I came inside for a minute.'

She ushered him in then marched out to the landing and shouted, 'All right, the show's over, folks. You can go back inside now.'

Shabbily dressed but shining with cleanliness, she was wearing a black outdoor coat and had grey woollen mittens on her hands.

'So what do you want with me?' she asked, moving into the room, its freezing temperature explaining her outdoor clothes.

'I'd like to talk to you.'

'Well, you'll have to be quick about it,' she said abruptly. 'I can't afford to stop work for more than a few minutes.'

'It won't take long.'

'All right, you'd better sit down then,' she said, moving a pile of children's clothes from a frayed armchair and putting them on to an equally shabby sofa.

He sat down near the fireplace which was unlit but laid with coal and sticks for a fire.

'I light it in time for the children to come home from school,' she explained, sitting down opposite him and hugging herself against the cold. 'Can't afford to burn coal all day.'

'You'll make yourself ill in this weather,' he said, appalled at her circumstances.

'Tell me something I don't already know.'

'Do you work all day in here?' he asked, glancing at the loom in the window.

She nodded. 'And most nights too now that I don't have a man's wage coming in.'

Her tone was brisk but not bitter, he noticed. She was merely presenting him with the facts. He thought her to be a proud and courageous woman without an ounce of self-pity. If he was any judge, all her energy went into looking after her children.

'And I suppose you think I'm to blame for that?'

'It's only natural. I mean, if it wasn't for . . . for what happened between you and my husband, he would still be here,' she said, the hardship of the last few months culminating in a ferocious need to hit out – to blame someone for the hurt she was feeling inside. 'And my children would still have a father.'

'Yes, I can understand how you must be feeling. It's a very sad time for you and your children,' he said kindly.

'What a gift you have for understatement,' she said coolly.

'Look, Mrs Carter,' he said in a conciliatory manner, 'obviously I'm very sorry indeed about what happened.'

'Not half as sorry as I am!'

'There's nothing I can do to change the past but I can do something to help you now, and in the future.'

'So you've come to offer me a job, have you?' she surmised.

'You can have a job at Verne's if you wish, certainly,' he told her, 'but that wasn't what I meant.'

'Oh . . . what then?'

'I'd like to help you in the only way I can,' he said earnestly. 'Practical assistance in the form of financial compensation.'

She threw him an icy stare. 'Well, well, this is a surprise.'

'I was thinking in terms of a lump sum that you could either draw on as and when you need it, or invest wisely to give you a regular income,' he continued.

Shrill laughter echoed through the room. 'If you think I'd even consider taking a penny of conscience money from the man who killed my husband,' she said, face pinched with cold but bright with anger, 'you must be crackers!'

'Oh, dear. I'm sorry you've chosen to see it that way,' he said, bruised by her accusation which reached a place inside him untouched by the hatred of the rest of the Carter family.

'Oh, come on. If that doesn't bear all the hallmarks of a guilty conscience, I don't know what does,' she said, Polly's influence having rubbed off on her at this vulnerable time.

'Naturally I don't feel good about what happened.'

'I should damned well hope not!'

She began to shake with silent laughter and he knew she was on the point of hysteria. Something inside him stirred. The gesture he had come here to make out of humanity to someone for whom he felt responsible now became a personal wish to help a woman he found himself admiring.

There was a kind of raw beauty about her that transcended the squalor of her surroundings. Her candid green eyes were stunning against her pale skin and black clothes. A few strands of blonde hair had escaped from the dark ribbon holding it back, and fell untidily across her fine-featured face. As her laughter changed to a look of sheer desolation, he found himself with an urge to take her in his arms and comfort her.

But he just said, 'I hoped you might feel able to accept the money whatever you think of me personally.'

'No chance,' she told him with a vigorous shake of the head. 'So why not do us both a favour and leave?'

Philip had been through a lot this last few months. He'd

taken cruel insults from members of the Carter family without argument because he knew how terrible they must be feeling. But seeing the savage accusation in her eyes was just too much for him to bear.

'I think it's time you faced up to the truth,' he said, dark eyes black with feeling.

'Oh, just get out of here and take your rotten money with you,' she commanded, her voice ragged with emotion as she marched to the door. 'Go on, get out of here . . . out . . . out!'

'I'm not leaving until you've heard me out,' he boomed, his commanding presence filling the room.

'I don't want to listen to what any killer has to say,' she said, hearing her mother-in-law in her own voice.

'Look, I know how dreadful you must be feeling and I can understand your wanting to put all the blame on me,' he told her fervently, 'but I'm not a murderer and I believe you know that . . . if you're really honest with yourself.'

She moved away from the door quickly and stood with her back to the window, near the loom.

'Keep your voice down, will you?' she said, lowering her voice. 'I'd rather not give the neighbours free entertainment and fuel for more gossip. So say what you have to say then get out and leave me alone.'

'Your husband killed himself as surely as if he put a gun to his own head,' he said with the brutal candour he considered necessary to bring her to her senses so that she would feel able to accept his help. 'He came to my office that night full of bloodlust. If I hadn't managed to get him off me, *he'd* have been the one on trial for murder.'

Biting her lip, she sat down on the chair by the loom and

165

clasped both hands to her head. 'I don't want to hear any of this. It was bad enough having to listen to it in court.'

'Is that why you didn't go to hear the verdict . . . because you couldn't bear to hear about it?'

She shrugged. 'That and the fact that I couldn't afford to take time off from work.'

'I think it's very important that you know the truth,' he said.

'All I need to know is that Stan is dead and you killed him. How it actually came about can't alter that.'

'Do you think you are being quite fair to me?' he asked.

'Why do I have to be fair to you?' she wanted to know. 'You're not involved in my life. My feelings don't affect you one iota.'

'Oh, but they do. They matter to me a great deal, as a matter of fact,' he said truthfully. 'I don't enjoy being thought of as a murderer.'

'You should have made sure that no one ever had cause to give you that title then, shouldn't you?'

'Do you think I haven't suffered over what happened? Do you think I haven't tortured myself over the last few months, sifting over every detail of the incident in my mind and wondering if I could have done anything to avoid the tragedy?'

'And?'

'Short of letting him kill me, there wasn't anything I could have done.'

'And why would Stan want to do that?' she asked, though she knew the answer.

'Because, with respect, he allowed his grievances to rule his life. He hated me with an unnatural fervour,' he told her.

'You probably knew him better than anyone. You must know that what I'm saying is true?'

'Only two people know what happened that night and one of them isn't able to speak for himself,' she said, more affected by what Philip had to say than she was prepared to admit.

'Your husband died unnecessarily,' he went on. 'He robbed his children of a father by letting his feelings get out of control and cause a tragic accident.'

She sat very still, looking at her hands clenched together in her lap.

'Of course, I can't force you to take what I am offering,' he said, 'but please don't deprive your children of a little material comfort by refusing help. If you don't want the money for yourself, take it for them.'

'I can't do that.'

'Why not?'

'It wouldn't be right.'

'Are you afraid you might be able to afford coal for the fire,' he accused her harshly, 'or that you might be able to eat decently? That you might be forced to stop playing the martyr . . .'

'That isn't fair!'

'I should have bought you a hair shirt,' he continued sarcastically, driven by his need to lessen her burden. 'Perhaps that would be more to your taste than the practical means to improve life for you and your children?'

Memories were filling her mind, of things she had tried to blot out since Stan's death because she didn't feel able to cope with guilt as well as grief. She recalled how violently Stan's paranoia towards Philip Verne had irritated her. Only the day before he'd died he'd accused her of taking the other man's side.

It would be all too easy for her to fall into the trap of self-castigation whilst her judgement was impaired by bereavement. But the same independent spirit that had driven her to express opinions that didn't coincide with her husband's, wouldn't allow her to ignore what her visitor was saying.

She stood up slowly and cast a close eye over her visitor, seeing someone as incongruous in this room as a duke in a doss house. He was expensively dressed and had striking good looks, a typical example of the uncaring capitalist classes that Stan had felt so strongly about. As she met those rich dark eyes, though, she perceived strength of character and genuine compassion. But she couldn't accept his offer. It didn't feel right to do so.

'All right, Mr Verne, I've listened to what you have to say,' she said with a kind of calm weariness, 'and I accept that you are sorry for what happened and genuinely want to help me. But surely you can see that I couldn't accept any offer of assistance from you? It would be disloyal to my husband . . . to his family.'

'I should have thought blind loyalty is a luxury you could ill afford.'

'You can think what you like.'

'Why not face the facts?'

'The facts as perceived by you, you mean?'

'You can't deny the truth of the matter,' he said grimly. 'That no matter how strongly you feel about loyalty to your husband, he isn't around to provide for you.'

'I hope your capabilities stretch beyond a gift for stating

the obvious,' she said cuttingly.

Ignoring this, he continued determinedly, 'And since his brothers saw fit to put themselves out of work on his behalf, quite unnecessarily in my opinion, his family are probably not in a position to help you much either.'

She shrugged.

He nodded towards the loom. 'You don't need me to tell you that there is only so much money you can earn as an outworker.'

Her temper was rising again because he was bringing thoughts and feelings to the surface she would rather keep suppressed.

'I think you must leave it to me to decide what I can and cannot afford,' she informed him crisply. 'Now if you'll excuse me, I have work to do.'

'Very well.' He walked to the door then turned back to her. 'If you do change your mind, you know where to find me.'

'Thank you for coming, Mr Verne,' she said politely.

'Not at all, Mrs Carter,' he said with a bleak smile.

On the way downstairs he realised that it had become vital to him to make things better for her. Conscience was undoubtedly a major factor because, no matter how provoking the circumstances, he *had* actually committed the act that had led to her husband's death.

But there was something else too: the woman herself. During their short meeting, he'd discerned enormous strength – a definite sense that life would never be allowed to grind Lizzie down.

He had noticed something else about Lizzie Carter too. As

far as he knew she'd been born into poverty and would never have known anything other than drudgery. Yet she looked as out of place in that miserable setting as he had felt. There was a kind of nobility about her that belied her humble circumstances.

Glancing at his pocket watch, he hurried towards the street door, realising that he was going to be late home for lunch. He tensed as he always did at the prospect of upsetting Emily. He tried never to keep her waiting because she fretted so if he was even a few minutes late. He hadn't expected to be so long with Lizzie Carter. Damned stubborn woman! he thought as he made his way along the hall and opened the squeaky front door.

He almost collided with someone on the way in, a woman he recognised as Stan Carter's mother. Even as he braced himself for the hostility he knew would come, he felt her spit in his face, then she went on into the house without a word.

Wiping his face with a handkerchief, he carried on out to his car, his skin smarting as though she'd cut it with a knife.

'What was that scum Verne doing here?' Polly demanded the instant she set foot over the threshold.

'Oh, he just called round to see me,' replied Lizzie.

'Well, of all the nerve!'

'That's what I said.'

'What did he actually say to you?' Polly was curious to know.

'As a matter of fact, he offered me financial help.'

'Never!'

'Yeah . . . a lump sum.'

'Thinks he can ease his conscience the only way his sort knows how, I suppose?'

'Maybe. Though I got the impression that he really does feel bad about what happened and wants to make amends.'

'Naturally you told him where to put his dough?' said Polly.

Lizzie nodded.

'I should think so too,' exclaimed Polly. 'He doesn't know us Carters if he thinks we can be paid off that easily, just so that he can get on with his life and forget what he's done to us.'

'I *really* don't think that was what he had in mind,' said Lizzie, surprising herself with her persistence. 'I believe he genuinely does want to help.'

'Huh, it's easy enough for someone like him to give out money, isn't it?' she snorted. 'But it won't bring our Stan back.'

Another one with a gift for stating the obvious, Lizzie thought wryly, but just sighed and said, 'Well no . . .'

'As if you'd accept anything from him,' rasped Polly.

It wasn't so much her words that annoyed Lizzie as her dogmatic attitude. Her bold assumption that Lizzie would automatically behave in the way she was expected to, jarred on her already sensitised emotions and she didn't feel able to let it pass.

'I told him I wouldn't accept it,' said Lizzie. 'But it was *my* decision, not *yours*.'

Polly flushed. 'My, my, we are touchy today. I don't know what's got into you lately . . . first you don't turn up in court to hear the verdict, now you're as good as telling me to mind my own business.'

'I didn't come to court because I was busy trying to earn a

living,' explained Lizzie firmly. 'Anyway, I saw no point. Stan is dead. Whatever had happened to Philip Verne couldn't have changed that.'

'There's such a thing as family solidarity, you know.'

'I'd have to be awfully dim not to know all about family solidarity after being part of the Carter family for so long, wouldn't I?' Lizzie told her brusquely.

'Well, this is all I need,' huffed Polly, her voice quivering on the edge of tears. 'After all I've been through lately, I come round here with a pan of tripe and onions for you and the kids to have tonight – and what happens? I get my head bitten off.'

An awkward silence settled over them. Compunction would not be stifled as Lizzie looked at the older woman's face which was more or less permanently blotchy from weeping these days.

'I'm sorry, I didn't mean to upset you. I'm a bit tired, that's all.'

'I should damned well hope you are sorry, too, my girl,' said Polly as though Lizzie was about five years old. 'We have to show a united front at times like this.'

'Yes, I know,' said Lizzie, giving her a conciliatory hug. 'Thanks for bringing us something for supper.'

'You're welcome,' said Polly stiffly.

'Got time for a cuppa?'

'Well, only if you can spare the time,' she said, her face softening.

'I can always spare the time for you,' said Lizzie, filling the kettle from a bucket and putting it on the gas stove to boil.

One day a few weeks later when Lizzie's employer came to collect her finished work, he took the loom away with him too.

'I'm expanding . . . taking over a factory in Essex,' he explained cheerfully. 'Shan't be using many outworkers. Any work I do put out will go to local people.'

'Expanding, eh?' she'd said. 'I didn't know things were that good in the silk trade.'

'They're picking up nicely,' he said. 'I've no shortage of orders, anyway.'

This may have been heartening news to entrepreneurs but it wasn't much help to Lizzie who knew it would take time to find a new source of outwork.

'You'll soon find something else,' said Polly encouragingly.

'I hope so.'

'And Will and me will try and help you with your rent till you're fixed up.'

Since Will's wages were already subsidising Luke's dole money, Lizzie knew that that was out of the question.

'Don't worry, I'll manage.'

In the event she found home employment with one of the remaining silk factories in East London who hadn't moved out to Essex. The pay was even lower than she'd been getting before. There were so many desperate women like Lizzie, looking for work after losing their wartime jobs, employers found exploitation easy.

If she got up at the crack of dawn and worked until late at night, she could just about manage to pay the rent and feed the family, albeit in spartan fashion. Clothing the children was her biggest worry. She couldn't afford to put more than a few coppers into her clothing fund each week so lived in dread of one of them needing something before she had enough saved to buy it.

One cold and wet day at the end of February that happened. The children came home from school shivering and soaked to the skin. When Lizzie noticed that Eva's shoes had reached the final stages of disintegration and were now soleless, she knew she would have to keep her at home until she could afford to buy her a pair from the second hand stall in the market.

Eva was a bright, gregarious child who enjoyed being at the centre of things. For the first few days she quite enjoyed her 'holiday' from school but soon became bored, especially as she was isolated from the children playing in the street after school. When, a few days later, the shoe leather deficiency spread to her brothers who were forced to take a holiday too, Lizzie was at her wits' end. It wasn't good for them to be cut off from everything like this, but what else could she do? Barefoot children weren't unknown on the streets of this area but, even apart from the humiliation for them, Lizzie daren't let them brave the winter weather without footwear for fear they'd catch pneumonia.

Despite her very best endeavours, she wasn't able to keep her predicament from Polly for very long, not with three talkative children about.

'What about getting them some shoes from the tally man?' suggested her mother-in-law one wintry morning.

'I've already thought of that but I won't be able to keep up the weekly payments,' explained Lizzie grimly.

'In that case, I'll have to try and pay something towards it,' said Polly, frowning worriedly. 'I can't have my grandchildren going without shoes. I'll help out as much as I can.'

Lizzie was silent as she wrestled with a dilemma that had

174

been giving her sleepless nights for some time. She made a sudden decision.

'You can help me right now by looking after the children for an hour or so.'

'Oh . . . why?'

'I have to go out.'

'Certainly, love. Where are you going?'

'I'll tell you when I get back,' said Lizzie mysteriously.

Lizzie went straight to the weaving department entrance at Verne's. It was the first time she'd been back to the factory since she herself had worked there. Nothing had changed. Still the same warm oily smell, the same clatter of machines. Having exchanged a few pleasantries with some of her old workmates and ascertained that Philip Verne was in his office, she made her way up the iron stairs and tapped on his office door.

'Well, this *is* a surprise. How nice to see you, Mrs Carter,' he said, ushering her in with courtesy that came naturally to him. 'Please sit down.'

'You can guess why I'm here, I suppose,' she said in a brittle tone. At the first hint of condescension she was off.

'Could you have had a change of heart about the money, perhaps?' he enquired pleasantly.

'A change of circumstances, actually,' she explained sharply. 'I wouldn't be here if I wasn't desperate.'

She explained briefly what had been happening to her since he'd been to see her. 'I've thought a lot about what you said . . . you know, about taking the money for the children's sake. If it was just myself, wild horses wouldn't have dragged me here but I can't have my children going without shoes when there's an alternative. It wouldn't be fair to them.'

'I'm glad you're able to look at it in that light now,' he said amiably. 'Think of it as a sort of death benefit payment.'

'No, I couldn't accept it on those terms,' she said.

'Oh?'

'No, I'd rather take it as a loan.'

'But I don't want the money back.'

'I'd feel better that way.'

'Look, I did *not* murder your husband but I *do* feel responsible for his death,' said Philip earnestly. 'So why not think of it as conscience money if it will make it any easier for you?'

She shook her head.

'Not even as it will come out of my personal account and have nothing to do with the family business?'

'No.'

'But why, for God's sake?'

'It's all to do with feeling beholden, you see,' Lizzie explained.

'There'll be nothing like that. You need never see me again after today if that's what you wish,' Philip said. 'I'll give you a cheque for five hundred pounds and you can forget all about me.'

'Five hundred pounds?' she repeated in astonishment.

'That was the figure I had in mind, yes. So you see, it would be very difficult for you to repay such a sum.'

She was too stunned by the amount to utter a sound.

'May I suggest that you keep some aside for your immediate needs and invest the rest? I know an excellent broker who will help you to place the money to ensure a good income.'

'I suppose I'll need to open a bank account,' she muttered to herself.

'That's right. If I can be of any assistance with that, and with your investments, I'll be only too happy . . .'

It was like looking at a different person as she faced him across the desk. The grim shadow of worry had dropped away and she radiated new energy. Her eyes shone resolutely, her cheeks were flushed, and that finely curved mouth was actually arranged in a grin. A real smile, too, that transformed her face – so different from the sarcastic and hysterical expression he had been treated to at their last meeting.

'No, I think I can manage to open a bank account myself . . . and as for investments, I have plans of my own, thank you,' she informed him.

'Might I know what they are?' he asked conversationally.

'You'll get to know in due course,' she said enigmatically.

'Oh, really?' Lizzie's mood was infectious. He found himself smiling with her. 'I shall look forward to it.'

'And as for repaying the loan,' she continued, 'it might take a very long time but with the plans I have I stand a good chance of doing it.'

'There's no need,' he repeated.

'For me there is.'

Philip's admiration grew. A different sort of person, her late husband for instance, would have grabbed as much as they could without the slightest compunction.

He took a cheque book from his desk drawer and a pen from the inkstand.

'I'll phone the bank and arrange for you to have some cash right away,' he said, head bent as he wrote. 'Just in case there's a delay while the administration is completed.'

'Thank you.'

'No trouble at all. I hope you're not going to insist on paying me interest, though?' he said as he turned the cheque over and pressed it against the blotting pad.

'No, I think that would be rather too unrealistic.'

Her smile faded into a more serious expression – almost, he fancied, as though she was ashamed of feeling happy.

He felt more cheerful than he had in a long time when he handed her the cheque. At least he wouldn't have hungry, barefoot children on his conscience now. But he knew there was more to this than just the silencing of that inner voice. He really did want life to be kinder to her and her children.

After she'd left, he sat at his desk staring into space and mulling over the rather startling realisation that he had been very sorry to see Lizzie go.

Chapter Ten

'I've something to tell you,' Lizzie told Polly gravely.

'Let's hear it then?'

'It's something you're not going to like.'

'I guessed that much from the look on your face.' Her bushy brows met in a frown. 'Well, spit it out then.'

Lizzie had just got back from her meeting with Philip and the two women were having a cup of tea together. The children had retreated to the bedroom to keep warm under the covers until this afternoon when the fire would be lit. Lizzie felt very tense about what she had to say to Polly.

'Well, actually . . . I've decided to accept help from Philip Verne after all.'

'You've done what?' exploded Polly, turning scarlet.

'I've taken that money he offered – five hundred pounds. I paid it into the bank on the way home from his office.'

Polly's flush drained away to leave her skin bloodless, her freckles emphasised by the pallor. 'So that's where you've been? To see *him*.'

'That's right.'

'How could you have done it, Lizzie?' she asked with real distress.

'For the children . . . I did it for them. It isn't fair to let a grudge that has nothing to do with them deprive them of a few home comforts.'

'Philip Verne killed their father and you say it has nothing to do with them!'

'I was referring to the Carter grudge against the Vernes.'

'It's all part of the same thing.'

'Maybe, but . . .'

'Do you think those kiddies would want anything paid for with *his* money?' Polly cut in tartly.

'I think they probably like having shoes to wear,' said Lizzie.

'You know very well I would have helped you to pay for their shoes . . .'

'Yes, I do know that and I'm grateful. But with the best will in the world, you simply can't afford it.'

'I'd have got the money somehow.'

'Only by scrimping and scraping and going without yourself,' said Lizzie, shaking her head. 'I'm just not prepared to let that happen, not when there's another way.'

Polly shook her head slowly. 'I just can't believe you'd stoop so low.'

'I've only taken the money as a loan.'

'Even so, the children won't thank you when they're old enough to understand the significance of where the money came from to clothe them,' said her mother-in-law.

'They will if they're not brought up with hatred in their hearts,' said Lizzie, adding quickly, 'The last thing I want to do is upset you but I really think I've done the right thing in accepting his money.'

'Right thing, my eye! You've made a mockery of Carter

values . . . we look after our own in this family. We don't take charity from those who seek to destroy us.'

'With respect,' said Lizzie patiently, 'until I paid that cheque into the bank just now, none of us had the means to look after ourselves properly, let alone anyone else.'

The other woman saw fit to ignore this. 'I'm bitterly disappointed in you, Lizzie,' she said, her eyes wet with tears.

Lizzie combed the hair back from her face with trembling fingers for she didn't oppose Polly lightly.

'Why not try to look at the situation from a different angle?' she suggested kindly. 'Try to see Philip Verne's action as a gesture of genuine regret.'

'He's only done it to ease his conscience!'

'Surely that's better than his just ignoring the consequences of what happened altogether?'

'I wouldn't touch a brass farthing of his money if I was destitute and I don't think you should either.'

'Surely you're not suggesting that I give the money back?'

'Yeah, that's exactly what I think you should do.'

Lizzie found herself weakening under the power of Polly's personality. Her uncompromising nature made her a tough opponent. Lizzie recalled all the agonising that had gone into her own change of heart and was determined not to be bullied into reversing that decision now. There would never be another chance to improve the quality of her children's lives. It was her duty to provide for them in the best way she could. If that meant a disagreement with Polly, then that's the way it had to be – however painful that was.

'I'm afraid I can't do that, Polly,' she forced herself to say.

'Won't, you mean.'

'All right, won't then.'

'Not even knowing how much it means to me?'

'Sorry, but it wouldn't be fair to the children.'

'You couldn't be more wrong.'

'This isn't a matter of right and wrong,' said Lizzie. 'It's simply a conflict of opinion. I see Philip Verne's offer of help as a way to make things better for us all. You see my accepting it as some kind of betrayal.'

'That's what it is.'

'I'm hoping to give us all a better life,' continued Lizzie ardently, 'and that includes you and Will.'

'It won't be any good you tryin' to sweeten us with Verne money 'cos we wouldn't touch a murderer's dough with a barge pole.'

'Philip Verne isn't a murderer, he was cleared of the charge.'

'Huh . . . he's certainly won you over!'

'It's the situation I'm in that has done that,' explained Lizzie, struggling to stand her ground against such powerful opposition. 'I just can't bear the idea of my children going hungry when they don't have to, that's all.'

'And you know they never will. Not while I'm alive.'

'But I've an opportunity for them to live decently instead of hand to mouth, and I'm going to seize it with both hands.'

'Poor Stan must be turning in his grave,' tutted Polly.

'Knowing Stan, he'll be giving me a round of applause.'

'That's enough of that sort of talk, if you please.'

'Be honest with yourself,' urged Lizzie, 'Stan's answer to this would be to take the bugger for every penny he's got. He certainly wouldn't want me to refuse the money.'

'That's where you're wrong,' Polly said hotly. 'My Stan had principles.'

'Indeed he did. But he would have seen compensation from Philip Verne as no more than his due,' she pointed out. 'And let's face it . . . as long as it was the upper classes who were shelling out the dough, that was all right by Stan.'

'You've changed. These aren't the values I brought you up with.'

'I'm twenty-eight years old, of course I've changed,' said Lizzie, her tone softening as she added, 'It's no criticism of you. We all develop our own ideas as we get older.'

'Family unity means everything to me,' declared Polly hotly.

'And to me,' said Lizzie with heartfelt sincerity, 'and my accepting this money hasn't altered that. If my plans work out the whole family will benefit.'

'I want nothing to do with anything come by in such a way.' She paused and looked at Lizzie curiously. 'Plans . . . what plans?'

'I want to set up in business,' she explained. 'To build a solid future with this money rather than just let it fritter away.'

Up shot Polly's brows. 'You can't be serious!'

'Never more so. I'm going to set up my own silk-weaving business. In a very small way to begin with, of course.'

'Well, I've heard some daft things in my time but that just about tops the lot!' came the cutting reply.

Lizzie had expected this sort of reaction but it was deflating just the same. 'Why is that, exactly?'

'That should be obvious to anyone with a fraction of sense.'

'It isn't to me.'

'Business is for men,' came the categorical reply.

'It doesn't have to be.'

'Come off it. What women do you know who are in business for themselves?'

'Well ... er ... none. Though there's a sweet shop in Notting Hill that's run by a woman.'

'Only because she took over from her old man after he died,' Polly pointed out. 'She didn't start from scratch like you're proposing to. Anyway, running a shop's a damned sight different to running a factory.'

'It'll only be a very small factory to start with.'

'Just the same, a woman's place is in the home ... biology sees to that,' insisted Polly. 'That's why they all flooded back into the home after the war.'

'They had to because there weren't enough jobs to go around when the men came back,' Lizzie reminded her.

'That just proves my point,' said Polly. 'If women were meant to take part in business, the men would be the ones at home.'

'Now you're just being deliberately stupid,' said Lizzie. 'There's no law to say someone of either sex can't go into business. As long as the children don't suffer.'

'The law of common sense is the only one to take notice of,' insisted Polly.

'Oh, really,' tutted Lizzie, frustrated by the other woman's refusal to look beyond her own narrow opinion.

'Use your head,' she went on. 'I mean, what do you know about business?'

'I know a lot about the silk business,' Lizzie pointed out. 'I've been in the trade for fifteen years including all the time I've put in working at home.'

'That's as maybe,' said her mother-in-law dismissively. 'Anyway, I thought you said you'd accepted the money for the children's sake, not for some madcap adventure of your own?'

'I have taken it for them.'

'Then why don't you use it for them, then, and put some of it away so they've something behind them later on instead of embarking on some cracked pot scheme and losing the lot?'

'Because this way,' Lizzie explained, grinding her teeth and trying not to be totally destroyed by this barrage of cynicism, especially as she was only too well aware that what she was planning to do was an enormous gamble, 'I can build something solid for them in the future and give us a decen income while I'm doing it.'

'You've got about as much chance of that as I have of appearing on stage at the Empire.'

'Thanks for the support.'

'There's no call for sarcasm, my girl,' snapped Polly.

'Well, it's so damned disappointing to have you dead set against me.'

'You must have known I would be. You know me well enough.'

'Yes, that's true.' Lizzie was close to tears. Being on bad terms with Polly was almost a physical pain. So much so that she was beginning to wish she'd never started along this track. But there could be no volte-face. The ambitions that had been forced to lie dormant for so long would not be stifled now. 'I suppose I hoped you might find it in your heart to encourage me, once you got used to the idea. You know how much I value your support. I . . . well, you've always been there to back me up in the past.'

'Not this time.'

'But this will be the only chance I'll ever have to make something of myself and give the children a decent life,' she implored. 'Can't you see that it would be criminal for me not to snap it up?'

'No, I can't see that.'

'Be happy for me and for the kids, please. It means so much to me.'

'Nonsense. If you cared about how I feel you wouldn't be doing this.'

Lizzie heaved a sigh. 'You make it sound as though I have a choice.'

'You do.'

'*Look*, there are three children in that bedroom when they should be at school. They're lying in bed because it's too damned cold in this place to do anything else,' said Lizzie, her patience severely tried. 'Thanks to Philip Verne I can now buy them shoes so that they can go to school tomorrow. I can also buy coal to keep the place heated for longer than just a few hours a day. How can that be wrong?'

Polly's blue eyes met Lizzie's steadily. 'Because in taking his money you are telling him that you forgive him, and that's one thing you should never do.'

'Oh, that's a very Christian attitude, I must say,' said Lizzie sardonically.

'What he did wasn't Christian.'

As there was no point in continuing along this particular road, Lizzie just said, 'Anyway, my taking his money does not give him absolution. It's simply a sensible solution to my problems. The man is keen to help me and I desperately need assistance, that's all there is to it.'

'Rubbish!'

Lizzie swallowed her tears and said in a muted tone, 'You're not the only one to miss Stan, you know, I miss him too . . . all the time . . . with a grinding ache.'

'Well, you've a damned funny way of showing it, that's all I can say.'

'Stan isn't here and his three children are,' Lizzie said gravely. 'Surely to God you must realise that I have to do my best for them in whatever way I can?'

'Not this way.'

'Oh, it's easy for you to be holier than thou about it,' said Lizzie.

'What's that supposed to mean?'

'I mean that we have both lost someone we love. The difference between us is, I was left with his responsibilities.'

'Oh, you do what you want,' mumbled Polly irritably. 'But don't expect me to take an interest. And don't ask me to look after the children while you're out working either. I helped out during the war because of the special circumstances. I won't do so again, on principle.'

'Fair enough.'

Polly rose abruptly, gathered her coat and hat from the back of the chair and put them on with stiff little movements.

'I'm sorry I've hurt you so badly,' said Lizzie with genuine regret.

'So am I,' said Polly with an elaborate sigh. 'You don't know just how much.'

When Polly had gone, Lizzie sank into a mood of gloomy introspection. There had been disagreements between them before, but this had been a watershed. Lizzie could feel the change; she knew she had taken the first step on a path that could lead to a permanent rift which was the last thing she wanted. But, no matter how strong the ties of love and gratitude were, as a parent herself, Lizzie's first duty must be to her children. She also considered that she had the right, as a self-respecting adult, to make the most of her own life too.

Anyway, to yield to Polly's wishes wasn't the way to a happy relationship. It would only lead to resentment and drive them even further apart. She wondered if, perhaps, they had to grow away from each other for a while before they could come together again as friends.

Glancing out of the window to see pale winter sunshine on the rooftops and drying the grimy pavements from a recent shower, she went into the bedroom.

'Right, kids, get yourselves cleaned up . . . we're going out to get you all fixed up with some new clothes.'

'New shoes?' queried Eva hopefully.

'Yes, darling. Shoes and warm coats and hats and woollies,' said Lizzie.

'Yippee!'

They were all so excited they fell over each other in an unprecedented rush to wash their hands and faces at the washstand.

Polly was in a reflective mood on the way home. She was losing Lizzie and it frightened her. It was so damned soul-destroying to see the woman she loved like a daughter behave in a way that was contrary to everything Polly had taught her. Polly was pleased she had managed to stop herself from reminding Lizzie of her debt to the Carter family. That would only have alienated her further. Anyway, Lizzie was an intelligent woman, she didn't need reminding of what they had done for a homeless eight-year-old. So why couldn't she see that accepting a handout from Verne was wrong?

Lizzie had changed. She wanted things that weren't proper for people like them. Business indeed! She'd be turning her back on her own kind before long. A traitor to her class as well as the Carter family. These unwanted thoughts caused an ache in the pit of Polly's stomach. She wasn't normally given to self-doubt so was surprised to find herself in the grip of a fleeting moment of uncertainty. Could Lizzie be right, perhaps, to grab what she could for her children – to put the past behind her and make something of her life?

This idea imbued her with light and hope for she hated being bad friends with Lizzie. Then a mental image of Stan lying dead on the cobblestones flashed into her mind and she knew that some things were beyond price. If the family meant anything to her at all, she'd give the money back to Verne.

In her heart Polly knew that wasn't going to happen. There had been a confidence and determination about Lizzie today that she had never seen before. She's growing away from us, Polly thought miserably, as she turned into Thorn Street.

'Starting a business . . . *you*?' said Bobby in astonishment, late that afternoon when Lizzie called to see him and June in their rooms in Case Street and gave them a brief outline of her change of fortune. The three Carter children, cutting quite a dash in their new clothes, were playing out in the street with the twins who had a natural gift for entertaining, even at this early age, and were performing some sort of comedy act for the local urchins.

'There's no need to sound quite so shocked,' Lizzie rebuked him lightly. 'I'm not completely thick, you know.'

'Of course you're not . . . but people like us don't start up in business.'

'Well, I'm going to. And what's more I'd like to offer you a job.'

'*Me* work for *you*?' he said with visible apprehension.

'That's right. I'd like you to help me set the factory up then manage it when we've got it up and running.'

'Well, I . . .'

'Such wild enthusiasm,' said Lizzie with playful sarcasm. 'It may not be the best offer you've ever had but it's gotta be better than being on the dole.'

'I'll say it is!' enthused June without a moment's hesitation. 'I think it's a terrific idea, Lizzie. If anyone can make a go of it, you can. You've always been the brightest among us.'

'It isn't that I'm not thrilled for you, Liz,' Bobby explained doubtfully. 'But I just can't imagine myself working for a woman, and especially you. I mean, how can I take orders from my best pal . . . the girl I always used to go after when we played kiss chase?'

'I shouldn't think it will be too difficult if you're getting paid well enough for it,' she told him crisply.

'There's no answer to that, is there?' he grinned. 'So it looks like you've just hired your first employee.'

'Good.'

'I'll second that,' said June.

'Seriously, though,' continued Lizzie, 'it'll be much more interesting for you than the job at Verne's because you'll be on the management . . . you'll have authority. I'm going to need a right-hand man right from the start, someone I can trust to be at the factory when I'm not there. Obviously, I won't be able to be there all the time because of the children.'

'I'll help out with them if you're stuck at any time,' offered June eagerly. 'They're always with the twins anyway.'

'Thanks, June, that'll be a great help. Obviously I shall tailor my working day to fit in with their school hours but there might be times when the two overlap.'

'It's bound to happen now and again,' agreed June.

'And Polly's not prepared to help.' Lizzie told them about her reaction to her plans. 'In fact, on thinking about it, I wonder if she'll disapprove of your working for me, Bobby, considering where the money's coming from to fund the project?'

'Surely she wouldn't let her feelings stand in the way of a man having a job?' said June.

'She's very strongly against me in this,' said Lizzie. 'So, if there is a problem and you'd rather not upset her, Bobby, I'll understand. I don't want to come between mother and son.'

'Ma knows I don't bear grudges,' said Bobby. 'I only gave up the job at Verne's because she was in such a state at the time of Stan's death. Now, six months on, and trying to keep a wife and two kids on the pittance I get from the state . . . well, it's time to be realistic. Anyway, Stan wouldn't want us to go without on his behalf.'

'Can I take it that you'll definitely accept the job then?'

'Try stopping me.'

'I think I'll leave it to you to tell your mum,' said Lizzie. 'I'm seriously out of favour with her at the moment.'

'Don't worry, I'll square it with her. Ma can be a stubborn old duck at times but her heart's in the right place.'

'You don't have to tell me that,' Lizzie was quick to point out, 'that's why I hate upsetting her . . . because I know she'd walk through fire for any one of us if necessary.'

'Trouble with Ma is, her opinions are set in stone. I think that must be where Stan got his hard and fast views from.'

'Very probably. I was thinking of offering Luke a job too, later on when the business is properly established.' Lizzie felt obligated to rescue Luke also from the misery of unemployment because of her loyalty to the Carter family. She didn't relish the idea, though, because she still found his presence intimidating.

'Good idea. Keep it in the family, eh, love?' said Bobby.

'That's the general idea. As long as Polly doesn't disapprove.'

'She'll come round, eventually.'

''Course she will,' agreed June.

'So when do you want me to start?' asked Bobby.

'Will straight away be too soon?'

'Not for me.'

'Good. Your first job is to find some suitable premises.'

'Right, I'll get on to it first thing in the morning.'

'If you can sort out the wheat from the chaff then I'll come with you to look at anything you think is promising.'

'I shouldn't think we'll have too much trouble finding a place,' he said thoughtfully. 'There are some industrial units down Hammersmith way that have been left derelict since the war.'

'We can't go for anything with a high rent, though,' Lizzie

told him. 'I'll have to keep within a strict budget so that I've capital to draw on until we start earning money.'

'Perhaps we can consider taking something that's really run down and doing it up, providing the terms of the lease allow it?' he suggested with his usual zeal. 'If Luke and I do the work ourselves, it'll save paying a builder.'

'Good old Bobby, I knew I could rely on you for a positive attitude.' Lizzie turned to his wife. 'You too, June.'

'I'm thrilled to have him in work again.'

'But I think I ought to warn you,' said Lizzie, 'that I'm probably going to be seeing more of your husband than you are while we get the factory organised. He certainly isn't going to be working normal hours for a while. So how do you feel about that?'

'Oh, Lizzie, you don't know what a relief it'll be to have him working again . . . to have a wage coming in,' she said with genuine delight. 'You certainly won't hear me complaining.'

'Thanks, June. Your support means a lot to me.' Lizzie made a face. 'I only hope I can pull it off, for all our sakes. It's a bit scary, a big risk to take.'

'You'll make a success of it or my name isn't June Carter,' she said with absolute confidence. 'All you needed was the wherewithal to get started. There'll be no stopping you now.'

Lizzie gave her an affectionate hug. She really appreciated the encouragement and support of her two oldest friends, all the more welcome after Polly's depressing attitude.

'Here's to the new firm then,' she said, raising her tea cup.

'We'll be celebrating with more than tea this time next year,' said June.

'To Lizzie's Silks,' said Bobby.

'To Carter's Silks,' she corrected hastily. 'I think I owe Polly that much.'

One blustery evening in March when Philip arrived home from work, Emily's companion, Mrs Oakes, greeted him anxiously at the front door.

'She's ill again, isn't she?' he surmised.

'I'm afraid so, sir.'

'Why didn't you telephone me?' he demanded, his face tight with worry. 'I'd have come home straight away.'

'Well, she's not been like it for very long, sir. I knew you'd be home soon so it didn't seem worth bothering you,' explained Mrs Oakes, but it wasn't true because Mrs Verne had 'gone peculiar' not long after her husband had gone back to work that lunchtime.

Mrs Oakes hadn't sent for Philip because she thought he had a dreadful life and had wanted to make it slightly more bearable by allowing him the afternoon in blissful ignorance of what was going on at home. His poor, wretched wife was sitting cross-legged on the sitting-room floor with a blanket over her head, rocking to and fro and whimpering softly. Convinced that someone was trying to kill her, she'd refused her medication on the grounds that it had been poisoned.

Frankly, Mrs Oakes thought Mr Verne was nothing short of a saint, keeping the poor demented soul at home when she should be in an asylum. But it wasn't her place to say so. Anyway, a lot of the time Mrs Verne was as sane as anyone else and then the job was an absolute gem, for Mrs Oakes was very well paid to do little more than keep Emily company.

'Has my wife had her medication?' he wanted to know.

'She wouldn't take it from me, sir. I just couldn't get her to have it.'

'All right, I'll take over. You get off home to that husband of yours.'

'Very well, Mr Verne,' she said. 'I'll see you in the morning.'

Collecting his wife's medicine from the first aid box in the kitchen, and half filling a tumbler with ginger beer from a stone bottle, he went into the sitting room and approached the tent-like shape near the piano which was quivering from movement within.

'Hello darling,' he said, lifting the blanket to look at her face.

The eyes that could melt icebergs when their owner was well, stared at him wildly. 'Is it time for my class?' she asked in a shrill, staccato tone. 'Are the children waiting for me?'

'No. It is time for your medicine, though,' he told her.

She squinted towards the bottle in his hand. 'Are you absolutely certain that they haven't tampered with it?'

He nodded because he had been advised to humour her when she was like this. 'Quite sure. Everything is in order.'

'Good. Only that Oakes woman is trying to poison me, you know,' she said in a conspiratorial whisper, letting the blanket drop to reveal the fact that she was naked. 'She's jealous because I'm such a good teacher and she can't control her class.'

Over the years it had come to light that his wife's mental illness had first shown itself to a minor degree during her adolescence. It had been kept well hidden by her parents who hadn't wanted to spoil their chances of getting her off their hands via a good marriage. Reading between the lines, he thought they'd probably not even admitted to themselves that there was anything wrong with her – after all, there were times when she seemed perfectly normal. Philip had had to prise information from them when it had become obvious to him that there was a serious disorder.

They'd admitted that she'd become very odd after their refusal to let her study as a teacher but claimed it had been only a temporary imbalance caused by the situation. According to the doctor who treated Emily now, her acute distress at being thwarted in her ambitions could have triggered the illness off but it would have happened anyway, eventually.

Her parents' lack of interest in their daughter filled Philip with fury. When he'd been courting Emily they had seemed to be such caring people – pillars of middle-class society. But in truth, they didn't want a dotty daughter disrupting their lives and ruining their reputation. The day she had married Philip, they had absolved themselves from all responsibility towards her, and for the last few years had ignored her existence altogether.

'Look, I've brought you a glass of your favourite drink,' he said.

'Yummy,' said Emily in an infantile manner that twisted his heart because it stripped her of her dignity.

'Now, you know the rules of this game.' He hated to patronise her but when her sickness took this form she responded only to this kind of parental-style persuasion. 'You can't have the drink unless you have your medicine first.'

Her answer to that was to flick a dismissive hand at the

tumbler so that most of the contents spilled on to the floor. Then she leapt up and ran to the door, pounding on it with her fists.

'Help me someone . . . open this door!' she shrieked in penetrating tones. 'Let me out . . . please . . . he's trying to kill me.'

Philip had taken the precaution of locking the door on the way in to prevent her from going downstairs to the kitchen and alarming the servants with her manic behaviour. Her insane distress could be heard all over the house, of course, but the less people who actually saw her in this pitiful state the better, for her sake. The poor dear had to face them again when she was better.

'Come on now darling, don't be silly. It's me, Philip.'

Staring at him with wild eyes, she asked, 'Where's Mummy? Is she going to let me study for my exams?'

'No.'

She threw herself at him, pummelling her fists into his chest and face. A sharp pain caught him above his eye as one of her rings cut his flesh. Ignoring the wound for the moment, he grabbed her firmly by the arms and pulled her to him, holding her close and whispering loving reassurance to her.

When she was calmer he gently helped her on to the sofa, put some cushions behind her head and covered her with blankets. After a while she lay still, singing a pathetic version of 'If You Were the Only Girl in the World'.

Holding his handkerchief to the cut on his forehead, Philip went to the telephone in the hall and called the doctor. Emily obviously needed something more than her usual medication this time.

* * *

Dr Alan Marchant was a general practitioner and a family friend. He and Philip had been at school together.

'Well now, what's my favourite girl been up to?' he asked, looking down at Emily who was still lying on the sofa, humming softly.

'Alan, what are you doing here?' Her voice was slightly more normal and her glance darted across to her husband standing next to him. 'What's happened? Have I been ill again?'

'Yes, just a bit under the weather, darling,' said Philip gently. 'Alan will give you something to make you have a nice long sleep. You'll feel much better when you wake up.'

She pulled the blanket up to her chin protectively and started to cry. 'You won't leave me, will you, Philip?' she wept. 'Promise you'll never leave me.'

He went down on his haunches in front of her and took one of her hands in both of his. 'Now, why would I do a thing like that? I can't manage without you, you know that.'

'You won't leave me?' she repeated, desperate for reassurance.

'No, I won't leave you,' he told her, suddenly overwhelmed by tiredness. After an exhausting day at the factory, the stress of dealing with Emily had sapped all his energy. 'Now, just let Alan put a little prick in your arm . . . there, that's it . . . that's my girl.'

When she was asleep, Philip and Alan carried her upstairs and lifted her into bed. Alan went downstairs while Philip got her into her nightdress and tucked the covers around her, then the two men had a companionable glass of whisky by the sitting-room fire.

'You won't reconsider, I suppose?' said Alan, referring to

something he had suggested to Philip several times.

He took a swallow of whisky, grateful for its soothing influence. 'Having Emily put away, you mean . . . certified insane?'

'Not necessarily,' corrected Alan. 'Just looked after by professionals.'

'No.' Philip was adamant.

'I've connections with a very good place across the river, at Clapham. She'd be very well cared for, you know.'

'An asylum for my wife? No, thank you very much.'

'These days we prefer to call them mental hospitals,' Alan informed him evenly. 'The one I have in mind for Emily is a small nursing home. It's expensive but the patients are made very comfortable.'

'Mental hospital or asylum . . . it would amount to the same thing,' said Philip. 'It would mean I was abandoning her.'

'Rubbish. You'd be able to visit her.'

'I just couldn't do it to her, Alan.'

'Some of the richest families in London have relatives in the nursing home in Clapham,' continued Alan. 'You'd be surprised.'

'I'm not surprised to hear that mental illness isn't something that afflicts only the lower classes,' said Philip abruptly.

'I meant that mental disorders are far more common than people realise,' his friend corrected patiently, 'because everyone tries to keep it hidden.'

'They reckon that a large percentage of the aristocracy is as mad as hatters, don't they?' Philip remarked lightly. 'But no, Alan, I couldn't send her away. You've seen how reliant she is on me.'

'There would be trained medical people to attend to her there. Anyway, she managed without you when you were away at war.'

'She's worse now.'

'Exactly. Which is why I'd like you to consider residential care for her.'

Philip shook his head, sighing heavily. 'No, Alan. You heard me promise never to leave her. Anyway, she isn't as bad as this all the time.'

'She could come home from time to time, when her condition is stable. I wasn't suggesting she stay there for the rest of her life,' explained Alan. 'But for your sake as well as hers, let her be cared for by trained people when she's sick. It isn't as though you can't afford the best care and attention for her. Unlike the poor who are packed into public asylums where the conditions really are quite horrific.'

'There's no cure for her condition, you've told me that.'

'Not a cure but there is treatment to help people like Emily. It's limited, I grant you, but it is available.'

'Padded cells . . . straight jackets? No thanks,' insisted Philip.

'Those things are used in extreme cases, yes,' he admitted. 'But that doesn't mean they'll be used on Emily.'

'I'm not having her institutionalised and that's final.'

Alan finished his drink and rose, picking up his black bag from the table thoughtfully.

'You are my patient as well as Emily, Philip. I do have to consider your health too.'

'Meaning?'

'You look terrible,' he said candidly. 'Running a business

and coping with a sick wife will put you into an early grave.'

'Nonsense, I'm in excellent health.'

'You and I are the same age, are we not, thirty-two?'

'Yes?'

'You're beginning to look like my father,' Alan told him frankly. 'The strain is really starting to tell on you, old boy.'

'So be it.'

'You have no life at all.'

'Emily is my life.'

'But she's sick, Philip, and you're not a medical man. There's only so much you can do for her.'

'I'm not sending her away, Alan, and that's all there is to it.'

'All right, we'll leave things as they are for the time being,' the doctor said gravely.

'The time being?' queried Philip, his brows meeting in a frown.

'I've gone along with your wishes so far because Emily hasn't been a danger to herself or anyone else,' Alan explained grimly, 'but I have to tell you, Philip, that if this changes and she does cause injury to anyone else, as is quite likely in these cases, I shall have to insist that she is hospitalised. It would be most unethical of me not to.'

'Emily wouldn't hurt a fly,' insisted Philip hotly.

'Not normally, of course not, but when she's ill . . .'

'What do you mean by that?'

'That cut above your eye didn't get there by your walking into a door, did it?' said Alan, throwing him a shrewd look.

'That was an accident,' he was quick to explain. 'She was struggling . . . she didn't know what she was doing.'

'Exactly my point, old boy,' persisted Alan, 'she doesn't know what she's doing or even who you are when she's sick. She wouldn't suffer if she went away but you are killing yourself by looking after her at home.'

'No, Alan. I just couldn't do it to her. I would be failing her.'

'So be it then,' said the doctor wearily. 'For the moment anyway.'

Chapter Eleven

Lizzie stood beside Bobby in the spring sunshine gloomily surveying a derelict building, a ruin of a place on the waterfront at Hammersmith in a rundown industrial area known as Sparrow's Yard.

'Don't you just love it, Liz?' enquired Bobby excitedly.

'No, I don't,' she said, frowning at the one-time light engineering factory with broken windows and rotting woodwork, its dilapidated interior horribly displayed through a gaping hole which had once housed double doors. 'Frankly, I think it's an eyesore.'

'It's a bit grim at the moment, I admit,' he was forced to agree. 'But it's got bags o' potential. Try to imagine it after it's been done up.'

'*Done up!*' she exclaimed, horrified at the prospect of setting up a business in such gruesome surroundings. 'We'll need to rebuild the place before it would be usable.'

'It isn't as bad as it looks,' he insisted, taking her arm and leading her eagerly inside. 'I mean, the walls are solid and the stone floor's reasonable apart from a few holes here and there . . . and there are plenty of windows.'

'Not a bit of glass in any of them, either,' she pointed out as the missing component crunched beneath their shoes as they picked their way around the wreck which had become a haven for local wildlife. Legions of spiders, beetles and stray cats had made their home here among the copious weeds and grasses that flourished in great bushes around the rusting metal and oily rags that littered the floor. A whole community of eponymous birds seemed to have taken up residence in the rafters, too.

'That's easily rectified,' Bobby informed her breezily as they stood at the bottom of an iron spiral staircase leading to the upper floor. 'It's a question of cutting our cloth, Liz. We're not gonna get a factory like Verne's for the rent we're prepared to pay.'

'I know that, but this!'

'This place is perfect for us,' he continued with unflagging optimism. 'Two floors, one for weaving, one for warping . . . office space at the end of the building . . .'

'It's far too big,' she informed him, staring glumly at some rusty gaslamps hanging from the cobwebbed ceiling. 'We'd only use a corner of it. We've already agreed to start off with just a couple of looms.'

'But we don't intend to stay that small for long, do we?'

'Well, no, but . . .'

'So where's the sense in taking the lease on a place with no space to expand?'

'Mmm. I suppose you have a point.'

'As I was telling you on the way here,' Bobby went on, 'the owner is prepared to waive the charge for the lease if we do the place up and the rent is well within our budget. I really think we'd be mad to let it go.'

'I'm still not so sure.'

He took her hand and led her into a shell of a room with pieces of metal lying around on the floor.

'This was used as an engine room for their machines,' he explained. 'It'll be just right for us. One loom or twenty, you still need an engine to run them.'

'That's true.'

She had decided that if this venture was going to be commercially viable, hand weaving was not really an option. Initially, she would be the sole operator of the power looms with Bobby doing the setting up, maintenance, delivering, and anything else that needed looking after until she had enough work coming in to warrant more staff.

It was a month since her momentous decision – four hectic weeks in which she and Bobby had tramped all over London looking at premises he thought might be suitable, all of which had turned out to be unsatisfactory. Those that fitted the bill were too expensive; the ones that suited their budget would have cost too much to put right.

This particular property had come to Bobby's notice through his huge network of acquaintances with an uncanny knowledge of what was occurring in the backstreets of London.

Much to her surprise, she was beginning to see possibilities here. Despite her doubts about the spaciousness of the building, it was still only a fraction of the size of Verne's.

'It's in a very good position too,' Bobby pointed out. 'The river might be handy for deliveries of raw silk.'

'All right. You can stop trying to sell me the idea,' she told him lightly. 'I think you might be right about this dump of a place.'

'No might be about it, Liz,' he told her, his warm brown eyes smiling earnestly into hers. 'Trust me, love. It might be a dump now but you wait till Luke and I have finished with it. You just say the word and we'll get started.'

'I suppose you know a glazier who'll do the windows cheap?' she grinned.

He angled his head roguishly. 'Naturally. And a carpenter who'll do the chippying for next to nothing as well as a few other specialists who'll charge us well below the going rate. They're all unemployed tradesmen glad of the chance to earn a few bob. Luke and I will do all the painting and decorating, though. He'll be really glad of the work till you're ready to take him on full-time.'

'You'd better get everyone organised then, hadn't you?' She smiled meaningfully. 'While I go ahead and sign the lease.'

'We're on our way, Lizzie,' he said, lifting her off her feet in an exuberant hug as he had done a million times before. 'You and me are really going places.'

'I hope so,' she laughed when she was back on the ground.

'Oh, there's something else,' he said. 'I know where to get hold of a second-hand gas engine cheap.'

'Yes, I thought perhaps you might.'

'A mate of mine knows a bloke out Essex way who's got one for sale.'

'You'd better go over and have a look at it then, hadn't you? I'll leave all of that side of things to you.'

'Righto.'

'I'd like to get the looms second hand too, if you can find any,' she said. 'Immediately the place is in reasonable enough shape to set them up, I'll get busy on some samples. I'll work out a few simple designs and get some Jacquard cards cut. Once I've something to show the punters I can start to find customers.'

'Leave it to me, sweetheart,' he grinned cheekily. 'You want second-hand looms? Then that's what you shall have.'

'I've never come across anyone with as many friends and contacts as you.'

'Well, us gregarious types collect people,' he told her lightly.

His buoyant company was very refreshing. He'd made the nerve-wracking business of opening a factory feel as exciting as a holiday. The years had dropped away from her this last few weeks as she'd basked in an atmosphere redolent of those carefree times when she and Bobby had been inseparable among the Thorn Street kids.

'So . . . now that we've found the premises, I think we ought to invest in a little motor van for all the running about you're gonna be doing to get it ready for business, don't you?'

'I won't argue with you about that,' he said, his eyes shining.

The task of transforming the shambles in Sparrow's Yard into a smart, workable factory was as nothing compared with the soul-destroying job of trying to obtain orders for cloth.

As soon as the actual building work was finished, but not the painting and decorating, Lizzie had Bobby set up the looms. Then she produced a variety of samples with which she toured the garment makers, department stores and fashion houses. Most buyers wouldn't even see her. Those who deigned to give her a few minutes of their time were briskly complimentary about her work but quick to explain that they were not looking for a new supplier of silk fabric at the moment, *thank you very much*.

Not only was it very disappointing, it was also extremely frightening for Lizzie, having invested so much money in the project. It wasn't as though she'd gone into it blindly, without first doing some research; she knew there was a market out there for good quality work. Breaking into it was the problem. She felt like a gormless amateur at sea among sharp professionals who were all too busy with their own careers to bother with someone new in the business.

It was becoming obvious to her that something more than talent was required to set up in business. To get started you had to have contacts. As well-connected as Bobby was among tradesmen, he had no influence at management level. Now that Lizzie had changed sides, so to speak, she could see that the lot of an entrepreneur was not an easy one.

'Don't worry, it'll happen,' said June one evening in April when Lizzie called at her place to collect the children after yet another exhausting afternoon of pedalling her wares unsuccessfully. 'All you need is one order to start you off. Once the word gets round about the quality of your work, you'll be inundated.'

'June's right,' agreed Bobby.

'How long is it going to take though, that's the problem?' said Lizzie, brushing her furrowed brow with a tired hand. 'I need to get into production . . . to have money coming in.'

'Oh, come on, we haven't even finished painting the factory

yet,' said Bobby. 'You'll have your first order by then. So stop panicking.'

Touched by their unwavering encouragement, Lizzie bit back the tears. 'I don't know what I'd do without you two,' she said.

'You're not going to have to do without us, so don't even think about it,' said Bobby.

'That's right,' agreed June. She looked towards the door. 'What on earth . . .'

The children piled into the living room from the street, Jed, Bruce and Eva with their twin cousins, Jamie and Keith, the former barely visible beneath a dark trilby hat and a huge black jacket that almost reached the floor.

'Jamie and Keith are doin' a show,' explained Bruce.

'It's the interval so we've come in for a rest,' said Jed.

'Jamie is takin' off Charlie Chaplin,' Eva informed them proudly. 'He's ever so good at it.'

'You've got the wrong style of titfer, son,' smiled his father. 'Charlie Chaplin wears a bowler hat.'

'I know, but you don't have a bowler, Dad,' Jamie informed him.

'Why, you little horror!' admonished Bobby. 'I thought I recognised those clothes. That's the jacket of my Sunday suit. Take them off and put them back where you found them, this very minute.'

'Oh, can't I keep them on for a little bit longer?' coaxed Jamie, a coaldust moustache smudging his upper lip.

'You heard what I said.'

'Aw, go on, Dad,' wheeled Keith. 'The kids are all waiting for the second half. Jamie's Chaplin impersonations are brilliant.'

'Show 'em, Jamie,' urged Bruce.

'Yeah, go on,' said Eva.

'Well, seeing as I'm in popular demand, take your seats, ladies and gentlemen,' said Jamie in an amusing parody of a showman.

As Bobby was no match for this sort of opposition, he settled back in his armchair to watch the show. Jamie's freckled face became fixed in a dead pan expression and he walked around the room with his toes and elbows turned out, emulating the stiff speedy action of film and swinging his mother's umbrella to represent the famous Chaplin cane.

No one could help but be amused by his natural showmanship and they all applauded heartily. Flush with success Jamie was then joined by his brother. The comical duo told a few childish jokes and ended the act with a rendering of the popular 'Don't Dilly Dally on the Way'.

'I reckon we've got a couple of budding stars in the family,' said Lizzie. 'They'll be on the halls one of these days.' She took two sixpenny pieces from her purse and gave one to each twin. 'That's for taking my mind off my troubles,' she told them. 'I hope you make many more of these by entertaining people in the future.'

'Crumbs,' gasped Jamie.

'Cor, thanks, Aunt Lizzie,' said Keith, breathless with delight.

'Can we keep the clothes for a bit longer, then, Dad?' asked Jamie.

'No,' he said, but it was only a token protest to prove that he wasn't a complete pushover with all his family.

'Aw, go on, Dad . . . please.'

'Not a chance.' Bobby managed to keep a straight face. 'But let's go and have a look in the wardrobe to see if we can't find something a bit more Chaplinish.' His face broke into a grin. 'You need a shorter jacket for a start.'

'Good old Dad,' the twins chorused.

'Not so much of the old, if you don't mind.'

'Hurrah for Uncle Bobby,' cheered the Carter children, and the whole gang clattered off to the bedroom with Bobby.

Lizzie and June were left smiling. 'He's wonderful with the children, isn't he?' remarked Lizzie.

'Yeah, he's a good dad,' said June. 'One o' the best is my Bobby.'

'Stan was never close to our kids,' said Lizzie. 'He was always too preoccupied with other things to have any fun with them. He missed a lot and so did they.'

'Well, you know Bob . . . he's naturally easygoing,' said June. 'He takes after his dad in that way. Stan was more like his mum.'

'Mmm . . . anyway, those lads of yours have really cheered me up,' said Lizzie. 'I feel able to fight another day now in the battle for orders.'

'That's the spirit,' replied June. 'You'll make it work, Lizzie, or my name's not June Carter.'

June was right. A few days later Lizzie talked her way in to the office of a small garment maker in Shepherd's Bush who specialised in silk waistcoats and ties for men. Not having been in business for very long, the proprietor was much more sympathetic to a newcomer than the larger, long established firms. He liked her samples and the fact that she was negotiable on price and gave her her first order with a firm promise of more to come if they were satisfied with the first. It was an order for silk fabric for men's ties and cravats.

Fired with new energy, Lizzie worked at the looms, weaving the design into the fabric on to broad cloth, through Jacquard cards. The finished material would be cut and made into men's neckwear by the garment maker. It was exhilarating to be working again . . . especially for her own firm.

'There you are, Bobby,' she said when the rolls of silk fabric were complete and neatly wrapped in good quality buff-coloured paper ready for delivery. 'All ready to go.'

'Well done, princess,' he said, lifting her up and twirling her round in his usual boisterous manner. 'You're one helluva clever lady.'

Giggling, she gave him a bow. 'And for my next trick . . .'

They both roared with laughter, caught up in a glow of success.

'This is just the beginning,' he said as they went out to the van together and loaded the goods into the back. 'When they see the quality of your work the orders'll come pouring in.'

'You've got the invoice, haven't you?' she queried.

'You bet.'

'With a bit of luck they'll pay on delivery,' she said. 'That's the arrangement I made with them, anyway.'

'I tell you what. Why don't we get a few bottles and have a drink to celebrate tonight round at my place?' he suggested. 'You, me and June and all the kids.'

'A good idea,' she said, with a broad grin. 'You think of everything, don't you?'

'I do my best,' he said affectionately.

'Well?' Lizzie said excitedly when he arrived back at the factory an hour or so later. 'Do you come bearing good news . . . payment in full and a hefty new order?'

He bit his lip and seemed lost for words – most unusual for him.

'Bobby,' she said, her smile fading, 'what's the matter? Weren't they pleased with the job?'

'Well . . .'

'Something's happened?' she said in a panicky voice.

'Er . . .'

'What is it?' she urged, clutching his arm and looking into his worried face. 'Tell me, for God's sake. They obviously weren't happy with the standard of the work.'

'Hey, hold on,' he said, gripping both her hands to steady her. 'There's nothing wrong with your work . . . it's first-class.'

'Why the long face then?'

He sighed and shook his head gravely. 'They haven't even seen your work,' he told her gently. 'It's still in the van.'

'But why haven't you delivered it?' she demanded urgently. 'Was it because the proprietor wasn't there?'

'Nobody was there . . . the place was empty . . . the firm's gone bust.'

'But that isn't possible,' she exclaimed, 'I was talking to the boss on the phone only the other day . . . he gave no indication . . .'

'Yeah, it's hard to believe the speed with which these things can happen,' Bobby agreed. 'I was talking to the guvnor of a small woodworking firm who was operating right here in Sparrow's Yard. It's happened to him too because he was undercapitalised when he started up. Same thing probably applies to our tie maker.'

'Oh God, Bobby, what am I gonna do? I've spent time and materials on that order . . . all wasted . . . all down the drain.'

'Calm down, you're not on your own with the problem, remember? I'm with you every step of the way,' he told her kindly. 'We'll get by. It's only a minor setback, not a major disaster.'

But she wasn't comforted. 'I should have done some research on the firm before taking the order,' she said, wringing her hands. 'I should have been more careful.'

'How were you to know they weren't stable?'

'They hadn't been in business very long,' she said. 'That should have made me wary.'

'That's exactly why people are wary of us,' he reminded her. 'And we don't like it one little bit, do we?'

'You're right, as usual.'

She let go of his hands and led the way into her small office tucked away to the side of the weaving sheds. She sat down at her desk, chewing the end of her thumbnail. He seated himself opposite and lit a cigarette.

'I think the best thing we can do is to try to recoup some of our expenses on that order,' she told him.

'Good idea . . . but how?'

'By selling the material half price or less to another garment maker,' she told him, her positive mood returning as a plan began to form. 'If the price is low enough we'll shift the goods.'

'At a substantial loss, though?'

'Yes, but at least there'll be some money to put into the bank,' she said. 'It isn't the way I want to do business but it's the only sensible thing to do in this instance. I'll just have to put this one down to experience and be more careful in future.'

'That's the stuff,' he said, his admiration for her growing.

'Come on then, you can drive me. I'll hawk the material around London till I do place it,' she said, adding as she clambered into the passenger seat of their little blue van, 'And you'd better teach me to drive this thing some time soon . . . just in case I ever need to.'

'Yes, ma'am,' he said, giving her a mock salute.

Lizzie's spirits were beginning to rise again because she was getting on and doing something!

That outing proved successful in that Lizzie sold the fabric to an old established workroom and gained another order for material to be made into dressing gowns. But as it was obvious that she was desperate they gave her a ridiculously low price and refused to negotiate.

As she said to Bobby, 'It's daylight robbery and I ought to have told them what to do with their order but it'll go towards our overheads until we get some decent work in. Whenever that may be. Anyway, I'd sooner be working for a pittance than not working at all.'

'Me too.'

'I'll keep trying to get work. I'll find the time to get out and about somehow, in between meeting this deadline.'

* * *

Philip called at his parents' house after work one evening in June to visit his father who was recovering from an attack of summer 'flu which had turned to bronchitis.

'How's the patient?' Philip asked his mother.

'Well . . . put it this way, dear, is there any chance of my moving in with you and Emily for a few days?' she grinned.

'As bad as that, eh?'

'Worse. You know your father. He's an excellent patient when he's actually ill . . . it's the recovery process that turns my hair white,' she explained. 'He's bad-tempered, irritable, demanding. Our poor little day girl's been run off her feet all day long, fetching him this, that and the other.'

'Sounds familiar.'

'One of his cronies from the association called to see him this afternoon and he's been in a thunderous mood ever since.'

'Why's that?'

'No idea. I didn't ask for fear it would start him ranting,' Meg confessed. 'I can only take so much of your father as a convalescent. Fortunately, it was my afternoon for the women's refuge so I was out for a while, thank God. Mrs Todd told me about it when I got back.'

Philip smiled. His father's behaviour in the sickroom was a family joke. Philip remembered it well from his childhood. Father booming out orders, Mother desperately trying to escape.

'Is he in bed?'

'No, in the sitting room,' she said and they went in together.

'Oh, it's you,' growled Humphrey, sitting hunched in an armchair in his dressing gown, observing Philip over the top of the evening newspaper. 'Come to give me an ear bashing about all the disasters of the day at the factory, I suppose?'

'Not at all,' corrected Philip. 'It's all plain sailing at the moment.'

'Well, that's a nice welcome when your son takes the trouble to come and see you, Humphrey,' admonished Meg. 'It would serve you right if no one came to visit you at all.'

'Suits me,' he said in a wheezy voice. 'Let 'em all stay away.'

'I understand you had a visitor while I was out this afternoon,' said his wife.

'Yes, old Bertie Smallwood called in for a chat.' He rolled his eyes and tutted. 'There ought to be a law against it.'

'Why, what's poor Bertie done now?'

'Not Bertie.' He threw his wife a withering stare. 'It's that damned Carter family again . . . nothing but trouble, the whole caboodle of them.'

'What have they done?' enquired Philip, eager for news of the family who had affected his life so profoundly.

'According to Bertie,' said Humphrey, 'the widow of the one that . . . that was killed . . . has only gone and set up in business . . . in the silk trade, would you believe!'

'Well, good for her,' said Meg who had often thought of Lizzie. She'd very much wanted to visit her after her husband's death but there had been such bad feeling between the two families, she hadn't thought she'd be welcome.

'*Good for her?*' repeated Humphrey sardonically. 'What are you talking about, woman? It's bloody ridiculous!'

'I don't see why,' said Philip.

'Surely you don't need me to spell it out for you?' snarled Humphrey. 'She has no experience . . . she'll give the silk trade a bad name and, God knows, we can do without that.'

'But she's very experienced in the trade,' Philip pointed out. 'She worked for us for enough years.'

'So she worked the looms,' was Humphrey's scornful reply. 'That hardly qualifies her to run a business, does it? Where did she get the money from, that's what I'd like to know?'

'I gave it to her,' Philip informed him calmly.

A shocked silence dropped like a stone over the room.

'You?' spluttered Humphrey at last. 'You . . . gave her money . . .'

'Yes, that's right.'

'Well, this is the first I've heard of it.'

'As it was money from my own account and nothing to do with the business, I saw no reason to mention it particularly,' explained Philip. 'I didn't deliberately keep it a secret. The matter just never arose.'

'Good God. Fancy throwing your money in that direction,' blustered Humphrey. 'What on earth got into you?'

'I feel bad about her,' said Philip. 'She's been left to raise three children on her own . . . because of what happened.'

'That's not your responsibility.'

'Not legally, but I can't help feeling responsible.'

'Huh. I bet the rest of that terrible family leapt on your action as a confirmation of your guilt,' said Humphrey.

'Yes, I expect they did,' said Philip evenly. 'That doesn't worry me. My only concern is that Stan Carter's widow and children should not suffer financial hardship as a result of his death.'

'And now she's wasting the money you gave her on some tin pot business venture,' exploded Humphrey. 'I hope she doesn't try to catch you for more when she's lost all that.'

Actually, Philip was pleasantly surprised to hear this news about Lizzie but a little worried too, knowing she would have difficulty getting started in the silk weaving industry without contacts. But he admired her courage. If anyone could succeed, it was her.

'She wouldn't do that, she isn't the type,' he said.

'How do you know what type she is?' demanded Humphrey.

'I could see how proud she was when I first approached her,' explained Philip. 'She refused help at first and only changed her mind later because she was desperate.'

'She's certainly got you fooled,' was Humphrey's opinion.

Philip heaved a loud sigh of frustration. 'You think what you like, Father.'

'I certainly will.'

'It's none of your business what she does with her money, though,' said Philip. 'Frankly, I always find it heartening to hear of someone new setting up in the silk trade. At least it helps to keep the industry alive in this country.'

'You don't see her as competition then,' said Humphrey.

'Good Lord, no,' exclaimed Philip. 'If we have to worry every time a new silk firm opens, after all our years at the top of the trade, then we shouldn't be in business at all.'

Meg had been sitting quietly listening to them in a chair by the window overlooking the rear gardens. The crazy paving terraces were inset with well-kept miniature lawns; dotted about were pots and tubs bright with summer flowers, producing an intensity of colour in the evening sunshine.

'I'm proud of you, Philip,' she said. 'You did right to give her that money.'

'Trust you to damned well agree with him,' snapped Humphrey. 'You two always take each other's side . . . against me.'

Philip and his mother exchanged glances, both guessing that Humphrey was remembering the son with whom he had felt truly bonded – the son for whom he still mourned.

'Nonsense,' denied his wife. 'I agreed with Philip because I think he did the right thing. If I hadn't, I should have said so and you know it.'

'Well, let's leave it at that, shall we?' said Philip swiftly, in an effort to lower the rising temperature.

'Good idea,' said Meg.

'I just called in to see how you were feeling, Father, but I mustn't stay too long,' said Philip, his expression darkening. 'Emily will be wondering where I am.'

'She will indeed,' said Meg. 'I popped in to see her earlier.'

'That was nice of you, Mother.'

'I try to call in on her most days, even if it's only for a few minutes,' she said. 'She is my daughter-in-law, after all. Anyway, I enjoy her company when she's well, which she seems to be just now.'

'Yes, she's not too bad at the moment,' he replied.

Meg noticed her son become tense as soon as Emily came to mind. Poor Philip – how troubled his life was, never knowing how his wife would be from one minute to the next, constantly on tenterhooks about her. Although it was a tragedy for Emily, the sheer nature of her illness protected her to a large extent. The whole thing was ghastly for them both nonetheless. Thank God young Toby was away at school most of the time.

What the future held for Philip and Emily, Meg dreaded to

think! One thing she was certain of, though, the situation couldn't continue as it was indefinitely. Philip was going to have to face up to that eventually.

Chapter Twelve

'Meg . . . Meg Verne, how lovely to see you,' said Lizzie in surprise, answering a tap on the office door to see the older woman standing there in a navy blue summer dress with white hat and gloves. 'Come on in.'

'Er . . . thank you.'

'Sit down,' said Lizzie with a welcoming smile, waving a hand towards a chair. 'I'll put the kettle on for a cuppa.'

'I heard through the grapevine that you'd recently set up in business,' explained Meg rather hesitantly because she'd been unsure as to how she'd be greeted. 'So I thought I'd just pop over to wish you well.'

'How kind of you,' said Lizzie, touched by the gesture. She filled the tin kettle at a tiny sink in the corner and put it on to the gas-ring to boil. 'Well-wishers are a bit thin on the ground around here. Most people think I need my brains tested to have done what I did and are just waiting to be proved right.'

'Mmm, I can imagine. It always causes a stir when one of us women tries to do anything the slightest bit out of the ordinary,' said Meg. 'Which is quite ridiculous when you think what we achieved during the war.'

'That's right,' agreed Lizzie, warming a small brown teapot with hot water from the kettle before scooping tea from the caddy and adding it. 'I think that work experience gave a lot of women confidence in themselves, though, even if they are back at home now. Who knows? Maybe I wouldn't have had the courage to start up in business if I hadn't had to stand up for myself when I was working on the trams.'

'From what I saw of you before the war, I think you probably would.'

Lizzie poured the tea and set the cups down on the desk with a plate of ginger biscuits. 'Well, that's something we'll never know for sure, isn't it? One thing's for certain though – I wouldn't have been able to do it if it hadn't been for your son.' She passed the biscuits to Meg, eyeing her warily. 'You did know it was Philip who loaned me the money?'

'Yes. I only heard about it yesterday, though,' she explained. 'He didn't say a word about it at the time.'

That didn't surprise Lizzie. Philip didn't strike her as the type who would go out of his way to make his generosity known. 'I was furious when he first approached me with the offer,' she confessed, stirring her tea thoughtfully. 'I suppose it must have been a mixture of pride and grief. You know, given the circumstances.'

'Perfectly natural.' Meg sipped her tea. 'But tell me, my dear, having decided to accept the money, what made you decide to use it to start a business?'

'It's something I've always wanted to do,' Lizzie explained. 'Well, it was more of a fantasy really since people of my class don't normally get the opportunity . . . and a lower-class woman almost never does. Knowing I would never get another chance, I thought I'd stick my neck out rather than take the safer option.'

'How do your in-laws feel about your accepting money from Philip?' asked Meg, her dark eyes observing Lizzie astutely over the rim of her teacup.

'Stan's mother doesn't like it one little bit,' Lizzie told her sadly. 'In fact, she's still cross with me about it.'

'Isn't she being rather shortsighted?' asked Meg impulsively.

'Perhaps,' returned Lizzie in a fiercely defensive over-reaction. 'But Polly has many other wonderful attributes . . . she's been very good to me over the years.'

'I'm sure she has,' said Meg, immediately perceiving the depth of Lizzie's feelings for Polly Carter.

'She's extremely firm in her views, though,' Lizzie continued less heatedly, 'and she took Stan's death very badly.'

Meg bit her lip. 'Yes, I didn't know if you'd let me over the threshold, actually,' she admitted, looking sheepish. 'That's why I didn't come to see you after your husband died. I wasn't sure if you shared the Carters' general animosity towards my family.'

'No, that's not my way at all. You might all be part of a whole,' Lizzie told her, 'but you're all people in your own right too. One member can't be held responsible for the actions of the others in any family.'

'You blame Philip though?' suggested Meg gravely.

Lizzie pondered on this for a moment. 'I don't blame him entirely, no. But naturally I feel . . .' She paused, trying to clarify her confused thoughts on this painful subject and identify the exact emotion which Philip Verne evoked in her. 'Sheer ruddy resentment, I suppose it is. After all, Philip did deal the blow that sent Stan to his death. Accidentally or not, that is the plain fact of the matter.'

'Yes,' agreed Meg miserably.

'There's no reason why you and I can't be friends though,' said Lizzie.

The other woman smiled. 'I'm very glad about that.'

They drank their tea in comfortable silence until Meg said, 'So how does Mrs Carter Senior feel about your becoming a businesswoman?'

'Her disapproval is total,' said Lizzie. 'She's a staunch believer in traditional values – thinks it's wrong for a married woman to work outside the home.'

'She's not alone in that. Many people feel the same.'

'I'll say they do,' agreed Lizzie. 'And I respect their right to their opinion. Personally, I think it depends on each individual's circumstances. I've no choice but to go out to earn money because working at home just doesn't pay enough now that I'm the sole breadwinner. At least being my own boss gives me flexibility in the hours I work, so the children don't have to be latch-key kids.'

'Sounds fair enough to me.' Meg cast a studious eye around the office which was basically furnished with a small desk, a filing cabinet, a wooden table in the corner with tea-things on it, a coatstand and a profusion of potted plants. The room was extremely clean and tidy – a little too tidy, in fact. 'So, how's the business going?'

'Pretty good, thanks,' lied Lizzie, trying to sound convincing. 'I've that many orders, I'm rushed off my feet a lot of the time.'

'I'll ask the question again, shall I?' suggested Meg, throwing her a straight look. 'How's the business going, Lizzie?'

'It isn't,' she admitted with a wry grin. 'I just can't break into the trade. Unless you've contacts in certain quarters no one wants to know.'

'Oh, dear. Aren't you getting any orders at all?'

'Just a few. And I only get those because I'm taking on jobs at sweated labour rates because it's the only work I can get,' she confessed solemnly. 'I'm only here in the office now because there's nothing to do on the looms until the next cheapjack job comes in.'

'That's awful,' was Meg's response. 'I'm so sorry.'

'So am I,' said Lizzie. 'More than sorry, I'm bloomin' desperate.'

'You must be.'

'I'm not making a profit so my capital is draining away on overheads and living expenses,' she continued, 'I still have to pay the rent on this place and our rooms and feed the kids whether I'm making money or not.'

Meg gave a sympathetic tut. 'I can't tell you how sorry I am,' she said.

'I *really* think you are too,' said Lizzie. 'And I appreciate it. As I said, there are plenty who can't wait to see me go under.'

'Some people seem to thrive on other people's misfortune.'

'Still, I'm not gonna give them the satisfaction,' declared Lizzie emphatically. 'Oh, no. I don't know how I'm going to get this thing off the ground since it seems to be out of my control but I'll do it . . . somehow.'

'I'm sure things will start to look up soon,' said Meg.

They sat in companionable silence, drinking tea and nibbling biscuits. It was amazing how at ease Lizzie felt with this woman, considering the difference in their background and age. But she felt able to talk to her about anything. Maybe it was because there were no emotional ties, as there were with Polly.

'You've not taken on any staff then?' Meg remarked eventually.

'Only my brother-in-law,' said Lizzie. 'He's overlooker-cum manager, delivery man and errand boy. He'll turn his hand to anything including the warping and winding, and I don't know what I'd do without him. In fact, he and his wife are my strength and salvation. They're both wonderfully supportive.'

'Where is he now?'

'Gone to collect some raw silk in the van to save the cost of delivery,' Lizzie explained. 'I'm expecting him back at any time.'

A few minutes later there was a rap on the door and on being told to enter, Bobby marched in.

'Talk of the devil,' said Lizzie, smiling at him. 'Bobby, this is Mrs Verne.'

'Yes . . . I know who you are,' he said, looking at Meg.

She rose quickly and gathered her handbag and gloves from the desk. 'Well, I think it's time I was off.'

'Don't go on my account,' he said breezily. 'I won't bite you.'

'Oh . . . um . . . well, I . . . er . . .' She was visibly embarrassed. 'I don't want to impose.'

'You've no need to worry, you won't get any abuse from me,' Bobby assured her with his usual lack of inhibition. 'I've no quarrel with you.'

'That's nice to hear,' said Meg, looking slightly more relaxed.

'Arguing about my brother's death isn't gonna bring him back, is it?'

'Well, no.' She cleared her throat. 'That's a very sensible way of looking at it. But I must be on my way just the same. I've things to do.' She pulled on her gloves, and as Lizzie stood up gave her an affectionate peck on the cheek. 'It's been lovely to see you again, my dear.'

'Likewise,' said Lizzie. 'Thanks for coming, it was very nice of you.'

'My pleasure. Goodbye.'

'Tata,' chorused Lizzie and Bobby.

'You seem to know her quite well?' remarked Bobby, after she'd gone.

'Not well exactly. I've chatted to her a couple of times, that's all. Ages ago, before all the trouble,' Lizzie explained. 'I like her though. She's a really nice woman.'

'Yeah, she seemed all right,' he agreed. 'Mind you, Ma would have a fit if she knew she'd been round here to see you.'

'Mmm . . . according to Polly I should have sent her off with a sizeable flea in her ear just to prove that I'm a true Carter.'

'That sounds like Ma.'

'But it just isn't in my nature.'

'Nor mine,' said Bobby.

Meg told her chauffeur to drive her straight to Verne's factory where she made her way to Philip's office and told him all about her visit to Carter's Silks.

'It's so damned unfair,' she fumed. 'I mean, there's a young woman with the gumption to set up in business on her own and she can't get started. Not because she has no sense or talent but because she has no contacts in the silk or rag trade.'

'I suspected she might find it difficult to break in,' he said. 'Buyers of silk fabric aren't willing to take a chance on someone new. It's safer to use firms they know.'

'What are her chances of ever getting started?' she asked.

'Well, the demand is there for someone who really knows their stuff and since she was trained by us I'd be conceited enough to say that she most certainly does. It's getting buyers to give her a chance that's the problem.'

'Being a female doesn't help either,' ranted Meg. 'Everyone in the trade knows that women make excellent weavers but when it comes to one of them actually running the show . . . out come all the knives. It's nothing short of scandalous!'

'All right, Mother, don't get back on your high horse,' he admonished lightly. 'At least women have the vote now.'

'Only those over thirty who have property,' she said. 'It ought to be given to every man and woman over twenty-one.'

'That'll come in time.'

'Maybe, but for the moment I'm more concerned about Lizzie Carter. Is there anything you can do to help?' Meg enquired. 'You've plenty of contacts. A word in the right ear from you could make all the difference to her. And it isn't as though she's any sort of threat to an old established, specialist firm like Verne's.'

'I'm the last person she'd accept help from,' snorted Philip. 'It was bad enough trying to get her to take the money.'

'She needn't know you're involved,' suggested his mother.

'There is such a thing as discretion, you know.'

Philip stroked his chin meditatively, sunlight through the window picking out the dark hairs on his hands. 'Mmm . . . that's a point.' He was deep in thought. 'Leave it with me. I'll see if I can think of anyone who might be interested in putting some decent work her way.'

Meg was beaming. 'Thanks, I knew I could rely on you.'

'Hello, Charlie, old boy,' said Philip into the telephone later that day. 'It's Philip . . . Philip Verne.'

'What ho, Phil? How are things in your neck of the woods?'

The two men exchanged pleasantries and chatted about business in general for, as well as being an old friend of Philip's, Charlie King was also one of London's most well-known manufacturers of high quality rainwear.

'But to get to the purpose of my call, Charlie,' Philip said after a while.

'And there's me thinking you phoned just to ask after my health,' said his friend with lighthearted irony.

'There's a new silk mill opened recently in Hammersmith,' said Philip, 'their work is first class. I wondered if they might be of interest to you for your raincoat linings? I know you only ever use silk fabric.'

'A friend of yours, is he?'

'It's a she actually.'

'Well, well, I didn't think you were the type, Phil.'

'Nothing like that, you fool,' laughed Philip. 'It's run by someone who was trained by us, that's all.'

'I see. Well, as you know, we use a firm in Essex as our regular supplier for lining material,' said Charlie.

'Didn't you say once that you sometimes get a sudden rush order that your usual weaver can't cope with?'

'That sometimes happens, yes, if one of the stores has a run on our stuff or a special promotion or something.'

'How do you overcome the problem?'

'Tear about to find someone who can produce the stuff in a hurry.'

'Perhaps you and she can do each other a favour, then?'

'She's Verne-trained, you say?' confirmed Charlie.

'That's right.'

'That's a recommendation in itself.'

'We do our best.'

'Well, give me her details and I'll bear her in mind next time I'm stuck,' said Charlie. 'I've nothing at the moment but I might have in a month or two.'

Philip provided him with the relevant information and was about to hang up when he had a sudden thought. 'Oh, by the way, old boy . . . I'd appreciate your not mentioning my name.'

'What if she asks who recommended her?'

'Oh, just tell her someone she left her business card with told you about her . . . or something.'

'Don't worry. I'll think of something,' said Charlie absently, his mind already moving on to other things.

'Thanks a lot.'

'Don't give it another thought, old boy. Cheerio.'

'Cheerio,' said Philip.

By the late-summer Lizzie was beginning to fear that she would have to close the factory. Bobby had broadened his skills to include salesmanship but even with both of them out pedalling samples they still had no orders on the books. There were a few possibles for the future but nothing concrete apart from the men's neckwear material they produced for ridiculous rates rather than have the looms standing idle. She hadn't articulated her fears to Bobby yet because she just couldn't bring herself to admit defeat.

One warm autumn afternoon she was at the loom tying a new thread into the weft when Bobby came in from the yard, where he'd been polishing the van, with the news that they had a visitor.

'Some bloke's just drawn up in the yard in a flash car . . . a Bentley no less.'

'Oh?' she said quizzically. 'I wonder what a Bentley owner wants with us?'

'He's on his way in so we're about to find out.'

'Mrs Carter,' said the visitor, a man in his thirties with a neat moustache and hair oiled close to his head beneath his Homburg hat which he removed on entering the factory. He was somewhat flamboyant in appearance, his dark business suit splashed with colour from a brightly-patterned silk waistcoat and dazzling tie. He offered her his hand. 'Charlie King . . . King's Rainwear.'

'Pleased to meet you,' she said, shaking his hand and feeling rather startled to receive a visit from the proprietor of such a famous company whose raincoats were only worn by the very well-heeled.

'I'll come straight to the point,' he said, casting a sharp eye around the factory, only a corner of which was in use. 'I need fifty yards of silk lining fabric urgently. We've had a rush order of raincoats for the new season and our usual supplier can't do it. Some sort of industrial dispute in his factory, I believe. A colleague of mine in the rag trade mentioned your name to me. You left your calling card with him, I believe.'

'Oh,' was about all she could manage.

'Thought I'd come along and have a look at your set up,' Charlie went on exuberantly. 'And to find out if you'd be interested in taking on the job, of course.'

Lizzie's cheeks were burning with a mixture of shock and excitement.

'We're interested,' she said, hoping she didn't sound too eager.

He frowned. 'I see you've only two looms though,' he said doubtfully.

'At the moment . . . yes.'

'And are there just the two of you on the staff?'

'Well . . . yes,' she was forced to admit, her nerves jangling for fear this might destroy his interest. 'But I'm planning to expand as soon as we have enough work coming in to warrant it.'

'A very wise attitude,' he said, adding doubtfully, 'As I have said, though, I need this material in a hurry. Do you think you'll be able to cope with that?'

'Most definitely. We could start on it immediately,' she said. 'No point in pretending we're busy as it's obvious we're not.'

'Mmm.'

'The length of time it will take us depends on the type of weave you require, of course,' she pointed out.

'Fifty-four inch cloth in standard King pattern,' he informed her. 'We can supply you with the Jaquard cards providing you undertake not to disclose the pattern to anyone else.'

'That goes without saying.'

'Are you sure you can manage it though?' he pressed. 'I'd rather you didn't take the job on if there's any doubt at all.'

'We might be small but we're highly efficient,' she assured him with confidence.

Charlie King was thoughtful. Time was of the essence with this job. He would lose the order for raincoats if she let him down. He hadn't realised it would be quite such a small set up when he'd agreed to do Philip Verne a favour. Still, Philip had been very complimentary about the quality of her work . . .

'Yes, Philip spoke well of you,' he said without thinking. 'The fact that you were trained at Verne's speaks for itself.'

She was too surprised to utter a sound for a few moments. 'I thought you said you heard about us from someone in the rag trade?' she said at last.

'Oh, dear,' he said, clapping his hand to his mouth. 'I've really let the cat out of the bag now, haven't I?'

'I'm afraid so.'

'Philip spoke to me about you a couple of months ago,' he explained. 'I didn't have anything to offer you at the time . . .'

'I see,' she said coldly.

'Me and my big mouth,' said Charlie guiltily. 'He asked me particularly not to let you know he'd had a hand in it, I've no idea why.'

Because he knew I wouldn't want to take any more of his charity, she thought.

'It doesn't matter who told Mr King about us, does it, Lizzie?' intervened Bobby, speaking to her with his eyes. 'The

235

important thing is that he needs a job doing, and we'd like to
do it.'

Lizzie's immediate reaction was to throw Charlie King out
and blast off at Philip Verne on the telephone for interfering
in her affairs and patronising her in this way.

'My feelings exactly, old boy,' said Charlie amiably. 'I like
to see a spirit of enterprise, myself.'

'Really?' she said stiffly.

'Yes. My grandfather built our firm up from nothing, you
know,' he informed her cheerfully. 'And God knows, we need
to keep the silk-weaving industry going in this country . . . too
much of the material used here is woven abroad. The craft of
weaving will disappear altogether here if we are not careful.'

'Quite right,' said Bobby, replying on Lizzie's behalf as
words seemed to be failing her.

'If we can agree on price and I'm happy with the finished
article,' Charlie was saying, 'there could be steady work for
you. My regular supplier has been most unreliable lately so I
wouldn't be averse to the idea of putting some of the work
elsewhere on a permanent basis.'

'I see,' said Bobby, struggling to behave like a professional
and not turn cartwheels of sheer joy.

'So . . . can we talk price, Mrs Carter?'

She was trying to justify accepting an order that had come
to her from an act of charity and not from her own efforts. But
Philip Verne hadn't wanted her to know so couldn't be accused
of being patronising, could he? And although the job had come
through someone else, whether or not she made the most of it
to get this firm established was in her hands.

'Lizzie,' said Bobby loudly. 'What do you say to that?'

'Certainly, Mr King,' she said at last, catching Bobby's pleading eye. 'Let's all go into my office for a chat, shall we?'

Thank Gawd for that, thought Bobby, heaving a sigh of relief. For one horrible moment he'd thought that damned pride of hers was going to lose them a nice juicy order.

'Hello, Mrs Carter,' said Philip when Lizzie turned up at his office later that day. 'This is a surprise.'

'I thought the least I could do was to come and see you personally, to thank you for sending some business my way,' she said, sitting down as he waved a hand towards a chair by his desk.

He should never have trusted Charlie not to spill the beans. She didn't look too murderous though. 'You wait till I see Charlie King,' he said.

'He didn't mean to tell me,' she said. 'It just sort of slipped out.'

'You're not angry?' He grinned and it made him look ten years younger.

'No, I've decided to accept the favour in the spirit in which it was intended,' she told him. 'Thank you so much.'

'All I did was make a phone call. I'm glad Charlie followed it up, though.'

'So am I.'

'He's giving you some worthwhile business, I hope.'

'Very. And he's paying a better than average rate for the job so that'll keep the wolf from the door for a while.'

'I knew I could trust Charlie to be fair or I would never have put him on to you.' He frowned. 'How rude of me not to offer you tea. Would you like some?'

'Thanks but I can't stop,' she said, eager to get back to the factory to get things organised. 'I came over right away because once we start on the order, first thing tomorrow morning, I won't have time to go anywhere.'

'I suppose not.'

'That's the trouble with being so small,' she said. 'You can't delegate.'

'Perhaps you'll be able to take on some more weavers before long?'

'I hope so.'

'It could happen sooner than you think,' he told her. 'This order from Charlie could be just what you need to set you going. Not only could he provide you with good steady work but there's the word of mouth element too . . . you'll be running several jobs at a time once the word gets round.'

'Ooh, the very thought of it! I want so much to make a success of my business.'

'Yes, I can see that.'

He was such a serious man, she thought, always looking as though he had the worries of the world on his shoulders. Still, it wasn't surprising if the rumours about his wife were to be believed. Such a smart and beautiful woman too on the odd occasion Lizzie had seen her years ago. She used to call in to Verne's sometimes when Lizzie worked there, to see Philip.

Heaven knows where the tales about her insanity came from, though the Vernes' domestic staff was the most likely source. It just went to show that things weren't always what they seemed to the casual observer. No one, not even the rich and privileged, got off scot free.

'If I don't, it won't be for want of trying,' Lizzie said.

'I believe you.' If it had been any other female Philip would have thought she was doomed to failure. Women in business were rare, especially women of her background. But her sheer bravery inspired such confidence in him, he couldn't imagine her failing at anything.

'Anyway, I must be off. Thanks again,' she said.

'My pleasure.' And Philip really meant it.

His father didn't share his enthusiasm.

'Why don't you just send a batch of our orders over to the damned woman and have done with it?' Humphrey said sarcastically the following Sunday when Philip and Emily were having lunch with his parents in Eden Crescent. He had just been telling his mother that his efforts to help Carter's Silks had finally reached fruition.

'Surely you don't begrudge my offering a helping hand to a colleague?' said Philip, pausing over his roast beef. 'It isn't as though we'd want to take on work for Charlie . . . we've a full order book in our own specialist field.'

'It would have created goodwill if we'd taken it on,' said his father. 'You never know when we might be glad of an order from Kings.'

'At the moment we can certainly afford to put a job someone else's way.'

'Anyway, there's always been a good community spirit in the silk trade,' Meg pointed out, picking up the gravy boat.

'Exactly,' said Philip. 'The day that business is so competitive you can't do a good turn, is the day I'll give up.'

'I can't understand why you're willing to help the Carter

family after the way they've behaved towards you,' said Humphrey.

'Why shouldn't I?' said Philip firmly. 'Their behaviour was perfectly understandable under the circumstances. But anyway, it isn't the Carter family I've helped collectively . . . it's just one member of it. An individual in her own right.'

'She certainly deserves a helping hand,' put in Meg. 'Being left to bring those three children up on her own.'

'As usual I can see that I'm completely outnumbered here,' remarked Humphrey, winking at his daughter-in-law with a sudden change of mood. 'Not unless I have an ally in you, Emily.'

'Not a chance, Father-in-law,' said Emily who had been enjoying a period of calm lately. 'Any woman trying to make her way in the world needs all the help she can get.'

'Hear, hear,' said Meg.

'I know how difficult it is from bitter experience,' said Emily with unexpected vehemence.

'Yes, quite right, dear,' said Meg uneasily, hearing warning bells in the tone of Emily's last remark.

'If only I'd been given a chance.' Down went her knife and fork with a clatter on her plate, the gravy spilling over the edge. 'It's so bloody unfair . . .'

'Language, dear,' admonished Meg as though Emily was any rational person. But they all knew the signs. A sudden show of temper, the uncharacteristic use of expletives, usually meant that violence was imminent.

Philip, who was sitting next to his wife, rested a steadying hand on her arm. 'All right, darling, don't upset yourself,' he said, hoping to avert an embarrassing scene.

'I'm not in the least upset,' she said but her voice was quivering. 'Just because I choose to voice an opinion, doesn't mean I'm in a state.'

'No one's suggesting it does,' he said gently, once again forced to tread the fine line between being protective or patronising. 'That particular subject usually upsets you, that's all. We all know how much you wanted to be a teacher.'

'Well, it hasn't upset me this time,' she informed him briskly, picking up her eating utensils and continuing with her meal as though nothing had happened.

He felt his muscles loosen with relief. He had thought her eruption heralded yet another drama. This was further proof of the unpredictable nature of her illness.

'Anyway, getting back to the redoubtable Mrs Carter junior,' he said, 'I've a strong suspicion that that lady is going to make a success of her business with or without my help.'

'I think you're probably right,' agreed his mother.

The order from Charlie King proved to be a turning point for Carter's Silks. The first order for the red, brown and green striped material that was King's trademark was finished ahead of time and Charlie was so pleased he ordered another batch right away. Word soon got around and almost simultaneously with the second order for King's lining fabric, they were asked to make a healthy amount of silk cloth for a firm who produced blouses and underwear.

Work from other clothing manufacturers followed. More looms were installed in the factory at Sparrow's Yard and by the summer of the following year they had ten looms and their staff included three weavers. Luke Carter was also on the payroll as a general handyman-cum labourer and factory assistant, relieving Bobby of some of the routine jobs and delivery work so that he could attend to his duties as manager.

Lizzie put a strong emphasis on teamwork, insisting that all her employees should be willing to turn their hands to tasks other than their main skills if it was warranted. She herself took time off from the administration to help out on the looms or on the warping floor if she was needed.

Her self-confidence and bank balance grew along with her business and by the Christmas of 1921 she and the children had moved out of their cramped rooms into a house all to themselves. Nothing very grand, just a little rented terraced house about ten minutes' walk from Bessle Street, but it had a tiny kitchen and a small garden for the children to play in.

Seeing their pleasure as they settled into their new home, Lizzie experienced her first real sense of achievement in that she had realised what had once seemed like an impossible dream. She had improved their living accommodation!

But her life was far from calm as she found herself faced with a dilemma that had nothing to do with her role of parent.

Chapter Thirteen

On Boxing Night the Carter family gathered at Lizzie's place for a combined Christmas and housewarming party.

'It seems to be going well,' remarked June, leaving the festivities in the sitting room to join Lizzie in the kitchen where she was making yet another batch of sandwiches.

'So's the food,' laughed Lizzie.

'You're telling me,' grinned June who had spent the afternoon helping her to prepare the party spread. 'All the sausage rolls have gone. Any more cheese straws?'

'In a tin in the larder.'

June took the container from the cupboard and began setting the contents out on a doily-covered plate. 'How are things between you and Polly lately?' she asked companionably.

'We keep up a front for the sake of appearances but she's very offhand when we're on our own,' explained Lizzie, pausing thoughtfully with the bread knife poised in mid-air. 'I don't think she'll ever forgive me for taking that money from Philip.'

'She's still not taking any interest in the business, I gather, even though you're doing so well.'

'None at all,' replied Lizzie, slicing a pile of ham

sandwiches into quarters. 'I wanted her and Will to share in my good fortune. God knows I owe them. I'm not exactly rolling in money 'cos I'm saving to repay the debt and I've taken on a higher rent with the house, but I've enough to put a bit their way. She won't take a penny from me, though.'

'Seems such a pity for you both,' said June who was thoroughly enjoying the fruits of Lizzie's success. She and Bobby had left their shabby rooms for a roomy ground-floor flat in a converted house just off the Portobello Road. 'Bobby and I have never been so well off as we are now that he's working for you.'

'Polly isn't on the breadline or anything,' continued Lizzie. 'She's a wage coming in from Will and Luke every week. But I wanted to treat them to some extras, new furniture for instance, and pay for them to have their place done up. But she just won't have it. It's her way of punishing me, I suppose.'

'She's one tough lady when it comes to making a stand.'

'You can say that again.'

They were interrupted by the noisy exuberance of youth as all five children clattered in, accompanied by a boozy version of 'Any Old Iron' drifting from the other room as the kitchen door was opened.

'Can we have some drinks, please, Mum?' asked Bruce.

'There's lemonade and ginger beer in the larder,' said Lizzie.

The youngsters clustered around the cupboard, chattering and laughing.

'Jamie and Keith are gonna do their act in a minute,' announced Eva.

'Wait till we come in then, won't you, boys?' requested Lizzie.

'We wouldn't start without you, Aunt Lizzie,' Jamie promised.

There was more giggling and teasing as they filled their glasses with ginger beer from a heavy stone bottle.

'Right, you lot, now you've got your drinks you can vamoose back to the sitting room,' said June lightly. 'You're in the way out here.'

After their boisterous exit, Lizzie remarked casually, 'They're dead on their feet but having a whale of a time.'

'Doesn't hurt them to stay up late once in a while.'

'No.'

Their conversation was halted again by the appearance of Bobby looking mildly squiffy. His jacket had been removed, his shirt sleeves were rolled up and his hair was boyishly dishevelled.

'Anything I can do to help, girls?' he offered, standing opposite them at the table, smiling benignly.

'Yes, you can go and see if everyone is all right for drinks,' said June.

'Right you are,' he agreed, and sauntered from the room.

'I'll take these into the other room, shall I, Lizzie?' suggested June, referring to the cheese straws.

'Yes, please, love. You might as well take that dish of pickled onions too.'

'Okey-dokey,' she said, and wandered off to join the party.

Lizzie arranged the sandwiches on a plate with an uneasy conscience. Dear, trusting June was happily unaware of the blistering emotions simmering beneath her friend's calm exterior. In an effort to analyse the worrying situation she now found herself in, Lizzie cast her mind back, trying to pinpoint the exact moment when her feelings for Bobby had changed. But the process had been so gradual this wasn't possible. All she knew was that at some stage during the course of her working relationship with him, she had begun to want more from him than friendship.

It had been an occasional stab of desire at first, usually triggered by a moment of physical contact, perhaps when they were sharing some high point in the business day with the sort of casual embrace they'd enjoyed all their lives. She'd told herself it was just a trick of nature, misplaced lust caused by sexual frustration, a mere side-effect of widowhood which would disappear if it lacked attention.

But with no conscious encouragement from her the feeling had grown and flourished, dominating her thoughts and ruling her life. When she'd found herself dreading the end of the working day, she knew she'd drifted into extremely dangerous waters. The uncomplicated, platonic love she had always felt for Bobby had become an aching, all-consuming passion.

If it had been anyone else but him there might have been a chance. But their sibling-like relationship added to the fact that he was married to her best friend made the whole thing unthinkable – even quasi-incestuous. The worst thing of all – and to her shame the most wonderful – was that she was sure her feelings were reciprocated.

Not a word had been said on the subject. Bobby was happy-go-lucky but not shallow. In fact, he was extremely uxorious with a strong sense of duty. His wife's best friend, a woman who was still thought of as his sister-in-law, would be strictly off-limits to him. His attitude towards Lizzie had changed accordingly. He avoided physical contact – the friendly embraces that had been a part of their lives no longer happened.

But he was a full-blooded man. She suspected that even the slightest encouragement from her would propel them gloriously to disaster. It had been like living on a bitter-sweet knife edge these last few months. For all the trauma, she still felt blissful in his company.

Looking back in the light of her present affections, it seemed odd that she had married Stan and not Bobby. They had always been close, far more of a couple than she and Stan in many ways. But somewhere along the line she had lost her direction . . . and this was the result.

Her reverie was interrupted by Bobby who reappeared carrying two empty glasses which he rinsed under the tap.

'Where's June?' she asked quickly, acutely aware of the danger of being alone with him in this festive atmosphere with their judgement impaired by alcohol.

'In the other room, singing her head off.' He took a bottle of brown ale from the larder and went to the sink where he began to pour some into a glass on the wooden draining board.

'You've got yourself the job of barman, then,' she said stiffly.

'Looks like it. Dad wants a beer, and a port and lemon for Ma.' He turned and gave her a lopsided grin. 'Christmas wouldn't be Christmas without Ma's port and lemon, would it?'

'No, it certainly wouldn't,' said Lizzie inanely, unable to avoid meeting his shandy brown eyes.

At this moment Bobby seemed to sober up instantly, his face becoming dark and serious. He put the bottle and glass down so hastily that the contents slopped over the top of the glass. He moved towards her.

'Oh God, Lizzie, what are we gonna do?'

'Do?' she said in a cracked voice.

'Don't come the innocent,' he said. 'You were terrified when I came in that door without June because you're as scared as I am of what might happen.'

'Happen . . . what can happen with a house full of people?'

'We can acknowledge our feelings, admit that they're there,' he informed her shakily. 'That's what can happen.'

'Oh, Bobby.'

And suddenly she was in his arms, melting against him, feeling his lips on hers.

'Stop it, this isn't right,' she said in a trembling voice, managing to tear herself away from him at last.

'I know, I'm sorry.'

They stood just inches apart.

'It's the drink,' she announced. 'It makes people do things they don't intend.'

'Yeah, I know that.' He looked at her in a way he had never looked at June. 'The booze might have made me step out of line and speak up about it, but it has nothing to do with my feelings. I love you, Lizzie.'

'Don't, Bobby . . .'

'I didn't want this to happen,' he confessed. 'God knows I don't want to hurt June.'

'And we mustn't.'

'But I want to be with you all the time, day and night,' he went on. 'I must be the only bloke alive who doesn't look forward to the end of the working day.'

'It's been like that for me for some time too,' she confessed.

'Oh, Lizzie.'

'How could things have changed so drastically between us?' she asked, her voice full of anguish. 'After all this time.'

'Have they changed that much, though, Lizzie?' he said.

'What do you mean?'

'Perhaps it was always there under the surface,' he said. 'We've always been a pair, you and me. I'd have married you like a shot if . . .'

'It was never like that between us,' she cut in quickly.

'Maybe not for you.'

She threw him a sharp look. 'You never gave any indication.'

'By the time we were old enough to bother about such things, it was obvious that Stan was the only one who stood a chance,' he explained.

'Mmm, I've been thinking about that a lot lately,' she said. 'I wonder why it was him I went for and not you.'

'Dunno but I wish you hadn't.'

'Perhaps it was because he was the older brother,' she said. 'Age is impressive when you're young.'

'Could be.'

'What attracted you to June?'

'She happened to be around, we just drifted into marriage,' he explained. 'But you were always the special one.'

Lizzie believed him. Recalling a conversation she had once had with June she knew that she was aware of it too. 'Your marriage has worked though, hasn't it?'

'Oh, yeah. June's a real doll, one of the best.'

'She told me once that she used to be jealous of me when we were children because you and I were so close.'

'We'll have to make sure we don't make her feel like that again, won't we?'

'Definitely.'

But even as their words died away so did their good intentions and somehow they were in each other's arms again.

An increase in the volume of noise from the other room indicated that the door had opened and someone was heading their way. They sprang apart and by the time June appeared with a tray of dirty glasses, Lizzie was already on her way out with the sandwiches and Bobby had resumed his task of filling a glass with beer.

'You two been havin' a business meeting out here or somethin'?' said June lightheartedly, unaware that Lizzie's knees were shaking and Bobby could barely keep his hand steady enough to pour the drink.

'Something like that,' he said. 'You know how dedicated we are.'

'You're a pair of ruddy workaholics if you ask me,' laughed June.

'We're coming back to join the party now,' said Lizzie.

'You'll be just in time for the twins' turn.'

'Good.'

As Lizzie made her way along the narrow passageway to the gathering in the sitting room, it occurred to her that she and Bobby could be found having the most intimate discussion without anyone suspecting anything untoward because they were all so used to their being together. That sort of leeway could be dangerous!

'This has to stop, Bobby,' said Lizzie, extricating herself from his embrace one afternoon a month or so later in her office.

'I know,' he sighed, drawing her back to him. 'But I want you so much.'

'The feeling's mutual, I can assure you,' she breathed. 'But someone's going to see us if we're not careful.'

'No one can see us . . . not in here,' he pointed out shakily. 'The window's too high to see into the back of this room from the yard.'

'Luke's got eyes everywhere,' she whispered nervously.

'Even he can't see through walls or wooden doors,' he told her, tracing her face lovingly with his finger.

'Don't bet on it,' she said with a weak little laugh.

A knock on the office door had them leaping apart. She adjusted her clothing and tried to smooth her hair down with her hand before sitting down at her desk and grabbing her pen. Bobby sat down in the chair opposite and picked up some papers in which he feigned to be deeply engrossed.

'Come in,' said Lizzie at last.

It was Luke. 'I've loaded the van with the finished order so if you can let me have the paperwork I'll go and make the delivery.'

'It's in my office, mate,' said Bobby, rising and walking towards the door. 'You've got to go to an address in Camden Town if my memory serves me correctly.'

As the door closed behind them, Lizzie took a deep breath and rested her throbbing head on her hands. The situation with Bobby was making her ill. Ever since Christmas they couldn't leave each other alone. This put her into a constant state of nervousness and compunction for what she was doing to June. It was no use. This thing had to end before things got out of hand and the inevitable happened.

* * *

Luke fought his way through the traffic in the West End on his way to Camden Town. A multitude of open-topped buses, taxi cabs, motor cycles, horse-carts, motorcars and bicycles were caught in a tangled chaos between crowded pavements and buildings draped with slogans advertising everything from Iron Jelloids to Exide batteries. The air was thick with dust, exhaust fumes and the heavy stench of horse-dung.

Turning into Tottenham Court Road, he found himself recalling the scene in Lizzie's office just before he'd left the factory. Those two were at it or his name wasn't Luke Carter. Oh, yes, he'd obviously walked in on something. Her flushed cheeks and the quiver in his voice were a dead giveaway. Everyone else might be blind to their antics because they'd always been such close friends, but Luke could see at a glance what was going on. Once upon a time Bobby and Lizzie might have been just pals but they were a damned sight more than that to each other now!

It was an interesting situation and one that was worth keeping an eye on. When he was certain of his facts, he would have a few words in a certain person's ear. Then he'd stand back and watch the sparks fly.

One day in February Bobby and Lizzie lunched together at a pub on the river.

'I want us to be together, Lizzie,' he said over coffee.

'We're together all day,' she said, deliberately misunderstanding him because there was no solution to the problem.

'You know very well what I mean,' he said. 'I want us to be a couple.'

'Me too,' she told him wistfully, 'but we both know that isn't possible.'

'We could make it possible,' he said, with a determined edge to his voice.

'Not without hurting June and the twins.'

'Look, I didn't ask this to happen,' he told her grimly. 'And neither did you. But it has happened and I want to be with the woman I love. Is that such a sin?'

'Wanting to isn't,' she said. 'Doing more than that is, though.'

'Oh, Lizzie,' he said. 'Do you always have to be so good . . . so sensible?'

'You wouldn't say that if you could read my thoughts,' she told him. 'I practically set the sheets on fire in bed at night. I want to grab this chance of happiness and to hell with other people, but . . .'

'But we have to be content with stolen moments in the office like a couple of naughty kids,' he cut in irascibly.

'That's right. And even that can't go on,' she told him. 'And it's no good you sulking. I didn't arrange things this way. I'm not the one who's married.'

'All right, don't rub it in.'

'Seems funny seeing you so serious,' she told him gently.

'Good old Bobby, eh? Always ready with a laugh and a joke,' he said bitterly. 'Well, I have feelings too, you know. Just because I don't walk about with my chin on the floor every time something goes wrong, doesn't mean I don't bleed the same as anyone else.'

'I know that,' she said, taking his hand across the table. 'This is Lizzie you're talking to, the girl you started school with, the one you used to come to when you were in trouble with the teacher or had a pasting from your dad. I reckon I know you better than anyone. Well, apart from June, of course.'

'Maybe.'

'But there isn't a future for you and me together,' she went on. 'You know that in your heart. You'd never leave June. Not in a million years.'

'You're right, as usual,' he said with a heavy sigh. 'Not now anyway. When the twins are grown up perhaps . . .'

'We'll be past it by then, which just goes to show that it isn't meant to be.'

'Oh, let's get out of here,' he said irritably. 'Let's go for a stroll.'

They walked along the riverside towards Chiswick. It was a cold day with watery sunlight gleaming on the muddy waters at high tide. A sharp breeze whistled through the skeletal trees, sending the smoke from the tug-boats sideways and causing the moored barges to creak and rattle along the grassy banks which were sprinkled, here and there, with orange and mauve crocuses.

'The irony of all this is,' she said thoughtfully, 'we're forced together every day by necessity. You've too much to lose to leave the firm and I'm too committed to sell out. With both of us having children to support, neither of us can make the grand gesture because we are both reliant on the income.'

'Mmm.'

They lapsed into silence until he made a sudden rash suggestion. 'Let's spend a night together, Lizzie.'

'Oh, if only!'

'We could.'

'It's a lovely idea but that's all it can ever be, an idea.'

'Not necessarily.'

'And how are we supposed to explain our sudden departure?'

'We could pretend to be going away on business,' he said. 'Up North somewhere, perhaps.'

'And who's going to look after my children?' she asked him.

'June, maybe,' he suggested without any real hope.

'I don't think either of us could sink that low.'

'No.'

'So there's only one option open to us,' she said resolutely. 'We must put this whole new situation between us out of our minds and try to return to the way we were.'

'Now you're the one who's being unrealistic!'

'We *must* turn back the clock, Bobby,' she said. 'We've no alternative.'

'Let's take a room in an hotel for an afternoon,' he said daringly. 'That can't hurt anyone.'

'You're not serious?' she exclaimed, unable to suppress a tingle of excitement.

'I am, you know,' he said, enthusiasm growing as the idea seemed workable. 'The business can survive for a few hours one afternoon without us, and our children are at school so that problem is taken care of.'

'Oh, Bobby, we mustn't.'

'You can tell the staff you're having lunch with a client in the West End,' he continued with rising eagerness. 'I'll say I've a special meeting with a firm of silk merchants we're trying to agree terms with. We'll leave the factory separately and meet at the hotel.'

'I couldn't do such a rotten thing to June,' she protested. 'I just couldn't.'

'I don't want to hurt her any more than you do, but what the eye doesn't see . . .'

'That doesn't make it right and you know it,' Lizzie admonished firmly.

He stopped and drew her into an alleyway between some houses where he pulled her into his arms. 'The way I'm feeling at this moment isn't right, Lizzie,' he said huskily. 'In a perfect world it would only happen for June. But this isn't a perfect world, and I've never claimed to be a saint.'

'Oh, Bobby, I don't know what to do,' she said miserably.

'Leave everything to me. I'll book a room. All you have to do is be convincing in your cover story.'

The rhythm of Lizzie's heartbeat was very erratic as she sat on the tube, smartly dressed in a navy and white low-waisted suit with a cloche hat in matching colours, all of which covered silk underwear specially purchased for the occasion. She'd popped home from the factory to bathe and change, glad of the fact that she had her own place now. She imagined getting ready for such an assignation from their rooms in Bessle Street with their primitive washing facilities and lack of privacy. That would have kept me on the straight and narrow, she thought wryly.

Getting off the train at Hyde Park Corner, she stood at the kerb waiting to cross the busy road, anxiety, guilt and eagerness fusing into a cocktail of feverish excitement. Dodging through the traffic, she crossed the road and made her way into the hotel, certain that the doorman knew her purpose here and was inwardly sniggering. She sat in the foyer as previously arranged beside a potted palm and waited for Bobby to arrive, staring at the marble floor in terror of being seen by someone she knew, the chances of which were infinitesimal.

'Hello, sweetheart.'

She looked up and there he was, stunningly handsome in his best suit with a stiff white collar and dark blue tie. 'Hello,' she said through dry lips.

'I've booked us in and got the key to the room but I thought you might like a spot of lunch before we go up?' he said, his breezy manner not quite ringing true today.

'Yes, that would be lovely,' she said, and they went into the restaurant together.

Having chosen the least expensive item on the menu, vegetable soup followed by lamb chops with redcurrant jelly, she whispered, 'I'd better pay for this. A meal for two here would feed your twins for a week.'

'Whoever heard of a woman footing the bill in a situation like this?'

'Please, Bobby. I couldn't live with myself if I took the food out of your children's mouths,' she persisted.

'Don't, Lizzie,' he warned. 'You're embarrassing me.'

'What on earth made you choose such a pricey place?'

'So that we could be sure of not being seen,' he explained. 'Nobody from our circle can afford to come here. Anyway, I didn't want our first . . . our initial . . . well, you know, to take place in some seedy joint.'

'It was a nice thought,' she said. 'But I feel bad enough cheating on June without taking money that's rightly hers, too.'

'Leave it, Lizzie,' he said sharply, because he too was

feeling terrible about it, especially as the cost of this whole exercise would pay for the new curtains June wanted so badly for their flat. Since they'd moved out of their rooms, all their spare money went on their flat. June lived for him and the twins and worked hard to make a comfortable home for them; and here he was selfishly indulging his own feelings. In a perverse kind of way, he felt worse about cheating her out of money than the actual adultery.

'All right. Sorry.'

An uncomfortable silence settled over them. Lizzie felt so tense she thought she was going to erupt into nervous laughter.

'You look lovely,' he said rather stiffly at last.

'Thank you. You're looking very handsome yourself,' she replied formally.

'Well, I couldn't very well come to a place like this in my working clothes, could I?' he pointed out. 'And no one suspected anything because I wouldn't be expected to go to a business meeting in overalls.'

'June fell for it then?' she said, feeling worse by the second.

'You know June . . . it wouldn't occur to her to doubt me.'

'No.'

They were served with the soup which could have been rainwater for all the notice Lizzie took of it. The second course wasn't much better. Bobby wasn't eating either. Most of his food was pushed to the side of his plate.

'Not hungry,' she said.

'Well, you know.'

She reached across and took his hand. 'I know just how you feel.'

'Look, why don't we skip the rest of the meal and go on up

to the room?' he suggested in a hurried, staccato manner.

For a while she didn't speak, then she gave a slow shake of her head. 'It isn't on, is it, Bobby?' she said.

'Don't say you've got cold feet now?' he said, angry because he felt so damned unequal to the situation.

'Not cold feet,' she said. 'Just a good healthy dose of common sense. You feel as bad about all this as I do. Come on, admit it.'

'It's just the place,' he claimed defensively. 'I'm like a fish out of water among all these toffs.'

'No, it isn't the place,' she told him gravely. 'It's us . . . you and me.'

'I love you, Lizzie,' he told her earnestly. 'Please believe me.'

'I *do* believe you,' she assured him. 'I also think you love your wife too, in a different way, perhaps, but you love her. Too much to be able to cheat on her.'

He combed his hair back from his brow with his fingers. 'June was never special to me, not like you were.'

'I think she is now, though.'

'Do you know what it was that put me off my stroke this afternoon?' he asked, lowering his hands and leaning towards her.

'Tell me.'

'It was the money I was spending that played on my conscience,' he explained. 'I'd promised June she could get new curtains . . . it sounds so bloody pathetic!'

'Not at all. It shows how much she means to you,' she said, imbued with a sudden sense of loneliness.

'Maybe if we'd gone somewhere cheaper . . .'

259

'You wouldn't have been able to go through with it wherever we'd gone, any more than I would,' she said. 'We're both too emotionally tied to June and the children.'

'Under different circumstances . . .' he began lamely.

'It wasn't meant to be, Bobby,' she cut in. 'If it had been we'd have got together all those years ago.'

'I've made a right mess of everything. Here we are with a room booked . . .'

'Why not go and cancel the room and then come back and we'll finish our lunch?'

'I'm so sorry, Lizzie. To have had you come here.'

'Stop worrying and cancel the booking,' she urged him.

Without another word he hurried from the restaurant.

When he returned to the table the atmosphere was easier. Neither of them wanted a dessert so they just ordered coffee. Lizzie was both relieved and disappointed. She'd known the minute they'd met in the hotel foyer that she couldn't go through with it. It wasn't only basic morality and the fact that he was married to June, as significant as these things were, there was more to it than that.

She was still confused about what had actually made the whole thing into a fiasco but thought that it probably had something to do with her love for Bobby having its roots in friendship. It had always been a joyful, wholesome thing. Not the stuff of illicit sex in some hotel bedroom but a thing to be celebrated openly. To have consummated it in such a shabby way would have belittled it somehow.

Along with this conclusion came the firm belief that there would be no more furtive fumblings in the office. It was over.

They had passed safely through the storm.

Reaching across the table, she took his hand with a half smile. A part of her would always be tormented by thoughts of what might have happened in that hotel bedroom today. But the affair that had never really happened was at an end!

'I'll settle for friendship,' she said gently. 'Since there isn't a choice.'

'Yeah, me too.'

Reeling with desire as his strong fingers curled around hers, she knew that they couldn't return to their former carefree relationship – not quite.

Although Bobby knew it had all worked out for the best, he was bitterly disappointed. He still wanted Lizzie but she was worth more than a quick tumble in a hotel bedroom and a spot of heavy breathing behind the filing cabinets. That was all it could ever be. Lizzie was right, he would never leave June and the boys, he was far too deeply indoctrinated with respect for family values. Today's farce had made him realise just how badly he'd been behaving, cheapening Lizzie and cheating on June because of feelings he hadn't tried hard enough to control.

There would be no more passion running riot at the factory. This miserable escapade had forced him to face up to the truth. Lizzie was a romantic dream. June was real life.

His hormones weren't so easily convinced, he realised, at the feel of her hand in his. He managed a weak smile. As Lizzie had said, they must settle for friendship. With a real effort they should be able to get back to their old lighthearted footing. But he knew he was deluding himself.

* * *

One spring morning, Luke was driving the van out of the factory yard on his way to deliver an order to a firm in Wandsworth when he decided to make a slight detour. It was high time he paid his sister-in-law a visit.

June was busy polishing the lino on the living-room floor when he knocked at the front door. She could have done without an interruption but politely invited him in.

'I was passing the end of your road,' he lied, 'so I thought I'd pop in and cadge a cuppa tea from my favourite sister-in-law.'

'I'll put the kettle on,' she said, managing to hide the fact that she was cursing him because she wanted to finish her chores and go down to the shops.

She left him in an armchair in the living room while she went to the kitchen to make some tea, hoping he didn't intend to stay long.

'So you're out delivering, are you?' she said, bustling in with a tray of tea and biscuits and setting it down on an occasional table. She poured the tea and handed him a cup.

'That's right.'

'I bet Bobby and Lizzie wouldn't be too pleased to know you'd stopped off for a tea break,' she said lightly but with the intention of deterring him from prolonging his visit.

'Huh! I doubt if those two would notice if I was gone all day,' he said, delighted to have found the perfect opening for what he had come here to say. 'In fact, the more I'm out o' the way the better they like it, these days.'

'What on earth do you mean by that?' she wanted to know.

'Well, they've more freedom if I'm not around.'

'Freedom for what? What are you talking about?' she asked, frowning darkly.

'Well, they wouldn't want me to know. With me being family,' he said with the subtlety of Syrup of Figs. 'I don't suppose they care what the workers think.'

'Think about what, for goodness' sake?' she asked, irritated by his obnoxious innuendo.

'Well . . .'

'Look, if you've something to say, Luke,' she snapped, 'I'd rather you came right out and said it instead of dropping hints.'

He sipped his tea and peered at her over the rim of the cup. 'Er, nothing,' he said, pretending to feel uncomfortable.

'There must be some reason for all these insinuations?'

'No, no. I've said enough already. It's nothing.'

June knew she was being manipulated. He had come round here for the sole purpose of imparting information. She was damned if he was going to tease her with it any longer. 'You can't leave it at that. What are you trying to tell me, Luke? *I want to know!*'

'I don't expect it's serious enough to be a threat to you. I mean . . .' He hesitated for a moment. 'I shouldn't think they're actually planning to go off together or anything. Bobby wouldn't do a thing like that.'

'What! You mean, they're . . .?'

'At it like rabbits,' he said, enjoying his moment of triumph. This would stop Lizzie at her little game. He was so keen to hurt her, he hadn't given a thought to how this would affect June who had turned a pale mushroom colour.

'They're not,' she gasped.

'They are.'

'How do you know?'

'It's written all over 'em,' he said. 'They can't leave each other alone for a minute at the factory. You daren't go into her office without knocking.'

'Bobby and Lizzie have always been very close, everyone knows that.'

'Not like this.'

'That's a wicked thing to say.'

'It's true, though.'

'I don't believe a word of it.'

'That's entirely up to you,' he told her casually. 'It doesn't matter to me one way or the other.'

'Why take the trouble to come round here to tell me, then?'

'Just doing my duty,' he said smoothly. 'I thought you ought to know what's going on behind your back.'

'You're just trying to make mischief,' she accused. She'd never been sure what to make of this member of the Carter family with his quiet ways and menacing eyes.

'And why would I wanna do that?'

'Who knows what goes on in that nasty little mind of yours?' she said hotly. 'But you're wasting your time because I don't believe you.'

'Ask them then,' he said. 'Let them try to deny it.'

'I wouldn't lower myself by taking notice of your mischief-making.'

'Suit yourself,' he said with studied nonchalance.

'So if you've finished your tea,' she said firmly, 'I'd like you to go. I have to finish my housework.'

'Certainly.'

He left feeling jubilant. She believed him, however much she denied it.

Chapter Fourteen

One Saturday afternoon in spring, the Carter children were playing in the back garden near the kitchen window while Lizzie prepared tea. Absorbed in thought whilst buttering some currant buns, their youthful chatter barely registered with her. She was remembering the ghastly contretemps with Bobby in the hotel a month ago, hardly able to believe she'd let things go so far. Thank God common sense and decency had finally prevailed.

Her pondering ended abruptly as something outside caught her attention.

'Right everybody, let's pick sides,' Jed was saying authoritatively. 'It's Vernes against Carters. Vernes are the baddies – they're wicked murderers. Bruce and Jamie can be Vernes, me and Keith'll be Carters . . .'

'What about me?' the indomitable Eva wanted to know.

'Girls can't play this.'

''Course they can.'

'No, they can't,' argued Jed. 'This is a boy's game.'

'Who says?'

'I do,' said her dictatorial brother. 'Anyway, if you join in, we'll have odd numbers.'

'Oh, let her play,' said Bruce. 'It isn't fair to leave her out.'

Jed gave his sister a withering look, sighing impatiently. 'Oh, all right. But don't start grizzling and spoil it for the rest of us if the game gets rough.'

'Come on, sis,' said the amiable Bruce with a gentle grin. 'You can be on our side.'

'I don't wanna be a Verne,' she wailed. 'I don't wanna be a murderer.'

'Oh, for goodness sake, Eva,' snapped Jed. 'It's only a game.'

'I don't care. I'm not gonna be a horrible old Verne.'

At that point Lizzie opened the window and issued a command. 'Jed, will you come in here, please?'

'Oh, do I have to, Mum? We're just gonna start a game.'

'Don't argue, just do it.'

He appeared in the kitchen exuding aggression, a replica of his father in sulky mood. He was told to sit down at the scrubbed wooden table whereupon Lizzie abandoned her task and sat down purposefully opposite him.

'What's this game Carters and Vernes all about?' she demanded.

'Goodies against baddies, like Cops and Robbers,' he told her with a scowl.

'Whose idea was it to name the sides Carters and Vernes?' she asked.

'Mine,' he said proudly. 'Isn't it stunning?'

'Indeed it is. I'm quite stunned by its awfulness.'

'Oh . . . why?'

'Because the Vernes are not a fictitious family of monsters, Jed,' she said gravely, 'they are a real family living in

London . . . and they are not bad people.'

'One of them killed my father,' he retorted, his cheeks flaming, blue eyes glistening with angry tears. 'And you say they're not bad!'

'Your father died in an accident,' she reminded him.

'No, he *didn't*! He was murdered by a man called Philip Verne, everyone knows that,' he said, shocking his mother with his vehemence. It might have been Stan sitting there intent upon vilification. How sad that his resentment lived on in his son.

'You shouldn't say things like that,' she told him.

'Gran says it. I've heard her lots of times.'

Ah, she might have guessed Polly was behind this. 'Well, I don't want to hear you saying it,' declared Lizzie. 'Mr Verne was found innocent of murder and we have to accept that.'

'You can but I'm not going to. If it hadn't been for him, my dad would still be here now,' he said, his young voice tight with anger.

'Oh, Jed,' she said, going round to him and putting her arm around his shoulders. 'We all miss your dad but we have to try to put his actual death out of our minds and remember the good times when we were all happy together. It's nearly three years now since he died.'

'I'll never forget my father,' he cut in, pushing her away and standing up, eyes hot with indignation. 'Even if you have.'

'I haven't forgotten him,' she exclaimed, aghast at the suggestion.

'You don't care about him,' he said, his face dark with accusation. 'If you did you wouldn't have taken Philip Verne's money.'

It was as though his fist had struck her right between the eyes. 'How did you know about that?' she asked.

'I heard Gran talking to Uncle Luke and Grandad about it,' he told her.

Lizzie wasn't prepared to justify her actions to an eleven-year-old boy, so she just said, 'Whatever I've done, Jed, I have genuinely believed it to be in the best interests of you children. You're too young to understand so I'm not even going to try to explain. There is going to be *real* trouble, however, if I ever catch you playing the Carters against the Vernes again. Is that clear?'

He shrugged his shoulders with an elaborate show of nonchalance.

'Jed?'

'All right.' He stared at her with blatant contempt. 'Can I go now?'

'Yes, off you go.'

Turning at the door, he threw her a parting shot. 'You might be able to stop me playing the game but you can't change my thoughts or stop me believing what I know is right.'

That's a fact, she thought sadly, recognising the signs of incipient adolescence as he went outside, slamming the door viciously behind him. But I *can* try to curtail the influence that is colouring his judgement.

As soon as she'd washed the tea things, Lizzie gathered the children together for a visit to their grandmother, stopping off at Bobby and June's on the way to deliver the twins.

'You coming in, Liz?' asked Bobby, standing at June's side at the front door.

'No, I won't, thanks all the same. I'm on my way round to Polly's.'

'As you like,' he said.

'Maybe I'll call in on my way home for a natter, though,' she suggested casually. 'If it isn't too late.'

'We're going out,' announced June sharply before her husband could reply.

Bobby gave his wife a quizzical look. 'It's the first I've heard of it.'

'Well, you know now, don't you,' she snapped and went back inside.

'Whatever's the matter with her?' asked Lizzie, suddenly becoming aware that June had been offhand with her rather a lot lately.

'Search me,' he said. 'Maybe she's feeling a bit off colour.'

Puzzled, Lizzie went on her way, deciding to have a talk with June some time in the near future. But her first priority was a frank discussion with another lady.

'Don't you dare tell me what I can and can't say in my own house,' rasped Polly, when Lizzie had recounted the incident with Jed and made it known she disapproved of Polly inflicting her views on her grandchildren.

'That isn't what I'm doing,' denied Lizzie. 'I'm just trying to . . .'

'Yes, you damned well are!' interrupted Polly, her cheeks angrily suffused. 'That's exactly what you're doing, and I won't have it.'

Lizzie took a slow, calming breath, wishing she could have a debate with Polly without her flying off the handle. The last thing Lizzie wanted was a quarrel but the issue was far too important to ignore. Fortunately, the two women were alone in the kitchen where Polly was preparing high tea for Will and Luke. The children had gone to play in the street and Luke and his father were in the parlour experimenting with a new toy, a crystal wireless set that Will had obtained cheap from one of his mates at the pub.

'I didn't come here to upset you,' said Lizzie, biting her lip.

'Huh! You could have fooled me,' was the barbed reply.

'But neither do I want Jed to grow up with hatred in his heart.'

'He's bound to resent the Vernes after what happened to his father. All the children will. It's only natural,' pronounced Polly, rinsing a piece of smoked haddock under the tap and putting it into a saucepan to poach on the stove. 'You can't blame me for that. I'm not responsible for what happened to their father.'

'Of course not,' agreed Lizzie, choosing her words carefully.

'Well, then.'

'But you can help the children to put it behind them and grow up with an open mind.'

'Oh, yeah. I'm full o' tricks.'

'Surely you don't want your grandchildren to start their lives burdened with bad feeling that's rooted in the past? And that is exactly what will happen if you constantly promote your own quarrel with the Vernes to them. You're a powerful force in their lives, they look up to you. Jed is particularly susceptible. Stan wasn't close to any of the children but Jed got on better with him than the others. He sees him as something of a hero, in fact.'

'Quite right too,' said Polly smugly, slicing bread on a wooden board on the table. 'That's how a boy should feel about his father.'

'Yes, but it isn't a good idea for him to grow up with all Stan's prejudices too.'

'My Stan wasn't prejudiced,' she said predictably. 'Anyway, no one should try to interfere with a boy's feelings for his father.'

'Maybe not, but we can influence him against the worst side of Stan's nature, can't we? Teach him by example not to hate,' was Lizzie's answer to that.

Polly stopped sawing into the loaf and looked across at Lizzie, who was sitting at the table spreading the cut slices with margarine.

'I just don't understand you,' she said. 'Anyone would think your name was Verne instead of Carter the way you carry on, taking their side, taking their money . . .'

'That isn't fair,' exclaimed Lizzie, tears of frustration smarting at the back of her eyes. 'I try to do my best for our family. You've all benefited from the loan I had from Philip. Bobby and Luke are earning good money now from the business that I was only able to start because of it. I've tried to help you and Will. The fact that you won't take it isn't my fault. Just because I don't want my children growing up burdened with quarrels from the past has nothing to do with my loyalty towards the Carter family.'

The other woman returned to cutting the bread. 'All right, you've had your say. But I'm not going to change my opinions just because they clash with yours,' she said with her usual vehemence. 'If you don't want your children to be affected by

273

my views then you'd better stop them from coming round here, hadn't you?'

'You know very well that's the last thing I would ever want to do,' said Lizzie, throwing down the butter knife and rising.

'There's no point in losing your temper,' admonished Polly.

'No point in continuing with the conversation either as you're determined not to give an inch . . . as per usual,' she said furiously. 'I'll collect the kids and go home.'

She rinsed her hands under the tap and dried them on a towel hanging on the door.

'All right, I'll try not to talk about my views on Stan's death to the children,' conceded Polly with an elaborate sigh. 'But I can't be held responsible for what they overhear when I'm talking to someone else about it.'

Guessing it would have cost her a lot to have offered even this crumb of co-operation, Lizzie sat back down and carried on buttering the bread, changing the subject to more general matters. Although she was encouraged by Polly's agreement she couldn't help wondering if it was too late – if the damage hadn't already been done.

About the only time Lizzie could be sure of being able to speak with June in private was during the week while the children were at school and Bobby at work. With this in mind, she took time off from the factory to visit her friend the following Monday morning, knowing she would catch her at home because it was washing day.

June's welcome was cool. She said she was busy with the laundry and didn't have time to stop for a chat. Lizzie said they could talk while June worked and followed her to the steamy kitchen which smelled of hot soap suds and was piled high with wet clothes; in the sink, in a tin bath, on the draining board. The copper was on the boil and a faded scrubbing board lay on the wooden table with a bar of well-used Sunlight soap.

Glancing towards the tin bath, June said aggressively, 'I was just going to take that lot outside and put it through the mangle before I peg it on the line.'

'I'll give you a hand,' said Lizzie, and followed her out into a tiny back garden, separated from the other tenants' by chicken wire. Sunlight shone through the washing that was already blowing in the spring breeze.

'I'm getting towards the end of it at last,' muttered June who had a wrapover apron over her clothes, and was looking noticeably dowdy in comparison to Lizzie in her smart business suit and court shoes.

'You put the clothes into the rollers, I'll wind the handle,' suggested Lizzie.

'I wouldn't want you to soil your hands with such laborious work now that you're a bigshot businesswoman,' said June sarcastically, her dark eyes heavy with resentment.

'Come off it,' retorted Lizzie. 'I have to do a family wash the same as you.'

'I thought you sent yours to the laundry these days?'

'Only the bed linen,' she explained. 'While you're putting your feet up of an evening, I'm up to my eyes in this sort of thing.'

'Oh, yeah, I suppose you would be,' mumbled June grudgingly.

'Look, you and I have been friends a long time,' said Lizzie giving her a hard look, 'so why don't you tell me what's the matter?'

'Nothing's the matter.'

'Oh, do me a favour,' said Lizzie. 'You've hardly had a civil word to say to me these past few weeks. I want to know what I've done to upset you. That's why I'm here.'

June pulled a tea towel through the mangle and added it to a pile ready for the line. 'Oh, all right . . . but let's go inside,' she said wearily. 'I don't want the neighbours knowing my business.'

They trooped into June's living room overlooking the back yard. It was a reflection of its owner, neat and homely, the floor and furniture freshly polished, a vase of daffodils on the sideboard.

Lizzie perched on a chair by the table. June, looking grim, stood just inside the door with her arms folded.

'So,' said Lizzie who had been hoping that June's cool manner was just her imagination, 'tell me what's troubling you?'

'I know all about you and Bobby,' she announced in a nervous, high-pitched tone. 'I've known about it for some time.'

'Oh, so that's it,' said Lizzie, wondering what June could have heard, since there wasn't really anything to tell.

'You don't deny it then?' said June, two spots of colour on her cheeks standing out in her pale, worried countenance.

'Give me a chance,' retorted Lizzie. 'I don't know what I'm being accused of yet.'

'You're having an affair with him, aren't you?' said June who'd been unable to ignore Luke's story which had nagged and festered in her mind until she thought she would go crazy with the pain. 'Luke told me all about it.'

'Ah, so Luke's at the bottom of this. I might have known . . .'

'What have you to say for yourself, eh?' Quite suddenly, June lost control. 'You cow! You rotten, cheating bitch! This is the way you treat your best friend. I trusted you. I've even looked after your kids while you've been out at work, and all the time you've been . . .'

She went for Lizzie in a vicious attack, hitting her across the head, pulling her hair, her own body heaving with loud guttural sobs.

Struggling to her feet and fighting off the blows, Lizzie managed to grab her by her upper arms.

'Bobby and I are *not* having an affair,' she bellowed, staring into her friend's face to make sure her words registered.

'Don't insult me by denying it,' June wept, trembling. 'I'm not a fool.'

'If you'll calm down for a minute and let me get a word in, I'll tell you exactly what happened . . . and why Luke might have got the idea that there was something going on.'

This seemed to quieten her and she sat down in an armchair, staring at Lizzie suspiciously, her face blotchy and tear-stained, her dark hair standing out wildly.

'It'd better be good,' she sniffed, rummaging in her apron pocket for a handkerchief and wiping her eyes.

Lizzie sank shakily into an armchair, taking a few deep breaths to calm herself. 'I'm going to be completely honest with you about what happened between Bobby and myself.'

'Something *did* happen then?' June assumed miserably.

'Yes, something happened.'

'How could you, Lizzie?' said June, holding her head in anguish. 'How could you?'

'Please let me finish.'

June shrugged her shoulders hopelessly and waited for Lizzie to continue.

'For a while Bobby and I fancied ourselves to be in love,' she began, and carried on to tell June the whole story, including the incident at the hotel.

'So you never actually . . .'

'No,' confirmed Lizzie, relieved that she was able to say that in all honesty.

'But there were . . . I mean, you must have had some sort of . . .'

'Some kissing, that's all,' Lizzie told her gravely.

'Oh. Oh, I see,' gulped June, looking wounded. 'Not quite nothing then?'

'It was nothing compared to what you and Bobby have,' said Lizzie. 'And it's over now.'

'But you're together all day.'

'Nothing happens, June, and nothing will. Not ever again,' she said with emphasis. 'Whatever we imagined was there between us has gone for good. It's you Bobby loves.'

'You're not just saying that to make me feel better?'

'What would be the point?' asked Lizzie firmly. 'If there was anything going on between Bobby and me, I would be trying to get you to accept it so that we could make our life together, wouldn't I? I wouldn't be denying it.'

'I suppose not,' admitted June without much confidence.

'It makes sense, June, if you really think about it.'

'Even so, I don't want to be wondering what the two of you

are getting up to the whole time you're together.'

'You've nothing to worry about, I promise you,' said Lizzie with feeling.

'Really?'

'Yes, *really*. I'm not saying there isn't something very special between myself and Bobby, because there is. You've always known that and you've been able to cope with it. But he and I are meant to be friends not lovers.'

'So what made it change into something else all of a sudden?' asked June.

'I'm not sure,' said Lizzie truthfully. 'I think it was probably a combination of things. Both of us being so bucked over the success of the business, the fact that I'd been widowed and all the emotional turmoil that entails. Our priorities got out of focus for a while.'

'And you've definitely reverted to just being friends now?' said June, needing further reassurance.

'That's right.'

Lizzie saw no purpose in telling her the whole truth, that her passion for Bobby had not died when they had made that momentous decision. Since it was to remain ungratified there was no point in hurting her unnecessarily.

'Oh, Lizzie, I've had a terrible time worrying about it,' said June. 'I didn't want to believe Luke but . . .'

'I can guess what you must have been going through,' said Lizzie with genuine sympathy. 'But it's over now. Do you think you can live with something that was nothing in comparison to the strength of your marriage?'

'It'll take more than a near miss to break me and Bobby up.'

279

'Yes, I really think it would too,' said Lizzie, feeling horribly lonely. 'You have something worth hanging on to.'

'I wonder why Luke was so keen to make mischief?'

'No idea, but I reckon he's done us a favour, don't you? I think it's better for us all to have it out in the open.'

'Definitely,' said June, her round face looking brighter as the strain of the last few weeks fell away. 'Have you time for a cuppa before you go back to work?'

'I need one after all that talking,' said Lizzie, smiling.

'Good. I'll go and put the kettle on then.'

Lizzie felt warm with relief as her friend left the room. She was really puzzled, though, as to why Luke would want to stir up trouble for them all. But she decided not to confront him with it. The least said about it the better!

Carter's Silks continued to thrive over the next couple of years, despite the continuing threat of foreign competition as French woven silks were still allowed into Britain duty free. Lizzie's success did not make her complacent, though. Well aware that a full order book could quickly become an empty one, she constantly strived to get the firm noticed.

Not content with producing fabric of the highest quality for their regular customers such as King's Rainwear and a host of other garment manufacturers, she also developed her talent for design, exhibiting patterned silks at trade fairs and art exhibitions.

In 1925 her design for evening wear material, silver flowers on a black background, won her a gold medal at an international exhibition in London. This was a tremendous boost for business as well as a personal triumph because her success received wide coverage in the trade press as well as the local paper.

The family were all terribly proud of her. The children were thrilled to see their mother in the paper and Bobby and June threw a party to celebrate the occasion. It turned out to be a doubly festive occasion as it happened because it coincided with good news for everybody in the British silk trade as the government imposed duty on imports of foreign woven silks at last.

Even Polly offered her congratulations to Lizzie.

'I don't hold with women in business, as you very well know,' she sniffed. 'And I am still dead against the way you got started. But you're making a damned good job of it, I'll say that much for you, and I take my hat off to you.'

This meant more to Lizzie than Polly would ever know.

On the advice of her accountant, who thought it a false economy for Lizzie to continue to pay rent on her living accommodation, she took out a mortgage on a house, a smart property in a quiet street in South Kensington.

In the summer of that year, Lizzie welcomed Jed into the firm after he left school and became apprenticed to the trade. He was not an easy adolescent because he had inherited his grandmother's propensity to strong views and his father's fiery temper. But he was a keen and interested worker for all that, and learned well under his Uncle Bobby's supervision.

By the time Lizzie had been in business for five years, the fund she had been building to repay her debt had reached the required amount. She decided to deal with the matter at the next Silk Manufacturers' Federation meeting.

Lizzie had joined the Federation as soon as the business began

281

to do well enough to justify spending money on membership fees because it was a very useful organisation to belong to in that it kept the members in touch with the trade in general. It had even been active in lobbying the government over import duties.

Having a family to look after as well as a business, however, she didn't manage to get to all of the meetings which were always held on a weekday evening at a Kensington hotel. She supported them as often as she possibly could, albeit that she felt completely incongruous in that she was always the only female there. When she did attend, she sometimes saw Philip Verne and they exchanged brief and formal pleasantries. The men always gathered in the bar after the meeting, at which point Lizzie made a diplomatic exit.

This particular November evening, she changed her plans.

'Might I have a word, Mr Verne?' she asked, waiting at the door of the assembly room as he emerged with a group of his colleagues.

'Yes, of course,' he said rather absently, and she noticed how haggard he looked. He had lost a lot of weight since she'd last seen him.

'Shall we sit down somewhere?' she suggested, as he stood aside from his colleagues who were drifting towards the bar.

'Can I buy you a drink?'

'Well . . . if it won't cause too much of a stir with the others,' she said with a grin. 'I've already put their backs up, invading male territory by attending the meetings. But daring to go into the bar afterwards! Well, that's nothing short of anarchy.'

'Don't worry, I'll see to it that they don't get violent,' he said, responding to her lighthearted mood.

They found a table in the corner of the smoky bar which had a musty smell about it and was dismally appointed with tarnished, gilt-edged mirrors, heavy mahogany tables and weighty chairs upholstered in muddy brown leather.

'So what's on your mind?' asked Philip, setting the drinks down on the table, a sherry for her, a whisky for him.

She gave him a half smile then took an envelope from her handbag and handed it to him.

Puzzled, he opened it. 'Well, well,' he said, taking out a cheque and looking at it. 'So you're out of debt then?'

'Yes.'

'Thank you.'

'It's I who should be thanking you,' she said. 'You made it all possible.'

'I only gave you the start, you did the rest,' he told her.

'Well, anyway,' she said, unexpectedly pleased that he had acknowledged her achievement. 'It's paid now.'

They chatted about the trade in general as they finished their drinks. She found him to be such pleasant company that they had had another couple of drinks and a lot more conversation before she even thought about the time.

'Good Lord, I didn't realise it was so late,' Lizzie exclaimed after a while. 'It's time I was making a move.'

'So soon?' he said, sounding genuinely disappointed.

'Yes, I must get back to the brood.'

'Parental responsibilities, eh?'

'Mmm. I've left my eldest in charge.'

'How old is he now?' Philip enquired in conversational manner.

'Fourteen, going on fifteen.'

'The same age as my son, Toby.'

'Just the one, you have, isn't it?'

He nodded.

'Has he left school and gone into the business with you?'

'No. He's still away at boarding school at the moment,' Philip explained, unintentionally reminding her of the class division.

'Oh, I see.'

'But he'll come into the firm eventually,' he said. 'He's very interested in design so he might do a course at art school at some point during his training.'

'Lucky boy. I enjoy design work myself and often wish I'd had some artistic training,' Lizzie told him.

'I've heard that evening classes are very good,' he suggested. 'If you're really keen.'

'No. My time is all taken up with the business and the family,' she told him. 'I'll leave it to my daughter to get formal art training when the time comes. She seems to be very keen on that sort of thing.'

'Lack of training doesn't seem to have hampered you, anyway,' he said, narrowing his eyes at a memory. 'Didn't I read something about you winning a medal for your design recently?'

'Yes, that's right.'

'Congratulations,' he said warmly. 'Albeit belatedly.'

'Thank you. It was a terrific thrill.' Lizzie looked at her watch again. 'I really must go.'

'Can I give you a lift home?' he offered.

'That would be a great help, thank you.'

She settled into the soft leather of his smart Austin Saloon, shivering against the cold, misty vapour that seemed to seep into everything.

'This beats waiting for a bus any day,' Lizzie remarked cheerfully.

'Especially in this weather.'

'Yes, it looks like it might be a real peasouper later on.'

'Indeed,' he said, keeping his eyes on the road which was crowded with traffic and shrouded with greyish, yellow mist.

'Your wife won't mind you being a bit late home, will she?' Lizzie ventured.

'Er . . .'

'She expects you to stay on for a few drinks after the meeting, I suppose?'

'Um . . . well . . . yes, I suppose she might do,' he said sharply.

It was obvious she'd touched on a delicate subject. Although she could only see him in profile she perceived his change of mood. He seemed to age before her eyes. His whole face seemed to harden and his shoulders became rigid.

'I'm so sorry,' she told him. 'I didn't mean to pry. I was only trying to be polite by making conversation.'

'No offence taken.'

'Good.'

'Er . . . my wife is away at the moment actually,' he said.

'Oh, a holiday at this time of year,' said Lizzie in an effort to lighten the atmosphere that had become uncomfortably tense. 'How lovely. I wouldn't mind one of those myself . . . even in this weather. Still, I expect Mrs Verne will have taken a trip on a liner to somewhere warmer.'

'No, nothing like that,' he said, and his manner was so abrasive she was embarrassed.

'Oh.'

'My wife is away convalescing,' he snapped because he couldn't bear to tell her the truth. 'She hasn't been well.'

'Oh dear, I'm so sorry. I hope she gets well soon.'

'She will,' he lied. 'It's simply a question of time.'

His grip on the steering wheel tightened as he recalled that terrible night two years ago when he'd woken in the night to find Emily lying in a pool of blood in the bathroom, having cut her wrists with his razor blade. All self-delusion had ended at that moment. The severity of her condition could no longer be ignored. He'd had to have her hospitalised for her own safety.

Alan Marchant had arranged for her to go into the clinic in Clapham. It was very comfortable, the best money could buy – unlike the public asylums of which one heard such gruesome tales. As it wasn't too far away he was able to visit her regularly. She even came home occasionally at weekends.

This didn't lessen his compunction about having her institutionalised. To add to his guilt was the fact that he dreaded having her home. It wasn't so much the strain of having to cope with the demands of her erratic behaviour or the fear that she might injure herself, as punishing as those things were. But the sheer agony of watching someone he loved reduced to an imbecile, albeit intermittently, was hard to bear.

His passenger's voice recalled him to the present.

'You turn right at the end of this road, Mr Verne, then Berry Gardens is first on the left . . . we're number fifteen.'

'You've moved since I last visited you in Bessle Street.'

'Oh, yes. In fact this is our second move since then,' she explained. 'We have our own front door now, thank goodness.'

They drew up outside her house in a neat row of stuccoed villas in a tidy street well-served with gas lamps, where shiny black railings and white-painted walls edged the tiny front gardens in which geraniums and marigolds flourished in summer.

'If there's anything I can do to help at any time,' she heard herself say, 'do let me know . . . even if you just need someone to talk to.'

At that precise moment he would have given anything to have bared his soul to her. It had occurred to him earlier that during the pleasant interlude in the bar with her, he'd felt relaxed for the first time in ages.

'I might take you up on that one of these days,' he replied lightly, knowing that he would do no such thing. She'd had quite enough problems of her own, she certainly didn't need to take someone else's on board.

'Any time at all. You know where to find me.'

'Oh, and by the way,' he said, as she went to get out of the car.

'Yes.'

'The name's Philip.'

'And I'm Lizzie,' she said warmly. 'Goodnight, Philip.'

'Goodnight, Lizzie.'

He's a really nice bloke when you get talking to him, she thought as she walked up to her front door. He's so sad though, so terribly forlorn. Behind the polite formalities, that man is going through hell.

Chapter Fifteen

'Cor!' said Jamie Carter, deeply impressed by his cousin Jed who had just lit a cigarette with great panache, cupping it in his hands against the blustery March winds which were gusting across the riverside this Saturday afternoon. 'I fancy having a go at that.'

'Me too,' said Keith who was a mere echo of his more dominant twin.

Jed put the packet of Goldflake back into his pocket and exhaled the smoke with an air of worldliness. Now fifteen and a wage earner, he saw himself as a sort of elder statesman to the younger Carter children, all of whom had entered their teens.

'Gonna let us all have a go, then?' suggested his brother Bruce, aiming a stone at the water and making it bounce across the surface.

'You're all too young,' announced Jed with aplomb, enjoying his seniority. A year's age difference was barely noticeable when you were all still in short pants, but once you left school and went out to work you were in a different league. He was only hanging around with the kids this afternoon because he had nothing better to do until he was old enough to pursue proper adult activities on a Saturday, like going to the pub at dinner-time and dance halls to meet girls at night. His spare time was a real drag at the moment because he finished work at midday on a Saturday which left him with the whole of the rest of the day to fill with boring juvenile pastimes like this.

'I'll tell Mum you've been smoking if you don't give us all one,' threatened Eva.

'Go ahead and tell her, I don't care,' said the rebellious Jed. 'She can't stop me . . . I'm not a kid.'

'You weren't half in trouble with her when she found out you'd been smoking that other time,' his sister reminded him.

'That was when I was still at school,' he said with casual contempt, his wild red hair blowing in the wind. 'She can't tell me what to do now. I paid for the fags with my own money. Anyway I couldn't care less what *she* says.'

Eva realised that she had no leverage in that direction because Jed was always quarrelling with their mother. 'Just give us a puff then?'

'I'm definitely not giving *you* one,' he declared. 'Girls aren't supposed to smoke . . . it makes them common.'

'Lots of women do it,' said Eva determinedly. 'I've seen them when I've been to the picture palace with Mum.'

'Only the tarty ones,' he stated categorically. 'Everyone knows smoking is for men. Dad used to smoke but I bet you've never seen Mum doing it, have you?'

She couldn't argue with that; neither did she really want to smoke a cigarette, she was merely trying to be equal with the others.

'I'm not too young,' said Bruce. 'I'll be leavin' school myself soon.'

Yes, unfortunately, thought Jed, who feared a challenge to his own exalted status when his brother joined the workers. 'Buy your own fags then,' he suggested with authority. 'Out of the pocket money Mum gives you.'

'Yeah, I will,' said Bruce without any real intention because his taste buds still lacked adult refinement and he would rather spend his money on gobstoppers than Goldflake.

The five of them mooched along the Hammersmith waterfront, passing Carter's Silk Factory then crossing the wooden footbridge over the creek and continuing upriver, the twins dribbling a stone with their feet, Bruce hurling pebbles across the surface of the water between passing boats and barges. He was careful to avoid the river wildlife, much to his brother's scorn for Jed thought it was great fun to aim for the swans and ducks and even the seagulls that swooped and dived in search of food. The youngsters had come to the riverside just to pass an hour or so until tea-time, street games having lost their appeal with the onset of adolescence.

As everyone seemed to have lost interest in his new habit, Jed decided to regain their attention by giving the boys a cigarette between them. The trio huddled together against the wall of a bakery and each took a drag.

'I don't know what you see in it,' gasped Bruce, his head spinning.

'I think it feels quite nice,' said Jamie, but his face had an eau-de-nil tinge.

'Yeah . . . me an' all,' declared his pale-faced brother.

'Anyway, Keith and me will have to smoke when we leave school,' announced Jamie gravely.

'Why?' asked Jed.

'Because we're going on the stage, o' course, and a lot of smokin' and drinkin' goes on in show business,' he explained seriously. 'They do it to soothe their nerves, you know. Performing can be very nerve wrackin'.'

'They get stage fright,' was Keith's contribution to this enlightening discourse.

'Show business, my Aunt Fanny!' jeered Jed. 'You've about as much chance as I have of becoming a Member of Parliament.'

'Don't be so mean, Jed,' admonished his sister hotly. 'The twins are really comical . . . they're gonna be famous one day.'

'I agree with you, Eva,' pronounced Bruce heartily.

'You would,' snorted Jed.

'What's your stage name gonna be, eh, boys?' asked Bruce, ignoring his brother's jibe.

'Dunno. The Carter Brothers, probably,' said Jamie.

'That's a bit ordinary, isn't it?' opined Bruce who thought his cousins were an absolute scream. 'Comedy acts usually call themselves something and something . . . like Naughton and Gold or Flanagan and Allen.'

'We've plenty of time to work something out,' said Jamie.

'No hurry,' agreed Keith.

They came to a small jetty on a quiet stretch of the river. Bruce bounded to the end of it and turned to face the others, pretending it was a stage. 'And now, ladies and gentlemen,' he said in a manner used by masters of ceremonies at the music halls, 'the hilarious, the multifarious, the astronomically talented, Carter Brothers!' He spread his arms and moved away to leave room for the twins who ran forward with gusto.

'Da-da-da-le-da-da-da-le-da,' was their introduction music

and they went straight into a soft shoe shuffle which came to a grand finale with each of them holding their caps as though they were straw hats.

There then followed a quick fire exchange of ancient gags about such ludicrous improbabilities as chickens going to psychiatrists because they were 'eggs-centric' and the awful old chestnut about the nasally challenged dog. It all got a bit wild and silly after that with some lavatorial jokes and the twins adding acrobatics to their act in the form of wobbly cartwheels and ending in a heap on the jetty, shrieking with laughter and kicking their legs in the air.

'And now, ladies and gentlemen,' announced Bruce, moving back on to the stage to bring some order to events, far too caught up in the hilarity to notice how dangerously close he had strayed to the edge, 'we come to our last spot of the show . . . Carter and Carter . . . that's it boys . . . that's what you should call yourselves . . . Carter and Carter will end with a song . . . er . . . oops!'

There was an almighty splash as he entered the water, bringing instant sobriety to the proceedings. Eva flew into an immediate panic about her beloved Bruce until Jed reminded her that he could swim and the water wasn't too deep there anyway.

A few minutes later, Bruce waded out to the bank and climbed up, muddy water trickling down his face and dripping from his clothes.

'Ugh!' he said, throwing himself down on the grass. 'I must have swallowed a gallon of water in there.'

'That's the least of your worries,' Eva wisely pointed out. 'Mum's gonna do her nut when you arrive home like a drowned rat . . . especially as we're not supposed to play near the river.'

'Ooh, crumbs, yes,' he said, shivering as the sharp wind whipped through his wet clothes.

Naturally Lizzie wasn't pleased when the tribe arrived home escorting their drenched companion, full of excuses as to how he came to be that way.

'It wasn't his fault, Mum,' explained Eva who was closer than any of them to Bruce. 'He just sort of tripped. Must have been an uneven board on the jetty or something.'

'Yeah, he wasn't doing anything daring, Aunt Lizzie,' explained Jamie.

'Nothing daring at all,' echoed Keith.

'He was standing there one minute and in the water the next,' said Jed, united with his companions against authority. 'It could have happened to anyone.'

'Only if they were near the river,' blasted Lizzie, angry that they had been playing off limits. 'You've been told enough times not to muck about down there. You're lucky it wasn't a lot worse than a ducking. He could have drowned.'

'I can swim, don't forget, Mum,' reminded Bruce, shivering violently as, assisted by his mother, he divested himself of his outer clothes and let them drop into a slimy heap on the quarry-tiled kitchen floor.

'You could still have been carried off by a current,' roared Lizzie. 'Now get the rest of those filthy wet clothes off you and I'll heat some water so you can get into a hot bath – before you catch pneumonia.'

It was early afternoon nearly two weeks later and Carter's Silks had just received an important order from a specialist London dealer who supplied silk fabrics to the theatrical world. He had ordered fifty yards of crimson taffeta which was to be used for the chorus costumes of a European opera company.

'I told them we'd get some samples done quickly for them to have a look at before we actually go into production,' Lizzie said to Bobby with great excitement, having just heard the good news over the telephone. 'Just in case they want any modifications to the design.'

'Good idea. I'll get that organised right away.'

'Thanks. If we can dazzle them with our efficiency, who knows what it might lead to?'

'Not half.'

The telephone rang on her desk. It was the headmaster from the school with the news that Bruce wasn't very well.

'He has a bad headache and stomach pains,' the teacher informed her seriously. 'He seems quite feverish too.'

'I'll come and collect him straight away,' she told him anxiously, all thoughts of the new order forgotten.

'I think that's best. It's probably just a chill but I think he'll be more comfortable at home.'

In the event, Bobby collected Bruce from school in the van while Lizzie hurried home to put a hot water bottle in the bed ready for him. Spring might well be on the way, but these March winds could be lethal.

'It's just a cold or a touch of 'flu, I expect,' said Bobby reassuringly after Lizzie had settled her son into bed.

'I'm calling the doctor in just to be on the safe side, though,' she told him. 'The best thing about being better off is that I can afford medical advice if I need it.'

'Do you want me to wait till he's been?'

'No, you go back to the factory and hold the fort.'

The doctor confirmed their diagnosis. 'Just a touch of 'flu. Keep him in bed with plenty of fluids and aspirin.'

'I thought that's what it was,' Lizzie said with relief. 'He's been a bit listless for a few days now I come to think of it, and he's had a couple of nose bleeds too so I guessed he must be sickening for something.'

The next morning, however, after a night of high fever and delirium, alarmingly significant symptoms had appeared in the patient. Small pink spots had erupted on his abdomen, chest and back as well as bluish blotches. He also had diarrhoea. The doctor was called speedily and confirmed Lizzie's worst suspicions.

'It's beginning to look like typhoid fever,' he muttered worriedly. 'Hasn't been swimming in the canal, has he?'

'Not that I know of,' she told him. 'Even my daredevil Bruce would draw the line at that in this weather.'

'You know what boys are like for devilment,' he said.

'The river!' she said, remembering. 'He fell in the Thames a couple of weeks ago . . . he must have swallowed some of the water.'

'Yes, that might be it,' said the doctor. 'He'll have to go to the infirmary.'

'Will he come through it, doctor?' she asked, pale with terror.

'Well, he'll be in the best place,' he told her non-committally. 'They'll do everything they possibly can.'

Lizzie, with Jed and Eva who had been kept home from school because of possible infection to other children, watched

Bruce carried out to the ambulance on a stretcher, muttering something about the amazingly funny Carter and Carter.

'That's what he thinks the twins should have as a stage name,' explained Eva tearfully to her mother.

The doctor wouldn't let Lizzie go in the ambulance with Bruce, or even kiss him goodbye because of the risk of infection. Numbly she went back into the house to carry out his instructions and sterilise Bruce's bed linen and towels and scrub everything he had touched with disinfectant.

She never saw him alive again. In the early hours of the following morning two policemen came bearing terrible news.

For Lizzie every day was an agonising expanse of time to be endured until she could crawl into bed at night and escape from her grief in sleep. Two things kept her sane, the children and the factory, both of which needed her attention regardless of her own feelings. All the Carter children were devastated by Bruce's death. The twins' misery was exacerbated by the idea that they were somehow to blame for playing on the jetty.

She assured them that Bruce's fatal soaking was an accident and not their fault. If blame was to be apportioned, it would be to herself for not keeping her offspring on a tighter rein, though common sense told her this was unrealistic. Youngsters on the brink of adulthood needed a certain amount of freedom to prepare them for the future.

But for all her sensible reasoning, her basic instinct was to scream and stamp her feet in fury at the unfairness of a young life taken so cruelly. The pain was deeper than anything that had gone before – worse than her grief for her parents or Stan. Losing a child was gut-crunching, heart-rending hell.

Sadness hung over the entire family in a dark, debilitating cloud. Everyone was so wracked with grief they could barely carry on. June turned to Bobby for comfort, Polly turned to Will, Eva and Jed were united by their youth. All of them, with the exception of Luke, tried to comfort Lizzie. All failed, though she pretended otherwise to make them feel better.

For the first time, she had a real insight into what it must have been like for Polly when she had lost Stan, and why she'd needed to blame Philip Verne for his death. When Roy had died from an unknown German's bullet there had been no visible recipient for her bitter feelings. In Philip Verne she'd had an easy target, an identifiable human being towards whom she could pour out all her anguish.

In really bad moments Lizzie felt compelled to do the same for Bruce. She wanted to scream 'Murderer' to the Thames, to hit out at her other children for letting their brother fall into the river, to blame the doctors for not saving him. But when reason returned she knew she must not let such irrational feelings overcome her as Polly had done.

Their sadness could have brought Lizzie and Polly together. But this didn't happen, even though they were both bleeding from the same wound. Physically they reached out to one another, spent a lot of time together drowning themselves in tea and sympathy, their differences put to one side. But emotionally they remained distanced. Maybe, Lizzie thought, because their own personal sense of loss was too all-consuming at the moment to be shared with anyone.

They were united in their gratitude to the local people for their kindness, though. People called to see Lizzie in their droves. Sympathy letters arrived from all over the manor, to the factory and the house. Even strangers sent their condolences.

Lizzie was touched to receive a letter of sympathy from Meg Verne. But the letter that moved her in particular was from Philip. It contained a standard message of condolence but there was an extra sensitivity about it somehow. 'You'll be deep in the bosom of your family at the moment so I won't intrude. But if there's anything I can do or if you ever fancy a chat with someone outside the family circle, you know where to find me.'

She didn't know him well, but well enough to realise that it was typical of him not to impose himself at a time like this but to leave her with an open invitation. His mother was rather less hesitant, however, and visited Lizzie at home, without prior warning, one Saturday afternoon in the early summer.

Unfortunately, Polly was already ensconced in one of Lizzie's cretonne-covered armchairs in her sitting room, a light and elegant place with soft peach walls and frivolous curtains patterned with orange and yellow flowers blooming among cool green leaves.

'I haven't been to see you before,' explained Meg, having been introduced to the scowling Polly, 'because I guessed you'd be inundated with visitors. I thought you might be glad to see a friend now . . . when things have probably calmed down a little.'

'It's very kind of you to call,' said Lizzie, having offered her guest a seat and poured her a cup of tea.

'Such a dreadful thing to happen,' sighed Meg, looking with compassion from Lizzie to Polly. 'It must have knocked you both sideways.'

'Yes,' said Lizzie.

'Naturally,' put in Polly sourly.

'I can imagine,' said Meg with a sad shake of the head. 'Are you beginning to get over the shock now that some time has passed?'

'What a ridiculous question,' said Polly viciously. 'Of course we're not getting over it.'

'Yes, I suppose it's still too soon,' replied Meg, brushing aside Polly's truculence. 'You must be absolutely devastated.' She shook her head again. 'Fourteen years old. There's no rhyme or reason to it, is there?'

'They say there's a reason for everything, don't they?' said Lizzie. 'But I'm blowed if I can see it – not at the moment anyway.'

Polly rose abruptly. 'Well, I'll be off now, Lizzie,' she said huffily. 'Seeing as you've got company.'

'Don't leave on my account,' intervened Meg speedily. 'I only popped in to say hello . . . the last thing I want to do is impose.'

'Why come round here in the first place then?' demanded Polly rudely, her cheeks brightly suffused.

Lizzie's face was burning too as she glared at Polly. 'Really!'

'Don't worry, Lizzie,' Meg said diplomatically. 'I only dropped by to let you know that I'm thinking about you.' She looked at Polly. 'Both of you, that is. My grandson is fifteen, I can imagine how dreadful you must feel.'

''Course you can't imagine how we feel,' said Polly with blistering hostility. 'How the devil can you if it hasn't happened to you?'

'You're quite right, of course,' said Meg, her breeding manifest in the charming way she was handling this contretemps. 'I can't speak from experience . . . at least the son I lost in the war lived to be an adult. Fortunately for us all, sympathy doesn't require practical experience, does it?'

'Thankfully, no,' said Lizzie.

Meg stood up. 'Anyway, the last thing I want to do is upset anyone. Lord knows you've enough on your plate.' She turned to Polly and put a restraining hand on her arm. 'You stay with Lizzie, Mrs Carter dear. I shall be the one to leave.'

'It's time I was going anyway,' growled Polly, stomping towards the door.

'Please don't go,' began Meg.

'Don't bother to come to the front door, Lizzie,' interrupted Polly gruffly as Lizzie stood up. 'I can see myself out.'

She was too angry to argue or even speak. She just stood where she was until she heard the front door close.

'Well, what can I say but sorry?' she said with a heavy sigh. 'I'm afraid she's taken Bruce's death really hard.'

'Yes, I can see that . . . the poor woman.'

'It's a peculiar thing,' confided Lizzie, 'but for some reason we don't seem able to help each other.'

'You're too emotionally tied, I expect,' suggested Meg.

'Perhaps.'

'A constant reminder to each other of what's happened.'

'Yes. You'd think trouble would bring people together, wouldn't you?'

'It very often does but everyone reacts differently to these things.'

Lizzie sat down in a big, squashy armchair that matched

the curtains. Meg perched on the edge of the sofa.

'I always feel as though I'm failing Polly, somehow, even over Bruce's death,' confessed Lizzie.

'In what way?'

'Because I can't be the sort of woman she wants me to be, even at a time like this,' Lizzie explained. 'If she had her way I'd close the factory and stay home all day moping.'

'Really?'

'Yes. She was horrified when I went back to work so soon after Bruce's funeral. But I had to, Meg. For one thing, I couldn't leave everything to Stan's brother, Bobby.'

'And the other reason?' Meg prompted curiously.

'Work is an escape from the misery I feel inside,' confessed Lizzie. 'It isn't that the pain goes away at the factory but it does take my mind off it for a while and eases the knots in my stomach.'

'I was the same when Neville died,' admitted Meg. 'I threw myself into my voluntary work with a vengeance.'

'We all cope with grief in our own way but I can't get Polly to understand that,' said Lizzie. 'She thinks I'm unnatural because I don't want to sit about the house all day thinking about Bruce and feeling sorry for myself. I've told her, Bruce is with me wherever I am.'

'You've broken away from the traditional female role as well, that's probably what she can't come to terms with.'

'Yes,' sighed Lizzie. 'But I wish she and I could become close again because I miss her for all that she's infuriating.'

'Yes, I can tell she means a lot to you.'

They chatted generally until Eva arrived home from a wander around the shops with her girlfriends. She was a slim, willowy girl with the same fair colouring as her mother. Lizzie had been encouraging her to go out with her friends these last few weeks as a break from the atmosphere at home.

'My daughter is just beginning to take an interest in ladies' dress shops,' explained Lizzie after making the introductions. 'She's keeping an eye on the situation for the future.'

'Young women's fashions are such fun these days, aren't they?' smiled Meg who was dressed in smart classic style in a navy and white striped dress and blazer. 'I only wish they'd been as interesting when I was a girl.'

'You don't disapprove then?' said Eva in surprise.

'Heavens, no. Why on earth would I do that?'

'Well, with respect, older people usually do.'

Her grandmother does, that was what she was trying to say, Lizzie guessed. Polly considered the new flat-chested, shorter length dresses that were so popular with younger women to be disgusting, yet she and Meg were of the same generation.

'Not me, dear.'

'I hope the Charleston is still in when I'm old enough to go out dancing,' said Eva.

She was obviously feeling comfortable in Meg's company, Lizzie noticed. It was good to see her smiling again, for she'd been terribly upset by her brother's death.

'If it isn't, there'll probably be something even more exciting,' smiled Meg.

The sound of someone coming in the back door heralded the arrival of Jed, home from an out-of-season football match. Warily Lizzie introduced him to Meg whereupon he proceeded to embarrass them all.

'What are you doing here?' he demanded rudely, his colour rising.

'I came to see your mother,' she replied calmly, though a strawberry flush on her neck and face betrayed her discomfort.

'We don't want anyone with the name of Verne in this house!'

'Jed,' rebuked Lizzie furiously. 'Apologise to Mrs Verne at once.'

'No bloody fear,' he said, throwing his mother an insolent look. 'Why should I?'

'Because I said so . . . and that's enough of that sort of language.'

'Look, Lizzie dear, I'll just slip away,' ventured Meg anxiously. She looked at Jed. 'I'm sorry you feel so strongly about my family, young man, especially as your mother and I get along so well.'

'We don't want your sort coming round here with your rotten do-gooding,' he exclaimed, making Lizzie want to die. 'Stick to your own kind, will you? We don't want any relatives of murderers in this house.'

'That's quite enough, Jed,' shouted Lizzie. 'Apologise this minute!'

'Never,' he said, marching from the room and thundering upstairs.

Lizzie was mortified and poor Eva's cheeks were flaming.

'I can't apologise enough,' said Lizzie as she showed the visitor to the door.

'Don't worry.'

'But it was so insulting . . . especially as you came here in the name of friendship,' said Lizzie. 'First my mother-in-law,

304

now my son. You must think us Carters are completely uncivilised.'

'Of course I don't.'

'I feel terrible.'

'It wasn't your fault. Anyway I rather like young people with strong views,' said Meg. 'It's better than the lethargy that hits some of them at that age.'

'He didn't have to be so damned rude,' put in Lizzie.

'Forget it.'

'How can I? He's my son ... my responsibility. His behaviour is a reflection of the way I brought him up.'

'He is also Polly Carter's grandson,' said Meg shrewdly.

There wasn't an answer to that so Lizzie just said, 'Thanks for coming, your visit was much appreciated ... by me, anyway.'

'A pleasure.' She gave a wicked grin. 'I won't promise to come again, though.'

Lizzie managed a smile. 'I don't blame you either but I really hope we can still be friends.'

'I'd be very disappointed if we couldn't,' said Meg.

Lizzie stormed straight upstairs to her son's bedroom where he was lying on the bed reading a comic.

'Don't you *dare* behave like that to a friend of mine *ever again*,' she said through clenched teeth, glaring down at him. 'And get up when I'm speaking to you.'

He got to his feet in a slow, defiant manner. 'How can you call a Verne a friend?' he asked lazily.

'Easily,' she told him acidly. 'By judging her for herself ... not by the surname she happens to have.'

His reply was a shrug of the shoulders and a sigh like a gale force wind.

'She's a very nice woman and I like her a lot.'

'Oh, well, if you're gonna have friends like that . . .'

'I choose my own friends. I don't need you to vet them.'

'Just don't expect me to be civil to people like her.'

'I not only expect you to be civil, I *demand* it,' Lizzie informed him crisply. 'And since you live under my roof you don't have a great deal of choice, do you?'

'The Vernes are scum,' he said, looking at her venomously.

Almost of its own volition, her hand went up and she slapped his cheek. 'That's what you've driven me to with your wretched bigotry,' she told him shakily.

He stared at her in stunned silence, shocked by her action. 'I just don't know how you can bear to have anything to do with anyone from that family, that's all,' he said at last in a subdued tone.

'And I don't know how any son of mine can be so damned prejudiced,' she retorted hotly. 'God knows I've always tried to teach you to live and let live.'

Unfortunately, it was a poor choice of words.

'Philip Verne didn't let Dad live, did he?' he was quick to point out.

Sighing deeply, she begged him from the bottom of her heart, 'Oh, Jed, please don't say such things. I need support from you at the moment . . . not aggravation.'

'Huh! I can't say that I've noticed it.'

'Don't let the past come between us at a time like this, when we're all sick with grief for Bruce,' she went on. 'Think badly of the Vernes if you really must but don't let me have to feel ashamed of you like I did just now. You're worth more than that, son.'

He looked achingly vulnerable, standing there, lanky and defiant. 'All right. I'm sorry I was so rude,' he mumbled sheepishly. 'I'll try not to show you up again. Just don't ask me to like the Vernes, that's all.'

'I wouldn't do that.'

'That's good because I never could,' he said, his tone hardening again.

She could feel a rift between them as palpable as the one that existed between herself and Polly. All she had to do was join them in their views about the Vernes and the barrier would disappear. But she couldn't do that because it would be going against everything she believed in just to win back their favour. This conflict was more than just a difference of opinion about the Vernes . . . it was about the right of an individual to be a person as well as a family member. It hurt terribly though, this ghastly division between herself and two people she loved so dearly.

'It'll all end in tears, you mark my words,' predicted Polly to Will and Luke over high tea that same evening.

'What will?' asked her husband, concentrating on removing a fine bone from a piece of kipper before popping it into his mouth.

'Lizzie moving out of her class, o' course,' she explained.

'Oh, that,' he said casually.

'Yes, *that*,' she said emphatically. 'It's downright ridiculous. Gawd knows what she thinks she'll gain from it.'

'What has Lizzie actually done?' asked Will evenly.

'She's only got herself on friendly terms with that Verne woman,' she explained affrontedly. 'On Christian name terms, would you believe? The damned woman came to visit her while I was there!'

'Well, I suppose Lizzie looks on those sort of people as equals now,' said Will.

'She may well, but they won't,' exclaimed Polly.

'They might.'

'Never in a million years.'

'She's in business same as them,' Will insisted because he'd always had a soft spot for Lizzie who'd been a sweet and gentle presence among the rough and tumble male exuberance when she and the boys had all been growing up.

'Don't be daft, Will. I mean, she's hardly in the same league as the Vernes, is she?' Polly pointed out.

'She has a good business,' he said. 'And she's comfortably off now.'

'There's more to class than that,' Polly informed him. 'It's all a question of breeding. Those sort of people have different values to ours.'

'Lizzie can be very charming, you know. She has a real way with her,' said Will. 'That's probably why she's attracted this Verne woman.'

'Delusions of grandeur, I believe they call it,' snorted Polly. 'If she had any sense of family loyalty at all she'd have nothing to do with those Vernes.'

'Could be that you're making too much of it, love?' remarked Will. 'You know as well as I do that people you hardly know come visitin' at a time of bereavement. Mrs Verne probably just popped by to pay her respects.'

'That's exactly what she did do,' confirmed Polly. 'But there's more to it than that. Lizzie has encouraged a friendship with her. They're as thick as thieves.'

'Get away.'

'Phew! You couldn't see me for dust I was out of there so fast,' she said. 'I couldn't bear to listen to 'em.'

'I don't know why you let Lizzie get to you so much, Ma,' put in Luke, adding a point he had made previously, 'I mean it isn't even as if she's family, is it?'

Polly looked at him in disgust, almost as though he'd cast some sort of aspersion on her marital status. 'Of course she's family,' she stated categorically.

'No, she isn't . . . not now that Stan's dead. She's not even an in-law legally.'

His mother gave him a hard look. 'Lizzie was a part of this family long before she married Stan,' she reminded him gravely.

'No, she wasn't, she was just a neighbour's kid,' he insisted.

'There's more to family ties than just blood.'

'I think your mother is talking about an emotional bond,' suggested Will.

'Lizzie has been a daughter to me since she was eight years old.'

'I've always thought she was a bit flighty myself,' interrupted Luke.

'Don't you *dare* say such a thing about her! Lizzie's a fine woman and I won't have a word said against her,' said Polly vehemently, her cheeks flaming.

'But you've just been . . .'

'Never mind what I've been saying,' said his mother

forcefully. 'That doesn't give you the right to criticise her behind her back.'

'But you've . . .'

'Yes, I know I have, but I won't have anyone else doing it.'

'I don't understand you,' said Luke. 'Why, for God's sake?'

'Because she's still my daughter in here,' she said, pointing to her heart. 'No matter what she does to hurt me or what I say about her, I will defend her to the ends of the earth before other people.'

'That doesn't make sense.'

'Matters concerning the emotions rarely do, son,' she told him with a depth of understanding unusual for her.

'It's all beyond me,' he said, turning his attention back to his food.

Polly was still smarting from the altercation with Lizzie and that dreadful Verne woman this afternoon. Something else had been nagging at the back of her mind lately too – something she found painful to think about. It was her failure to reach Lizzie, to comfort her in her grief. She'd tried as hard as she knew how but somehow it hadn't happened. They were still as far apart as ever. If only Lizzie would stop associating with those damned Vernes and be a true Carter again, everything else would fall into place.

But although a woman of limited perception, even Polly could recognise the flimsiness of that theory. Lizzie had altered too much for things ever to be as they once had been between them. Maybe though they could have a new relationship – be more like friends then relatives, she thought with a flash of hope. But despair soon followed because her vision was obscured by her inability to love anyone without wanting to own them.

Chapter Sixteen

When Bobby emerged from the conference room after a Federation meeting, one December evening, he found Philip Verne waiting for him in the reception area of the hotel.

'Fancy a quick one in the pub round the corner?' Philip invited, nodding towards the crowded hotel bar. 'We'll never get served in there.'

'Sounds like a good idea to me, mate,' said the amiable Bobby.

He'd got to know Philip quite well through the Federation meetings, which he'd been attending since Bruce's death in place of Lizzie whose overly zealous approach to her work as a means of solace left her too exhausted to go out anywhere of an evening. Although complete opposites the two men enjoyed each other's company and usually concluded the evening with a companionable drink.

To happily married Bobby it was a pleasant but unimportant interlude; to Philip it was a vital respite from the lonely existence he endured as the husband of a schizophrenic.

They walked round the corner to The Coach and Horses, and went into the saloon bar where they were greeted with a rush of warm, smoky air and a clamour of conversation.

Background music was coming from a piano in the corner but could barely be heard above the raucous hilarity from the public bar.

'Sounds like they're having a high old time in there,' remarked Philip as the two men stood at the bar with their drinks, a whisky for Philip, a pint of mild and bitter for Bobby.

'A blue joke, I bet,' surmised Bobby with a grin. 'Sounds like someone's come up with a corker.'

'You reckon?'

'Yeah. The public bar's always rife with 'em.'

'Is it?'

'Never get many women in the public, a bloke can let himself go.'

'Yes.'

'My old man would think I was bein' a traitor to my class if he could see me now,' remarked Bobby. 'The only time he goes into the saloon bar of a pub is when he takes Ma out for a drink, and that isn't very often.'

'Really?'

'Dad much prefers the rough and ready atmosphere of the public bar when he's out without his missus.'

'How about you?' asked Philip who was a newcomer to the finer points of working-class pub protocol. 'Do you like the public bar?'

'Not half. I really enjoy a game o' darts or shove-ha'penny in the public with my mates,' replied Bobby lightly.

'If you'd rather go in there now . . .' began Philip.

'Oh, no, it isn't for the likes of a gent like yourself,' laughed Bobby.

'Don't you mean middle-class twit rather than gent?' suggested Philip shrewdly. 'Or is that one and the same thing to you tough public-bar types?'

'If I didn't know you it might be,' admitted Bobby with a rueful grin. Philip's lack of pretension made him a likeable companion. It hardly seemed possible to Bobby that he'd once seen him through the jaundiced eye of an employee. 'But, no, it's just a question of what you're used to, innit? I mean, your sort would probably go to a men's club for male company. We go down the local.'

'Yes. Generally speaking, I suppose that's how it is.'

They drifted on to the silk trade, exchanging views on the various subjects that had been raised at the meeting.

'Lizzie'll be pleased to hear that imports of raw silk for weaving have increased in the trade in Britain as a whole,' remarked Bobby.

Philip nodded. 'The duty the government introduced last year has certainly made a big difference.'

'Too true.'

'But tell me,' said Philip, looking at him over the rim of his glass, 'how is Lizzie now?'

Becoming thoughtful, Bobby drew deeply on his cigarette. 'She seems to be coping well enough, on the surface anyway. She's not the sort to mope about, not Lizzie.'

'She's never struck me that way.'

'God knows what she must be feeling like inside, though. I mean, how do you get over the loss of a child, eh?' He paused, closing his eyes and shaking his head as though in pain. 'I feel bad enough about it and young Bruce was only my nephew.'

'I'm sure you must do.'

315

'Poor Lizzie, though,' said Bobby. 'She's had it really rough one way and the other.'

'First her husband, now her son.'

'It goes back even further than that too,' said Bobby, and went on to tell him about Lizzie's early background.

'She seems to be a very strong character,' remarked Philip.

'A real diamond,' said Bobby with such emphasis Philip wondered if there was, or had been, anything romantic between them.

'I wrote to her when her son died but I haven't seen her,' said Philip.

'No?'

'No. It seemed such a private matter, I didn't want to intrude.'

'Well, it is private, o' course,' agreed Bobby, 'but the initial shock's over now. She might be pleased to see a colleague like yourself . . . for a chat.'

'You think so?'

'Sure.'

'Wouldn't it seem a bit presumptuous of me to turn up at her house?'

'If you feel it might, why not pop over to the factory one day when you get a minute?' he suggested casually. 'It will do her good to have someone outside of the family to talk to for a change. Us Carters are a very clannish lot and it can get a bit overpowering at times.'

'I might do that,' said Philip, pleased at the prospect.

'Philip, how nice to see you,' said Lizzie a week or so later when he knocked on her office door. 'Are you playing truant?'

'No, I'm taking a proper lunch break for a change,' he informed her brightly. 'And I wondered if you'd like to join me for a bite to eat somewhere?'

'It's nice of you to offer but I planned to have sandwiches in the office.'

'Feed them to the ducks and come with me.'

'I don't think so.'

'Nothing fancy,' he persisted, 'just a spot of shepherd's pie or something at a local hostelry. The Ship perhaps?'

She was about to repeat her refusal when she realised just how welcome a break and some fresh company would be.

'You've talked me into it.'

Pausing only to run a comb through her hair and slip on her coat and hat, Lizzie followed him through the factory and out into the yard, sniffing the cold winter air heavily spiced with sooty smoke. They walked briskly along the towpath towards the ancient riverside inn, the leafless trees swaying and creaking in the wind, a scattering of lingering autumn leaves scudding across their path.

'I didn't telephone first to invite you out to lunch in the normal civilised way because I was relying on the element of surprise,' confessed Philip later as they sat at a table by the window, looking out over the water, angry and wind-tossed in the raw December blasts. Iron grey skies added an air of desolation to the scene, despite the bustle of river traffic chugging to and fro.

'I'm very glad you persuaded me. I needed a breather away from the factory.'

'Mind you, I risked life and limb when I entered your premises,' he said with a meaningful grin.

'Jed?'

'Yes, Jed. I think he wants me at the bottom of the Thames . . . securely weighted.'

Her expression darkened. 'Yes, I'm afraid you're right. He's still very upset about his father's death.'

'It was insensitive of me to mention it. I'm sorry.'

'Apologies aren't necessary. You haven't told me anything I don't already know.' She smiled determinedly. 'But I'm not going to let my difficult son spoil my lunch.'

'That's the spirit.'

The barmaid bought them steaming hot shepherd's pie with carrots and cabbage which they ate companionably.

'I think this is probably the first food I've actually tasted since before Bruce died,' she told him. 'The change of scenery must have done me good.'

He smiled at this and they ate in silence for a few minutes.

'How are you feeling now that some time has passed since the tragedy?' he asked.

'Fine.'

'Really?' he asked, sounding unconvinced.

'No. Actually, it still hurts like hell.' She stared across at him, her eyes filling with tears. 'Sheer torture. I just don't seem able to get to grips with it at all even though I pretend to.' The tears rolled down her cheeks and she didn't feel at all embarrassed. 'I miss Bruce so much.' Philip handed her a large white handkerchief which still had a faint scent of soapflakes about it when she put it to her face. 'But I'm being pathetic, spoiling your much needed lunch break.'

'Don't be silly,' he said. 'I asked you to join me so that you could talk to someone outside your own grief-stricken circle . . .

someone with whom you don't have to pretend.'

'Oh, you don't know what a relief it is to let myself go! Not to have to put up a brave front for once,' she said. 'I have to be strong for the children.'

'Of course. But with me you can be the way you are really feeling,' he said. 'And I'm not in any hurry to leave.'

So she told him all about Bruce's illness, reliving it with every word. He listened without offering advice or sympathy. It was wonderfully therapeutic.

'Anyway, that's enough about me,' said Lizzie when she had exhausted the subject. 'How are things with you these days? The last time we spoke your wife hadn't been well.'

'That's right.'

'She will have recovered by now?'

'Sometimes she's better than others but she'll never be totally well.'

Noticing an absence of the spikiness that had been present the last time his wife was mentioned, Lizzie decided to chance her arm. 'To echo your words, I'm not in any hurry to leave.'

Apart from his mother and the doctors, Philip never discussed Emily's condition with anyone. But, somehow, he found himself telling Lizzie all about it now.

'They look after her very well at the hospital,' he explained, 'and there are still times when she seems as normal as you or I. She comes home for short periods then.'

'That's nice.'

'Not really,' he said. 'It unsettles her terribly. She's like a visitor in her own home now. I think she feels more comfortable in the hospital environment. She nearly always has to go back sooner than planned anyway. It's awful for her.'

'It must be very hard for you, too?'

'I can't deny it. The worst part is not being able to help as you can with a disease of the body,' he said. 'I can't reach her when she's sick, you see. She's in a world of her own which cuts her off from the rest of us. I feel so terribly inadequate . . . as though I'm letting her down.'

'Sounds to me as though you've done everything humanly possible.'

'I tell myself that but it doesn't seem to help.'

'Pity.'

'Emily had everything when we got married,' he went on, his eyes softening with affection. 'She was beautiful, clever, charming . . . then this bastard of an illness came and ruined her life. It's such a damned waste. She's an extremely intelligent woman, actually, though that's hard to believe when she's sick.'

'Do they know what caused it?' Lizzie asked with interest.

He gave her a brief outline of Emily's background and thwarted ambitions. 'But according to the doctor it's a biological thing so it would have happened anyway at some point. Unfortunately there's little interest in mental illness. It's just something that's kept hidden away.'

'Mmm.'

'I suppose I'm as guilty of that as anyone else,' he confessed, speaking to Lizzie as he had never spoken to anyone before. 'I try to keep her condition secret. I tell myself it's for her sake but is it for me too? I often wonder. Am I embarrassed by something that isn't her fault?'

'Maybe you are . . . sometimes,' she suggested with candour. 'But we're all only human. We can't help but be affected by the attitude of the society we live in.'

'There is that, I suppose. But you don't seem to have been affected by it unduly,' he remarked. 'It certainly didn't stop you breaking out of the usual female role and going into business.'

'That's true. But breaking the mould doesn't make for an easy life,' she said. 'I would have had a less stressful time just investing that money you loaned me.'

'I doubt if you'd have been happy, though.'

'I would probably always have regretted not having a shot at it,' she admitted thoughtfully. 'We are what we are. I have this perverse need to follow my instincts.'

'I've noticed!'

'It's caused no end of trouble with the woman who brought me up.'

He didn't comment on this and they lapsed into silence while their empty plates were removed by the barmaid and replaced by dishes of treacle pudding and custard.

'I should imagine that you and your mother are quite close,' she remarked. 'Am I right?'

He nodded.

'How about your father?'

'Nothing between us at all.'

'Oh, how sad.'

'He's never had any time for me. I used to be hurt by it but not now.'

'You learned to accept it?'

'You get used to anything if it goes on for long enough.'

'Yes.'

'Anyway, there's no law that says a parent has to like their offspring.'

'True.'

'Fortunately, I like my son very much,' he said. 'Well, most of the time. Except, perhaps, when he's being an unbearable know-all . . . the arrogance of youth, I think they call it.'

'Don't remind me,' she said with a mild grimace. 'I've got a couple like that at home.' She gulped back the tears. 'I'd give everything I have just to hear Bruce's youthfulness about the place too. I wouldn't care how noisy . . . how stroppy . . .'

'I'm sure.'

Looking into his face, she recognised the depth of character behind those dark eyes. A stunningly handsome man by any standards, he wouldn't be short of feminine comfort in his wife's absence if he so wished. She had no idea if he was the adulterous type. She did know, however, that he would never make a pass at her. A business colleague and a friend, yes, but anything else was out of the question and they both knew it. She had no intention of getting involved with a married man again.

When it was time to leave, Lizzie said, 'Thank you so much for lunch. It made a nice change, a real tonic.'

'Perhaps we could do it again sometime?' he suggested lightly.

'Yes, that would be lovely,' she replied casually.

They made a habit of lunching regularly together after that. Every month or so he would telephone and suggest it. Their meetings were easy and companionable and entirely without sexual connotation. Unfortunately, however, not everyone believed them to be so innocent.

'You'll get yourself a bad name,' Polly pointed out one

Saturday afternoon in spring when she called in to see Lizzie after shopping in Kensington High Street.

'For doing what exactly?' Lizzie wanted to know. Because of the harmless nature of her friendship with Philip, it had not occurred to her that it might be misconstrued. She had never tried to keep their meetings a secret, even from Polly and Jed who openly disapproved of her having *any* sort of association with Philip.

'For going out with a married man, o' course,' Polly informed her.

The implied suggestion was so ludicrous that Lizzie emitted a dry laugh. 'I'm not going out with him. We have lunch together sometimes, that's all. If people want to make something of a thing like that . . . well, they must have very empty lives.'

'Oh come on, Lizzie, you must know what it looks like – a married man with a sick wife keeping company with a widow.'

'There's nothing like *that* about it,' she said firmly.

'I should damned well hope not,' said Polly, adding quickly, 'I mean, I wasn't suggesting there is. All I'm saying is, that it might look bad to other people.'

'The man is simply a business colleague whose company I happen to enjoy,' she said, seeking to reassure for she guessed that it was Polly's personal concern rather than fear for Lizzie's reputation that was the reason for this conversation. 'We both run silk factories in the area, naturally we have plenty to talk about. There's nothing more to it than that. Philip is devoted to his wife.'

'She isn't much use to him, though, is she?' said Polly crudely. 'Everyone knows the poor soul has been put away.'

'I don't know what he does in his private life,' said Lizzie crossly. 'Maybe he has a mistress . . . I wouldn't dream of asking.'

'Oh.' Polly dunked her biscuit in her tea and ate the soft part. 'You know that Jed is pretty miffed about you seeing him, I suppose?'

'I'm not *seeing* him as such,' insisted Lizzie. 'But, yes, I am well aware of Jed's feelings on the subject. He's an expert at letting me know.'

'Doesn't that bother you?'

'Yes, of course it does,' said Lizzie. 'I don't enjoy upsetting any of my children. But I simply cannot allow a sixteen-year-old boy to tell me who I can have lunch with.'

Seeing a chance to make a point yet again, Polly said, 'It's only natural he wouldn't like it. And he'd be absolutely devastated if he thought you and Verne were . . . well, you know. I mean, none of us would be able to take that, him being who he is.'

'I am *not* sleeping with Philip Verne!' declared Lizzie.

'Must you be so vulgar?'

'That's what you want to have spelled out for you, isn't it?' she asked acidly. 'So let me make it perfectly clear – I am *not* having an affair with Philip Verne, nor have I any intention of doing so at any time in the future.'

'As if you would,' interrupted Polly in a warning tone.

Objecting to the veiled threat, Lizzie said, 'But if I were to, it would be *my* business. Not yours or Jed's, just *mine*.'

'I don't know how you can even say such things, Lizzie,' reproached Polly. 'You're getting to be so hard and selfish lately.'

'If being hard and selfish is staying out of this quarrel you have with the Vernes, then that's what I am,' said Lizzie.

'Oh, really, there's no talking to you these days.'

'Well, be honest, there wouldn't be all this fuss if I were occasionally to have lunch with some other man.'

'All right, I admit it.'

'So could you *please* stop going on about it, then?'

'How can you even bear to pass the time of day with Stan's killer?' said Polly. 'You are his widow, after all.'

'Yes, I am Stan's widow,' conceded Lizzie patiently. 'But that isn't my only function in life. I am also the proprietor of a business, the mother of two children, and a person with feelings and opinions of my own. You and Jed should respect that. You should allow me to be myself. And if that means counting Philip Verne and his mother as friends, then so be it. You've no right to interfere.'

'You won't stop seeing him then, even to please me?' persisted Polly.

Lizzie could feel her own strength ebbing against the power of this lifelong influence. It was not easy for her to oppose people she cared about, knowing she was hurting them. To be perfectly honest her lunchtime meetings with Philip Verne weren't that important to her. She enjoyed them certainly, but they were not vital to her happiness and were merely a congenial respite during her busy working life. She could agree to give them up this minute and feel only mild regret. In fact, at this precise moment she was tempted to do what Polly wanted and revert back to their former state when her mother-in-law's word was law to Lizzie.

But that would mean a life of total domination. Because it

wouldn't stop with the Philip Verne issue. Oh, no! If she was successful in this, Polly would try to persuade Lizzie to give up the business, would want to choose her friends and have a say in where she lived. There would be no end to it.

'No, Polly,' she said determinedly, breathing deeply in an effort to purge herself of compunction. 'I won't stop seeing him . . . not even to please you.'

Although unemployment remained high in such old established industries as shipbuilding and the cotton mills of the north, many new factories were beginning to appear in London and the surrounding areas. These provided work for many people, manufacturing a variety of modern commodities including cars, aircraft and synthetic rubber. New houses were proliferating, too, in the 'ribbon' developments on the fringes of the capital, and new forms of cheap entertainment, such as wireless sets, gramophones and lush new cinemas were readily available to those who could afford them.

1928 was a memorable year. As well as the first talking picture reaching British screens, the right to vote was made available to all women of twenty-one and over. This year, too, Lizzie recognised Bobby's valuable contribution to the continuing fortunes of Carter's Silks by making him a director of the company.

This gave him the confidence to take out a mortgage on a house, and he and June chose a smart but modest property in South Kensington, close to Lizzie.

'You might have guessed we wouldn't be far away,' laughed June, whose friendship with Lizzie had strengthened after the severe testing it had taken back in 1922.

'You're all going up in the world and moving south of the area. It'll be tuppence to talk to you soon!' said Polly without a trace of envy.

For all her faults, Lizzie didn't believe Polly had a materialistic bone in her body. This made it easy for her to refuse Lizzie's offers of financial assistance which she still did on principle. Since Lizzie had declined to cancel her lunch meetings with Philip, Polly treated that particular matter with disapproving silence. The relationship between the two women remained as it had been for several years – superficially friendly with simmering undertones.

Whilst Jed was content to work his way up in the traditional way in his mother's business, his sister had more creative ambitions. When Eva was seventeen, having spent some time gaining practical weaving experience in the factory, she went away to study textile design in a college in the North of England, in the weaving town of Macclesfield.

Over a period of time, Lizzie grew into the habit of discussing all her major business decisions with Philip. Being experienced in silk but an outsider to her firm, he was able to give her a considered but unbiased opinion, unlike Bobby or June.

Things seemed to go from strength to strength for Carter's Silks as the new decade got underway, even as the depression became a slump according to the newspapers. With a full order book, the economic problems affecting so many other people seemed far away.

Until one grey autumn morning in 1931 when they received an unexpected visit at the factory from Charlie King.

'To what do we owe the pleasure?' asked Lizzie after

formalities had been exchanged and she and Bobby were entertaining their visitor to coffee and biscuits in her office. Charlie had become a firm friend to both her and Bobby over the years but they didn't see a great deal of him because most of their business discussions were conducted on the telephone. This personal call was an indication of something important. Something to their advantage, Lizzie hoped.

'Well . . .' began Charlie, and his obvious reluctance to reply made her spirits take a dive.

'There's nothing wrong, is there, mate?' enquired Bobby.

Charlie made a face. 'This isn't a social call, put it that way,' he said. 'I didn't want to tell you on the phone . . .'

'Tell us what? Come on, Charlie, let's have it,' said Lizzie stiffly.

'The truth is,' he said soberly, 'business isn't good at the moment. We're just not selling the same amount of rainwear that we were even a few months ago.'

'You surprise me. I didn't think the market for high quality rainwear would be affected all that much by the state of the economy,' said Lizzie. 'I mean, the people who can afford to buy your raincoats are from the upper classes, and they're not gonna go short.'

'Don't you believe it!' he said gravely.

'Oh?'

'Admittedly, it's a relative thing – they're not in nearly such a bad way as the manual workers. But there's a lot of belt tightening going on, even among the toffs.'

'Get away!' said Bobby.

'It's been getting steadily worse since the Wall Street crash. A lot of rich men lost a great deal of money over that.'

'Mmm,' murmured Lizzie, dreading what was coming next.

'Anyway, to cut a long story short, we're going over to artificial silk for our linings.'

Both Lizzie and Bobby were too shocked to speak for a moment. King's Rainwear was famous for its high quality silk linings.

'I can hardly believe it,' muttered Lizzie at last. 'You're well-known for your pure silk linings. I can't imagine your customers being satisfied with anything less.'

'Maybe not but there aren't enough of those sort of customers about these days,' he said. 'So we're going to aim for a different market . . . bring out a cheaper range to appeal to the managerial types in the new factories.'

'We'll be quite happy to make artificial silk fabric for you, of course,' said Lizzie, relieved that the news wasn't worse. 'We do quite a bit of it for our customers nowadays . . . that and blended weaves to cut costs.'

The look on Charlie's face sent a shiver of alarm up her spine. 'There's something else, isn't there?'

'I'm afraid so,' he confirmed, rubbing the side of his face with his thumb nervously. 'The order for our lining material is going to a firm in the North of England.'

'What, all of it?' burst out Bobby.

'That's right.'

'Oh, Charlie,' exclaimed Lizzie, unable to hide her distress. 'You might at least have given us a chance to give you a price for some of it.'

'I have to give the firm a contract for sole manufacturing rights or they won't give me a cheap enough price,' he explained.

'We could have.'

He shook his head. 'They're a huge firm, Lizzie, they specialise in mass production. You would never be able to compete with them. Honestly, I really am very sorry.'

'So are we,' said Bobby harshly.

'This is a terrible blow to us, Charlie,' said Lizzie, inwardly trembling at this news for King's order was one of the mainstays of their business, providing a regular income every month.

Charlie shook his head sagely. 'You don't have to tell me that. I feel really bad about it which is why I came to tell you in person,' he explained. 'We're all beginning to suffer from the slump. It's eating its rotten way into everything.'

'Is there nothing at all we can say to make you change your mind?' she asked with little hope.

'I only wish there was,' he told her sadly. 'But I'm afraid it's a question of adapting to the current climate to stay in business.'

'Yes, I understand,' Lizzie managed to say with dignity. 'Thank you for taking the trouble to come over to tell us in person.'

In the same way that gaining Charlie King's order had set Lizzie's business in motion back in 1920, so losing it seemed to be the catalyst to send it plummeting to ruin. Garment makers they dealt with on a regular basis began to cut their orders drastically or cancelled them altogether as the depression deepened.

The ready-made garment industry was booming at the moment, but they tended to eschew silk in favour of cheaper fabrics.

'I'll just have to go out foot slogging to find some orders,' said Lizzie to Bobby one day early in the New Year. 'I'm damned if I'll stand by and let this firm go under.'

'We'll have to lay off some of the weavers if things don't start to pick up soon,' he said worriedly.

She looked straight into his face. 'I'm carrying a huge responsibility. I've a mortgage to pay, a daughter at art college, and a factory full of workers relying on me for their pay. Do you think I'm going to let you all down?'

'Not if you can possibly avoid it.'

'Stop worrying, then.'

'Even you can't work miracles.'

'I can have a damned good try though,' she told him.

Just for a fleeting second, the old magic flared between them. It happened like this sometimes but less often than it once had. She guessed that a flame of desire would always burn for him somewhere deep inside her.

'If anyone can do it, you can,' said Bobby, sounding more positive.

'So it looks like you're going to be holding the fort around here most of the time while I get my best hat and coat on and get out there touting for business!'

A month later Lizzie was crushed, exhausted and desperate. But not quite defeated.

'It's absolutely soul-destroying,' she confessed to Philip at one of their lunchtime meetings. 'I've tramped all over London trying to drum up business . . . and not a single bite.'

'Oh, dear.'

'I've tried everywhere,' she sighed wearily. 'Garment

factories, department stores . . . but you can't even get in to see the buyers, let alone talk business.'

'Things are bad for a lot of firms, I know.'

Because Verne's produced very specialised household fabrics and had long established contacts with suppliers to the aristocracy, whereas Lizzie dealt mostly in silks for the clothing industry, they were not in competition. This meant that she could use him as a confidant.

'I would never have believed that things could change so suddenly,' she told him. 'One minute we've so much work we can hardly cope with it. The next I'm out there begging for orders like a cheap commercial traveller.'

'That's the way it is in business. There are always peaks and troughs.'

'Even for a firm as long established as yours?' she queried.

'Everyone has highs and lows and we've had our share of lows over the years,' he told her. 'The slump has affected us, of course, but because we're so big, and in a specialist part of the market, I think we'll be able to ride it out.'

'I wish I could say the same thing about us.'

'Why don't you try the couture fashion houses?' suggested Philip. 'They'll always stay with quality fabric like silk. If you make a breakthrough into that field, it could be the making of your firm. Word spreads among the fashion houses, the same as in any other trade.'

'A lovely thought,' sighed Lizzie wistfully, 'but I did my damnedest to break into that market when I first started up in business . . . and it was a complete dead loss.'

'It's not an easy nut to crack, I grant you,' he agreed. 'But think how much more experienced you are now than when you first went out pedalling your wares. You could charm your way into Buckingham Palace now, if you set your mind to it.'

'You really think so?' she said, encouraged by the compliment.

'I certainly do,' he confirmed. 'And if you can get a foot in the door in couture, you'll never look back.'

'I won't?'

'No. Because no matter how far-reaching the depression gets, or how much the ready-made trade increases to the detriment of made-to-order clothes, there'll always be those people who can afford to have exclusive clothes made for them.'

'You could be right.'

'No question about it,' he said with confidence. 'Couture fashion houses will always need good quality silk material simply because their customers will demand it.'

'I suppose so.'

'So get out there and make yourself known to them, and you'll soon be wondering why you worried about losing King's order.'

'All right,' she told him with renewed hope. 'I'll give it a try.'

A month later she reported back to him. 'Nothing doing.'

'No interest at all?'

'Just a few "we'll let you knows if we ever think of changing our supplier" . . .'

'Oh, what a pity.'

'I managed to distribute a lot of my business cards but I'm no further forward as far as actual business is concerned.'

'Something might come of it in the future,' he said. 'It's all good groundwork.'

'That doesn't solve the immediate problem though, does it?'

'No.'

'Looks like I've come to a dead end.'

'I still think you should pursue the couture idea further.'

'How?'

'You need to get in with someone new . . . a designer who's just starting up in business and making a name for themselves. They're usually more sympathetic to a new fabric supplier.'

'The last time I went along that road it cost me a lot of money,' she pointed out, and gave him a brief outline of the men's neckwear manufacturer who had gone out of business before even taking delivery of the cloth he had ordered.

'We all have to take risks from time to time,' said Philip, stroking his chin thoughtfully. 'Inevitable in any business. I still think you should find someone who's just beginning to get known . . . someone who's attracting publicity.'

'I don't know of anyone,' she confessed gloomily. 'Well, only that designer who's been in the newspapers lately . . . Jeanne Marat, I think her name is.'

'Why not try her, then?'

'Don't be silly.'

'What do you mean?'

'Her fashion house is in Paris,' she informed him gloomily.

'So?'

'You think I should send some samples to her?' she said in surprise.

'No.'

334

'What then?'

'If you want to beat the competition, you'll have to go and see her . . . meet her in person.'

'You're *not* serious?'

'I certainly am,' he told her. 'You must show her your samples yourself. If you send them, they might get lost in the pile of others she probably receives every day.'

'All the way to Paris – me?'

'Why not?'

'I've never been further than Southend,' she admitted.

'Now's your chance to broaden your experience and get a foothold in the export market at the same time,' he told her with enthusiasm. 'Travel broadens the mind and all that.'

She gave him a close look, realising how narrow her perspective was compared to his. Travel was an everyday event to someone of his background. For people like her it was simply something you read about.

'You make it sound so easy.'

'It isn't a particularly difficult journey,' he said casually.

'It's abroad, though.'

'I'm talking about France not the Australian Outback!'

'Even so . . .'

'It's only across the water. You get the boat train from Victoria and it takes you right to Paris,' he informed her cheerfully. 'You'd have to get a passport, though.'

'But you don't understand . . . it isn't just the travelling.'

'What else is bothering you?'

'Well, the whole idea of going abroad. I mean, people like me just don't go swanning off to foreign parts.'

'That's just where you're wrong. People like you can do

anything they set their mind to, Lizzie,' he stated categorically. 'And that includes travelling abroad.'

'Hey, this is *me* you're talking about?' she said with a question in her voice.

'Yes, *you*. You must remember that you're not just an outworker any more,' he reminded her. 'You're the proprietor of a good business that's going to go under if you don't pull out all the stops. You must follow any lead, however tenuous.'

'Your faith in me is very flattering,' she said, excitement rising despite all the obstacles.

'But?'

'But we must be realistic.'

'Go on then, be as realistic as you like. I'm listening.'

'All right, so I take the plunge and travel to Paris on my own? Bobby can't go with me because he'll have to stay here and look after the factory while I'm away.'

'Yes, I accept that. So?'

'So how am I going to talk my way into any fashion house, let alone do business with them, if I can't speak the language?'

'Ah, yes, you do have a point,' he admitted thoughtfully.

'Oh, well, so much for that idea then,' she said, feeling ridiculously disappointed.

'Not necessarily,' he said with a gleam in his eye. 'I know of someone with very good French who would make an ideal travelling companion for you . . .'

Chapter Seventeen

'What do you think of it?' asked Meg Verne of a rather bewildered Lizzie as they lingered over coffee in the cool dusk at a crowded pavement cafe in the Champs Elysées.

'Wonderful,' she enthused, overwhelmed by the noise and colour of this busy boulevard, gloriously green with chestnut trees and resonant with the lyrical clamour of foreign voices on this balmy May evening.

'Yes, I think Paris is rather special too,' agreed Meg.

'You certainly seem to know your way around,' remarked Lizzie, recalling the aplomb with which the other woman had carried herself since they'd alighted from the train at the Gare du Nord a few hours ago. In what sounded to Lizzie like an unfaltering command of the language, she had chatted to the railway porter, the taxi driver and the hotel staff. She'd explained to Lizzie that she'd been offering them her sympathy for the assassination of their President who'd been murdered recently at a charity event where books were being sold for the benefit of ex-servicemen authors. Apparently, President Paul Doumer had been talking to one of the writers when a man pushed through the crowd and pulled out a revolver.

'I ought to, my dear. I've been here enough times over the

years,' said Meg, her voice softening with memory. 'I'll never forget my first visit, though.'

'Oh?'

'I was just seventeen,' she continued dreamily. 'I came with a girlfriend to stay with friends of her parents who lived in Sèvres. That's a small town just outside Paris, very famous for its fine porcelain.'

'Sounds fascinating.'

'It was . . . though at that age I had other things on my mind rather than porcelain,' said Meg, her dark eyes gleaming wickedly.

'That follows.'

'I met my first love here.'

She fell silent and seemed to drift into a world of her own. Lizzie noticed her fine profile, so much like Philip's, her ebony-coloured eyes and olive complexion complimenting her cream linen suit and mane of silvering black hair swept back into an elegant bun. She must be turned sixty and her skin was heavily lined but she was still an extremely striking woman.

'How romantic,' said Lizzie, though she wasn't sure if the comment registered.

Meg looked at her with a wistful smile. 'Yes it was. Very romantic.' She seemed consciously to change her mood. 'But that's all in the past. The present is what we must concern ourselves with.'

'Indeed,' agreed Lizzie, still astounded by the fact that she was actually here. Two weeks ago Paris had been just a name, a place synonymous with chic and glamour. She'd never dreamed she would see it for herself.

But this was how life was for people like the Vernes. Imbued with the confidence of established wealth, they thought nothing of crossing the channel to France. How different their attitude was to that of Lizzie's own people. Poor Polly had been horrified to learn that she was going abroad. Even dear supportive Bobby had had serious reservations.

'I don't like the sound of it at all,' he'd said when the family were all gathered at Polly's place for Sunday tea. 'Two women going abroad on their own . . . that could be dangerous.'

''Course it could,' agreed Polly wholeheartedly. 'You'll get robbed, assaulted even. You can't trust those Froggy men. They're a hot-blooded lot, so I've heard.'

'Take no notice of them, Lizzie,' said June. 'You go and enjoy yourself. I'd be off like a shot if I had the chance.'

'I'm not going there to enjoy myself,' she'd reminded them, 'I'm going on business. Anyway, Meg's a seasoned traveller, she'll know how to avoid trouble.'

Jed didn't so much disapprove of the trip as of her travelling companion. Although he didn't say anything, his feelings were obvious.

The twins were quite excited about a member of their family going abroad. 'Can you find room for us in your suitcase, Aunt Lizzie?' laughed Jamie.

'There's supposed to be a lot of street entertainment in Paris,' chimed in Keith. 'It would be smashing to see some of it.'

Now Lizzie found herself smiling at the thought of her nineteen-year-old nephews who had refused her offer of a job at Carter's Silks on leaving school. Obsessed with the idea of a career in showbusiness, they'd found menial work in the theatre, doing anything from backstage labouring to cleaning the auditorium. They were currently employed at the Chiswick Empire as general dogsbodies but were at the back of the stalls at every opportunity, studying the technique of professional comedians. The variety theatre was a magnet to them. All their spare time and money was spent on tickets for shows all over London.

She was recalled to the present by the sound of Meg's voice. 'Share the joke then.'

'Not a joke,' said Lizzie. 'I was just thinking about my twin nephews who want to go on the stage . . . they're natural comics.'

'Still thinking about home when you have Paris at your feet?' said Meg in a tone of lighthearted reproof.

'Ours is that sort of family.' She laughed. 'They don't come into the "out of sight, out of mind" category, I'm afraid.'

'So I've gathered.'

'Your husband doesn't mind you going off without him, then?' suggested Lizzie.

'No . . . he'll be well looked after by our housekeeper,' she said. 'I don't suppose he'll even notice I'm not there.'

They lapsed into companionable silence while they drank their coffee, idly watching people strolling past. Plump, gregarious pigeons stalked among the tables pecking for crumbs.

'So let's go over our plans for tomorrow, shall we?' suggested Meg.

'Yes, the first thing is to get an appointment with Jeanne Marat,' said Lizzie. 'Obviously, I shall have to leave that to you.'

'And if she won't see us?'

'Then we'll have to force our way in,' laughed Lizzie. 'I'm not going back to London without seeing her, even if we don't do business. I wouldn't be able to look Philip in the eye if I didn't get that far.'

'Don't worry, we'll get an appointment. Somehow.'

Lizzie yawned. 'Right now, though, I'm ready for bed.'

'Me too.'

They had booked accommodation for three nights on the Right Bank because it was close to the fashion houses. Meg had been in favour of a longer stay – she'd wanted to make a holiday of it – but Lizzie had neither the time nor the cash and had only agreed to stay this long in case they failed with Jeanne Marat and needed time to approach other designers.

Lizzie hadn't said anything to Meg but she was extremely apprehensive about the task ahead because there was so much depending on it. This trip had been costly by her current standards, even though she'd insisted on a reasonably priced hotel and Meg had insisted on paying all her own expenses. If Lizzie returned home empty-handed it would be to a very bleak future indeed for Carter's Silks.

The smallish, family-run hotel was off the main thoroughfare and overlooked a leafy square flanked by shops and cafes. The building was ancient but the interior was very clean and comfortable. They each had a single room on the third floor, reached by means of a wheezy lift. Lizzie's room was basically equipped with dark furniture and a washstand with a bowl and jug patterned with pink roses. The floor was highly polished and the snowy white bedlinen was lavender-scented. Paintings of vineyards and sunny French terraces adorned the walls and a wooden crucifix hung over the bed.

Although Lizzie was exhausted, sleep eluded her. She got up and sat in an easy chair by the window well into the small hours, watching people milling about in the square, surprised to see the cafes still doing a roaring trade.

If she thought too deeply about the situation she was in, it seemed the height of irresponsibility to have come all this way without so much as an appointment with Jeanne Marat. But on the other hand, there *was* a chance, however slight, of putting her business back on its feet, and if she failed it wouldn't be through lack of effort. This was Philip Verne's gift to her – faith in herself to attempt the seemingly impossible!

Having finally drifted into a fitful sleep, Lizzie was awake at dawn to watch Paris coming to life from her window. The scent of newly baked croissants and fresh coffee wafted up to her as she watched the pavements being swept and washed down, water gushing along the curbs and glinting in the early sun. In the distance the white domes of the Sacré Coeur towered above the city, their decorative lines etched against the steel blue sky.

Later, as she and Meg breakfasted on the hotel terrace, blinds were being raised all around the square as shopkeepers prepared to start the day's business. City workers thronged the streets in a hurrying tide bound for their offices and shops. There was more than a sprinkling of old men in berets and darkly-dressed, elderly women carrying shopping baskets, black shawls covering their heads.

'Perhaps when our business is finished, I'll introduce you to the Left Bank,' suggested Meg. 'It's where all the students hang out . . . very bohemian. All the intellectuals gather in the bars and cafes there.'

'This is the Right Bank then?' said Lizzie still too dazzled by her new surroundings to be sure about them.

'Yes, this is the centre of business. All the big department stores are around here.'

'At the moment I feel as though I'll never get used to where we are now, let alone exploring other parts.'

'You will,' said Meg. 'We can't let you go home without seeing some of the sights.'

'First things first, though, eh?' said Lizzie, finishing her coffee and gathering her bag ready to go upstairs.

She dressed with care in an outfit she had had made for the occasion in a variety of silk fabrics of her own designs produced at her factory. It was a stunning creation, a soft black suit in plain silk worn with a cream satin blouse with a self colour floral pattern. The lapels and pocket trims of the jacket were patterned to match the blouse. On her head she wore a large brimmed hat in cream, extravagantly trimmed with silk chiffon, her blonde bobbed hair shining beneath it. The girlish beauty of her youth had matured into stunning sophistication in middle age. Not excessively fussy in appearance but very stylish.

'Wow!' approved Meg when she tapped on the door to say she was ready. 'You'll knock her dead in that. It was a very good idea of yours to wear your own fabrics.'

'It's a bit dressy for a business meeting,' said Lizzie. 'But I want to show off the different materials.'

'You look really good,' said Meg who looked pleasantly smart rather than glamorous in a plain linen suit in pale blue.

'What better way of displaying my samples than by wearing them?' said Lizzie. 'I'm hoping it will do the trick.'

'Fingers crossed.'

'There's so much hanging on this meeting, I'll use every trick in the book to get an order from Madame Marat.'

They exchanged a wry grin because subterfuge had already been used by Meg. Given the animosity of many people towards anyone with things to sell, she had obtained an appointment with Jeanne Marat by pretending that they were clients, insisting that they would deal with no one but Madame herself.

'Let's go then!' said Meg. 'I've asked reception to order a taxi for us.'

The cab bumped and rattled through smart boulevards into narrow side streets flanked with quaint little shops with colourful awnings, past markets and parks and public gardens resplendent with flowers and fountains. Everywhere there were cafes, trees and people. Eventually they turned into a cobbled street of houses that at first glance appeared to be residential with lace curtains and window boxes. The driver stopped outside a house in a biscuit-coloured terrace of town houses with stone steps winding down to the basements and wrought iron balconies to the upper rooms.

'A lot of these houses have been converted into business premises, I suppose,' remarked Meg as they walked up to the front door of the house with 'Jeanne Marat' written with a flourish in gilt-edged letters across the ground-floor windows.

The door was opened by a young woman oozing panache. She was tall, slim and blonde and dressed in a plain navy blue suit and crisp white blouse. Her hair was bobbed and her immaculate make-up gave her face a doll-like look. The overall effect of her simple attire was so striking, it made Lizzie feel as though she herself must look as though she'd just come off a stint in the fields, hop picking or something, despite all the attention she'd paid to her appearance that morning.

They were shown into a carpeted hallway which led to a waiting room tastefully appointed with easy chairs and an array of pot plants and magazines, the walls liberally hung with Parisian paintings. The receptionist invited them to sit down then disappeared through the glass door.

'I suppose Madame's office is through there?' said Lizzie, nodding towards the door.

'And the fitting rooms, I should think,' remarked Meg.

'There's probably an army of seamstresses down in the basement,' said Lizzie. 'Behind the glamour of haute couture there's a great deal of hard, unglamorous labour.'

'This is very nice, though,' said Meg, sinking into a soft leather chair.

'Mmm,' agreed Lizzie ruefully. 'But it's really for the benefit of bona fide clients, not fakes like us who are here to sell not buy. Do you think she'll throw us out?'

'That'll probably be her first impulse,' said Meg wryly. 'So we'll just have to be very persuasive and capture her interest before we find ourselves out on the street.'

'It was a low trick.'

'Desperation calls for desperate measures.'

'We can't even give her an order either because it's too far to come for a fitting,' remarked Lizzie guiltily.

'Chin up, Lizzie, it's too late for cold feet,' said Meg. 'We're in the door and we have to make the most of it.'

'Yes, I know.'

After a while they were shown through the glass door into another passageway and finally into a room where a small, colourful woman of about thirty was sitting. Her black hair was shoulder-length with a startling blonde quiff at the front. Her face was brightly adorned with scarlet lipstick and vivid blue eye shadow which matched her eyes and blouse. Numerous gold bangles jangled noisily on her wrists and she was wearing a pair of enormous gold hoop earrings. Lizzie had never seen anyone so outrageously made up before.

Meg spoke to her in French and to Lizzie's surprise she replied in a soft English voice with a slight Northern accent.

'I'm English,' she explained, 'from Manchester originally.'

'Well, I'll be blowed!' said Lizzie, hardly able to believe her luck.

'Marat is my married name. I made France my home after marrying a Frenchman ten years ago.' When the introductions were complete, she leaned back in her chair and Lizzie noticed that the blouse she was wearing under a beige lightweight suit was made of silk. 'So, ladies.' She looked from one to the other, her glance lingering for a moment on Lizzie's outfit. 'What can we do for you here at the House of Marat? Something for the autumn season, perhaps?'

Lizzie and Meg exchanged anxious glances. Lizzie took a deep breath. 'Well, actually . . .' She cleared her throat nervously and put one of her business cards down on the desk in front of Madame. 'Er, the truth is . . . we're not clients. I am, in fact, a producer of silk fabric.'

'You mean you tricked me into seeing you?' she said in a surprisingly even tone.

'I'm afraid so.'

Her brows rose and she picked the card up and studied it. 'Lizzie Carter of Carter's Silks. So you have come here to sell me something, not the other way around?'

'Yes, that is the case,' said Lizzie, feeling really bad about it now. 'I'm sorry about the deception. We thought we'd be fobbed off if we said who we really were.'

Jeanne Marat looked at Lizzie. 'Your name is Carter. Are you representing your husband's company, or is it your father's firm perhaps?'

'Neither. Carter's Silks belongs to me,' she explained.

'Did you inherit it from your father?'

'No, I set up the factory myself,' explained Lizzie.

'Well, well, that *is* a novelty,' she said, sounding impressed. 'There aren't many female factory proprietors about. It's normally the lot of our gender merely to work in them.'

'Yes, that's right,' said Lizzie, her nerves taut as she waited to see which way this interview was going to go.

'Lizzie isn't the type to run with the pack,' Meg informed her proudly. 'Rather like yourself, I should imagine.'

'You are related?' said Madame, her questioning glance moving from one to the other.

'No, just friends,' said Meg. 'I'm here as translator. Not necessary in your case, as it happens.'

'No.'

Lizzie felt almost numb with tension. At any moment she would either be asked to leave, or to stay and do business. There would be no shilly-shallying with Madame Marat if Lizzie was any judge of character.

Madame placed the forefingers of both hands under her chin and looked at Lizzie meditatively. 'Have you been doing the rounds of all the fashion houses in Paris?'

'No, just you.'

'Why me?'

'I've read about you in the newspapers at home,' she explained.

'Nothing bad, I hope?'

'Not at all. They all speak highly of your work,' said Lizzie. 'I must admit, though, that my motivation in coming all this way to see you was the fact that you haven't long set up in business on your own. I thought you might be more approachable than the long established firms.'

'At least you're honest in that, anyway,' she said pointedly.

Lizzie had the grace to look sheepish but just said, 'Everything I am wearing is made from fabric produced in my factory.'

Jeanne Marat smiled. 'A neat move on your part.'

'I thought it would give you an opportunity to see the fabrics made up.' Lizzie lifted her attaché case from the floor and rested it on the desk. 'But I have a comprehensive range of samples here for you to look at too.'

Madame Marat rose to reveal a close-fitting suit on a reed-like figure. She came over to Lizzie and took a studious look at the clothes she was wearing. Lizzie removed the jacket and handed it to her.

'Such beautiful material,' said Madame, feeling it gently between finger and thumb then looking closely at the blouse. 'Quite exquisite. I noticed it as soon as you walked in.'

'Yes,' said Lizzie who had observed the other woman's interest. 'That was what I was hoping for in wearing it.'

The other woman went back to her desk and sat down. 'You've come all this way just to try to get me to place an order with you?'

'That's right.'

'What is known as "playing a longshot".'

'You have to take an occasional chance in business,' said Lizzie. 'As I'm sure you very well know.'

'Indeed. Tell me, Mrs Carter,' she said, tapping her chin idly with a pencil, 'why should I buy silk fabric from you when I can buy any amount of the stuff here in France?'

'For several reasons,' said Lizzie, slipping her jacket back on and sitting down. 'First and foremost, the quality.'

'That isn't in question,' admitted Madame. 'But there are many producers and dealers with good quality fabric to offer me here in Paris.'

'There is also the price,' said Lizzie, having rehearsed this speech many times beforehand. 'I'm not a one-man band by any means, weaving by hand in a garret. But neither is Carter's Silks a huge company that will only set up a loom for orders of a certain size and then charge the earth to cover their overheads. We are small enough to be flexible. We can do short runs of one type of silk fabric and still keep our prices reasonable.'

'And?'

'Dealing direct with me will cut out the dealer's commission,' she said. 'Naturally, we will pay the carriage charges from London to Paris.'

'Tell me more,' urged Madame.

'We are very reliable.'

'Anything else?'

'Well, there's the one upmanship element,' Lizzie pointed out. 'Paris leads the world in fashion, I know. But some people, particularly those who wear exclusive clothes, might find a certain added glamour in having their outfits made from foreign silk.'

'Mmm.'

'And my final argument is this: I would really enjoy producing the material that goes into making Jeanne Marat clothes, so you would be assured of good service at all times.'

Jeanne laughed, a warm, throaty sound that was music to Lizzie's ears. 'I think you and I have been shaped in the same mould,' she said. 'I had to fight every inch of the way to be accepted as a businesswoman too.'

She told them that she was from an ordinary working-class Northern family and had won a scholarship to art school. This was followed by a bursary which had given her a year in Paris studying fashion design, during which time she met her husband and decided to make her home here. He had been very supportive when she decided to set up in business on her own after years of making clothes for other designers.

'The fashion industry is terribly competitive.'

'So I've heard,' said Lizzie, and went on to talk about her own business and how the loss of the raincoat lining order was the reason for her visit to Paris.

'I think it's time we talked serious business,' said Madame. 'I always keep a good stock of silk fabric so let's see what you've got to show me in that case of yours.'

Not only did Jeanne Marat give them a good order, she invited them to join her for dinner that evening. They dined on oysters and coq au vin in a small lively restaurant in St-Germain-des-Prés at which Jeanne, as they now addressed her, was a regular. They all got along famously and the occasion was an unqualified success. Lizzie and Jeanne finalised arrangements for transporting the goods from London to Paris, but their talk was mostly lighthearted and personal.

'It's been quite a day,' said Lizzie as she and Meg arrived back at their hotel.

'It certainly has.'

'I can enjoy the sights tomorrow with an easy mind now that we've achieved what we came here for.'

'A day isn't even long enough to scratch the surface of this city.'

They did their best though. The next morning after breakfast they walked the length of the Champs Elysées, window shopping and having morning coffee in the rooftop cafe of one of the big stores. They sat on the grass in a shady spot by the Seine to recover, eating fruit they'd bought from a street barrow, then took a trip to the top of the Eiffel Tower and visited the Notre Dame Cathedral. Then it was the Métro to Montmartre to watch the artists at work and have a very late lunch of baguettes and wine at a cafe crowded with people, some of whom seemed to be arty types.

A group of young men at the table next to theirs were having a heated discussion while chain smoking. Meg said they were talking about Germany and Adolf Hitler and the increase in power of the Nazis. When their voices rose to an angry roar and it seemed as though they might come to blows, the two women skipped coffee and took a walk through the back streets, browsing among the interesting little shops and choosing presents to take home.

By the time they got back to the hotel to change for the evening, they were so exhausted they almost took to their beds. But, somehow, they managed to summon the energy to take a taxi to the Left Bank where they dined in a small, unpretentious restaurant, cool and verdant with plants and reputed to be patronised by poets and other members of the literati. They had hors d'oeuvres followed by entrecôte bordelaise which the untravelled Lizzie discovered was a juicy steak with a rich wine sauce.

In true French tradition they drank wine, rather too much as it happened, and giggled all the way back to the hotel in the taxi.

'Oh, what fun we've had,' laughed Meg. 'I feel like a girl again.'

'You *are* a girl.'

'At sixty-one?' she said, erupting into fits of laughter.

'You can be a girl at heart at any age, it's all in the mind,' said Lizzie lightly. 'I mean, look at me. I'm forty going on seventeen.'

Meg was prevented from answering by an attack of hiccups.

'I'm supposed to be a mature and responsible businesswoman,' continued Lizzie, overly chatty with drink, 'and I come all the way to Paris on the offchance of finding business. Some people would call that highly immature.'

'Others would call it enterprising,' drawled Meg.

'It was all Philip's idea.'

'Three cheers for Philip,' said Meg merrily. 'I'm having a marvellous time.'

Back at the hotel, they wandered out on to the terrace and ordered coffee, the loud, hilarious stage of inebriation mellowing into quiet drowsiness as they watched the world go by on the gaslit boulevards.

'How about us staying on for an extra day?' suggested Meg.

'What about our tickets for the boat train tomorrow morning?'

'Forget those and get some for the following day,' said Meg. 'We can book another night here. It'll be my treat.'

Softened by the wine and the lighthearted atmosphere, Lizzie was tempted. 'I ought to get back to work.'

'One more day won't make any difference,' Meg woozily pointed out.

Lizzie had weakened to the point when she was about to agree when they were interrupted by the waiter. He said something in French which Meg managed to translate despite her condition. Apparently there was a long-distance telephone call from England for Lizzie.

Instantly sober, she hurried inside to the hotel reception area, wondering fearfully who it could be. It must be urgent. No one would telephone abroad unless it was, especially as she was due back home tomorrow.

'Hello, Lizzie, it's Philip.'

Of course, she should have guessed. Telephoning abroad was probably quite ordinary to someone like him.

'Hello,' she said brightly. 'Couldn't you wait till we get back tomorrow to know if I pulled off a deal with Jeanne Marat?'

There was a silence. All she could hear was crackling of the line. 'Philip . . . are you still there?'

'Yes, I'm here.'

'I think there must have been a misunderstanding. The hotel people called me to the telephone but you probably want to speak to your mother?'

'No, I want to speak to you first. I'll speak to Mother in a minute.'

'Oh?'

'The thing is, Lizzie, I've some bad news, I'm afraid.'

'Oh, my God!' Her legs felt weak. 'Is it one of the children? Has Bobby asked you to telephone me?'

'No, it isn't your family,' he explained. 'It's mine . . . my father.'

'Is he ill?'

'He's . . . well . . . he's dead. A heart attack this afternoon.'

'Oh, Philip, I'm so very sorry.'

'Yes, it is a blow,' he said. 'Collapsed in his office at the factory. Died even before the ambulance arrived.'

'How awful!'

'Dreadful. Actually the reason I wanted to have a word with you before Mother is . . . well . . . so that you were warned.'

'I understand.'

'Would you mind being there with her when I tell her, in case she passes out or anything? It will be a terrible shock for her.'

'Of course I will.'

'I didn't know quite what to do,' he confessed, and she could tell how worried he was. 'Naturally I didn't want to telephone Mother with such horrible news, but in the end I decided it was my duty to let her know right away. I couldn't just let her come home to face such a ghastly blow.'

'Don't worry, Philip,' she assured him warmly. 'You did the right thing. And I'll look after her here.'

'Thanks, Lizzie.'

'Shall I go and get her?'

'Please.'

'Hang on then.'

She put the instrument down and picked it up again almost

at once. 'Bear up, Philip,' she said gently.

'I will. Thanks.'

It was the oddest thing but she felt extraordinarily close to him as she went to bring his mother to the telephone.

Chapter Eighteen

Considering the lack of rapport between Philip and his father, it was hardly surprising that compassion for his mother by far outweighed his own feelings of grief. More so because of the pluckiness with which she coped with her trauma, stoically striving to adjust to widowhood, determined not to be a burden to anyone.

Philip thanked God for Lizzie Carter whose friendship did more for his mother than he ever could. Believing a long period of strict mourning to be pointless, Lizzie persuaded Meg to return to her charity work quite soon after the funeral. Also a firm believer in the medicinal qualities of light entertainment, she dragged her off to the theatre or cinema some evenings.

As the healing process became manifest in his mother and his filial concern became less all-consuming, Philip found himself considering his own feelings for his father. Although he couldn't pretend to be traumatised by his death, he was sad that he had never managed to improve their relationship. In this mood of introspection, he was able to admit that he'd never given up hope for some sort of a bond to be forged between them.

During his father's lifetime, Philip had never felt able to

discuss the matter with his mother – perhaps because it had been too painful. Now he found himself wanting to do so and broached the subject one evening in the late autumn when he was dining with her at her house in Eden Crescent.

'I've never understood why Father disliked me so much,' he remarked over coffee in the drawing room, softly lit and cosy with red armchairs set around a log fire which was gently crackling and exuding a pale orange glow. 'And it's no use denying it because we both know it's true.'

'I'm not going to deny it.'

'Oh!' He was surprised. He had expected her to leap to his father's defence.

'How can I when he made his feelings so obvious?' she said, her face pale and solemn in the flickering firelight.

'Do you know why he was like that to me?'

She stared into her coffee cup, running her forefinger over the rim.

'Am I so repulsive?' he asked when she didn't reply. 'Am I so difficult to like?'

'It wasn't actually *you* as a person he disliked,' she said.

'Why did he spend his life finding fault with me, then?'

Stiffening, she leaned forward and put her coffee cup down on a small polished table, staring silently into the fire.

'I hoped we might have become friends after Neville died,' he said when she didn't enlarge on her previous comment. 'But no . . . he wouldn't have it.'

Still she looked towards the orange tongues of flame darting up the chimney, the undulating light gleaming on her silvering hair. Tension was noticeable in the rigid set of her shoulders.

'I mean, we all know Neville was his favourite son,' he

continued, feeling the need to pursue the subject that had haunted him for so long. 'I can see that that would make him like me less. But I'm at a loss to know why it should have made him loathe me as much as he did?'

'Neville wasn't the favourite son in the usual sense,' said his mother.

Philip emitted a dry laugh. 'Oh, come on, who do you think you're kidding?'

'He was Humphrey's *favourite*, son, Philip,' she uttered shakily into the fire, 'because he was his *only* son.'

Baffled, he stared at her, absently putting his coffee down on the table. 'What on earth are you talking about?'

She bit her lip, staring into her lap. Then she looked up and met his eyes resolutely. 'Humphrey wasn't your father.'

'Of course he was,' Philip said instinctively. He leaned forward, his eyes narrowed quizzically on her. 'Wasn't he?'

'Your father was French.'

He flopped back in the chair as though he'd been physically pushed. 'I don't believe I'm hearing this!'

'It's true. I met him on holiday with a girlfriend at the home of friends of her family just outside Paris,' his mother continued. 'He was an artist, a lot older than me. I was just seventeen and very impressionable.'

'Well, you seem very calm about it, I must say!'

'I suppose that's because I've lived with it for such a long time,' she said. 'I don't see the point of making a drama out of something that happened so long ago.'

'You might have had the decency to tell me the truth when I was younger . . . that I was a bastard child!'

'What good would it have done? Anyway, you were born

inside wedlock, all respectable and above board.'

'Even so,' exclaimed Philip, frowning deeply. 'Don't you think I had a right to know the truth about myself?'

'Humphrey and I agreed that you wouldn't be told,' she said. 'I promised him. We both thought you were better off not knowing.'

'It might have stopped me being so hurt by his obvious dislike of me if I'd known the reason,' said Philip, angry at her deceit. 'As it was, I grew up thinking there was something wrong with me, that I'd done something to make him hate me.'

'Yes, I'm very sorry about that, Philip,' Meg said gravely. 'Many times I was tempted to tell you but I was afraid it would make things worse if it was out in the open. Be a reminder to Humphrey . . . a reminder to us both. I always tried to think of you as his child, you see. Anyway, I really believe it would have done you more harm than good to have known when you were a child.'

As the full implications of this revelation began to register properly, he realised that he was feeling happy. In fact, it was as though a long and tiresome illness had suddenly gone away, leaving him lighthearted with relief.

'You can't possibly know how good it feels to know that his hatred of me wasn't personal.'

'I can imagine.'

'I suppose I should be feeling devastated but I'm actually elated now that it's sinking in!'

'Humphrey tried hard to love you,' she explained, her eyes glazed with memory, 'but once Neville arrived . . . well . . . it just didn't seem to be possible for him. I suppose you were a constant reminder of something he didn't want to remember.'

'Yes.'

'I often quarrelled with him about it, you know,' she said. 'It hurt me deeply to see the way he treated you.'

'Yes.' He could believe that. 'So what happened to my real father?'

'I've no idea.'

'That seems a bit bizarre, Mother.'

'I suppose it must do,' she admitted. 'But it was just a holiday romance and I never saw him again after I came back from France. He never knew I was pregnant with his child. I didn't know myself until I got home to England.'

'What happened then?'

'Oh, the usual story. Young girl from respectable family brings shame on horrified parents,' she said. 'They were positively apoplectic when they found out who was to blame for my condition. A stranger, and a bohemian type at that. An artist . . . and not a very successful one, though both he and his lifestyle had seemed very glamorous to a young girl from a conventional middle-class family.'

'Didn't your father hot foot it to Paris with a shot gun?'

'Good Lord, no, the man wasn't my parents' idea of good husband material. He was far too disreputable in their eyes. He had no money, no prospects . . .'

'*And* he was a seducer of young girls,' Philip interrupted.

'Oh, no! He didn't force me into anything,' his mother was quick to point out. 'I was infatuated with him and a willing party. Actually, he was a very kind and charming man. But he didn't conform to conventional standards. He liked to think of himself as a free spirit. I suppose that's why I fell for him . . . because he was so different from anyone I'd known before. Marriage to me was the last thing he would have wanted.'

'So where did Father . . . the man I knew as Father, fit in?'

'Humphrey was the son of a family friend and awfully sweet on me,' she explained. 'He would have done anything to get me, and proved it by stepping in to protect my reputation and avert a family scandal.'

'I see.'

'Are you terribly shocked?'

'If all this had come to light twenty years ago, I might have been. But you're not so easily shocked as you get older.'

'Don't you even feel a little ashamed of your wayward mother?'

'Well, one does tend to think of one's mother as being a cut above that sort of thing – unreasonable as that is,' he admitted with a wry grin. 'But at my age I'm hardly going to throw a fit or start making judgements.'

'Do you feel any great longing to trace your real father?'

'No. At the moment I can feel nothing beyond relief that I didn't fail the man I knew as Father in what I did . . . only in who I was.'

'Well, you may not have fared very well as a son but you certainly seem to be doing better as a father,' she remarked. 'You and Toby are awfully close.'

'Yes, we are. Probably because there's only been us two for so long. Emily hasn't been around for most of his life.'

'He's grown up into a remarkably balanced young man, despite that,' remarked Meg. 'Much more of a happy-go-lucky type than you ever were.'

'You're telling me,' agreed Philip. 'He's a real young man about town.'

'Gregarious, certainly.'

'Rather too much so at times.'

'Is he?'

'Yes. He's in with a really boisterous crowd at the moment,' explained Philip. 'He met up with an old school pal of his who's turned out to be a real socialite. He's introduced Toby to his friends and they're out at all the fashionable night spots in London most nights of the week.'

'That won't hurt him. At twenty-one he should be having fun.'

'I might have guessed you'd take his side.'

'A grandmother's prerogative.'

'If you say so.'

'Perhaps he gets his arty ways from his biological grandfather?'

'He certainly doesn't get them from me,' smiled Philip.

'You've always had your feet planted firmly on the ground.'

'Young Toby works hard at the factory so I suppose I shouldn't complain if he likes to play hard too.'

'He's like his Uncle Neville was.'

'Yes, not a bit like me. Life has always struck me as such a serious business.'

'And the situation with Emily must have added to it?'

He frowned. 'Yes. Poor, dear Emily . . . such a tragedy.'

'I thought she seemed a lot better when I last went to visit her at the hospital.'

'You know how she fluctuates,' he told her. 'One day I'll go to see her and she'll seem well enough to come home and live a normal life. The next time I go she doesn't even know who I am.'

'Still, she's happy where she is. Happier than you in that she's oblivious to what's going on a lot of the time. And at least she is well looked after.'

'Thank God I can afford to have her decently cared for,' he said. 'It makes my blood boil to think of the appalling way the poor and mentally ill are treated.'

'Yes.'

'Mental health charities are top of my donation list,' he said. 'And I'll never give up hope of a cure for Emily.'

'Me neither.'

They lapsed into thoughtful silence before he went back to something they had touched on earlier.

'I don't enjoy being such a serious person, you know.'

'No?'

'Oh, no. I really envy these cheery extrovert types,' he confessed. 'I suppose that's why I enjoy Lizzie Carter's company so much . . . and her brother-in-law Bobby.'

'Lizzie is very resilient,' said Meg. 'She can put up a cheerful front even when she's in the depths of despair.'

'She never seems to let life get her down. I don't know how she does it.'

'Frankly, I don't know what I'd have done without her this last few months,' admitted Meg. 'She's been such a wonderful companion to me, spending all her spare time cheering me up and encouraging me to get out and about and face life without Humphrey.'

'I think you ought to know that Polly thinks that Meg Verne

has taken her place as the mother figure in your life,' June announced to Lizzie one afternoon early in 1933 when she called to see her sister-in-law at her office.

'Oh, does she? Well, that's just nonsense,' denied Lizzie hotly.

'Is it, though?' queried June, breaking some dead leaves off a potted plant on Lizzie's desk and dropping them into the waste-paper basket. 'I mean . . . you are very pally with Mrs Verne, aren't you?'

'She lost her husband. I've been giving her some moral support, that's all,' explained Lizzie. 'She doesn't have a daughter to turn to and her daughter-in-law can't help.'

'There's Philip.'

'It isn't the same as having another woman to talk to, though, is it?'

'Oh, I dunno . . .'

'Come on, June. There are times for every woman when a spot of female company is the only thing that will do.'

'All right, I'll admit it,' she said. 'But it's perfectly understandable that the green-eyed monster has got to Polly, considering the amount of time you spend with Meg these days . . . and her son, come to that.'

'Oh, so that's what all this is about, is it?' objected Lizzie. 'All I do is have lunch with Philip now and again.'

'Isn't he at his mother's place when you go there, too?' said June.

'Sometimes, yes,' said Lizzie defensively. 'But it doesn't mean anything.'

'No?'

'No. There's nothing going on between us, if that's what you're implying.'

'Methinks the lady doth protest too much,' teased June.

'Leave it out, June,' snapped Lizzie. 'I thought you of all people would take a more liberal view. It's bad enough having to put up with insinuations from Jed and Polly.'

'I'm not criticising you, I just wondered if you fancy him.'

'The old cliché "we're just good friends" really is true in this instance.'

'At the moment,' said June suggestively.

'He's a married man.'

'He doesn't have a normal marriage though, does he?'

'Not in the accepted sense of the word, no,' admitted Lizzie. 'But he still loves his wife. He's told me so. Many times.'

'Are you sure he isn't trying to convince himself?'

'Oh, for goodness' sake!'

'I'm only being realistic,' said June. 'After all, it must be hard for him to stay on the straight and narrow the way things are with his wife. No matter how much he loves her.'

'Maybe it is,' agreed Lizzie. 'But I'm certainly not putting temptation in his way. I've no intention of getting involved in that way with a married man . . . not ever again.'

'No?'

'No. But if you and Polly and Jed are determined to believe otherwise, you'll carry on believing it whatever I say.'

'All right, all right, keep your hair on.'

Lizzie could have told June that Philip had become very important to her. But as any such confession would be immediately misconstrued, she deemed it wise to remain silent.

'Anyway, I thought we were talking about Polly?' said Lizzie.

'We were.'

'Is she really getting herself into a state about my friendship with Meg Verne?'

'You know Polly when it comes to you, she's always been very possessive.'

'I'll go and see her,' said Lizzie. 'Try to reassure her. She's a good sort, I don't want her to be hurt unnecessarily.'

Lizzie called to see Polly the next day in her lunch break, knowing she would be alone because both Will and Luke took sandwiches for lunch and ate them at work.

Polly made tea and set about cutting cheese sandwiches for herself and Lizzie. 'What brings you here during a working day?' she asked as Lizzie sat down at the kitchen table.

'Oh, I just thought I'd pop in for a chat.'

'Slumming, aren't you?' said Polly, slicing great doorsteps off the loaf on the bread board. 'Don't you usually have dinner, or lunch as you call it now that you've gone up in the world, with your posh friends?'

'Only now and again.'

Polly made sandwiches as thick as encyclopaedias and handed one to Lizzie, then sat down opposite her at the table and poured tea from the large brown pot. The familiarity of it all gave Lizzie a pang of nostalgia. The big kitchen table, the sooty warmth of the range, the stew gently simmering on the stove, the steamy smell of clothes airing around it, brought her childhood back so vividly, her eyes smarted with tears. You hadn't been able to hear the stew bubbling in those days, though, not with everyone gathered round the table talking at once.

Achingly homesick for those times, she nibbled her

sandwich. When she looked across at Polly it was as though she was seeing her for the first time after a long absence. Quite suddenly, the effects of the passing years registered with startling clarity. The hair that had once been so bright red was completely white now and thinner, her face lined and jowled. Only her eyes retained their sharp vitality.

The years had not been kind to her as they had to Meg who wore her golden years with elegance. Polly had no cleverly applied cosmetics to disguise the effects of time, no smart clothes to reduce the years. Nor would she want them. Lizzie had offered her money to spend on herself on countless occasions, but that wasn't what Polly cared for. She had only ever wanted one thing: to have an ordinary life with her family around her. Not being a person of any guile or sensitivity, her primal instincts drove her to achieve this with domineering tactics.

So much of Lizzie came from this woman. Here, in this house, she'd learned about the sharing and caring of family life. Polly had taught her about basic morality, had made her feel loved.

What could have happened to her if Polly hadn't taken her in, didn't bear thinking about. So having to fight for her independence was a small price to pay for so many years in the care of this intransigent woman.

'Actually I do have a special reason for coming to see you,' said Lizzie.

'Oh?'

'I have something to tell you.'

'Get on with it then,' said Polly sipping her tea, her blue eyes watchful over the rim of the cup.

'I want you to know that my friendship with Meg Verne has not altered the way I feel about you.'

'That June's been blabbing!'

'Yes, she has, and I'm very glad she has because I don't want you being unhappy over my thoughtlessness in not explaining the way things are.'

Chewing her sandwich slowly, Polly waited for her to continue.

'I'm very fond of Meg, here in my mind,' she said, touching her head. 'What I feel for you is in my heart . . . in my blood. You're the only mother I can remember, and that will never change.'

Polly sniffed to hide her embarrassment then said shakily, 'Well, that's nice to know.'

'I thought it needed saying.'

'You've changed, though,' said Polly, rapidly recovering her composure. 'I mean, all this business with the Vernes . . .'

'I like them, Polly,' Lizzie said ardently. 'I enjoy their company. You would like Meg too if you got to know her.'

'Huh!'

'Why not? You're about the same age, you're bound to have something in common. You could even become friends.'

'You know perfectly well that I would never make a friend of anyone in *that* family,' declared Polly hotly.

'Yes, I do know that,' sighed Lizzie wearily, saddened by Polly's stubborn prejudice which couldn't be an easy burden to have borne for so many years. Pity wasn't an emotion one normally felt for Polly but Lizzie felt sorry for her now. Sorry she was wasting her autumn years in bitterness when she deserved tranquillity.

'I should think so too.'

'You want me to stop having anything to do with the Vernes, don't you?'

'I think it would be right and proper, yes,' said Polly. 'Considering their connection with our family. But I can't tell you what to do . . . those days have long gone.'

'Yes, they have,' agreed Lizzie. 'But you can still be the best friend I ever had.'

Polly's eyes were bright with tears. 'Actions speak louder than words.'

Lizzie reminded herself of the price she would pay if she did what Polly wanted and gave up her freedom to choose her own friends. Life would become a prison, colourless and empty. She would soon begin to hate herself – and Polly!

'I'm sorry but I can't let you bully me into ending my friendship with them,' she said. 'It wouldn't be right for either of us.'

After Lizzie had gone, depression settled over Polly in a sickening tide as she washed the dishes, her movements slowed by the heaviness of her gloom. The sensible part of her mind said it was time to put the past behind her. Stan had been dead for nearly fourteen years and the bad feeling between herself and the Vernes only came between her and Lizzie. Then she remembered her dear son who had lost his life needlessly and was so agonised she could scarcely endure it.

Why didn't Lizzie share her pain? How could she bear even to be in the same room as the man who had killed her husband, let alone share a table with him? It was quite beyond Polly's understanding. Lizzie claimed there was nothing going on between them and Polly believed her. But if she ever found out different . . . well, that just didn't bear thinking about. The mere thought of him and Lizzie together like that . . . ugh! The idea of it revolted her.

The sound of something breaking startled her. A saucer had smashed into pieces in the sink. She was shocked to realise that she was to blame. She had thrown it down with such force in the anguish of the moment. As she picked the fragments up and took them out to the dustbin in the yard, tears were streaming down her cheeks. Oh, how she longed to be free from the horrors in her mind! How she longed to have Lizzie back!

Philip had become very adept at inventing plausible excuses to call at Carter's Silks for a chat with Lizzie and Bobby.

'I've just heard that imports of raw silk are still rising,' he'd say to Bobby, breezing into the factory and catching him on the factory floor or in his office.

Or: 'I was just passing and wondered if you'd seen this article about the boom in silk stockings in the hosiery factories in the Midlands,' he'd tell Lizzie, putting a trade magazine on her desk.

He was lightly ribbed by them about not having enough to do at Verne's but no matter how busy they were, he was always given a cup of tea and a few jovial words which sent him on his way feeling better for having come. He'd learned to ignore the scowling hostility of Lizzie's son, Jed, and the tacit enmity of Luke Carter.

One day in February, however, he was forced to face up to the vehemence of young Jed's feelings for him.

'Oh, it's you again,' he said as Philip appeared at the entrance to the factory where Jed just happened to be on his way out.

'That's right.'

'I thought there was a rotten smell around here all of a sudden.'

'No need to be like that, old chap,' said Philip, more affected than he cared to admit.

'Don't "old chap" me,' growled Jed, and as he glared at Philip his striking likeness to his father was uncanny.

'Is there really any need for all this hostility?' Philip asked mildly.

'Too right there is,' said Jed, standing in front of him and blocking his way.

'Surely not?'

'Shut up!'

'Oh, charming.'

'Don't be clever with me,' said Jed. 'You're scum and it's my duty to stop you from turning up here and polluting the air around our factory.'

'Let me pass, please.'

'No fear. You just sling your hook . . . you murderer!'

Philip knew that if they had been within earshot of Jed's mother, this wouldn't be happening. She'd told him that she had warned Jed about this sort of behaviour.

'I'm not going to take orders from you,' Philip told him.

'And I'm not gonna stand by and let you sniff round my mother,' rasped Jed.

'Your mother is a grown woman . . . old enough to choose her own friends.'

'Have you no brains at all?' rasped Jed. 'Are you too thick to realise you're not wanted around here?'

'Oh, act your age, for goodness' sake.'

The young man took a sudden lunge at Philip, grabbing his lapels and glaring viciously into his face.

'Now, for the last time . . . are you gonna clear off and never come back?'

'Certainly not!'

'Right, you've asked for it and don't say you haven't been warned!'

Jed was dragging Philip across the yard, threatening to impale him on the factory railings, when Bobby made a timely intervention.

'Hey! That's quite enough of that, Jed,' he said, pulling his nephew away from Philip and observing him with cold authority. 'What do you think you're doing?'

'You're just a bloody Verne-lover like my mother,' Jed snarled at his uncle, his freckled face angrily suffused as he stomped off across the cobbled yard.

'Sorry about that, mate,' said Bobby. 'He's as hot-headed as his father used to be.'

'You're telling me.'

'He'll grow out of it.'

'I certainly hope so,' said Philip, straightening his lapels.

'Do us a favour?' said Bobby.

'If I can.'

'Don't say anything to Lizzie about this little fracas,' he said. 'No point in upsetting her unless we have to.'

'What little fracas was that?' asked Philip meaningfully.

'Good man, Phil.'

'Will you do something for me too?' he requested.

'If it's legal and within my power, 'course I will.'

'Will you tell me truthfully if I ought to stop coming to your factory?'

'Definitely not,' stated Bobby categorically.

'No?'

'Oh, no.' He was adamant. 'Once we allow a stroppy youngster like Jed to make the rules, who knows where it'll end?'

'As long as you're sure?'

'Absolutely positive,' he confirmed. 'When Lizzie tells you to stop coming over, that's the time to stop. Until then, you call in whenever you feel like it, mate.'

'Thanks.'

'Come on through to the office. Let's see if we can find you a cuppa tea.'

'I was hoping you'd say that,' said Philip, falling comfortably into step beside him as they went inside and headed for the offices.

'Are you going to the Federation meeting tomorrow night?' asked Bobby.

'Yes.'

'Good. I'll buy you a drink afterwards to make up for my nephew's shocking manners.'

'There's no need.'

'I'll buy you one anyway.'

'In that case, I'll look forward to it.'

Chapter Nineteen

'You look lovely, Eva,' Lizzie told her beautiful daughter who was dressed ready to go out in a clingy white dress with a low-cut back.

'Thanks, Mum.'

Lizzie turned to her son. 'Doesn't your sister look gorgeous, eh, Jed?'

'You'll look even better when you put the rest of your frock on, sis,' he told her with typical sibling humour.

'Very funny,' tutted Eva.

'Bit scanty though, you must admit,' he said, peering at her rear. 'They've forgotten to put a back in the top half.'

'That's the style, you dope,' she said with playful impatience. 'Honestly . . . you're so old-fashioned.'

'You wanna be careful, going out looking like that,' he warned her more seriously. 'You're asking for a seeing to.'

'Must you be so vulgar?' objected Eva, fiddling with her shoulder-length hair before the gilt-edged mirror over the sitting-room fireplace. 'Speak to him, will you, Mum?'

'Don't be so coarse, Jed,' said Lizzie. 'Low-backed dresses are fashionable and Eva looks very nice in hers.'

'Don't blame me if some bloke gets the wrong idea.'

Despite the fact that Lizzie's success had taken the family into a different social class, Jed clung determinedly to the lower echelons, moulding himself with great dedication in his father's image. Not for him the nightspots of the West End to which his sister was drawn for entertainment. He preferred, or professed to prefer, a pint and a game of darts at the local with the mates of his childhood in Bessle Street.

'The people I go out with are all far too civilised to do that,' she retorted. 'They know what's what ... unlike a mindless clod like you!'

At twenty, Eva Carter had the same blonde prettiness as her mother had had at that age, but the income which enabled her to present herself stylishly created a stunning effect. Lizzie was very proud of her independent daughter who had chosen to make her own way rather than go into the family business when she'd finished at college. She'd found a job in the design department at Reed's of Brentford, a large company of textile manufacturers who also carried out research into new man-made fibres which many people in the silk trade believed might be developed eventually to become the fabrics of the future.

Eva bore little resemblance to her brother, either in looks or personality. Whilst he had inherited his father's brooding nature and dwelt on the wrongs of the past, Eva lived for the present and wouldn't know how to bear a grudge. Being naturally gregarious, she'd soon made friends at Reed's, in particular with a young woman of her own age called Ruth. She had introduced her to the crowd of well-heeled friends she went about with and Eva had become one of the gang.

On this warm summer evening she was waiting for them to collect her and go on to the Moonbeam Club in the West End.

'You shouldn't allow her to go out dancing, Mum,' said Jed, his mood becoming solemn.

'And how am I supposed to stop her, even if I wanted to, which I don't?' smiled Lizzie. 'I can't tell her what to do. She's twenty years old and earning her own living. Anyway, I was married and a mother at that age.'

'She's still officially underage,' Jed reminded her.

'Ooh, hark at the old man,' smiled Eva, turning to her brother and slapping his cheeks with both hands playfully. 'Just because he's got the key of the door.'

'Your friends are here,' said Lizzie, seeing a car draw up outside.

Eva grabbed a white silk wrap and a dainty sequinned bag, brushed her mother's cheek with a kiss, and said, ''Bye, then. See you later.'

'Don't be too late now,' said Lizzie, without much hope.

'I won't.'

'Have a good time.'

'You know me.' Eva grinned and hurried out of the front door, leaving an evocative cloud of perfume behind her.

Watching her from the window as she tripped lightly down the front path, Lizzie found herself smiling. Eva was such a delight with her modern outlook and fun-loving ways. Fortunately her insatiable appetite for pleasure hadn't diminished the gentle, warmhearted side of her nature.

'I suppose she'll roll home in the early hours?' said Jed in a doom-laden voice.

'Very probably,' agreed Lizzie who derived vicarious pleasure from her daughter's hectic social life, having had nothing comparable in her own youth. 'But her friends will bring her home in the car so she'll be quite safe.'

'All she cares about is having a good time,' he grumbled.

'That isn't true,' protested Lizzie. 'Just because she likes to have fun, that doesn't make her selfish. She pulls her weight at home and she cares a great deal about all the family, including her grandparents.'

'Be that as it may, I still think she'll end up in trouble, the way she's carrying on.'

'Not Eva,' exclaimed Lizzie. 'She's far too sensible.'

Eva was doing the rhumba with a lean, loquacious young man called Bertie, with floppy fair hair and teeth like tombstones. She was enjoying herself enormously, not least because the hip-swaying movements of the dance gave her the perfect opportunity to show off the figure-hugging effect of her dress.

'Quite a good band, isn't it?' remarked Bertie, dancing with panache, his long-limbed figure smartly accoutred in a black evening suit.

'Not bad at all,' she agreed, moving in time to the music. 'I enjoy the rhumba . . . and the tango.'

'Bags I the next tango!' he said.

'It's a deal,' she laughed, greeny-brown eyes shining.

The club was in a cellar in a side street near Leicester Square. It was softly lit and intimate with a small dance floor surrounded by candlelit tables. There were six of them in Eva's party, three of each sex, the sons and daughters of successful business or professional people. They were not paired off particularly, and changed partners at will. It was all very lighthearted and casual.

When the music ended she and Bertie went back to the

table, laughing breathlessly. They sipped cocktails then Eva glided into a foxtrot with someone called Peter who worked in his father's printing firm. On the way back to their table after the dance, he spotted someone he knew and insisted on introducing her.

His friend was sitting at a table with a group of other young people and brief introductions were made. But the only one who registered with Eva was someone called Toby who had dark wavy hair and the deepest brown eyes she had ever seen. He was nothing short of gorgeous and she couldn't take her eyes off him. He seemed to be having the same trouble with her and they stood gazing at each other as small talk went on around them.

She and Peter still hadn't returned to their own table when the band struck up a waltz. Much to Eva's delight she found herself being swept on to the dance floor by the handsome Toby, leaving Peter and the other members of Toby's party looking on.

'That wasn't very polite to the people you're with,' remarked Eva.

'They won't mind . . . we don't have to stay together just because we came together,' he said, moving back slightly and smiling into her eyes.

'That's all right then.'

'Are you and Peter . . .?'

'No, he's just part of the crowd I go around with.'

'Good.' She seemed to shimmer luminously before him with her bright hair and laughing eyes. 'You're lovely.'

'Thank you. You're not shy!'

'Not when I meet someone like you.'

'Do you have an answer for everything?'

'No, not everything.'

'That's a relief.'

His tone became more serious. 'Would your friends be annoyed if we just sort of disappeared?'

'I don't know if they would or not but I certainly wouldn't be rude enough to behave in such a way,' she told him.

'Yes, I thought you'd say something like that,' he said with a wicked grin.

'Anyway, I want to stay. I like it here. It's good fun.'

'In that case, I shall snap you up for every dance until the end.'

'You won't get any objections from me.'

'No?'

'No,' she confirmed, feeling almost unbearably excited when the music ended and he escorted her back to her friends.

Back at the table Eva was confronted with exuberant raillery.

'Looks like Toby has put us all out of the running,' teased Bertie.

'He's no right to be so handsome,' complained Peter with mock regret.

'He looks very smitten to me,' laughed Ruth. 'Is that right, Eva?'

'Maybe,' she said coyly.

'I hope you're not going to tell us that you were talking about silk?' laughed another member of the group.

'No . . . why would I do that?'

'Because you're both from a silk family, of course,' he said.

'I didn't know that,' grinned Eva. 'His family was the last

thing I had on my mind while we were dancing.'

'His family own Verne's Silks,' Bertie informed her.

'Oh, no!' she exclaimed, her interest fully aroused. Of all the families in London, he had to be a Verne.

'What's the matter?' asked Ruth.

'Nothing,' she said because she didn't want to bore her friends with the tedious tale. 'It's just a coincidence, that's all . . . us both being from a silk background.'

'It seems we have a connection,' she said to Toby later as they quick-stepped around the floor.

'You feel it too then,' he whispered, close to her ear.

'Apart from that.' She grinned. 'I mean . . . our families are in the same line of business. They know each other.'

'Do they really?' he said, moving back and eyeing her quizzically.

'My surname is Carter.'

He looked thoughtful for a moment. 'Carter's Silks?'

She nodded. 'That's right. Lizzie Carter is my mother.'

'Well, I'll be blowed. I've met her several times at my grandmother's house. She's a friend of hers.' He gave her a studious look. 'I can see the likeness now.'

'She's a good friend of your father's too, I believe.'

'Better and better,' said Toby with genuine delight.

'Worse and worse,' she corrected. 'There's bad feeling between the two families. You must have heard the story?'

'Yes.' He narrowed his eyes. 'Something happened years ago. There was a fight, wasn't there, your father got killed?'

'That's right.'

'But your mother can't possibly be on bad terms with us or

she wouldn't be so friendly with Gran and Dad.'

'No, she isn't. But the fact that she isn't has caused no end of trouble between her and my grandmother . . . and my brother,' she explained. 'You daren't even mention the name Verne to them for fear of an explosion.'

His expression became grave. 'So how does that affect us? I mean, if I were to ask to see you again?'

'It won't make any difference.'

He gave her a happy smile. 'That's a relief. I thought perhaps I was going to lose you before I'd even got to know you.'

'No. What took place is all ancient history as far as I'm concerned,' she said. 'I can't let something that happened when I was six years old affect my life.'

'I should say not.'

'If you were to ask me out, though,' she said with a devilish grin, 'it would be easier if you don't come to my house to call for me.'

'Oh?'

'I wouldn't want to expose you to my brother's wicked tongue.' she explained. 'He has tunnel vision when it comes to this particular subject. He's got a real thing about my father, you see, sort of hero worships his memory.'

'He won't bother me,' said Toby. 'I can put up with anything if it means seeing you.'

'It's very noble of you to offer,' she said, 'but it would only cause a family upset. My brother quarrels enough with my mother about her friendship with your family . . . there's no point our adding to it unnecessarily.'

'You wouldn't tell him you were going out with me then?' he said.

'Oh, yes, I would tell him,' Eva declared firmly. 'Who I go out with is my business.'

'So why keep me hidden away?'

'I'd rather not give him the chance to embarrass either of us.'

'If you'd prefer it that way . . .'

'I would. For the moment anyway.'

'We can always meet at my place?' he suggested. 'I have a small flat in Chelsea.'

'Really? How very adult.'

'Yes. When I was twenty-one I thought it time I got from under my father's feet and struck out on my own.'

'A man can do that and no one turns a hair, but if I took a flat as a single woman it would raise a few eyebrows.'

'Yes.' But as this was no time for a debate on women's rights, Toby put the conversation neatly back on course. 'Anyway, at least we have somewhere to meet if the need should arise.'

'We'll take it one step at a time, though, shall we?'

'Sorry. Was I rushing you?'

'A little,' she said, but it was only a token protest for the chemistry flowing between them was undeniable.

'How about coming to see a film with me tomorrow evening then?' he suggested when the music ended.

'Thank you, I'd like that,' she said, smiling up at him.

Lizzie thought Philip seemed rather preoccupied when they lunched together a couple of weeks before Christmas.

'Is anything wrong?'

'Not wrong exactly,' he said vaguely.

'Something has your attention, though,' she chided. 'And it certainly isn't me.'

He shook his head as though to bring himself back to the present. 'You're right,' he told her. 'Am I being lousy company?'

'I've had more scintillating lunches,' she admitted candidly.

'Sorry.'

'Only teasing,' she told him. 'Is there anything I can do to help?'

'No, it's good news really,' he explained. 'Emily is coming home for Christmas.'

'Oh, that *is* good news, Philip,' she said because she knew how much he cared about his wife.

'Yes, it is.'

'Why so worried then?'

'Her stays at home usually end in disaster,' he said. 'I don't know who's more pleased when they come to an end – Emily or me.'

'Yes, it's bound to be a strain for you both.'

He sighed. 'There's nothing I'd like more than for it to be a success, especially at Christmas, but past experience has made me wary.'

'What's brought it about this year?' Lizzie wondered aloud.

'The hospital only has a skeleton staff on duty over Christmas,' he explained, 'so they try to get as many patients home for the holiday as possible.'

'She's not been back for a while, has she?'

'No. Because it was always such a failure the doctors thought it best not to disrupt her again,' he explained. 'However, she's been better lately and they are particularly short staffed this

Christmas so they want to give it a try. It's only for a few days . . . the day before Christmas Eve till the day after Boxing Day.'

'Nothing much can go wrong in that short time.'

'Don't you believe it!'

'Will you have Christmas Day at home?' she asked.

'No. We'll go to my mother's for Christmas dinner,' he said. 'And all problems aside, it will be very nice for Emily to have a proper Christmas with the family.'

'Yes, it will.'

'What about you, what are you doing over the holiday?'

'We'll all be going to Polly's for Christmas Day,' she told him.

'Do you enjoy that?'

'Yes . . . well, it's traditional,' she explained. 'I wouldn't dream of going anywhere else, even if I wanted to.'

'Christmas is a family time whether we like it or not!'

'I know one person who would rather be somewhere else this year, though.'

'Who?'

'My daughter. She'd much rather be with Toby on Christmas Day.'

'She's welcome to our celebrations. Mother's taken a real shine to her.'

'I know but it would break her grandmother's heart.'

'It would?'

'Definitely,' she affirmed. 'Polly would see it as the ultimate betrayal if a member of our family was to spend Christmas with the Vernes.'

'She knows that Eva is seeing Toby though, doesn't she?'

'Oh, yes, Eva doesn't try to hide it, but she makes sure her grandmother knows that there's nothing serious between them,' Lizzie explained. 'She's careful to stress that they often go about in a group . . . good friends and all that.'

'Sensible girl.'

'And as she keeps him well away from the family, it's easier for Polly to put it out of her mind.'

'I suppose it must be.'

'I think Eva is protecting Toby rather than the family, though. Jed in particular would go out of his way to make him feel uncomfortable.'

'The balloon would really go up if they decided to get married, wouldn't it?'

'Phew! That doesn't bear thinking about,' Lizzie agreed. 'Fortunately it isn't likely to happen. They're both far too fond of hitting the highspots to want to settle down.'

'Yes, they certainly are two of a kind in that respect.'

'They've all sorts of social occasions lined up over the festive season, I gather,' she told him. 'Parties, dances and so on right up to the New Year. Eva'll need Christmas Day with the family as a rest period.'

'Sounds as though they both will.'

'Anyway, marriage is one problem we needn't anticipate.'

'It wouldn't worry me . . . but it's probably just as well for your sake.'

'Yes.' She was thoughtful for a moment before changing the subject. 'Well, Philip, I won't be seeing you again until after the holiday.' She raised her wine glass. 'So here's wishing you a very happy Christmas. I really hope all goes well with Emily.'

'Thank you.'

As their glasses touched, she reached out with her other hand and grasped his in a gesture of encouragement for the difficult task that lay ahead of him. Their eyes locked in a bond of feeling she couldn't quite identify. Was it just the warmth of friendship magnified by the emotion of the season, or something deeper?

'Merry Christmas, Lizzie,' he said, and as she reluctantly removed her hand from his, she found herself wishing that they were spending some time together over the holiday.

'I have to go into the factory for a couple of hours this morning, Emily,' said Philip over breakfast on Christmas Eve. 'But I'll be home by lunchtime, and Mother is coming over to keep you company.'

'It's sweet of you to organise it with your mother, Philip, but I don't need a nurse,' she told him sharply.

'No, of course not,' he told her, treading the fine line between husbandly concern and over-protectiveness. He had deliberately continued with his usual Christmas Eve visit to the factory to keep things as normal as possible, but had felt compelled to enlist his mother's assistance because he daren't leave Emily in the house on her own.

'I'm not ill now,' she reminded him. 'If I were they wouldn't have let me come home.'

It was so difficult to strike the right note in his attitude towards her. His natural instinct was to protect and pamper her, his respect for her dictated otherwise.

'Treat her like a normal person,' the doctor had advised him.

'But she isn't a normal person, is she?' he'd pointed out grimly. 'If she was, she wouldn't have to live in an institution.'

'She seems to be fairly stable at the moment, Mr Verne,' the doctor insisted. 'So treat her accordingly.'

'Can she go out of the house?' he'd asked.

'Yes, it will do her the world of good to go out. Not on her own, of course.'

'That goes without saying.'

'Just take it as it comes. Any major problems, let us know. There'll be someone on duty over Christmas.'

To a casual observer Emily looked ordinary enough, though years of hospitalisation had given her a rather defeated look. Her movements were either very slow and laboured or fast and jerky, depending on her mood. Her beauty had faded but Philip could still glimpse the woman she'd once been in her smile and fine bone structure. Over the years, his mother had seen to it that she didn't become too dowdy by shopping for clothes for her. This morning she was wearing a scarlet twinset over a grey skirt, and her near white hair was dragged back into a bun. Sometimes she wore make up, even at the hospital; other times she had no patience with which to apply it and lipstick tubes and powder boxes were sent flying in a fit of rage.

Today was one of her calmer days and she was wearing a little powder and rouge. She looked pleasant and normal, like an ordinary middle-aged lady. But Philip saw a strangeness about her . . . a heaviness about the eyes, due partly to medication, partly to a life without variety or challenge.

'I know you're not ill, darling,' he said now in reply to her, 'but I thought it would give you and Mother a chance to have a good old woman-to-woman chinwag without me around.'

Her face brightened. 'Perhaps we could go and have a look round the shops?' she said with a look of childlike pleasure.

'It will be packed everywhere on Christmas Eve,' he pointed out, aware of her vulnerability out on the crowded streets.

She narrowed her eyes as though remembering, then looked at him, smiling. 'It's Christmas Eve, of course! That's even better. I used to love the shops on a Christmas Eve. I could get presents for everyone.'

The look on her face pierced him with pity and reminded him of the times when they had had a proper marriage. There had been so much life then; the love, laughter, arguments, reconciliations, were all vivid in his memory. Even the weather seemed to have registered with more clarity then: driving rain, dazzling sunshine, gustier winds. Was it all just an illusion, though, age looking back on youth through the distorted vision of nostalgia? Would it be remembered just as gloriously even without Emily's disability?

Returning to the present, he dismissed his reservations about the shopping trip as Emily would be in his mother's capable hands and said, 'Yes, all right, if you'd like that. I can see no reason why not.' He could hear a supervisory note in his voice which he didn't like but supposed was inevitable. 'You can arrange it with Mother when she comes.'

Toby, who was staying at the parental home in honour of his mother's visit, breezed into the dining room.

'Good morning, folks,' he said with his usual joie de vivre. 'Anything left for me to eat or have my ageing relatives gorged it all?'

'Not so much of the ageing,' joked Philip. 'And, yes, we've

saved something for you, though it's probably dried to a cinder by this time.'

'As long as it tastes all right,' he said, helping himself from the tureen on the sideboard.

'You look tired, dear,' his mother remarked absently.

'That isn't surprising, the hours he keeps,' grinned his father with forced lightheartedness, grateful for his son's cheery company to ease the strained atmosphere. 'Since he's out nearly every night.'

'It *is* Christmas,' Toby pointed out, sitting down and eating heartily.

'It's Christmas all the year round for you,' admonished Philip lightly.

'Well, you're only young once, as they say,' he said, giving his mother a rather hesitant grin as though realising he must include her in the conversation. 'Isn't that right, Mother?'

'Yes . . . yes, of course,' she said stiffly, as though she didn't know how to reply.

'You'll have to get used to this boisterous son of yours, Emily,' said Philip. 'He's like a ruddy tornado about the place . . . always rushing off somewhere. It's a good job he's got his own flat. He'd wear me out if he lived here permanently.'

'Any minute now I'll be rushing off to the factory,' said Toby, for he was as enthusiastic about his work as he was for his play. 'Are you coming with me, Dad?'

'No, I'll be along later,' he said. 'I'll wait until your grandmother arrives.'

'Your father doesn't think I'm fit to be left here alone,' said Emily.

The ensuing hiatus betrayed the fact that Toby didn't feel as at ease in his mother's company as he was pretending. Encouraged by his father, he had visited her at the clinic every so often over the years but was obviously finding her presence here in the house a strain.

'Er . . . well, that's Dad for you, isn't it?' he said jokily. 'Ever the supervisor. Don't you let him bully you.'

'All right,' she said, missing the joke and sounding awkward because she was out of the habit of family banter and felt miserably incongruous in its crossfire.

When Toby had roared off to the factory in his car, Philip and Emily had another cup of coffee and she lit a cigarette with fast staccato movements, her fingers brown with nicotine stains. Over the years of her illness she had become almost a chain smoker. Philip struggled with a supply of small talk, trying to avoid the silences which were stretched uncomfortably. He hoped things would improve as they got used to each other again.

Emily's illness had distanced them so effectively, they were more like strangers here in this house than at the hospital. It was one thing exchanging little anecdotes during the transient atmosphere of hospital visiting and quite another trying to sustain a normal adult conversation in a family environment after such a long time apart.

'I know I've caused you a lot of trouble by being ill, Philip,' she said uncertainly.

'Nonsense,' he said, stabbed with compassion at her constant need for reassurance.

'But I feel quite different now,' she said excitedly. 'I can't tell you how much better I feel. Honestly, I'm really optimistic.

I'm going to be all right this time, I can feel it.'

'Yes, I know, darling. And so do I.' He'd heard it all before. In her better times she always thought it would last forever. In earlier times he used to think so too.

'I promise you.'

It both irritated him and broke his heart to hear her making promises about something over which she had no control. He detested the way she apologised to him for her illness as though any of it was her fault. But he felt duty bound to humour her when what he really wanted to do was to scream at her to stop being so humble.

'Stop worrying about it and try to enjoy Christmas.'

She leaned across the table and put her hand on his. To his shame he felt nothing but an overwhelming need to escape.

'It's all going to be like it used to be . . . you and me . . . just like the old days. It is, isn't it, Philip?'

His stomach was knotted with tension. He wasn't sure if he had that much hope and patience left in him. He struggled to keep a tight rein on his inner feelings and not let them show. To be perfectly honest, he didn't know if he could turn the clock back on their marriage if it ever did happen that he needed to. So much time had passed. Was it possible for any marriage to be resurrected after so long?

'We'll be a family again, you, me and Toby,' she said, and when he didn't answer immediately added, 'We will, won't we, Philip?'

'Yes, dear, of course we will,' he said at last, hearing the empty ring of his words and hating himself for it.

He was relieved when his mother arrived. The emotional strain of being with Emily was appalling. Philip lived in fear that her behaviour would change suddenly and drastically. She'd been away a long time; he was out of the habit of coping with her sudden mood swings.

'Emily fancies going out to the shops,' he told his mother.

'Oh . . . er . . . that will be nice,' said Meg, unable to conceal her doubts.

Fortunately Emily didn't seem to notice and shuffled from the room to get ready for her outing.

'Don't look so worried, Mother,' said Philip. 'The doctor has assured me that it will do her good to get out of the house. She does seem to be having a very calm patch at the moment.'

'Yes, of course,' said his mother, biting her lip. 'It's just that . . . well, it'll be so crowded everywhere. I don't mind going with her in the least normally but she's out of the habit of shopping. I'm afraid it might be too much for her.'

'Mmm, that was my first reaction to her suggestion, too,' he said, 'but it seems a pity to deprive her as she really wants to go and seems so well.'

'Yes.'

'At the first sign of distress, just get straight into a taxi and come home.'

'Don't worry, she'll be fine.'

'We have been professionally advised to treat her like any other person, after all,' he said, trying to quell his own fears.

'I'll keep a close eye on her to make sure she doesn't get lost in the crowds,' said Meg. 'I'll get the taxi to drop us outside Harrods. She can do all her shopping there.'

'Good idea. You can put everything on my account so there'll be no problem with Emily's trying to handle money.'

'I was just wondering how I was going to get over that one,' confessed his mother.

'The poor love's been out of circulation for so long, she doesn't know the difference between a shilling and a threepenny piece.'

'No.'

'Try not to let her see you being too protective of her though,' he said. 'It's so terribly demeaning for her.'

'I don't think she notices it any more than a child would,' said Meg.

'What do you think I should get as a Christmas present for Toby?' Emily enquired of Meg as the two women pushed their way round the menswear department at Harrods.

'How about a nice pair of leather gloves?' suggested Meg.

'That's a good idea,' agreed Emily.

The transaction was completed without too much trouble. The only awkward moment was when Emily rummaged through all the gloves the assistant put out on the counter with such enthusiasm most of them ended up on the floor. At which point she got down on her hands and knees to pick them up, apologising with embarrassing vehemence.

She also bought a gold watch for Philip, and Meg helped her choose some pearl earrings as her own gift.

When Emily was satisfied with her purchases, they made their way to the restaurant for hot buttered toast and coffee. Meg was feeling more relaxed now that they had reached this homeward stretch of the outing without a hitch. It was so pleasing to see Emily on such good form.

'Are you enjoying yourself?' asked Meg, sipping her coffee.

'Very much, Mother-in-law,' she said, her eyes shining a little too brightly. 'I'm having a wonderful time.'

Meg smiled a bitter-sweet smile, remembering other shopping trips she and Emily had had together. Meg hadn't had to watch over her then and put her up to date with all the latest fashions. It had been the other way around then for Emily had been one of the smartest women in London. Still, that was all a very long time ago. Fate had seen fit to deal her this blow and all the reminiscing in the world wouldn't change it.

Emily was in unusually high spirits and chattered on about the golden future when she would be coming home for good. Meg went along with what she said to please her. She had, in fact, rather enjoyed their morning out together, and thought how much she would like to do it again sometime.

'We'll have to be going home soon,' she said when she'd finished her coffee.

'Oh, already?'

'I'm afraid so,' said Meg. 'I still have some last-minute bits and pieces to see to for Christmas dinner tomorrow.'

'All right,' said Emily, and began gathering her bags.

'I'll have to pop into the ladies' room on the way out.'

'Me too,' said Emily.

There was quite a crowd and they had to wait their turn. Emily went into the cubicle first and Meg went into the one next to her a few moments later, delighted at the way the morning had gone. When she came out of the cubicle the crowd had dispersed and there was no sign of Emily. Nor in the wash area or by the mirrors. She wasn't still in the cubicle either – a stranger emerged from there.

'Do you know what happened to the woman who came in

here with me?' Meg asked the attendant who was sitting at a small table drinking a cup of tea and reading a magazine.

'The one in the green coat and hat trimmed with black fur?'

'That's right.'

'Washed her hands and went.'

'Oh, no!'

'Is she really a schoolteacher?'

'*A schoolteacher?*'

'Yeah, reckoned she was going to school . . . she had a class waiting for her, or something,' explained the woman without much interest. 'It didn't ring true with me, though, 'cos the schools wouldn't be open on a Christmas Eve.'

'Thank you,' said Meg, and hurried out into the store to search for her poor disturbed daughter-in-law among the crowds.

Emily was worried sick about being late for her class. She couldn't imagine why she had stopped off to go shopping on her way to work. In fact, why she was here in a crowded store at all was a mystery to her. In desperate need of fresh air and anxious to get to work on time, she asked someone where the exit was. After a great deal of pushing and shoving, she managed to find her way out into the street where she was immediately buffeted by crowds so dense she could hardly move or breathe.

She felt extremely muddled. Where was the school from here? She couldn't remember. In fact she couldn't remember the name of where she was now either. It looked vaguely familiar, though. So much traffic, so many people rushing in all directions. Where were they all going? It was all so frightfully confusing. Maybe she might be able to get her bearings better if she crossed the road. It didn't look quite so crowded over there. Yes, that's what she'd do. Perhaps everything would seem clearer from the other side of the street.

Having made the decision, she felt happy and free. It was good to be well again and working in her old profession of teacher. Such was her joy she wanted to sing. She burst into a rather tuneless chorus of 'Always', completely oblivious of the curious glances being cast in her direction as she threaded her way slowly through the crowds to the road.

People were gathered at the kerbside, waiting for a gap in the traffic so that they could cross. Well, they might have time to wait about but she didn't have all day – she was a busy woman with an important job to do. With a tremendous feeling of well-being and confidence, she stepped into the road – right in front of a car . . .

Chapter Twenty

Lizzie's contribution to the Christmas Day festivities at Polly's was the food for tea and supper which she prepared in advance at home. This arrangement had been in place for many years and major culinary efforts on the afternoon of Christmas Eve were as much a part of the festive season as holly and mistletoe. Mountains of mince pies and sausage rolls were produced, an enormous ham boiled and glazed, and a joint of pork roasted and left cold for sandwiches. The top of the rich fruit cake Lizzie had made beforehand would be transformed with great dollops of icing into windblown snowfields inhabited by little plaster robins and waxen holly leaves.

The kitchen was in pleasant uproar, every surface strewn with baking tins and cooking pots, and flour covering everything. The house always had a special feel to it on Christmas Eve afternoon, Lizzie thought. The collective aromas from the kitchen added to the growing pile of lumpy packages under the tree in the sitting room and a florid abundance of paper chains made the whole place quiver with the excitement of the holiday.

Eva had never lost her childhood enthusiasm for the 'great bake', and on this particular Christmas Eve afternoon was happily ensconced in the kitchen with her mother while Jed was out doing some last-minute shopping.

'It's a wonder we get a present from that brother of mine,' remarked Eva, sitting at the kitchen table spooning mincemeat into pastry cases. 'I mean, fancy leaving your Christmas shopping this late.'

'We always do get something though, don't we?' Lizzie pointed out. 'He never actually misses the shops.'

'More by luck than good judgement.'

'Anyway, tell me about this party you're going to this evening,' urged Lizzie.

'It's at the home of a friend in Pimlico,' said Eva. 'There's a whole crowd of us going . . . it should be fun.'

'You'll be with Toby though?'

'Oh, yes.'

'You've been going out with him for a while now.'

'Six months.'

'And still not the tiniest bit serious?' probed Lizzie lightly.

'If you're hinting at wedding bells, Mum, you can forget it,' she replied quickly. 'Toby and I get on really well and have a lot of fun together, but we're not thinking of anything as bourgeois as marriage.' She began putting the pastry tops on the pies and pinching the edges with water to seal them. 'We're far too young and immature. Neither of us is ready to settle down.'

'Most girls of your age are thinking in terms of marriage.'

'But not me,' stated Eva categorically. 'Which makes me a bit of a nonconformist, I suppose . . . like you.'

'Me!' exclaimed Lizzie, looking up sharply from the savoury pastry she was cutting into long strips for cheese straws.

'They didn't come more conventional than me when I was young. I was married and settled down at eighteen.'

'Yes, but you didn't exactly conform to the norm later on, after Dad died, did you?' she pointed out. 'I mean, not many widows set up in business on their own.'

'Maybe I was a bit different in that way,' admitted Lizzie. 'But I've always been a great supporter of marriage.'

'So am I,' Eva hastily pointed out. 'When the time and circumstances are right . . . and neither is for Toby and me at present.'

When the last batch of pies was cooking in the oven, they made a pot of tea and sat down at the kitchen table to drink it with a warm mince pie. Chatting companionably, they were about to have a second cup of tea when the telephone rang in the hall.

'I'll get it,' said Eva, flushed from the heat of the oven and the festive atmosphere. 'It'll probably be Toby to finalise the arrangements for this evening.'

As she hurried to the telephone, Lizzie poured herself another cup of tea, relishing the simple pleasure of an afternoon spent with her daughter. Like most people, she and Eva had the occasional bust-up, but compared to Lizzie's stormy relationship with her son, their association was positively tranquil.

Her thoughts moved on to tomorrow. Christmas Day at the house in Thorn Street wasn't wildly exciting but it did have a certain boisterous charm. There was nothing quite like a gathering of the Carter clan at Christmas to evoke the spirit of the season. This year, also, the festivities would incorporate a welcome home for the twins who'd been away most of the year performing in working men's clubs the length and breadth of the country. Some of the venues were real dives according to June, but the boys would rather scratch a living this way than abandon their dream and settle for an ordinary job.

Finishing her tea, she turned her attention to the oven, and was putting the steaming mince pies on to a cooling rack when Eva came back into the room.

'Well, is everything set for tonight?' Lizzie asked without looking up.

When her daughter didn't reply Lizzie glanced up to find out why.

'Whatever's the matter?' she asked, perceiving a drastic change of mood.

'It was Toby,' she said distantly.

'And?'

'His mother was knocked over by a car outside Harrods this morning,' she said, looking very shaken.

'Oh dear, is she badly hurt?'

'She's dead.'

'Oh my God!'

'She just walked out into the road without looking, according to witnesses.'

'What a dreadful thing.'

'Mmm.'

'How is Toby?'

'He sounded pretty much in control,' she replied. 'He'll have to keep a grip on himself because of his father . . . the poor man's devastated apparently.'

'Bound to be.'

'Toby told me to go to the party without him but I'm

not going to. It wouldn't be the same.'

Lizzie was already untying her pinafore. 'I'm going over to Philip's place to see if there's anything I can do.'

'I'll come with you,' said Eva.

'Poor old Philip won't be having much of a Christmas this year then,' Bobby remarked to Lizzie the following evening in Polly's kitchen where they just happened to find themselves. She'd wandered in here from the sitting room to wash some crockery and he was filling his glass with beer from the barrel which was perched on a wooden stool in the corner. No one stood on ceremony at Polly's on a Christmas Day; everyone just helped themselves to food and drink and mucked in with the chores.

'He certainly won't,' she replied sadly.

'It's a rotten business,' said Bobby, holding his pint glass firmly under the tap of the barrel. 'I know he and his missus hadn't had any sort of life together for years . . . but it's still a terrible shock for him.'

'I can't get it off my mind, to tell you the truth,' she confessed. 'That's why I'm washing up . . . to keep myself occupied.'

'Have you seen him?'

'Yes. I went over to his place yesterday as soon as I heard. Just to offer my condolences and see if there was anything I could do to help,' she explained. 'Eva came with me. She wanted to see Toby.'

'Was it suicide?' he asked, finishing at the barrel and taking a sizeable swallow of beer from the filled glass while leaning companionably against the draining board.

'No one knows for certain but they're almost positive it wasn't,' explained Lizzie. 'Meg thinks she'd drifted off into one of her fantasies and wasn't in her right mind when she stepped into the road.'

'Sounds plausible.'

Lizzie emptied the washing up bowl and began drying some glasses with the tea towel. 'I don't know who's blaming themself the most . . . Philip or his mother.'

'But why would they do that?'

'Well, Meg is castigating herself for not keeping a closer eye on her daughter-in-law while they were out shopping together, and Philip is giving himself a hard time for letting her go out shopping in the first place.'

'They could hardly keep the poor woman in chains when she'd come home for the holiday, could they?'

'Exactly. The doctor told Philip she was well enough to go out, but apparently you never know from one minute to the next with the sort of illness she had.'

'Poor old Phil,' he said again.

'Yes, we shall have to do what we can to cheer him up.'

'He's a good bloke.'

'He certainly is.'

'His wife's death alters things for you and him, I suppose?'

'No. Why should it?'

'Don't be coy.'

'I'm not,' she said truthfully. 'There's never been anything except friendship between us.'

'Really?'

'Yes, *really*.'

'Not for the lack of interest on his part, though, I bet,' he said with a knowing smile. 'But he's far too much of a gentleman to try anything when he already has a wife.'

'Not like you.'

'No, not like me,' Bobby admitted, his expression darkening. 'I admit it, I'm a real bastard. I started something that I wasn't prepared to finish.'

'We were both to blame,' she pointed out. 'It wasn't all on your side.'

'Maybe not.'

'Anyway, has Phil said anything to bring you to your conclusion?'

'Not in so many words, no. He's far too principled to discuss something as personal as that.'

'What makes you think he would want more than friendship, then?'

'It's obvious to anyone with half a brain. Anyway, I recognise the signs,' he said. 'I've been there myself, remember?'

Lizzie gave a hint of a smile, meeting his eyes. 'Will I ever forget?'

'I still . . .'

'Me too. Sometimes.'

'If things had been different . . . you and me might have . . .' His voice tailed off.

'That's something we'll never know, isn't it?' she said. 'And because things were left unfinished, so to speak, I suppose there'll always be certain undertones to our friendship.'

'Quite the philosopher.'

'Perhaps all the Christmas booze has gone to my head,' she said with deliberate levity because she didn't want the conversation to become too serious.

They were smiling at each other when June walked in carrying a tray of used crockery. She came to an abrupt halt just inside the door, her eyes darting from one to the other. 'Well, what's all this then? You two setting the world to rights or something?' she said.

'Not really,' explained Lizzie speedily. 'We've been talking about Philip Verne, actually.'

'Oh.'

The flash of suspicion in June's eyes when she'd entered the room to find Lizzie and Bobby alone together, hadn't passed unnoticed. Lizzie supposed there would always be doubts for her, in the same way as she herself would always feel something extra for Bobby. But it was incidental to the main body of their lives now – just a background thing like the weather that you were aware of but not completely in thrall to.

'Oh, yeah. His poor wife. What a dreadful thing to happen, eh?' said June, sounding relieved. She went over to the sink, put the tray down on the draining board and starting putting the crockery into the sink. 'Brings you up short when you hear about something like that, dunnit? It's certainly made me count my blessings.'

Philip was glad to see the back of Christmas, a feeling he guessed was shared by his son who dutifully stayed at the family home all through the holiday but clearly found the atmosphere depressing and missed the company of his friends. He had been as delighted to see Eva on Christmas Eve as Philip had been to see her mother.

The funeral was a very low key affair. Just some of the

staff from the hospital, and a few old friends joined Philip and his family to bid Emily a final farewell. When everyone had left after the funeral tea, including his mother who had gone home to bed with a sick headache, and he and Toby were in the house alone, Philip said to his son, 'Don't feel you have to stay here with me again this evening.'

'It wouldn't be right for me to go out, would it?' said Toby hopefully.

'Obviously it wouldn't be respectful for you to go out to a party on the day your mother was buried,' he said, 'but I can see no harm in your going home to your own place, and perhaps seeing your girlfriend.'

'Well . . . are you sure you don't mind being here alone?'

'Certain.'

'I'll give Eva a ring then,' he said unable to conceal his joy.

'Fine.'

'Thanks, Dad.'

'Thanks aren't necessary,' Philip told him. 'Go on, off you go.'

After he'd gone, Philip settled in a chair by the sitting-room fire, staring into the flames and drinking whisky. So it was all over. A wretched life had come to a tragic end. People had tried to comfort him with the usual clichés of bereavement; that she was at peace now, that she had suffered enough, and so on.

Maybe they were right. But that didn't alter the fact that her death needn't have happened. He'd lived with her illness for a very long time, he knew how unpredictable it was, he should have known better than to let her go out without him. For the second time in his life he had the death of another person on his conscience.

His reverie was interrupted by his housekeeper, telling him he had a visitor.

'Lizzie,' he said, rising as she appeared in the doorway. 'What a lovely surprise.'

'I thought you might fancy some company,' she explained.

He stood still, gazing at her, almost reduced to tears of joy by the sight of her. Just the prospect of her cheery presence to assuage his aching gloom on this darkest of all days, lifted his spirits.

'How clever of you to know,' he said with a smile. 'Do you have telepathic powers?'

'No, but I do have a daughter who is friendly with your son,' she said lightly.

'Oh. I hope Toby didn't make you feel obliged to come over?'

'Not at all. He just happened to mention to Eva that you were on your own when he telephoned,' she explained, 'so I decided to pop over for an hour or so. But feel free to ask me to leave if you'd rather be alone?'

'No, I'd like you to stay. Very much,' he assured her at once. 'But I'm probably quite sozzled.' He lifted his glass. 'God knows how many of these I've got through in the course of the day.'

'I wouldn't mind one myself, actually,' she told him.

'Certainly.'

He went to a collection of bottles set out on a small table and filled a glass for her. They sat either side of the fire, chatting. Loquacious with drink, he told her again that he felt responsible for his wife's death.

'If anyone is to blame, surely it's the doctor who said she was well enough to leave the hospital? But, frankly, I don't think it was anyone's fault.'

'You don't?'

'Certainly not. You've told me that Emily's behaviour was impossible to predict. So, unless you had physically made her a prisoner, it could have happened at any time,' said Lizzie. 'Anyway, you don't have to be mentally ill to get run over by a car, Philip. It's happening to people every day with the number of cars that are on the roads now. You take your life in your hands trying to get from one side of the road to the other, especially in the West End. It's no wonder the government are copying the Americans and bringing in traffic lights to try to control the chaos on the roads.'

'You're right in what you say.'

'But it doesn't make you feel better about what happened?'

'Not really.'

'The death of a loved one is never easy. I remember feeling guilty when I lost Bruce. I blamed myself for not keeping a closer eye on him . . . tore myself apart wondering why such a terrible thing had happened to us. But in the end you just have to accept the fact that it *has* happened and all the agonising in the world can't change that. Apportioning blame only prolongs the pain. I think that might be what happened to Polly, you know. All of her energy went into bitterness towards you instead of actual grief for Stan. Perhaps that's why she's never been able to come to terms with his death.'

'It's more than just Emily's death,' he said. 'I feel bad about her life too. I should have tried harder to make things better for her.'

'I don't see what else you could have done,' she said. 'According to your mother you kept her at home with you much longer than was sensible. Meg told me once that you had the patience of a saint with her.'

'That was all on the surface,' he admitted. 'Inside I was often furious . . . fed up with the whole damned business. I can even remember feeling as though I hated her when she was being really violent.' He closed his eyes. 'God, I feel such a bastard.'

'But you still did everything you could for her, despite the way you were feeling, that's the important thing.'

'Did I do enough, though? I keep asking myself that.'

'Frankly I think you are being unnecessarily hard on yourself.'

'I can remember being irritated by her the very morning she died,' he continued, almost as though Lizzie hadn't spoken. 'And she wasn't even being particularly difficult, just very insecure. Poor Emily couldn't help the way she was.'

'Oh, well, if you're going to start punishing yourself for being human, you might as well book a bed in the hospital at Clapham for yourself,' she told him firmly. 'Because you'll drive yourself nuts with that line of thought.'

'I can't stop the thoughts and memories coming.'

'No . . . but you can stop them getting too much of a hold.'

'And the worst thing of all is that I won't miss her as much as I feel I should,' he went on, 'because we haven't been together for such a long time.'

'You can't force feelings,' she reminded him. 'Personally,

I think you expect far too much of yourself.'

He swallowed some more whisky. 'It's all such a mess.'

'Are you a masochist or something?' she admonished firmly. 'Blaming yourself for Emily's life . . . her death . . . even the illness itself. Why not go the whole hog and blame yourself for her birth too? Oh, Philip, you're not God. You're just an ordinary man who did his best in an impossible situation.'

She was right. His whole marriage had been based on guilt. From the day he had married Emily, he had considered it his job in life to protect and provide for her in every way, emotionally as well as financially. Her happiness had been more important to him than his own which was why he seemed to have fallen short in every way but financially.

'I always felt as though I'd failed her,' he said. 'It was the worst moment of my life, having her put into an institution.'

'Yes, I'm sure it must have been. The important thing to remember is that you did what was right . . . you did what you could for her . . . and her illness was *not* your fault.'

'I'll try to bear that in mind.'

'I shall remind you, don't worry.'

He blinked as though having difficulty keeping her in focus. 'And you . . . you've had more than your share of trouble, but you always manage to keep smiling.'

'It's all an act,' she admitted frankly. 'But putting up a front becomes such a habit you begin to believe it yourself in the end.'

'You have an answer for everything,' he said with a slow smile. 'You and that ex brother-in-law of yours.'

'We're both from the same stable.'

'I've often wondered about you and Bobby, you know,' he

said, his voice becoming more slurred by the syllable. 'You do seem to be . . . er . . . very close friends.'

'That's exactly what we are . . . very close friends.' Because she felt so relaxed with Philip, she found herself adding, 'We nearly had an affair once but managed to pull back before any harm was done.'

'Oh . . . dashed rude of me to mention it,' he said in a very slow voice, his eyelids drooping. 'I'm awfully piddled . . . probably coming out with a load of old drivel . . . no offence meant.'

'None taken.' He looked as though he was about to doze off. 'Well, I think it's time I made tracks.'

'Yes, of course.' He rose but was so unsteady he fell back into the chair.

'Don't worry, I can see myself out.'

Even as she reached the sitting-room door, he was fast asleep.

The next morning he telephoned her with profuse apologies. 'I hope I wasn't too much of a pain last night?'

'You weren't.'

'Didn't get too personal, did I?'

'Don't worry, I'd have soon put you in your place if you had. But your behaviour was perfectly acceptable.'

'Thanks for coming over,' he said. 'I really appreciated it. I might have been drunk but a lot of what you said registered.'

'Good. Any time you need a listening ear, you know where I am.'

'How about lunch one day next week?' he promptly suggested.

'Yes, I'd like that.'

* * *

Although the economic depression kept its hold in many regions of the country, the new industries of the South continued to thrive. The silk trade enjoyed a boom and production figures had never looked healthier at Carter's Silks. The factory was efficiently run under Bobby's supervision with Jed now sufficiently experienced to make a valuable contribution.

With the children off her hands and the business under reliable management, Lizzie was able to have a life of her own. The monthly lunches she had enjoyed with Philip for so long became weekly affairs as he struggled to come to terms with Emily's death. Lizzie tried to help him to get his over-inflated sense of responsibility towards Emily into proportion, and to like himself a little. She sensed that he needed her and enjoyed the feeling. They began to have dinner together in the evenings, too, as the trees in the London parks and squares turned acid green with new growth and the flower-beds became emblazoned with tulips and daffodils.

Sometimes they would dine out at a restaurant, other times they ate at his place, never at hers because of Jed who still lived at home and could be relied upon to make Philip feel uncomfortable. At weekends they often went on outings to the country together, walking in the woods and lunching at some village hostelry. It seemed the most natural thing in the world for two unattached, lonely people to keep each other company.

As gradually and as tangibly as the changing season, Lizzie's feelings for Philip deepened into love. When she finally admitted it, she realised it had been lying dormant inside her for a very long time. Only when he'd become free had she allowed her feelings to develop.

The watershed happened one summer evening when they were walking beneath the elms in Kensington Gardens. The evening was soft and clear with late sunshine filtering through the rustling greenery and making a dappled pattern on the path. There were no ostentatious declarations of love, no fervent embraces. Just the mutual acceptance of a truth as gentle and inevitable as the dusk.

'I don't feel as though I have the right to be this happy,' remarked Philip, putting her hand to his lips as they lingered by the round pond, its shimmering surface fragmented with gold from the setting sun.

'I know the feeling,' said Lizzie. 'You get suspicious of happiness when you've had a lot of trouble in your life.'

He turned to her. 'Now I feel I can tell you . . . I started falling in love with you long before Emily died.'

'Yes, I think I knew that,' she told him. 'But I pretended not to, like I pretended it wasn't happening to me, too.'

A summer breeze disturbed the trees and rippled across the surface of the pond. A procession of ducks glided by, followed by a child's toy yacht on the end of a string, its white sails billowing in the wind.

They walked on arm in arm, pausing by the statue of Peter Pan, its fairy tale image outlined against the sky.

'Did you know that this statue was erected secretly in the gardens overnight so it would appear as though by magic the following morning?'

'No, I didn't.'

'It's true. It happened back in 1912.' She gazed up at the

mythical figure on his plinth. 'The boy who never grew up. I suppose most people have times when they envy him?'

'Indeed.'

They strolled on in comfortable silence until Philip said, 'I couldn't have offered you anything more than friendship before so I kept my feelings to myself.'

'Friendship was enough for me . . . then.'

'And now?'

'Now I'm ready to move on, to let nature take its course.'

They went back to his place and made glorious love in the dusk in one of the spare bedrooms. Lizzie couldn't bring herself to go into the bedroom he had once shared with Emily.

Lizzie hadn't expected to find love again at her age. She had loved two men before. Both had been deeply important to her. But the mature love she felt for Philip made everything that had gone before seem like a mere rehearsal for the real thing.

'I suppose there are people who would say this is wrong,' he remarked as they languished beneath the sheets in the fading light. 'Especially as Emily hasn't been dead for a year yet.'

'Oh, yes, there'll be no shortage of disapproval,' she agreed, snuggled into the crook of his arm. 'But anyone with a ha'porth of sense would realise that your situation is different to most, that it's time you had some happiness. God knows, you've waited long enough.'

'I'm serious about you, Lizzie,' he said. 'I want to marry you.'

'Oh.'

'Well, don't sound so surprised.'

'I'm not. I was taken aback for a minute, that's all.'

'So . . . will you?'

She sat up and leaned on her hand, looking down at him, pleased to see the handsome face that had looked so strained and haunted for so long, softened now with contentment. 'Yes, of course I will.'

'Thank you.'

'That's the most romantic thing that anyone has ever said to me.'

'What . . . thank you?'

'No, you fool.' She slapped his cheek playfully. 'The proposal, of course.'

He frowned. 'But your husband must have proposed.'

Lying down again, she stared at the ceiling.

'No, Stan and I drifted into marriage. Helped along by his mother.'

'Really?'

'Yes. It was a set procedure,' she explained. 'After we'd been courting for a while, it was assumed we'd marry and wedding arrangements were made. Stan just went along with it. I was very keen on him but he was always far more interested in other things than he was in me. To Stan, marriage was a thing that automatically happened at a certain point in your life and you did it without giving it any real thought. He wouldn't have known how to be romantic.'

'You didn't have a bad marriage though, did you?'

'It was as good as many others in our class, I suppose,' she said thoughtfully. 'Times were hard, there wasn't much money about. Romance doesn't stand much of a chance when you're living in squalor.'

'I suppose not.'

'Stan did what he thought was expected of him as a husband. He supported us financially with a little help from me,' she explained, 'but he wasn't a family man. Never took much interest in me or the kids.'

'Oh.'

'Actually, it's always puzzled me why Jed has put him on such a pedestal,' she said. 'Because he wasn't a loving father by any means. He was hardly ever at home, to be honest.'

'Perhaps that's why. The fact that he wasn't around much has given him a certain mystique in Jed's eyes.'

'Could be. Anyway, that's all in the past. We have the future to look forward to now.'

'Yes, and I think we should get married as soon as possible.'

'Not too soon, though,' she said. 'We ought to leave the actual wedding until a decent period has elapsed after Emily's death.'

'You're probably right. I think we should bring things out into the open with our families though, don't you?'

'Well . . .' She sounded doubtful.

'I suppose you're expecting a lot of opposition?'

'Phew, not half!' She had kept him away from the house because she hadn't thought it was worth causing a major argument with Jed when she and Philip were just friends. Now it was different. 'Because Jed is so opposed to you, I know he'll be very hurt.'

'Hurt, not just angry?'

'No, not just angry. He'll think I've betrayed him, you see.'

'Oh.'

'But I shall have to tell him about our plans now that we have some.'

'There'll be fireworks.'

'Explosions of earthquake proportions, I should imagine.'

'There's your mother-in-law too,' he pointed out.

'Strictly speaking Polly hasn't been that since Stan died,' she reminded him. 'That title will officially go to Meg.'

'Polly won't like that.'

Lizzie frowned. 'She certainly won't . . . and that really does worry me.'

'Not just her losing her title?'

'No, the whole thing of you and me and Polly,' she said. 'She's always been a mother to me and that means a lot to me . . . but I'm terribly afraid that marriage to you will rule out any sort of relationship with her.'

'You never know, she might surprise you and give us her blessing.'

'I doubt it,' she said. 'As I've said before, she's never been able to accept me as anyone other than Stan's widow.'

'And her opinion really matters that much to you?'

'Yes, that much. But even apart from my feelings for you, I can't let her rule my life. In the same way as I can't allow Jed to. They just don't have the right.'

'I agree.'

'I shall talk to Polly though, try to get her to see reason.'

'That's all you can do.'

'At least there are no problems on your side, thank goodness,' she said. 'Your mother's a real pal of mine, and I get on well with Toby too.' She paused thoughtfully. 'Marriage, though. Do you think he'll be happy with that?'

'Frankly, I think Toby is too wrapped up in his own life at the moment to bother too much about what I do.'

'Yes. Eva is pretty taken up with her own affairs too,' said Lizzie. 'She'll be pleased for me though, I'm sure.'

'I'm not saying that Toby won't be . . . just that he's very busy being a man-about-town at the moment. Anyway, it won't really affect him all that much since he lives away from home.'

'Fortunately for us,' giggled Lizzie, flapping her hand across the bed. 'I certainly wouldn't be here now if he were in residence.'

Philip saw the funny side of that and they laughed together. It relaxed them and made all the peripheral problems of their love affair seem less important.

'They're still seeing each other, Toby and Eva,' said Lizzie.

'Yes, so I gather. Though obviously I can't keep quite so up to date as you as he doesn't live here.'

'They seem to be having a whale of a time,' she said. 'But Eva still insists it isn't serious. Anyway, they're both too busy enjoying themselves to worry about us.'

'If only it was that simple with that son of yours.'

'Indeed. I'll have a chat with him about it sooner rather than later, I think,' Lizzie promised. 'No point in putting it off . . . not now.'

'Would you like me to be with you for moral support?'

'No,' she said quickly. 'It'll be better if I break the news to him on my own.'

'I'd rather be there if he's going to give you a hard time.'

'Thanks, but it will be easier if you're not.'

'I'm not happy about it, but if you're really sure . . .'

'I am. And don't worry. Jed will make a lot of noise at first but he'll come round eventually.'

But her positive manner didn't reflect her true feelings. Lizzie knew she was going to have a real fight on her hands with that young man, and she was dreading it!

Chapter Twenty-One

'How can you even think of doing such a thing?' exclaimed Jed rhetorically, his face white with temper. 'It's disgusting.'

His uncanny resemblance to his father was startling to Lizzie at that sensitive moment. The angry blue eyes glaring at her from beneath a mop of bright red hair might have been Stan's. He had the same eloquent hands, too, that moved continuously as he was speaking. He even walked like his father, his overall size making him somewhat ungainly. Unfortunately, he had also inherited Stan's infuriating inability to see anyone's point of view but his own.

'As I said,' she continued, trying not to be deterred by his enmity, 'we won't be getting married for a while yet . . . but I thought you ought to know that it's on the cards for sometime next year.'

'I never thought you'd stoop so low,' he growled.

'Can't you put your own feelings to one side for once and be pleased for your mother?' interrupted Eva who was delighted to hear Lizzie's news. 'It's about time Mum had some happiness.'

'She won't find it by marrying scum like Verne,' rasped Jed, pacing up and down the room.

It was a warm, stuffy evening in late-summer. Outside in genteel Berry Gardens all was serene. Insects buzzed and hovered; birds chirped and fluttered in the plane trees. A white poodle, ludicrously adorned with pink ribbons, trotted haughtily towards the park with its smart lady owner in tow. A bowler-hatted man, with a rolled umbrella hooked over his arm, strutted past the window on his way home from the city.

Inside this tastefully furnished room, the atmosphere was very different.

'I'd rather you didn't speak about Philip in such insulting terms,' said Lizzie, struggling to stay in control. This was hurting more than she had expected. Jed, the man, was still her child. He meant a very great deal to her because nothing was more instinctive than the basic maternal instinct. But to give in to her son on this issue would be to condone a kind of tyranny.

'How do you expect me to refer to the man who murdered my father?' he shouted.

'Oh, not that again,' she sighed. 'It really wasn't like that.'

'Can you deny that he was responsible for my father's death?' he demanded, his voice guttural with emotion.

'It wasn't so simple.'

'Did he or did he not push my father . . . your husband . . . so that he fell through the window to his death?'

'Well, yes,' she was forced to admit.

He spread his hands to emphasise his point. 'So how can you even bear to talk to him, let alone marry him?'

'Oh, for heaven's sake, why don't you stop living in the past?' intervened Eva who was standing with her back to the ornate marble fireplace, her blonde hair reflected in the overhanging mirror. 'Daddy's death was a long time ago. It was an accident, not murder, and keeping up a hate campaign against Philip and his family isn't going to bring him back.'

'Shut up, you.' He shot his mother a cold look then turned back to his sister. 'You're as bad as she is. Going around with that poncey Toby Verne with his flash car and stupid accent.'

'Don't you dare call one of my friends poncey,' she protested fiercely.

'I'll call them what I like,' he growled. 'If you will hang about with scum you must be prepared for the flak.'

'How dare you call my friends scum!' she protested, lunging at him and pummelling her fists against his chest.

'Now then, that's enough, both of you,' commanded Lizzie. 'That's no way for two grown-up people to behave.'

'But he . . .' began Eva.

'Enough,' pronounced Lizzie firmly, placing herself between them.

Her authority must still count for something, she thought, for they moved away from each other. Eva flopped into an armchair; Jed stood with his back to the window, glaring into the room.

Lizzie addressed him gravely. 'I'm really sorry you don't feel able to accept Philip into our family.'

'And I'm not the only one,' he informed her sharply. 'Gran will be very upset.'

'Yes, I know.'

'My feelings are obviously not important to you but don't you care about her? She is Dad's mother.'

'I care very much.'

'You've a funny way of showing it, then,' he snorted.

'As much as I love her, I can't live my life according to her rules,' Lizzie informed him. 'If your grandmother had had her way we'd still be living in squalor and I'd be working for a pittance somewhere.'

'At least Gran has principles.'

'Don't interrupt.' Although weakened by her feelings for him, she was strengthened by fury at this blatant hypocrisy. 'If I hadn't stood up for myself against her, you wouldn't have a good job in the family firm with a partnership in the offing. Eva wouldn't have been able to go to college which landed her the job at Reed's.' She waved a hand towards the room which bore all the hallmarks of success. 'We would have none of this . . . a comfortable home and money to spend.'

'Money isn't everything.'

'Oh, come off it, Jed,' said Lizzie irascibly. 'Don't try to tell me that you'd rather live in a hovel than live decently . . . that I was wrong to strive for the best for us all . . . because I won't believe you.'

'Of course I'm not saying that,' he muttered, faltering slightly, 'but it would have been better if you hadn't done it with his money.'

'And how else was a widow without a penny to her name supposed to get started?'

'We would have managed. What we'd never had we wouldn't have missed.'

'Oh, it's easy to criticise me now, isn't it, Jed?' she said, both angry and hurt. 'When it's all a fait accompli . . . when you've been living well for a good few years . . . when a high standard of living has been established and isn't likely to be taken away from you.'

'All right, so maybe it wasn't entirely wrong to make him pay for what he'd done,' he said, sounding slightly less sure of himself. 'But surely you don't expect me to accept him as a stepfather?'

'I do expect that, yes,' she told him. 'I've brought you up to be tolerant, to accept people as they are, and I hope that will come to the fore in the end.'

'So you are really going to marry him then?'

'After a decent interval, yes.'

'In that case I'll get out of your life and leave you to it,' he snapped, stamping across the room to the door.

'Jed, don't be hasty, we can talk about it,' called Lizzie.

'Don't be so stupid, Jed,' reproached his sister. 'Come back and discuss it in a proper civilised manner.'

'There's nothing more to discuss,' he said, his tone ominously calm as he spoke to his mother. 'I don't want that man in my life, and as he is going to be a part of yours, you leave me with no alternative.'

'Let's just talk about it.'

'I'll be out of this house within the hour.' He opened the door then turned back to face her. 'And you'll need to get someone to replace me at the factory, too, because I won't be coming in again . . . ever!'

'But, Jed . . .'

'A clean break is the only thing,' he said coldly. 'It will leave you free to do what you like without any interference from me.'

Leaving Lizzie and Eva in a state of shock, he stormed from the room. Lizzie started to go after him but was stopped by Eva's restraining hand on her arm.

'Let him go, Mum,' she said shakily, slipping a reassuring arm around her mother's shoulders. 'If he's going to be that damned selfish, you'll be better off without him.'

'He's my son, Eva,' she cried, her voice thick with emotion. 'I love him for all his faults. I can't just let him go.'

Eva moved back and looked at her mother, face flushed, eyes glistening with tears. 'How you handle this is up to you, of course, Mum,' she said sagely, 'but supposing you do manage to stop Jed from leaving . . . what then? Are you going to give Philip his marching orders? Give up the right to a life of your own?'

Lizzie was too shaken to be sure of anything at this precise moment. 'I don't know,' she said. 'The only thing I am sure of is that I don't want the family split up because of my personal arrangements.'

The young woman ushered her dazed mother into a chair by the unlit hearth where carnations ascended in a shower of pink and white from a tall vase in front of the fender.

'All right,' said Eva, perching on the edge of a chair opposite and leaning forward. 'Let's look at the problem logically. So you finish with Philip and make it up with Jed? Where does that leave you in the long run? Jed will probably get married eventually and have a family of his own. And even if he doesn't, is he going to be there for you in the same way as Philip is?'

'Well . . .'

'Of course he isn't,' said Eva with harsh frankness. 'He'll be far too busy getting on with his own life while you'll be lonely, having given up the right to yours.'

'I can see the sense in what you say,' said Lizzie, her hands clenched tightly together in her lap. 'But it's just too painful to have him leave like this.'

'I think you'll have to let him go . . . either that or you'll have to live by his rules for the rest of your life. Being bullied by him, because that's what he's doing – bullying you.'

'He doesn't mean to,' she said, following her primal instinct to defend him. 'He really does see Philip as a murderer.'

'Well, it's high time he grew up and looked at the matter rationally,' said Eva crossly. 'Fancy judging someone for something that happened when he was just a kid. Honestly I've never heard of anything so ridiculous.'

Lizzie knew that Eva meant well but she couldn't possibly know how awful the prospect of losing a son felt to his mother.

'Perhaps I should go upstairs and talk to him,' she said.

'And have him stay on his terms? Giving up your own chance of happiness so that he becomes even more of a bigot!' exclaimed Eva. 'Well, if you do, it will be the biggest mistake of your life.'

'But I couldn't be happy with Philip if Jed and I were separated,' began Lizzie.

'All right, leave your own feelings out of it for a minute,' said Eva. 'Do you think Jed has a right to treat the Vernes so badly?'

'Of course not.'

'You've always taught us to stand up for what we believe in.'

'Which is what Jed is doing.'

'Yes, but you have also taught us to respect the other person's point of view. If you give in to him over this, you're going against your own standards.'

427

'I suppose you're right.' She sighed and pointed to her heart. 'But, oh, Eva . . . it hurts so much . . . here.'

'I know it must be hard but if you let him go, he stands a chance of coming to terms with this thing,' she said. 'Persuade him to stay on his terms and he never will.'

'I know.'

'Don't worry, he'll come round eventually, Mum,' said Eva in a gentler tone. 'Because he really does care about you.'

'I believe he does too, underneath all that anger.'

'When he does come to his senses, maybe he'll have learned something about the tolerance you've told us so much about.'

Lizzie still hoped her son would change his mind and stay but less than an hour later he came downstairs carrying a suitcase. She waylaid him in the hall.

'You're really going then.'

'You've left me with no alternative, have you?' he said coolly.

'I'm sorry that's the way you see it.'

'So am I.'

'Where will you go?'

'I'll stay with a pal until I find a place of my own,' he said, and without another word opened the front door and marched down the street. Watching him from the window, Lizzie knew that without Eva's common sense to deter her, she would have gone after him.

Polly's reaction to the news was worse than Lizzie had expected.

'Of course the boy has left home,' the older woman exclaimed. 'What the devil did you expect him to do when you tell him you're going to marry his father's murderer?'

'Oh, I give up,' said Lizzie. 'You're as bad as he is.'

'You're asking too much of him,' said Polly. 'Too much of all of us.' She shook her head. 'God knows what sort of a hold this Verne bloke has over you, for you to give up your son for him.'

As there was no point in trying to make her understand, Lizzie just said, 'Not everyone is against me marrying Philip. Bobby and June are quite happy for me . . . so is Eva.'

'Well, that's up to them,' she said. 'As long as you don't expect me to accept it.'

'Your blessing would mean a lot to me,' confessed Lizzie.

'You're gonna have to face facts, Lizzie,' said Polly harshly, 'and realise exactly what you will be giving up by marrying that man.'

'Jed will be back, I'm certain of it,' Lizzie told her.

'Maybe he will . . . only time will tell,' said Polly. 'But if you go ahead and marry Philip Verne, you'll no longer be welcome in my house.'

Lizzie had expected a battle, she had expected undertones of hostility from Polly for a long time into the future. She had known that Philip wouldn't be welcome at the Carter family home in Thorn Street. But she had *not* expected actually to be cast out of Polly's life altogether.

'Don't you think you're being a bit hard on me?'

'What you're planning to do is hard on me,' was the tart reply.

'But I'm forty-two years old . . . surely who I marry is for me to decide?'

'Of course it is,' agreed Polly sharply. 'In the same way as

429

it is for me to decide who I associate with and allow into my home. Forty-two or ninety-two, you'll not get a foot over my threshold while you have that man as a husband.'

'Oh, really!' rasped Lizzie.

'It's no good you adopting that tone with me,' Polly went on. 'You've plenty to say about the freedom to choose . . . that doesn't just apply to you, you know. I have the right to choose too.'

'But that's emotional blackmail!'

'Call it what you like,' said Polly with solid determination that struck fear into Lizzie's heart. 'But it's more than just a threat to get you to change your mind. It's something *inside of me*. I know you've been seeing him, of course, and I could just about cope with that as long as I didn't have to see you together. But the idea of him actually taking my Stan's place – *him of all people* – no, I just can't take that, Lizzie, so I'd rather not see you at all.'

'This hurts.'

'It hurts me too.'

'Can't you find it in your heart to have a little more humanity?'

'Not over this,' stated Polly categorically. 'It just isn't possible.'

Philip told himself he was imagining things. He tried to convince himself that nothing had changed between him and Lizzie, that she was just as keen on him as she'd been when they had first acknowledged their feelings back in the summer. But as Christmas drew near, he could no longer pretend that she was as eager to discuss their future together as she had once been.

'What's the matter, Lizzie?' he asked, one day in December when they were lunching together at a restaurant in Kensington.

'The matter?'

'Don't pretend,' he urged her. 'You've been keeping me at a distance for months. Have you had second thoughts, is that it?'

She decided he deserved her honesty.

'You're right,' she admitted, 'there is something wrong. Basically, I'm weak against those who oppose me.'

'Weak is the last thing you are,' he told her with emphasis. 'You wouldn't be where you are today if you were.'

'In business maybe . . .'

'Jed and Polly are getting to you, I suppose,' he said for she had told him briefly about that situation.

'I'm afraid so,' she confirmed. 'I didn't think it would be so hard to bear. It isn't that I can't stand my ground against them because I can, but I miss Jed so much . . . and I dread the idea of not having Polly in my life. She's been an important part of it for so long.'

'So what it boils down to,' he said gravely, 'is that you're going to have to decide who you will miss most, them or me?'

She reached across the table for his hand. 'I don't want it to end between us.'

'But?'

'But . . . well . . . oh, I don't know, maybe I need more time.'

'The last thing I want to do is to pressure you into anything,' he said, 'but neither of us is a spring chicken.'

'No.'

'Anyway, what difference will time make? Unless, of course, you're hoping that when Jed hears that you haven't

431

married me, he'll come running back to you.'

'No, no, I'm not that feeble, and it isn't that simple,' she said. 'Oh, I don't know, Philip . . . I just can't bring myself to take the final plunge that will sever my connections with him and Polly. I'm afraid that without them in my life, I'll be miserable and take it out on you. I think our life together might turn sour because of the price I have had to pay for it.'

'I'm willing to take that chance,' he assured her.

'Oh, Phil, there's just too much bitterness . . . too much pain. Can we just cool it for a while?'

He was so deeply disappointed he hardly knew how to bear it. After the emptiness of his marriage to Emily, he'd tasted happiness only to have it snatched from him. 'You want us to stop seeing each other then?'

'Not altogether.'

'You can't have it both ways,' he said bitterly. 'We can't go back to being just friends who have an occasional lunch together. It just won't work. It's expecting too much of anyone.'

'It seems I am expecting too much of everyone,' she said miserably. 'You . . . Jed . . . Polly. I can't tear myself in two.'

'No, you can't. And I think you've made your choice,' he said sharply. 'You can't expect me to hang around until the time is right for you . . . until they give their permission.'

'You want to stop seeing me altogether?'

'It's the last thing I want but friendship isn't enough for me . . . not any more.'

'I'm sorry.'

'So am I. You don't know the half of it,' he said.

Neither of them could manage any more of their lunch.

They left the restaurant together in silence, then said goodbye rather stiffly before going their separate ways.

Christmas Day at Polly's was more of a punishment than a party for Lizzie. She just wasn't in the mood for Carter camaraderie. She found herself feeling resentful towards Polly. This was followed by guilt, then a kind of confused rage for allowing herself to be buffeted by other people's feelings like a raft at sea in a storm. Quite frankly, she was sick of being at the centre of an emotional minefield.

Jed, who was living in Essex and working at Courtauld's, was spending Christmas at his grandmother's. He kept in regular contact with Polly but he and Lizzie hadn't seen each other since his departure. There was no sign of a reconciliation between mother and son, despite the ending of her affair with Philip. Too much resentment still simmered between them, most of it on Lizzie's side because she couldn't quell her anger towards Jed for forcing her into a life that felt incomplete without the man she loved.

'I understand from Gran that it's all off between you and Verne?' he'd said when he and Lizzie exchanged a few words alone in the kitchen after dinner.

'That's right.'

'You've seen him for what he really is at last, then?'

'Not at all,' she informed him sharply, furious at his arrogance. 'I was merely worn down by all the pressure.'

'Oh, well, as long as he's gone . . . that's all that matters.'

It wasn't at all but she didn't have the energy for another fight. Her vitality had noticeably diminished since she'd parted from Philip. The atmosphere between herself and Jed was charged with acrimony. She changed the subject to ease the tension.

'How's the job?' she asked.

'Fine. In fact, I'm rather enjoying it . . . it's very good experience for me to be working with other fabrics,' he told her. 'I really think that man-made fibres could be the big thing of the future, you know.'

'Let's hope not for the sake of my company.'

'There'll always be a demand for silk, of course,' he said quickly, 'but you might find you'll need to diversify into other fabrics at some point in the future.'

'If I need to, I will,' she said. 'I've never been afraid of change.'

'That's true.'

'So how are you getting on, fending for yourself?'

'I'm managing. It was time I left home anyway.'

Maybe, but not under those dreadful circumstances, she thought, but just said dully, 'Yes, I suppose it was.'

She knew he would never come home to live again. The time for that had passed even without the problems that had hastened his departure. She desperately wanted him to be part of her life again but not with his present attitude. Nothing had really changed. Philip still stood between them. She realised now that she couldn't have a normal relationship with Jed or Polly unless they learned to see beyond their own prejudices.

It was too late to resurrect her relationship with Philip. She had hurt him enough already by rejecting him so cruelly. She certainly had no right to approach him with the news that she'd been wrong – that she missed him more than she'd thought possible and wanted him back whatever the consequences with her relatives. The only decent thing she could do for Philip now was to leave him alone.

The New Year was bleak for Lizzie. Added to the bitter cold weather and her deep personal loneliness there was trouble at the factory. They had a spate of problems with the machines which held up production and cost the firm money in materials and labour.

The bolts on the looms kept working loose and upsetting the tension. This resulted in faulty material which wasn't acceptable to the customer so had to be done again. Why it kept happening was a mystery because the machines were very well maintained.

'Oh, no,' said Lizzie, arriving at the factory one freezing February morning to find Bobby examining one of the looms yet again. 'Is it the bolts again?'

'No, this time it's more serious,' he told her gravely. 'The Jacquard harness has collapsed.'

'But I don't understand it,' she exclaimed. 'I mean, you expect trouble with machines now and then, but not every week.'

'I know.'

'How could the harness have collapsed when you check the machines regularly?'

'It's been cut.'

'What? You mean . . .?'

'I'm afraid so. This has confirmed my suspicions. I don't think these things have been happening by accident.'

'Sabotage!'

'That's what it looks like to me,' he told her solemnly.

'There've been too many faults for them to be accidental. It was always the same thing . . . the bolts loosened just enough to affect the tension but not enough for the weaver to notice it in time to stop a considerable amount of cloth being ruined. Now the culprit is getting more ambitious. A new harness will be expensive and it'll take days to set up.'

Lizzie could hardly believe it. 'But who would want to do a thing like that to us?'

'You tell me. Someone with a grudge, I suppose,' he said. 'Who, though? I've been racking my brains to think of anyone we might have upset recently.'

'Someone we had to dismiss, perhaps?'

'That's the first thought that springs to mind, yes,' he said. 'People can resent something like that for years.'

'There haven't been many, though, have there?' she reminded him. 'We're too careful about who we take on.'

'True.' He lapsed into ponderous silence. 'But if you think about it, Liz, it must be someone who's actually working here because the place is locked and bolted every night and there's no sign of a break in.'

'But that's crazy! I mean, why would any of our workers want to sabotage their own living?' she pointed out. 'If we lose orders over it, jobs could be lost.'

'Yes, it's a real puzzle,' he agreed. 'But someone's doing it . . . and that someone must have a sound knowledge of the looms.'

Lizzie's heart lurched under the impact of a sudden suspicion so horrible it was barely conceivable. So devastating she couldn't even tell Bobby about it, at least not until she was sure of her facts. But the more she thought about it, the more certain she was she knew the identity of the culprit.

'Oh, well, we'll just have to keep our ear to the ground, won't we?' she said deviously. 'Keep an eye out for anyone behaving oddly around the factory.'

'Yes . . . that's about all we can do for the moment.'

But it wasn't all that Lizzie was going to do. She knew she must confront the person she was sure was responsible. A daunting task indeed!

Chapter Twenty-Two

That same afternoon, after Bobby had gone to a meeting with a silk merchant, Lizzie asked Luke to come into her office.

Having offered him a seat, she came straight to the point, her calm exterior concealing her sick apprehension. 'Is it you who's been interfering with the looms?'

'Cor! What a thing to say,' he said, observing her with distaste from his seat across the desk. 'Bloody cheek!'

Despite his apparent outrage, she knew he was laughing at her, his thin lips hinting at a smile, beady eyes gleaming with satisfaction. This was an expression she recognised from childhood when he'd watched her suffering from the effects of one of his odious pranks.

'It is you, isn't it?'

'Now why would I wanna do a thing like that?'

'Why, indeed? I can only think it must be because of some perverse wish to make trouble for me,' she told him.

With slow, lazy movements, he rummaged in his overall pocket for a packet of cigarettes, took one out and lit it in a leisurely manner.

'What makes you think I wanna make trouble for you?' he asked, striking a relaxed pose with his head tilted back slightly as he inhaled the smoke, as though to emphasise how unperturbed he was by her accusation.

'Because you don't like me,' she said. 'You never have.'

'Is that a fact?' he drawled.

'The foul things you used to do to me when we were children was proof of that.'

He didn't reply, just watched her, drawing heavily on his cigarette.

'You deserved it,' he said suddenly, surprising her with this admission, his eyes becoming glazed as he thought back over the past.

'Why?' she wanted to know. 'What did I ever do to you to make you want to hurt me?'

'You humiliated me.'

'I humiliated *you*?' she said in astonishment. 'It was the other way around as I remember it. I can recall a particularly degrading incident when you tied me to the bedhead by my hair . . .'

'Well, if I did then you must have driven me to it.'

'In what way?' she asked, beginning to realise that this man was deeply disturbed.

He fell silent, eyes clouded with pain, purple-tinged face working against tears. 'I worshipped the ground you walked on.'

'What!' She couldn't believe it. 'You hated me . . . you've always resented my being a part of your family.'

'It was always Bobby you wanted and then Stan,' he said as though she hadn't spoken. 'You never had any time for me.'

'Of course I didn't, because you were always so hateful to me.'

'Only because you ignored me,' he told her sadly. 'It was very painful to a young boy . . . being disregarded like that. I had to pay you back the only way I knew how.'

To her utter astonishment, he sank into hopeless despair, tears meandering slowly down his cheeks. The arrogant and cruel man she had never quite lost her fear of was crying like a baby.

'But that was all a very long time ago, Luke,' she reminded him, forcing herself to stay calm. 'So why suddenly start trouble for me now?'

He shrugged his shoulders, mopping his tears with a handkerchief and sniffing loudly. 'I suppose I had some crazy idea that you might turn to me for help,' he explained. 'But I should have known you'd go to Bobby.'

'It's natural I would . . . the machines are his responsibility.'

'It was always him you loved really, even when you were married to Stan.'

'Ah . . . so jealousy was your motive in telling June that Bobby and I were having an affair, then?' she suggested.

Nodding miserably, he said, 'My feelings for you didn't go away when we grew up. Why do you think I've never married?'

'Oh, Luke,' she said in distress. 'What a terrible waste of your life. I could never have thought of you in the way you wanted me to . . . even without Stan and Bobby. But we could have been friends if you hadn't been so horrible to me.'

'It just festered away inside me . . . day after day . . . year after year.'

'For all those years?'

'Yes.'

'How dreadful for you.' Despite everything, she felt a stab

of pity for him but didn't think it wise to let him know. The more distance there was between them, the safer she would feel. 'Fortunately, no major damage has been done to the firm with this latest escapade. There would have been, though, had it gone on much longer.'

'I wouldn't have let it go on.' He blew his nose and became more composed. 'I'm a fool when it comes to you but I wouldn't have put jobs at risk.'

'That's something, I suppose.'

'Oh, well, I've blown any chance of respect from you now, I suppose,' he said. 'Snivelling like a two-year-old.'

Lizzie leaned back in her chair, watching him squirm. It ought to give her pleasure, considering the misery he had caused her in the past, but she felt so terribly sorry for him. Respect for such a miserable example of humankind, however, was another matter.

'Tears are nothing to be ashamed of,' she said.

He bowed his head. 'I'm sorry, Lizzie, for what I've done.'

'I should damned well hope you are.'

'God knows what Bobby's gonna think of me . . . and the rest of the family.'

'There's no need for anyone to know that you were the saboteur,' she told him. 'It can remain an unsolved mystery as far as everyone else is concerned. This time next week it'll all be old news anyway.'

He looked up quickly, his eyes narrowed suspiciously. 'Why would you cover up for me after everything I've done?'

She put her fingers under her chin meditatively. 'I can see nothing to be gained from making your treachery public.'

'No?'

'No. If your mother were to hear about it, she'd be shattered. I'd rather leave her with her illusions about you. I'd sooner have the firm stand the cost of the broken harness if it will save her from being hurt.'

'You mean, we can just carry on as though nothing has happened?'

'Oh, no.'

'Ah . . .'

'I wouldn't feel comfortable working with you after this,' she explained.

'No, I suppose not,' he said gloomily. 'I've really screwed up, haven't I?'

'As far as this firm is concerned, yes. But your life isn't over yet,' she reminded him. 'You've a good knowledge of the silk trade. I could put in a word for you at Verne's, if you like?'

'No, I wouldn't work for them,' he said, seeming to drift into a mood of grim acceptance. 'I think my best bet is to leave the district altogether . . . for a while at least. I shouldn't still be living at home at my age, anyway.'

'I won't argue with that.'

'It was the soft option,' he confessed. 'Mum made it so comfortable for me I just didn't get around to moving on.'

'It happens. But where will you go now you have decided to make the break?'

'Dunno . . . it needs some thought.'

'Why not try the Midlands?' she suggested helpfully. 'I've heard that the hosiery factories up there are booming at the moment because of the demand for silk stockings caused by the shorter skirts that are so fashionable now. You might be able to get a job in one of those.'

'I could give that a try, I suppose.'

Lizzie fiddled with some papers on her desk and studied her finger nails as an awkward silence settled on them. She was trying not to feel bad about taking such a firm line with him.

He stood up. 'Well, thanks for being so good about everything.'

'That's all right. I'm glad we've cleared the air, at last.'

'I'll finish here at the end of the week, shall I?'

'Yes . . . and as far as anyone else is concerned, you just fancy a change, all right?'

'Thanks,' he said, and left the room.

Lizzie let out a gusty sigh of relief as the door closed behind him. Luke had been a threatening presence on the periphery of her life for as long as she could remember. Now he had gone, she felt as though a heavy weight had been lifted from her shoulders.

One blustery March afternoon, Polly was sitting in an armchair by the fire in the parlour, knitting a pullover for Will and listening to the wireless. The wind was howling around the rooftops and rattling the windows with such force she had to turn up the volume of the wireless.

The news seemed to be dominated by Germany and that Hitler fella, lately, she thought, as the announcer outlined plans by the British government to expand the army, navy and airforce to counter the threat of Germany's massive rearmament programme, alleged by Parliament to be putting peace at risk. All this talk of unrest in Europe was very depressing. But she cheered herself with the thought that no one would be stupid enough to let war happen again – not after the last carnage.

She had a vivid recall of the weekend preceding the last declaration of war. You wouldn't have been able to hear the wind rattling the windows then for the clamour of voices as the whole family had been here for Bank Holiday tea.

Sadly, her family was diminished now, something that had been exacerbated last week when Luke had upped and left – right out of the blue. But she knew he would keep in regular touch. Both he and Bobby were loyal to their parents; neither of them would see her and Will go short. When Will retired, later this year, she knew she could rely on them if they found it hard to manage.

It was odd how she felt able to accept money from the boys but not from Lizzie who paid them from a business that had been started with *his* money. If Polly thought too much about it she could see that it was a bit hypocritical.

Thinking along these lines brought on the nasty little ache that had been nagging away inside her a lot lately. It came from missing Lizzie. Oh, she hadn't gone anywhere in the geographical sense. She still lived in Berry Gardens and regularly came to Thorn Street to see Polly and Will. But the person Polly knew as Lizzie was missing. In her place was a stranger who made polite, superficial conversation. Her vital spark seemed to have faded since she'd given up that Philip Verne.

An uneasy feeling tightened Polly's muscles. It was her damned conscience again. It had been playing her up a lot recently, and for no good reason. After all, it was perfectly natural she would feel unable to accept Lizzie if she married

Stan's killer. Lizzie had no right to expect it to be otherwise. Blasted Vernes. Polly was sick and tired of their troublesome presence in her life. But remorse continued to bother her just the same.

Polly had been right about Lizzie's mood. Having had her life enriched by romance, it was hard to adjust to singleness again, to the state of being special to no one person. Her son never so much as sent her a postcard, and her normally delightful daughter might have been a potted plant about the house for all the company she was just lately.

In fact she was so touchy, Lizzie's patience finally snapped one evening in the summer after having her head bitten off yet again.

'What *is* the matter with you?' she demanded crossly. 'You've been like a cat with a sore tail for weeks.'

'I haven't.'

'Yes, you have, and this evening you're absolutely unbearable.'

'Nothing's the matter with me,' denied Eva hotly, then promptly burst into tears.

'Is something wrong between you and Toby?' Lizzie probed gently, her attitude becoming more sympathetic the instant she realised that something really was the matter. She sat down on the sofa beside her sobbing daughter. 'It sometimes helps to talk about these things.'

Eva blew her nose and made a defiant announcement.

'I'm pregnant.'

Lizzie's immediate impulse was to shriek at her daughter about restraint and morality and downright stupidity, as every mother's nightmare erupted around her. But realising that that sort of attitude would change nothing, she just muttered numbly, 'Oh . . . oh, I see.'

'Why aren't you shouting?'

'Not much point, is there, as the deed is already done?'

'Well, no . . . but I thought you would, anyway.'

'Just be glad that I'm not!'

'Humph.'

'Does Toby know?'

'Yes.'

'And is he going to stand by you?'

'If you mean by that dreadfully bourgeois question, is he going to marry me,' said Eva irritably, 'the answer is no.'

'Ah, so that's why you've been in such a state?' assumed Lizzie. 'Well, that young man will have to be told a few home truths about facing up to his responsibilities.'

Eva shook her head. 'No, Mum, you've got it wrong. It's *me* who doesn't want to get married. Toby is all for it.'

'Oh,' said Lizzie in surprise. 'Why don't you want to?'

'I don't want Toby tied to me just because of the baby.'

'Has he said that's how it would be for him?' she wanted to know.

'No, of course not, he's far too nice to come right out and say a thing like that. But it's obvious. I mean, he enjoys his bachelor life, he doesn't want a wife and kid to cramp his style.'

'Your view, not his?'

'Yes, but I know him. I've been going out with him long enough.'

'There is the little matter of choice and the lack of it,' Lizzie pointed out with brutal candour. 'I mean, what's the alternative to marrying Toby?'

'I'll have the baby and stay single,' her daughter informed her.

'Oh, Eva,' said Lizzie, her voice deep with feeling. 'I don't think you realise just how hard it will be for you.'

'Not if Toby helps financially,' she said. 'That is all I am prepared to ask of him.'

'Money isn't the main problem,' said Lizzie. 'I wouldn't see you go short, you know that. I'm talking about the other aspects of it. You'll be the subject of gossip, you'll be shunned by society, and what about the baby as it grows up?'

'It'll be better for it to grow up with just a mother to love it than a father who resents it because it's forced him to do something he didn't really want to do.'

'A very noble attitude, love, but . . .'

'I'm not doing it to be noble, Mum,' said Eva decisively. 'I'm doing it because it's the best thing.'

'You're in an emotional state,' tried Lizzie. 'You'll probably feel differently later on.'

'I am feeling emotional, yes,' she admitted. 'Women usually are in the early stages of pregnancy, aren't they? But the reason I've been so miserable lately is not because of the pregnancy but because I've been worried that people might try to force us into marriage because of it.'

'I see.'

'The reason I've been so edgy this evening is because I knew I had to tell you before bedtime. Toby is going to tell his father too. We agreed to be simultaneous about it.'

'Ah.'

'My decision not to get married isn't just a whim, it's something I've thought a lot about – something I believe is the right thing for Toby and for me. I'm sorry about the scandal it'll cause for the family, but I can't do something I think is wrong just to stop people talking.'

Although a staunch believer in marriage and family values, Lizzie couldn't help but admire her daughter's spirit. She recognised the determination in Eva's tone – she had heard it in herself many times and knew that all efforts at persuasion would be fruitless.

'Well, in that case, all I can do is to offer you my support,' said Lizzie. 'Obviously I would prefer my grandchild to be born in wedlock but if that isn't to be, then I want you to know that you won't be on your own. I'll be there for you.'

'Thanks, Mum.' Eva hugged her tight, tears of relief beginning to fall. 'Sorry to do this to you. I know it must be really hard for you, the disgrace and all that.'

'These things happen,' said Lizzie. 'You're a damned fool but I'm proud of you for standing up for what you believe in.'

But she knew that the future would be a lot harder for Eva than she realised, and dreaded to think what life would be like for the baby growing up with such a stigma. They would all have to do everything they could to ease the child's way.

'Hello, Grandad,' Lizzie said into the telephone the next day.

'Lizzie,' said Philip with a smile in his voice, 'I was going to ring you later.'

'Well . . . have you recovered from the shock yet?' she asked lightly.

'Not really. How about you?'

'I've aged twenty years.'

He laughed heartily. 'It had the same effect on me.'

'Look, we need to talk,' she said. 'How about forgetting our own personal differences and meeting for lunch?'

'Good idea.'

They went to a place in Kensington High Street and immediately they'd ordered, she came right to the point.

'How do you feel about them not getting married?'

'Not happy.'

'Nor me.'

'Toby says Eva has made up her mind and won't be persuaded.'

'He is definitely willing to marry her, then?'

'Oh, yes. He's quite hurt that she won't agree.'

'Eva's convinced he isn't ready for marriage,' Lizzie said.

'He'd damned soon adapt with a wife and baby to look after!'

'I think that's what she's worried about. That he'd have his wings clipped and resent it later on.'

'Well, all I know is that he's thrilled about the baby and wants to make it all legal and above board,' Philip told her.

'My daughter can be stubborn when she likes. If she's got it into her head to go through with this thing alone, nothing in the world will change her mind.' She sighed. 'Still, at least it's a novelty . . . in these cases it's usually the man who needs persuading to do the decent thing.'

'It isn't surprising she's turned convention on its head, though, is it?' said Philip, with a chuckle. 'Given that she's your daughter!'

'My children were all born the right side of the blanket,

thank you very much,' said Lizzie in mock offence.

'Yes, but while every other woman was back in the home after the war, you were out there with the men building a business. I mean, it was hardly the done thing.'

'All right, I admit it.' After thrashing about in bed all night, sick with worry, Lizzie suddenly felt so much better.

'Oh, Philip, it *is* good to see you again.'

'Likewise,' he said with a wide grin.

One evening a few weeks later Jed Carter left his grandmother's house in a fury and headed for the nearest pub. What was it with his mother and sister, he asked himself, that they found those Vernes so irresistible?

This was the last straw – his sister pregnant by Toby Verne. This would tie the two families together by blood. And if that wasn't bad enough, they weren't even going to get married. Eva was going to stay on at the house in Berry Gardens and raise the baby on her own – and bring disgrace on the whole family in the process. Just to add to the bizarre situation, it was *her* idea to stay single – not his, according to Gran. Honestly, if Eva had to go and degrade herself, the least she could have done was to spare the family the shame. That would be Toby Verne's influence, he'd obviously given her queer ideas.

Jed usually visited his grandparents at least once a month, to see how they were and to keep up to date with family news. On hearing about this latest scandal, his visit had been cut short by an urgent need for copious amounts of something to soften the blow.

He was normally a beer drinker rather than a spirits man,

but tonight he ordered a double Scotch, drank it almost in one swallow, and followed it with another.

'Someone's got a thirst,' remarked a man who was also drinking alone at the bar, a stockily built chap in middle age.

'Anaesthetic, mate,' said Jed, staring broodily into space.

'Live round here, do you?' asked the man chattily.

'Yeah. I mean, no,' said Jed absently. 'I was brought up round here but I moved down to Essex last year.'

'I used to live round here too, till I moved up North,' said the man.

'You moved back for good then, have you?' asked Jed without any real interest.

'No. I've got a wife and kids in Macclesfield,' he explained. 'I've been down here for my mother's funeral.'

'Oh, sorry to hear that.'

'That's all right. She was turned eighty.'

'A good innings then?'

'Yeah.' The man finished his drink and turned his brown eyes on Jed. 'What are you having?'

'That's very civil of you,' he said, soothed by the whisky. 'I'll have the same again, please.'

One drink led to another and, mellow with alcohol, the two men chatted like old pals. Jed gave the stranger a detailed account of why he had needed to come here to get drunk.

'You'd think they'd have more respect for my dad's memory, wouldn't you?' he said, having told the man about both his mother and sister's involvement with the Verne family. 'I mean, this kiddie my sister's carrying will be the grandchild of my father's murderer. How could she do it, mate, how could she?'

The last time Arthur Brown had seen Jed Carter he'd been a boy of nine, but Arthur had known the instant Jed walked into the pub tonight that he was Stan's son. Apart from looking like his father, he had the same swaggering walk. It had given Arthur quite a turn. He hadn't told Jed who he was because it would inevitably have led to talk of Stan's death and that wasn't something he liked to think about. In fact, his dislike of the subject was the reason he had never kept in touch with the Carter family.

All these years he'd been plagued by guilt for not speaking up about Stan's intentions on that fateful night. He'd consoled himself with the thought that it was all so long ago the Carters would have stopped calling Philip Verne a murderer by this time. But instead of that the hatred had passed on to the next generation.

'How can you be so sure that Verne actually murdered your father?' asked Arthur. 'Your mother and sister could be right, you know, it could have been an accident.'

'Not a chance.' Jed's voice was thick and slow. 'They're just deluding themselves so that they won't feel guilty about hobnobbing with those Vernes. My gran isn't afraid to speak the truth, though. She knows what's what.'

'Does she?'

'Oh, yeah. She's been straight with me about it since I was a kid.'

'Your grandmother thinks he did it deliberately then?'

'Cor, not half! You should hear her going on about it.'

'Really?'

'Yeah. It's only because of Gran that Mum called it off with Philip Verne,' he said. 'She wouldn't get rid of him because I objected. Oh, no, nothing like that. She let me walk out of her life sooner than break it off with that load o' rubbish. That hurt mate, that really hurt.'

'But you've made it up with your mother now, surely?' asked Arthur hopefully.

'No, not really.'

'I thought you said . . .'

'I speak to her if she's at Gran's place when I'm there,' he explained, 'but I don't go to see Mum at home. Oh no.'

'But if she broke it off with . . .'

'Philip Verne still stands between us, even now,' Jed interrupted. 'She won't hear a word against him. Carries on as though I'm the one who's in the wrong instead of him.'

'I see.'

'Anyway, she's started seeing him again now, so Gran says, because of my sister's condition. Talk about a bloody mess!'

'How does your gran feel about your sister not getting married?' asked Arthur.

'She'd rather have a bastard in the family than someone with the name of Verne.'

'Oh.'

As inebriated as Arthur was, he knew the time had come for him to break silence. But not to Jed. That would be far too complicated. He would go straight to the horse's mouth.

Chapter Twenty-Three

Arthur found it very hard to get to the point of his visit when he called on Polly the following afternoon. He hadn't expected to feel so emotional on seeing her again, though, having once been practically one of the family, he supposed he should have been prepared.

'I've often wondered how you were getting on, Art,' she said as they drank tea at the kitchen table. 'You've never been to see us in all these years.'

'Well, I . . .'

'Never mind that now.' She smiled. 'You're here, that's the important thing.'

'Actually I came to . . .'

'Going back up North tomorrow, you say?' she cut in, loquacious with excitement at this unexpected visit.

'That's right.'

'You'll stay long enough to see Will, I hope? He should be in soon.'

'Um . . . well . . . I'm . . .'

'He's retired from the railway now, you know,' she went on as though he hadn't spoken. 'Still manages to make a few coppers on the side though. Well, you know Will and his little earners down the pub.'

'Yeah. Look, I . . .'

'Still, it keeps him occupied and out of my hair.'

'That's good.'

'How many children did you say you have, Art?'

Stifling the temptation to leave certain things unsaid, he finally managed to halt her inexorable flow.

'The thing is, Mrs C,' he almost shouted, 'I have something important to say to you.'

'Have you indeed?' she said lightheartedly. 'Well, if it's money you're after, mate, you're out o' luck.'

Oh, if only it was that simple, he thought, but said, 'No, no . . . nothin' like that.'

'Spit it out then, Art,' she urged, leaning forward expectantly.

He began by telling her about his meeting with Jed the previous evening, and how troubled he had been to hear that the boy had fallen out with his mother because of Philip Verne.

'That was bound to happen, wasn't it?'

'Given the information Jed's grown up on, yeah, I suppose so,' said Arthur, forcing himself to continue.

'And what's that supposed to mean?' she asked, her eyes narrowing quizzically.

'Well, the fact is, Mrs C, that information just isn't correct.'

'What *are* you on about?'

'Er . . . well . . .' He faltered, feeling like a monster for doing this to her. 'Well, truth is, Stan was the one with murderous intent that night.' The words came out in a rush before his courage gave out on him.'He told me he was going to fix Philip Verne for good and all after work that evening.'

'Don't you dare say such a thing about someone who can't defend himself!'

'Please here me out,' interrupted Arthur.

'Not if you're gonna come out with rubbish like that.'

'It really is vital for you and your family that you listen to what I have to say.'

'Oh, well,' she mumbled reluctantly. 'You'd better get on with it then, hadn't you?'

Feeling horribly callous, he gave her an account of the events preceding Stan's death, describing his deliberate attempt to provoke Philip Verne by smoking a cigarette on the factory floor that day.

'Stan had become obsessed with him,' Arthur explained solemnly. 'He spent all his time thinking of ways to upset him.'

Polly's sunny expression had hardened into one of sneering disbelief as she waited, in stony silence, for him to continue.

'Anyway,' he went on in a quick, nervous manner, 'when Stan and I were eating our sandwiches at dinner-time that day, after his barney with Verne over the smoking, Stan told me he was going to beat Verne up that night after everyone had gone. He had it all planned. He seemed . . . well . . . sort of excited about it. I told him not to be a fool. I was scared he'd end up in court for assault and lose his job. O' course, I never dreamt how terrible the outcome would be or I'd have stopped him somehow.'

'You've got a cheek coming round here telling me my son was a potential murderer,' said Polly, her face so pale it looked as though it was covered with chalk dust.

'I know it must seem rotten of me, and I'm sorry, Mrs C.

It's been a real bugger, having to do it. I should have spoken up about it years ago. But you were so upset . . . we all were . . . I just ran away and tried to forget all about it after the trial,' he confessed. 'I never dreamt you were going to canonise Stan.'

Polly's eyes widened and her breathing became rapid, knuckles turning white as she gripped the edge of the table.

'*Canonise him?* Is that what you think I've been doing?'

'You do seem to have given him quite a halo from what I can make out.'

'Is it wrong for a mother to think the best of her son?'

''Course not,' he replied speedily.

'Well, then.'

'But encouraging your grandson to continue his vendetta isn't right, and I think you know that in your heart.'

'You're presuming too damned much, Arthur Brown!'

'Be that as it may, young Jed should be told the truth.'

'Your truth,' she said, her voice leaden with agony.

'It's what happened, Mrs C.'

'You were Stan's mate, I dunno how you could say such things about him.'

'You know I wouldn't say them unless I had to. Stan was a good bloke, my best mate for years, I wouldn't lie to you about him,' he said, swallowing to ease his constricted throat. 'But good friend though he was, he certainly wasn't the saint you're makin' him out to be.'

'My Stan was a man of the people,' Polly insisted, clutching at straws because she couldn't bear even to consider the idea that what Arthur said was true. 'All he cared about was trying to better things for his workmates. That's why he was so much against the Vernes.'

'Once upon a time that was true,' agreed Arthur sadly, 'but he changed. In his last years, socialism took a back seat to his paranoia about the Vernes. All he seemed to think about was making trouble for Philip. Honestly, he was like a man possessed.'

'Stan was hot-headed, I admit, but there was no malice in him.'

'Not normally,' agreed Arthur, 'but when it came to the Vernes, Philip in particular, he was very malicious.'

Polly shook her head, her face working against tears. 'These are terrible things you're saying to me, Art. Why can't you just let my Stan rest in peace?'

'God knows, I want to. But none of us can until you do.'

She stared silently at the centre of the table, her eyes focusing on the maroon knitted cosy over the tea-pot.

'Do you think I wanna drag all this up again?' said Arthur, his voice gruff with feeling. 'Don't you think it would have been easier for me to go back up North without having said a word?'

'I dunno,' she mumbled, in a voice so low it was barely audible.

'If I hadn't happened to meet young Jed last night, that's exactly what I would have done,' he told her. 'I had no intention of coming round here, upsetting you. But after listening to what he had to say, I couldn't stay quiet and let him go on living in the shadow of his father, driven by anger and hatred and looking on Stan as some sort of a hero. If Jed isn't put right, this thing could ruin his life. He'll get to be as bitter and twisted as Stan was.' He paused, meeting her eyes with compassion. 'Your Stan wouldn't have wanted that . . . or to have his family torn apart because of him.' He brushed his greying hair from his brow with short, stubby fingers. 'He must be turning in his grave to know that Jed has turned against his mother because of him. Stan was just an ordinary bloke, Mrs C, with faults like everybody else. His biggest mistake was letting his feelings for Philip Verne get out of control . . . though I honestly don't think he could help it in the end. It was that weakness that cost him his life, not any malicious intentions on the part of Philip Verne.'

'All right, Art, you've made your point,' Polly said miserably. 'So what happens now?'

'That's up to you.'

'You want me to tell you to go ahead and tell Jed all this, I suppose?'

'Oh, no,' he was quick to point out. 'He wouldn't accept it from me any more than he would from his mother. He'd just think I was out to make mischief.'

'What then?'

'I reckon you're the only person he'll listen to on this subject. At least, that was the impression I got last night.'

'And if I don't choose to say anything?' Polly said dully.

'Then things will stay as they are.'

'But I thought . . .'

'I've done my bit in telling you about it,' he said. 'What you do next is between you and your conscience.'

Polly seemed to go into herself; stared into space as though she'd forgotten he was there. When he stood up and said he was leaving, she didn't reply. He slipped quietly from the house feeling a whole lot worse, instead of better, for having done his duty.

* * *

Polly was only vaguely aware of Arthur's departure. She sat where she was at the kitchen table, forcing herself to look back over the years to see if she could make sense of this latest revelation. She thought of her big lumbering son with his red hair and radical ideas. She'd been so proud of him when he'd first shown signs of a social conscience. Now she wanted to linger in the sunlit days of his youth – to luxuriate in memories of his passionate idealism and innocent belief that he could change the world. This was how she had always remembered Stan, because, she finally admitted, it had been preferable to his later years when he'd become so morose and difficult.

She put her hands to her head as though to stop the flow of tormenting images. But they just kept on coming. Vivid mental pictures of Stan complaining about every little thing: his impatience with the children and Lizzie, his constant criticism of Philip Verne.

Resting her head on her hands, she succumbed, weeping at the agonising destruction of her self-delusion and for the pain her blind loyalty had brought on others. Loudly and violently, she sobbed for the loss of her firstborn son as finally she let him die.

As the tears subsided into grinding emptiness, she glimpsed a particle of light in the blackness of her mind. With a shock, she recognised it as relief. It had been a wearisome burden, carrying a grudge all these years. Now it was time she put things right – if it wasn't too late.

461

Chapter Twenty-Four

It was Lucy Carter's birthday and she was far too taken up with the birthday celebrations to notice the tension that was mounting among the adults who had gathered here today at the house in Berry Gardens where she lived with her mother. Daddy was here a lot of the time but he didn't actually *live* here with them.

Everyone was making a great fuss of her. All the relations had come to the party. Mummy and Daddy had given her a shiny black doll's pram and Nana Lizzie and Grandpa Phil had given her a baby doll to put into it. Great-Granny Carter and Grandpa Will were here as well as Great-Granny Verne. There were the Great-Uncles Bobby and Luke, Aunt June, and Uncles Jamie and Keith.

There had been a special birthday tea with rabbit-shaped jelly and chocolate blancmange and a pink and white birthday cake with three candles on it which they'd all helped her to blow out. After that they'd played musical chairs and ring-a-ring-a-roses, and Uncles Keith and Jamie had made everyone laugh with magic tricks and jokes.

It had been good fun but now she was feeling sleepy. Luckily, the grown-ups were so busy chattering about something they'd heard on the wireless, no one was saying anything about bedtime so she could sit here on the sofa next to Uncle Jed with the cuddly bear he'd given her.

Through a somnolent blur, Lucy noticed that everyone had stopped talking. She heard a man's voice coming from the wireless set, then after a while they all started speaking again – only more loudly.

Lucy looked across at Nana Lizzie who was sitting opposite in an armchair. She winked which meant she wouldn't remind Mummy about bedtime. Nana Lizzie and Grandpa Phil were lovely. They took her to the park and to the river and sat with her sometimes while Mummy went out somewhere with Daddy. They sang to her and laughed a lot. Nana Lizzie wasn't laughing now, though. In fact she was looking a little bit cross.

At that precise moment Lizzie was desperately trying to assimilate the awful news that had just been announced: that Hitler had repudiated the Munich Agreement and marched into the remaining part of Czechoslovakia, thus making war a real possibility now.

'Oh, Philip,' she said to her husband, who sat perched on the arm of her chair. 'It's really beginning to look grim, isn't it?'

'I'm afraid so,' he said with a sigh. 'We're all going to have to face up to the inevitable.'

For months war preparations had been in evidence in the capital. Millions of gas masks had been distributed as well as underground air-raid shelters. Philip had answered the call for volunteers to the ARP, and his mother, undeterred by age, had responded to Lady Reading's appeal for recruits to the WVS, dragging a somewhat bewildered Polly along with her.

The unlikely friendship of those two white-haired ladies, after all the years of acrimony, had surprised everybody, including themselves, Lizzie suspected. Glancing across at them now, as they sat next to each other by the fire, chattering comfortably, she saw them as two opposites drawn together by outside forces and united by one major factor, mutual adoration for their great-granddaughter.

It hadn't been an overnight conversion for Polly. She'd been very wary of Meg at first. But being forced to be civil to her at various family functions, after Lizzie's marriage to Philip and Lucy's birth, the ice had gradually melted. To Lizzie's knowledge, Polly had never had a woman friend outside the family before, and for the first time in her life she had a social life of her own. Nothing too adventurous – just lunch out in a restaurant with Meg now and then, and tea at Eden Crescent quite often. She could even be persuaded by the indomitable Meg to see a show or a film occasionally.

It was more than three and a half years since Polly had arrived at Lizzie's door, sick with contrition. Lizzie had never seen her in such a state. After the emotional outpouring with Lizzie, and another one with Jed, she had been very subdued for several months. She'd hidden herself away, sleeping a lot and shedding copious tears. It was as though she was grieving for Stan all over again. But then, quite suddenly, she'd come out of it and been healthier and cheerier than Lizzie had ever seen her. She seemed charged with new energy and purpose in life, enthusiastically encouraged by Meg.

Jed had taken longer to recover from his shattered illusions. For a while he'd even refused to accept the truth about his father's death. But, eventually, he'd moved back to London, taken a flat in Chelsea and come back to work at the firm. Like his father before him, he wasn't given to great shows of feeling, but his presence at Lizzie's wedding to Philip had spoken volumes.

His relationship with his stepfather wasn't ideal, even now. Lizzie didn't think they would ever become friends. But at least Jed made an effort now, on the surface anyway. Since the two silk firms had merged to become V and C Textiles, and both men were on the board and in constant touch, a civilised working association was essential.

The decision to join forces in business had seemed the logical next step to their personal union. Because of the increasing threat of artificial silk, they had decided to expand their operation to include a wider range of fabrics. The silk trade had also been made vulnerable recently by news of an invention in America of a new material called nylon. This made commercial diversity even more imperative.

Both factories still operated separately under the new name. Lizzie, Bobby and Jed were responsible for the Hammersmith factory while Philip and Toby looked after things in Kensington. Though for how much longer this arrangement would continue if war came, Lizzie had no idea.

She looked across at Eva and Toby who were standing by the door, engrossed in conversation, happy and comfortable together but still unmarried much to Lizzie's disappointment. Eva had continued to scandalise the neighbourhood by refusing to get married though Toby was a regular overnight visitor at the house in Berry Gardens which Lizzie had vacated when she'd moved into Cedar Square with Philip after their marriage.

Shouldering new responsibilities had changed Toby. He provided well for Eva and Lucy and was at the centre of their existence. Lucy's arrival hadn't destroyed her parents' penchant for the highlife completely, though naturally their daughter had become their raison d'être. There was no shortage of babysitters when they felt like a night out on the town to blow away the cobwebs of domesticity.

Lizzie was recalled to the present by the sound of Bobby's voice. He was standing in the centre of the room calling for silence.

'I thought you might like to know that although the news from abroad is bloomin' awful,' he said when he finally had the company's attention, 'June and I have something a bit more cheerful to tell you.'

'Blimey! Don't say you've a nipper on the way at your age?' said Will crudely.

'Trust you to lower the tone, Dad,' admonished Bobby jokily. 'But no. Actually it's the twins' news but they have given me their permission to tell you.'

'Get on with it, then, for Gawd's sake, before we all die of old age,' said Polly.

'Yeah, come on bruv,' said Luke who had come down from Nottingham, where he now worked in a hosiery factory, especially for Lucy's birthday celebrations.

'Well, as you all know, our lads have doggedly pursued a career in show business and have suffered to this end, playing rough working men's clubs all over the country.'

'Yeah, yeah, we know all that,' said Polly, eager for him to get to the point.

'I think you'll all agree that they deserve success?' he said, pausing again just to tantalise them.

'Spit it out, Dad,' said Jamie. 'Before they all lose interest and go home.'

'Well,' continued Bobby, 'the lads, alias Carter and Carter, are booked to play at the Shepherd's Bush Empire next month!'

There was a general whoop of delight and a lot of back slapping and hugging. Toby organised some drinks for a toast and when the excitement had finally subsided, he had an announcement of his own to make.

'Actually, Eva and I have some news too,' he said, grinning.

Lizzie was puzzled. Eva had said nothing about any news. It sounded very much like the second patter of tiny feet to her. Lizzie loved Lucy to distraction and dreaded what society would do to her when she was old enough to appreciate her position as an outsider. Surely her bohemian daughter wouldn't inflict the same future on another child as well?

Toby swept Eva into the limelight, his arm around her shoulders. 'Well, folks, I hope you're all free on April the twentieth . . . because you're all invited to a wedding. Eva has at last agreed to make it legal!'

'Well, you're a dark horse!' said Lizzie to her daughter when the congratulations were over and everyone was chatting among themselves. 'I had no idea you were even considering it. You've always been dead set against marriage.'

Eva shook her head. 'No, Mum. I've never said I wouldn't marry Toby . . . only that I wouldn't marry him just because of Lucy.'

'And?'

'I think he's more than proved his feelings for me, don't you?'

'No doubt about that,' she readily agreed. 'I only wish it hadn't taken you so long to realise it.'

'There's more to it than just that,' explained Eva.

'Oh?'

'Yes. We've got to know each other properly now,' she explained. 'We're both more sure of our feelings. I suppose we've grown up at last. Anyway, I don't think I could ever be accused of forcing him into marriage.'

'Hardly!'

'I'm so happy, Mum.'

'And I'm happy for you . . . for all of you.'

'Life is going to be uncertain enough for all of us if war does break out,' said Eva, her expression becoming grave. 'It makes sense to put our personal affairs in order.'

Toby appeared at their side. 'Look at Lucy, bless her,' he said fondly. 'She's right out for the count.'

They all looked across at the sofa where tousled locks of curly red hair swept across the face of the sleeping child curled up in the corner with her teddy bear.

'I'll try and get her up to bed without waking her,' said Toby gently.

'I'll come with you,' was Eva's reply.

Watching them leave the room together with Lucy cradled in Toby's arms, tears rushed into Lizzie's eyes.

'Good news, innit?' said Polly, appearing at her side as she rummaged in her handbag for a handkerchief.

'Wonderful.'

'I never thought I would say it but they're lovely together, Eva and Toby.'

'Yes.'

'And little Lucy's a pet.'

'I'll say.'

'She's certainly got Stan's colouring.'

'I can see quite a bit of Carter in her, actually,' said Lizzie.

'The Carter influence is a strong one,' grinned her mother-in-law.

Lizzie looked across at Bobby who was engaged in conversation with June and the twins. Something must have amused him because he emitted a familiar roar of laughter which peeled away the years, reminding Lizzie that there was still a corner of her heart that would be forever his.

She smiled at Polly. 'It certainly is . . . and in more ways than just Lucy's colouring.'

'Meaning?'

'Well, I know my name is Verne now but a part of me will always be Carter.'

'I know I don't deserve it,' said Polly, 'but I'm very glad to hear it.'

As Polly was drawn into conversation with Luke, Lizzie caught her husband's eye across the room. Full of the gentle glow of contentment, she went to join him.